The Gambler

Chris Johns

Herndon, VA

ISBN 78-1-934187-22-7

Published in the United States
STARbooks Press
PO Box 711612
Herndon VA 20171
Printed in the United States

Many thanks to graphic artist John Nail for the cover design. Mr. Nail may be reached at: tojonail@bellsouth.net.

Book and text design by Milton Stern. Mr. Stern can be reached at miltonstern@miltonstern.com.

Chapter 1

A Slave Is Born

Yes, I guess the title sums me up perfectly.

Twenty years old, four years experience in my job with a natural flare, and a gambling addiction.

"You are going to be one of the top chefs in this country in another couple of years, Charlie, if you don't fuck up," my boss said.

Praise indeed, I was first commi at a Roux Brothers Restaurant. My boss thought I was good – better than good. What he meant when he said as long as I don't fuck up had nothing to do with my cooking. He knew that I was in way over my head with gambling debts. I loved the wheel at the local casino, but only the house wins in the end.

A couple of days after that, I was at the wheel again when the manager sent for me.

"You owe the Casino nearly a quarter of a million, Charlie. What are you going to do to repay that debt?"

"I'm sorry, sir, I can't think of any way that size debt is ever going to get paid unless I get really lucky," I said.

"What do you think a slave would fetch in a modern day auction, Charlie, when they fetched about $2,500 before abolition?"

"Probably enough to pay my debt to you," I laughed, wondering where this conversation was going.

"I agree. Easy then, I'll keep my boys away from you, but you will have to sign this agreement. It puts you into slavery to the owner for the next ten years. The alternative is my boys take out £250,000 from your hide – very painful – chance of recovery, zero. You choose."

I signed.

The document was long and complicated, worded in legal mumbo jumbo. The gist though was simple. The owner of the Casino would have the use of my body for any purpose for the next ten years. He could use me or abuse me in any way that suited him.

"Good. You will need your passport and be clothed for a flight, Charlie. You won't need anything else. Tell your landlord he can have the remainder of your things in lieu of notice. Come back here when you have them. We will inform your place of work that you are finished there."

No messing, I was on a private jet to somewhere about two hours later.

My parents were dead, and I had no siblings, so I could disappear and no one would be looking for me. Not a nice situation to be in not knowing where I was going, and as a slave, I had no rights.

The flight plus a helicopter ride brought me to a private island in the Grenadines, a bit like Mustique where the Queen's sister had a home for years.

I was taken to see the owner and was surprised to be confronted with a young guy, maybe five years older than I.

"Charlie, I need a first class chef and a body to exhibit as my fuck slave. I have paid a lot of money to get two in one. Now, take your clothes off, all of them. Let me have a look at what I have bought."

"Yes Sir."

I felt a bit foolish as I stood in this opulent study naked. I covered my genitals with my hands only to be told to remove them so that he could see if Dan's assessment was true. I was gob smacked. It turns out that the last trick I turned before becoming a slave had been a set-up so that this guy could decide if I was what he wanted. I was rigged like a donkey.

"Good. So that you are not surprised by what happens to you, I will tell you that in the next few years you will be subjected to group sex with my friends. I will be fucking you frequently during this time as well, as long as you please me. I will beat you if you're bad and reward you when you're good. You'll work out in the gym because I want a fit body to fuck. I am going to humiliate you and hurt you today so that you know what you can expect if you displease me in any way. Whatever I do to you or ask you to do will be done immediately and without protest. I will use this on you today, but normally it will be the whip. Do you understand?"

"This" was a paddle like the ones they used to use in slave days, plenty of pain but no permanent markings.

While he was talking, he had walked round his desk and started to fondle me to get me hard. He achieved it with no problem.

"Yes Sir," was all I could say really. I had fucked up big time, and now I was going to lose ten years of my life to pay for it.

"You will be the boss in the kitchen. You will have several hours during the day to work out in the gym, swim and play squash with me if you are any good. Are you?"

"I'm not bad, Sir."

"Good. The rest of your waking hours when I don't need you will be spent as a slave to the rest of the house staff. When I am away, you will be under the orders of my estate manager. You will need to be a diplomat in the kitchen. Otherwise, your staff can make life uncomfortable for you when they are off duty. You are the only slave here and will be clothed accordingly. That means just a pair of shorts, a watch, pager and this whip – no top, no shoes. Do you understand?"

The whip was a short one that coiled and hung easily from a clasp on the belt that my pager was on.

"Yes Sir."

He rang a bell, and a very striking black man, about 30 years old and immaculately dressed, came in.

"Cloud is my head of house. He will take you to your room to get your shorts. They are white, and you have a dozen pairs. They are always to be immaculate, as will be your chef's aprons. Your body will be the same, inside and out. I expect you to give yourself an enema everyday to ensure your inner cleanliness, which is why you have a private bathroom. I also want all of your body hair removed. You don't appear to have any except for under your arms and your pubic bush so that shouldn't prove too difficult. I will arrange for you to be shaved in the near future. Afterwards, you will do it yourself or arrange for someone else to do it. Cloud will show you around the estate when you have completed those first things. I want you back here in two hours when I will detail your routine and introduce you to the rest of the staff. Take your clothes with you, but you will not need them again for some time"

My room was terrific. It was either the last one on the owner's wing or the first one on the staff wing, whichever way you wanted to look at it. A double bed was the main feature, and I loved that. I had my own bathroom and fantastic views over the island. It would have been idyllic if I were a free man.

The estate was beautiful. The house was enormous with every possible facility – Olympic pool, gym and squash court. All of the staff were male, young, beautiful and black, except me. They wore tailored uniforms that showed off their bodies, all of which were gorgeous. Even the boys in the kitchen were dressed immaculately with pristine white aprons, covering their uniforms.

You can imagine the surprised looks I got when the boss paraded me before them wearing just a small and very sexy pair of white shorts. I called them hipsters, and they did nothing to hide my monster dick, which lay up my right side not quite reaching the waist band of the shorts. My owner introduced me to the staff in one go. They were assembled in the entrance hall. They all stood in a semi circle, so they had an uninterrupted view of me.

"This is Charlie. He is the new chef. He doesn't wear any other clothes so that you are all aware of his lowly status. He is a slave, and apart from the kitchen where he is the boss, he is lower than the garbage boy. During his off duty periods when he is working for me, you will leave him alone. When he has no other duties, you can use him as a slave, which means he does anything you want him to. I don't expect you to mistreat him, unless he disobeys you or is unsatisfactory in some way, in which case you can use the whip he carries on his belt. I want no permanent marks on his body, so watch how enthusiastic you get. You will all get a copy of his rota so that you can book him for chores. He will carry a chores and punishment book that you are to fill in if you use the whip or ask him to do tasks for you.

"Charlie is new to slavery, and you have never had a slave in the house, so I am going to give you a small demonstration of how subservient he is outside of the kitchen."

I was beginning to dislike my new role already. Chef and sex slave to the boss I could handle. Fuck slut for his friends was a step I would have been pleased to avoid. Slave to the rest of the house staff meant I probably would not be getting a lot of rest, and unless I was careful, I would live with a sore ass as well. I looked over all of the staff, trying to assess which ones would be most likely to give me a hard time. I guessed most were a year or two younger than I. Cloud, the senior housekeeper, and the permanent nurse were older. A very striking guy who I found out later was my first assistant in the kitchen was older, and that was about it. I thought some of the younger ones might get me doing chores for them for the novelty of it. Cloud, the Housekeeper and the Nurse I guessed would leave me alone. My deputy was the only one I felt I needed to be wary of.

The Master was 26. I found out very quickly that he looked so good because he was a real jock. His body was really something. He was about six feet tall, topped with jet-black hair, the most incredible piercing blue eyes, and a perfectly defined but lightly muscled body. Just the right amount of chest hair to look sexy and a nicely proportioned box, which I soon found out expanded to about seven or eight inches. His father, like mine, had died when he was in his late teens, but there the similarity ended. Mine had left me nothing. His had left him about six billion dollars. He was gay, as was I. The house staff were all gay as well and had been chosen for their looks and the equipment they carried between their legs.

I, on the other hand, was about as different as it was possible to be – five foot seven, dark brown hair, and some said beautiful green eyes. My body was similar to the Master's. I worked out a lot as well and swam, played squash and tennis, could even swing a reasonable golf club. I had no body hair except my pubes and under my arms, and luckily, despite my light colouring, I took a tan well. My box and my butt were my biggest assets in this world of size queens. My cock is about six inches soft, uncut, twice that erect and thick, and it settled in very comfortably just on my lower ribs when erect. I was a natural bottom because my butt was to die for, and very few guys wanted to take my cock in their love chute when they saw it.

Living in London and being grossly oversexed, I had accumulated a wealth of experience in the four years since leaving school. I was a bit of a slut if truth be told. I loved sex, almost any sex. I could get a steaming hard on at the drop of a hat, unusual for someone of my size with my equipment. I didn't think the Master would have much to complain about in bed, and I knew he wouldn't in the kitchen. I had never been involved in group sex, and I had never been with a black guy. If they were rigged like me and I had to take them, I was going to be sore for a while until I got used to it.

Introductions over, Cloud informed me that I would address him as Sir and the owner as Master. The remainder of the staff I could address by their first names.

The Master was carrying the paddle, so I was waiting apprehensively for the next move. It wasn't long in coming. The master moved the paddle into position to use and said, "Remove your shorts, Charlie."

I stood there not moving. It was bad enough being clad in tiny shorts that hid very little, but to be completely nude was too embarrassing for words.

"I said remove your shorts, Charlie, and if I ever have to repeat an order again, you will be extremely sorry."

I took my shorts off and quickly covered my genitals with my hands. I was blushing to the roots of my soul.

"Put your hands behind your head, Charlie, and stand with your legs astride."

I did, and he moved close to me and started to play with my cock. I had never felt so humiliated in my life as I reacted to his ministrations. As my cock passed the horizontal, he removed his hand, and everyone could see my foreskin pull back over the head as I reached full erection. There were a few gasps as it finally stopped growing and hugged my belly.

"Now, turn round, Charlie, spread your legs wide and bend over to grip your ankles."

This was too humiliating. With my legs spread and my body bent over, the staff would be able to see my hole clearly. Again, I hesitated. The Master gave me a hard smack across my ass with the paddle. It hurt like hell, and I was in the new position in no time.

"You can spread them wider than that."

As he said it, I felt a finger penetrate my rectum.

I did as I was told, almost dying of shame.

"I am going to give you ten licks with the paddle, Charlie. I want you to count them and after each one, say, 'Thank you, Master.' If you move while I am doing it, I will start again."

I knew what to expect from the quick one I had received, but bent over and with the Master properly positioned, I could not believe how much the first one hurt. The pain was horrendous, and I screamed. When I had recovered, I said, "One, thank you, Master."

The next one if anything was worse.

By five, I was barely able to speak. By ten, I could not speak at all and was just about to fall down when the Master said, "Now carry on with your duties, Charlie."

With that, everybody left. I remained in the hall naked, humiliated and in more pain than I could ever remember.

Winston was the first one I met when I was shown the kitchen. He had been doing the Chef's job for some time, so I was not popular with him and paid for it.

"I hope we can work together, Winston. I am sorry if I have stepped on your toes by coming here, but it wasn't my choice."

"Charlie, I will do the best I can for you here, but I will make you pay for it when you are on free time."

Obviously, he didn't have to tell me in what way I would pay. I could guess, and he didn't keep me guessing long. As soon as we finished lunch and the preparation for dinner, I was free, and Winston knew it. He had my rota and was aware of my workout times, swim time, etc.

As we left the kitchen, he said. “Come with me, Charlie, I have a couple of chores that I want you to do for me.”

His room was smaller than mine was but still adequate and very neat.

“Charlie, my shoes need cleaning, the cleaning kit is in the bottom of the wardrobe. They have to be immaculate. I am going out tonight after dinner.”

How much of a piss off is that – your assistant one minute, your master the next? I wasn’t great on shoe cleaning, which pleased Winston.

“Not good enough, Charlie, if you don’t do better I will have to punish you.”

He lay back on his bed and watched me do them again. They looked OK, to me, but when I finished, he pointed out three things wrong with them and said, “I shall have to punish you, Charlie, to make you understand the standard I require. Give me your whip. Take your shorts off and bend over the chair.”

I had no choice. The Master had made it quite clear the staff could beat me for unsatisfactory performance of chores. Bent over the chair with my hands gripping each arm, Winston told me to spread my legs wide. He ran his hand over my ass cheeks and said, “You have a cute butt, Charlie. It’s a pity to add to its already bright colouring.”

He continued between my legs and started to caress my balls and my cock. Of course I got hard, and that was worthy of more comment.

“That is a monster, Charlie. Let’s see how long it stays hard.”

With that, he stood to the side of me and delivered a stinging blow to my ass with the whip. The pain was unbelievable. I gasped with the shock. The second one made me yelp, and I jumped up to avoid any more.

“Get back where you were, Charlie. If you move again, I will take you to one of the outhouses and string you up to finish the punishment.”

The third one was even harder, and I broke.

“Please, Winston, don’t beat me anymore. I’ll do anything for you, but don’t whip me again.” I was sobbing quite hard. The pain was awful.

“OK, Charlie, I would normally give you six. That’s what you get in English Public Schools isn’t it? Instead of the other three, you can undress me and give me a blowjob.”

His cock was gorgeous. Smaller than mine, but not by much, cut and straight as a rod. His balls hung low and large. I had no problem tackling the whole package with my tongue and mouth. I loved his balls. I could just get the pair in my mouth and suck on them, swirl my tongue round them and generally enjoy the feel of them. When I had them slick, I let my hand take over playing with them, rolling them between my finger and thumb. I let my tongue lick up the underside of his gorgeous dick and engulf the tip swirling my tongue round it and using my other hand to wank him gently. He was gurgling with pleasure, which almost made me laugh. Little baby sounds coming from this big guy was the last thing I expected to hear.

I was very quickly rock hard again myself. Winston saw it and as I was sucking him, he started wanking me between his feet. It was very erotic. I could feel him expanding ready to cum, and he pulled my head onto his cock more so that I had to take his man juice in my mouth.

"Swallow it all, Charlie, or I shall have to beat you again."

I thought he was never going to stop pumping cum down my throat. It just went on and on. When he eventually did stop, he fell back on his bed and said, "That was some blow job, Charlie. I think you may have a permanent chore to do after lunch each day. But I won't let you get bored. What do you think of Darren?"

That was a strange change of conversation.

"He's a nice lad. He worked really hard for lunch, and he doesn't need a lot of supervision."

"Very funny, Charlie, I meant sexually."

"Sorry, Winston, stupid of me. He looks very sexy, and when he took his apron off it looked as though he had an amazing piece of equipment between his legs."

"He has. But I think you may have the edge, not by much though. Tomorrow after lunch, we will both have a chore for you. You will obviously do it unsatisfactorily, and we will have to beat you, or spit roast you, or both. Darren will want your ass I'm sure. You had better get going now, Charlie. I think you are supposed to be swimming with the Master in about five minutes. You'll be starting to get your all over tan then as well."

He laughed as he said it, so I guessed I was in for some more surprises.

I slipped my shorts back on and headed for the pool. It really was a beautiful setting. The Master was lying on one of the sun beds wearing a towelling robe.

"Hello, Charlie, you are just in time. Take your shorts off and come sit with me."

I took my shorts off dropped them on the floor and slid onto the bed next to him.

"How was your first session with the kitchen crew?"

"Not bad, Master, they don't really need me there. Winston is very competent, and Darren is a good worker. I'm not sure about Ryan and Johnnie, yet there wasn't really much for them to do. I think I will use lunch times as a training meal to get them all into my system ready for production of dinner, which should be where our major effort takes place."

"That sounds good to me. Do you think you will be able to work with Winston then?"

"It's going to be bloody difficult. I know I have put his nose out of joint, and he has already shown me how he intends dealing with that."

"Hmm, stand up, Charlie, and face away from me. Ah, I thought so. But why only three stripes across your ass, the boys all think in terms of six of the best like your old school system of Corporal Punishment?"

"I'm sorry, Master. I couldn't stand the pain and begged him for an alternative which he offered."

"I see. Unusual situation isn't it, Charlie?"

"Yes Master, Boss one minute issuing orders, slave the next taking them and receiving punishment from your underlings."

"I can see I am going to have an interesting time watching how you handle yourself. Now, I think we ought to see how good you are outside the kitchen. Come over here, Charlie, get me excited and make me cum, but I want you to make me last a long time."

With that, he took his robe off to reveal one very sexy body and a beautiful piece of man equipment that was partially erect. I worked on him with enthusiasm giving his balls and cock special treatment early to get him fully aroused. After that, I kept him on the boil using his nipples and his asshole. He was the easiest guy to arouse and bring to the boil. My tongue worked overtime all over his body, licking and slurping, particularly on his nipples and behind his ball sac. I didn't believe he went without, so I just assumed he had a very high sex drive. Either way, he was not going to be hard work.

I kept him simmering for about half an hour. His breathing was very ragged, and he was gasping.

"Let me cum, Charlie, now."

"Sorry, Master, I can't do that. You have some more pleasuring to come first."

"Let me cum now, Charlie, or I will beat you."

Decision time, do as I'm told or make him hang on and hope the eventual orgasm is so mind blowing he will forgive me. As a gambler, I take my own course. I left him completely alone until he had pulled back from the brink.

"You'll pay for that, Charlie."

Then I went back to pleasuring him bringing him up to the edge again, and again, and again.

"Oh God, Charlie, please let me cum, please, Charlie."

So I did. His orgasm was cataclysmic. I must have swallowed a pint of cum. He just kept jetting into the back of my throat. I had to withdraw from him a whole lot to stop from spilling any.

It took him about ten minutes to recover enough to speak.

"Charlie, I ought to thrash you for disobeying me, but that was one fantastic orgasm. Be careful though. You walk a very fine line when you ignore a command from me."

"I know, Master, but I am here to pleasure you to the best of my ability. That was it. To have let you cum before then would have been second best. You won't get that from your kitchen, and you won't get it from your bed while I am filling both roles."

He laughed and said, "OK, Charlie, go for a swim if you like or just lay here and soak up the rays."

"Thank you, Master, I'll swim. I need to unkink from all that travelling."

I enjoyed the rest of the afternoon, and my tan started to show as well.

"I shall not need you after supper tonight, Charlie. You can spend an hour with Cloud after you finish in the kitchen and let him show you things like the laundry and talk you through how the house system works. After Cloud and the Senior Housekeeper, you are the next most senior member of my household staff. I will introduce you to Mac in the morning. He is overall boss when I am away, but he does not interfere in the house at all, except for you of course. He runs the estate."

The boys really dug out for me at dinner, and I knew it was a big success. The Master had a couple of guests who sent their compliments down to me.

When we had finished, I decided to bite the bullet and let the boys know how I stood. I had been thinking about it since my session with Winston.

"Winston, guys, I'd like a word before we leave. I am aware our situation is weird. I am also aware that because of it, you may think you can influence my actions here as your boss by making me pay dearly for it when I am your slave. Well, that isn't going to happen. You can make my life extremely painful if you decide to, and I can make your work time unpleasant. I hope neither situation is going to develop. What I have seen from you so far impresses me. Please keep it up. I doubt I shall be as impressive as a slave, but you can teach me hopefully without tearing my ass up too much with this whip. I understand the Master eats little in the mornings but is particular about his eggs. I think tomorrow Winston, Ryan and I will do for breakfast, Darren and Johnnie, about ten for lunch preparation, OK?"

"OK, Charlie, goodnight."

Ryan and Johnnie left then. Winston and Darren remained.

"Charlie, the Master doesn't need you tonight, and you will only be with Cloud for about an hour. We would like you to come to my room afterwards to do a couple of chores."

I looked from one to the other. Darren looked uncomfortable, but I guessed he would not take long to get over that.

"OK, Winston, I understand."

I liked Cloud. He was very proper but also extremely sympathetic to my situation. He treated me with the respect accorded to my professional status not like the slave that I was, and let's face it dressed in jut a sexy pair of shorts was not the best dress to be wearing if you wanted respect. When we finished, he left me in the entrance hall with a "Welcome to Lara's House and Goodnight, Charlie."

"Goodnight, Sir, and thank you."

He winked at me as he walked back through the house to his quarters. I walked up to my room first, dead tired but had a quick cold shower, hopefully to wake myself up for whatever the two boys had planned. Clean shorts, and not forgetting my belt with pager and whip, I walked next door to Winston's room. They were sitting on the bed both dressed in just their boxers.

"Come in, Charlie, you can start your chores straight away. Darren has a pair of trousers there that need sharp creases in them for a dinner he is going to tomorrow. Press them for him, will you?"

I didn't have a clue as jeans were about my limit. I tried but failed miserably, as I am sure they knew I would.

"Sorry, Charlie, that isn't good enough. I shall have to punish you. I understand from Winston that you have to learn to be a good slave as well as a good chef. Six of the best is standard in your country, so I guess that is what I have to give you. Is that right, Winston?"

"Yes, that's correct, Darren, on the bare bottom of course."

I knew by the smirk on his face he had put Darren up to it, and with both of them there, I knew there was more to follow. Winston had humiliated me by making me cry and beg this afternoon. It would be a hundred times worse with a junior like Darren.

Winston had already swung his chair into position so that there was space for the action.

"Give me your whip, Charlie, and take your shorts off."

I did and was told to bend over the chair. It was only when I had leant over with my hands on the arms that I saw the ropes. Winston secured my wrists, went round behind me and spread my legs wide before securing them to each of the chair legs.

"Don't want you jumping up like you did this afternoon, Charlie. So we've just secured you in case."

Winston stroked my butt again and played with my cock and balls – very repetitive this boy.

"I thought you might like to see how big his cock is again, Darren, only close up this time. I think he outclasses you, but as soon as you hit him, it deflates very quickly. We need never let him stay hard if it annoys you. So off you go."

Darren stroked my buttocks with the whip before bringing it down hard. The pain was as I remembered it that afternoon, and I bit my lip to stop crying out. Darren moved around a little further for the second one so that he could see my face as he delivered it. I think he was shocked at the look of agony as the second one bit deeper into my buttocks. On the third one, which was much harder than Winston's, I screamed and bucked to try and get away.

"Is he alright, Winston, should I stop now?"

"No, Darren, he has to learn. Three more, and we can try him again with a chore."

On the fourth, I broke and begged them to stop. Darren was quite worried, but Winston made him give me the other two. My whole body was a sea of pain, and I could not stand when they released my bonds.

"If he can't stand to do his chores, Darren, perhaps we ought to give him another six."

"Oh no, Winston, can't we do something else with him?"

"Yes, why don't we spit roast him. You can let him suck you first so that he knows what he is going to get up his ass, and then he can blow me while you fuck him."

Darren's cock was enormous. I would not take bets on mine being bigger. I was made to suck him and get him very wet. Winston went round behind me and started to finger fuck me opening me up as much as he could to get me ready for Darren. The humiliation was unbelievable. Despite my pain, I just wanted to die. My own staff were abusing me like an animal. Then they swapped round and Darren entered me. I screamed again with the pain, but Winston held me down and told him to keep it in and feed me a little at a time until I had it all. Winston's cock was the next thing to enter me and now unable to make any noise, I had to endure a severe fucking from Darren. He was so turned on he forgot to be gentle, and I endured a vicious face fucking from Winston until they both came filling both orifices with loads of cum. Winston made me lick him clean, which I thought would be the end of it, but he had other ideas.

"Darren, come round here and let him lick you clean as well."

He was a little shocked but was used to doing as Winston told him. It was disgusting, and I wanted to throw up.

"Get down on you knees now, Charlie, lick Darren's feet and beg his forgiveness for not getting his trousers right. Make it very sincere, Charlie, or I will have to punish you some more."

I crawled to Darren still in great pain and feeling very humiliated. I started licking his feet and begging his forgiveness.

"Not sincere enough, Charlie," and as he said it, I received another vicious swipe across my butt. Easily the hardest yet, and I screamed. This one came from deep in my gut and was obviously heard round the whole of the servants' wing. I begged Darren's forgiveness even more sincerely and pleaded with Winston not to hit me again. I then received my last one of the night. The hardest of the lot and this time the blood flowed freely along with the loudest and longest scream of the lot. The pain was unbelievable, and I collapsed on the floor unable to move.

"Get back to your room now, Charlie. You have deserved everything you got in here. You have stolen my position in this house. I'll never forgive you."

He threw my things at me including a very bloody whip just as the door burst open and Cloud stood there aghast at the sight before him.

"My God, man, what have you done?"

Darren was shocked, and Winston just looked defiant.

"He needed punishing for being a worthless slave, and I punished him," Winston said.

"Darren, help me get this boy to his room. Winston, you get the first aid kit from the pantry, and hurry. Bring it to me in Charlie's room."

I was tended to and put to bed by Cloud.

My alarm was the next thing I remembered, and I tried to get out of bed. It was very painful and took me a long time. I looked at my ass in the full-length mirror and saw that it was heavily strapped. I washed and put on another clean pair of shorts. I was now late and decided in the interest of speed to use the main stairs instead of the staff ones. I nearly made it, too. I was just clearing the entrance hall when the Master came out of the study and saw me limping. He also saw something else that shocked him.

"Charlie, stop."

I did and turned round.

"I'm sorry, I'm late, Master. It won't happen again."

"Never mind that. What is the matter with your ass?"

"Nothing, Master."

"Don't give me that shit, Charlie. Turn round and drop your shorts."

I could not bend, so I discarded the shorts with some difficulty. I could see the blood on them. My cuts were bleeding again.

"Undo that bandage, Charlie."

I couldn't do anything else but obey. When I had it off, I saw that it was well soaked with my blood. I heard the Master's sharp intake of breath.

"Who on earth beat you like that, Charlie."

"It was an accident, Master. I'm sure he didn't mean it."

"Who did it, Charlie?"

"Winston, Master."

"He was responsible for yesterday's lunch times marks as well wasn't he?"

"Yes, Master."

"Cloud," the Master almost screamed, and Cloud came running. "Get this boy's wounds dressed properly. Have him taken back to bed, get two security guards here and Winston in my study now."

I just stood while the rest of the house erupted round me. Two houseboys eventually half carried me upstairs. The resident nurse dressed my wounds, administered painkillers, and I was out of it for the next 24 hours. When I woke, Darren was by my bed.

"I'm sorry, Charlie," he said when he saw me open my eyes. "I'm really sorry. Winston hated you and used me to further humiliate you and punish you. I didn't want to do it. I just wanted to say sorry before I leave. The Master allowed it. Winston was taken away yesterday."

"You are being made to leave as well?"

"Yes, Charlie, I deserve it just the same as Winston. We shouldn't have beaten you like that."

I managed to get out of bed and put on my shorts.

"Stay here until I get back, Darren. Do not leave this room."

I went and found the Master.

"How are you, Charlie? You should still be in bed."

"I know, Master, and I'll go back as soon as you tell me you will let Darren stay."

"What, he beats you half to death and you want him to stay. Don't be ridiculous."

"Please, Master, it wasn't his fault. He wasn't the one that drew blood, and what he did was at Winston's behest. Besides, I need him in the kitchen."

"Are you serious, Charlie?"

"Yes, Master, he is a good lad, I really do need him in the kitchen."

"You have him, but if anything goes wrong because of him, I will draw blood from your ass as well. Do you understand?"

"Yes, Master, thank you."

Back in my room, I looked very sternly at Darren and said, "The Master has released you into my care. Go and ask Cloud if you can have Winston's old room and then go and unpack your things. You are now my assistant in the kitchen, but I am still your slave outside of it."

He looked at me as though I were mad but went to do my bidding.

"See me in the kitchen when you are finished."

I had my kitchen back on my terms now, and it was worth the beating. Ryan and Johnnie were as cooperative as could be, and lunch was prepared by the time the Master found me and reamed me out for being out of bed.

"Honestly, Master, I'm fine. The boys won't let me do too much. Would you like me to join you after lunch for a swim?"

"We need to talk, Charlie, so yes, I think you had better."

At the pool, the Master was in swim briefs topping up his tan.

"Take your shorts off, Charlie, I like to see you naked. You are a very cute guy, and I love to see that appendage of yours. There is an air cushion on the other sun bed. I hope it is soft enough for you."

I tried it very gingerly and sighed as I sat on my butt for the first time in a day and a half.

"Charlie, I owe you an apology. You were never meant to take that kind of punishment Winston meted out to you. The whip is for gentle chastisement to remind you of your status in this house – not to maim you. The remainder of the staff are now aware of the limitations on punishing you.

Nurse tells me you should be fully fit in about four more days. Make the most of this leisure period to improve your all over tan. I don't like white lines, although I will have to accept your butt being a little white for a while."

The next few days were perfect. It was like being on holiday. The Master ate out every night that week and was not in fact on the island, so it was just breakfast lunch and staff meals. I started working out gently in the gym with the Master's personal trainer and continued to swim every day and sun bathe. The only blemishes on my skin were the two whip lines where Winston had broken it, but they healed quickly, and I was as good as new when the Master returned to the island briefly.

"Charlie, now that you are fit again, it is time we removed your body hair. I want you in the First Aid room after lunch preparation today. 10:30 will be good."

My first thought was what a strange place to shave me when I could so easily have done it myself in my bathroom. I understood why when I arrived.

The Master was there talking to two young men who looked like twins. They were wearing little brief shorts similar to mine and showing very adequate bulges in the front. They were very pretty and looked too young to be employees. In fact, they were pantry boys. The Master was carrying a camcorder that I was unhappy about. Was I going on film being humiliated with these two boys present?

"Charlie, take your shorts off and get up on the examination table. Peter and Paul are going to carry out the shaving task."

I was blushing bright red lying face up with Peter one side of the table and Paul the other. Peter lathered my pubic hair and started to shave me while Paul held my cock clear of my belly caressing it until I was very hard. There were stirrups hanging over the table, and Master told me to put my feet in them after my pubic hair was gone. Once in, my legs were pulled further back and wider allowing unfettered access to my balls and ass. Master was filming continually from all different angles.

"I thought the film might make amusing watching, Charlie, at sometime in the future. Hold Charlie's ass cheeks apart Paul so that Peter can shave his crack."

I felt even more humiliated than at the public flogging when I first arrived. The two boys were so close, and Paul was pulling my cheeks apart giving both of them a very close up view of my hole along with the eye of the camcorder. Once I was hairless, Peter ran his hands over my abdomen to check while the Master unclipped part of the table and pulled it aside leaving my ass dangling over the end.

"That looks very professional boys, as a reward you can both do what you like with Charlie now. Take your shorts off, and I will adjust the table height to suit so that he can suck you first before you fuck him."

They were gorgeous, but they had to be the youngest members of staff, and it was so humiliating. Peter was obviously the leader. He came around to the head of the table and told me to pleasure him using my mouth and hands.

"Paul, while Charlie is pleasuring me you can start opening him up ready to take my cock, and then you can take my place."

Peter's ball sac was lovely to lick. I was soon in cock heaven licking and kissing his balls and a beautiful silky shaft. I tongued his glans making him gasp and used my hands to caress the soft skin of his belly, sliding a hand round to do the same to two gorgeous butt cheeks. He was a delight, and I soon stopped worrying about the Master and his camcorder. Paul was playing with my cock and balls with one hand and using plenty of lubrication opening me up gently ready to take Peter when he was ready. When they eventually changed places, Paul was as delightful as Peter, and I was being fucked by another gorgeous cock. I orgasmed with Peter without touching myself and did the same thing sometime later as Paul fucked me. They were two very cute guys, and I immediately christened them Pinky and Perky in my mind.

The Master watched and recorded the whole thing with a shit-eating grin on his face. When they had both cum, Master slapped my ass quite hard with his bare hand five times. It hurt, but not as much as the embarrassment as I watched the faces of Peter and Paul.

I met Mac that afternoon when he came to check the pool at the same time as I arrived. He was the only other white man on the staff.

"Charlie, you are a very cute guy. Are you really a slave to be used by all the staff in any way they choose?"

"Yeah, I'm afraid so. I owe the Master such a huge sum of money the only way to pay it off was to become a slave for the next ten years. Outside of my duties as chef and whatever else the Master wants, I am at the disposal of everybody else to use and abuse as they please. I expect you heard about the Winston incident. He just went over the top with the whip, but everything else he and Darren did was within prescribed limits. A bit embarrassing really to be able to order people around at work, who can then abuse you and humiliate you afterwards."

"So if I took you to my cottage, I could fuck you, or get a blow job or anything else I wanted provided I don't impinge on your work time."

"Yes, that about sums it up, Mac."

"Phew, OK, how about dropping your shorts for me right here."

So I did, and stood with my hands covering my genitals, still a little shy about stripping, I guess.

"Very nice, Charlie, put your hands behind your head and stand with your legs astride."

Mac started to play with my cock and balls with one hand and stroke my butt with the other. When I was erect, he looked at it a little slack jawed and said, "Crikey, Charlie, you make us mere mortals look positively puny down there. Put your shorts back on. I don't want to do anything else to you. On the other hand, perhaps you had better leave them off and keep that tan going." He walked round behind me and patted my ass as he said it.

"I'm glad that cute butt is healing well. It would be a real shame to permanently mark that." Then he was gone.

Darren was becoming a real ace in the kitchen, and Ryan and Johnnie learnt very quickly how I liked food prepared and to keep the surfaces and floor immaculately clean.

They began to relax with me, and the atmosphere in the kitchen was very pleasant. I was a tough cookie where standards were concerned, but I didn't throw tantrums or anything like that. Master got me a new boy to bring us up to strength, and I found it easy for Ryan to teach him the basics while I concentrated on Johnnie who was the more talented of the two.

The new boy was also named Winston, only 18 and as cute as a button. The boys had to explain about my position and the whip and the old Winston, and we had a good laugh about it. He was more than a little surprised at the liberties he could take with me if he wanted to, and of course it wasn't long before he decided to try.

The Master had been called away on business, so I still had not done anything with him except for my first day blowjob. Other members of staff had looked a lot, and I had even done a couple of chores for them, but no sex and no beatings.

Winston had been with me about a week when Darren said he had a chore that needed doing after lunch.

In his room, he said, "Take off your shorts, Charlie, I want to suck your cock."

No argument there from me.

"Lie on the bed, on your back, legs wide open and bent."

He climbed between my legs and took my cock in one hand and my balls in the other. Gently playing with them and using his tongue and mouth as well, he said, "This is a more practical way of saying sorry for what I did to you, Charlie, and when you are ready you can ram this monster up my ass and really fuck me like you mean it."

I pulled him down to my chest and kissed him.

"I'm not going to do that, Darren. I don't want to hurt you, and as I am the slave, don't you want to fuck me?"

"Of course I do, Charlie. You have such a cute butt. Every day when you walk into the kitchen in those sexy little shorts, I want to fuck you."

"Well go ahead then, no argument from me. Just try not to do it as though you want to kill me this time will you."

"I'm sorry, Charlie. You are such a turn on though."

He was good. He had himself and me climbing the wall before he lubed me up and entered me. His cock moved around inside me as he changed his position frequently. I was gasping.

"Oh crikey, Darren, where did you learn to use your cock like that? It is driving me crazy. Please fuck me hard now, fuck me to hurt, fuck me like it's your last."

He did and my own erection got harder, if that was possible, before I shot loads all over his bed and myself. He followed, keening as he spasmed inside me. When I had finished milking him and he me, he rolled off me and lay alongside me. I took him in my arms and kissed him all over his face.

"That was wonderful, Darren, you can call me here for chores anytime you like."

"Thank you, Charlie, you are the best boss a guy could wish for." Laughing as he said it, I soon joined him. This was a really nice way to finish lunch.

"Charlie, I think you are going to get a slave summons after lunch tomorrow. Winston really wants to try out this slave thing. He has been quizzing me mercilessly this week. He was amazed at the liberties Winston and I took with your body and the whipping. Don't worry he knows if he marks you, he will be out of here."

I was ready for it the next day. Lunch was cleared away, and dinner for the staff was all prepared. I thought I would make it easy for Winston. There was no point in doing anything else really. He was more likely to get antsy if I made it difficult for him, and I had the feeling he would not do much. I was after all his boss at work, but the overriding factor was that he was as cute as they come, and I would take great delight in pleasuring him.

"I will see you all at six guys. Winston, would you stay for a moment?"

"Yes, Charlie, what do you want?"

"Just to see how you are settling in. I'm happy with your work, but have you got any worries about it that I can clear up for you?"

"No, everything is fine, Ryan is looking after me, and the rest of the guys are great."

I peeled off my apron while he was talking, and he could see the whip attached to my belt.

"You're lucky, Charlie, only having to wear shorts, our uniforms can be a bit hot in the kitchen."

I laughed, "I'm not lucky, Winston, not with the baggage I carry with them. OK, if there is nothing else, I will see you at six."

"Well actually, Charlie, there is. I have a couple of chores for you if you have time now."

He wouldn't look me in the eyes, and I felt so sorry for him. I nearly hugged him and told him it was OK. Instead, I made it as easy as possible.

"Oh, yes Sir, I can be your slave now until work time."

Calling him Sir really made him stand up straight and become a proper slave master.

"Follow me, then," very commanding!

His room was much like all the others. It was very neat except for his wardrobe, and I guessed that he had deliberately messed that up.

"I never seem to be able to keep that thing tidy, Charlie. Sort it out for me, will you."

He took his shirt and trousers off, gave them to me and plonked himself down on the bed in just his boxers and sandals that he soon kicked off.

I hung his work clothes and started on the rest.

"I'll take your belt, Charlie, and I don't think you really need your shorts on either. You can come over here and take them off."

I stood in front of him and said, "Yes Sir." As I undid the belt passed it to him and took my shorts off dropping them on the floor by his bed.

He unclipped the whip and uncoiled it.

"That is very untidy, Charlie, just dropping your shorts instead of picking them up and putting them somewhere tidy. I think I shall have to chastise you. I understand that six is the normal. Turn round, bend over and grip your ankles."

I did and he gave me six, but they were quite gentle and in fact were erotic enough for me to get an erection. When he had finished, he dropped back on his bed, and I hoped to be able to walk to the wardrobe straight away and not let him see my boner, but he told me to turn round again. My erect penis was at eye level, and he gasped when he saw it.

"Gosh, Charlie, that is amazing." He looked up at me and smiled as he said, "I can't let you work with that. I think I had better get rid of it."

He gave me a beautiful blowjob, nothing sophisticated, just a mouth jack really with a bit of ball play. He also got a real boner on. When he had finished me, I said. "Winston, you can't possibly supervise me with that, so I think perhaps I had better get rid of it for you, don't you?" I was smiling as I said it.

He looked adorable as he looked into my eyes and said very softly, "Would you, Charlie?"

I dropped to my knees in front of him and pulled his body toward me so that I could kiss him. A gentle start and then two hard ones. When I pulled away, his eyes were so wide, I'm sure they were ready to pop out.

"Winston, you are adorable. I'll do anything you like. After all, I am your slave."

I was smiling, and he returned the smile.

"I'm sorry I beat you, Charlie, I just wanted to see if I could. What I really want is for you to make love to me. Will you?"

"Nothing would please me more. Why don't we go back to my room? I have a bigger bed, and I have some sex aids that we might need."

Chapter 2

Learning about Winston

I am so pleased I did not have to do anything else that afternoon. Winston was an absolute delight. As soon as we entered my room, I took him in my arms again and kissed him deeply, running my hands over his body as I did so. I moved my head down and gently licked each of his nipples that became rigid little knobs in seconds. He gasped, but not as loudly as he did a couple of minutes later when I slid my hand under the waistband of his boxers and grasped his cock in my fist.

I pulled his boxers off completely and guided him to my bed. Once he was lying on it, I just looked at him for an age.

"What's the matter, Charlie, don't you like what you see?"

I lay on the bed beside him and propping myself on my left elbow, I leant over and very gently kissed his mouth, working from left to right and then all in one pushing my tongue between his lips to explore inside.

"Winston, there is so much of you that I like it would take me the rest of the afternoon to tell you. What I am going to do instead is take a very long time to explore the whole of your body, and then if you would like to you can fuck me."

"Oh no, Charlie, I want you to fuck me."

"That would be wonderful, but you know I would hurt you so much if I tried to do that."

"I don't care, Charlie, I want you to take me, punish me for beating you. I want you to hurt me with that monster."

I took my time and licked his body all over, particularly his beautiful little puckered love hole. I had him on his back with his legs spread wide and bent with both of my pillows under his ass. He was amazing. He sported a very pretty eight or nine inch cock that I would have loved inside me. Instead, I used a ton of lube and my fingers to open him as wide as I could. At the same time, I played with his cock and balls, sucking and licking him, driving him to the edge and backing off, driving him there again and again not letting him cum until he was begging me to fuck him and let him orgasm. When I was sure I could not get him any more relaxed, I positioned myself between his legs and very gently pushed my cock head against his sphincter until he let me in. He screamed with pain, and he was gasping when he said, "Please, Charlie, stay inside me and just give me a little while to adjust."

"Oh Baby, let me take it out, the pain isn't worth it."

"No, Charlie, please give me some more, I want to feel all of you inside me. It just hurts so much because you are the first to fuck me."

I was flabbergasted. This adorable child was taking my monster as his first cock. I don't know how long it took, but I continued to feed my cock into his wonderful love chute. Eventually, he had all of it, and I rolled forward, so that I could kiss him all over his face without moving my cock inside. The pain receded, and eventually he let out a huge sigh and said, "That is wonderful, Charlie, please fuck me now."

He wanted me to fuck him hard, but I couldn't. I knew that the pain level of a hard fuck with my monster would have been unbelievable. When we both came, it was exquisite, not spine shattering, just exquisitely erotic and satisfying.

He saturated his chest and belly with cum, and I rolled into it as I fell on him, and he moved his legs off my shoulders to wrap around my waist so that I could not slide out of him.

"Stay inside me, Charlie. That was wonderful."

We fell asleep in each other's arms for a little while, recovering. When he woke, I was already propped up on one elbow again gently kissing his face.

"Charlie."

"Yes Baby."

"Can I be your sex slave?"

I was overcome with that request.

"Oh Winston, definitely not, but I would be delighted if you were my lover. The Master has first call on me for everything, but after him I would love to satisfy you every day if I can. You can sleep with me every night as well if you like when I am not sleeping with him."

When we returned to the kitchen for dinner, I think that every one realised that there was something very different from a few hours prior. It was not very many days before they all realised that Winston and I had become lovers.

My problem was what David was going to say and do when he found out, which he surely would.

When David returned to the island, I was almost the first person he sent for.

"Charlie, you have been here for nearly a month now, and I have only experienced a blow job from you. I think it is time we changed that. Come and take a shower with me. I need someone to scrub my back, and I need to make a very close inspection of my slave. Are you horny, Charlie?"

"Always, Master."

"You mean the boys have not been enjoying your body while I have been away?"

"Not many of them Master, but I am sure it will not be long before the ones that have taken advantage convince the others they can make free with it."

"Who, precisely?"

"Just Darren and Winston from the kitchen, and two of the houseboys ganged up and played with me a bit while I did a couple of chores for them, but I think they were a little scared. They won't be next time, so I expect I shall have another two dicks to experience shortly."

"It doesn't appear to faze you at all, Charlie. Don't you feel humiliated being at everyone's beck and call for sex?"

I laughed, "Are you kidding, Master. Have you not noticed how gorgeous every one is on your staff? In London, I would have given my right arm to take anyone of those guys to bed. Here they come looking for me. This is one part of being a slave I am really beginning to like."

"Mmm, what if I ban you from having sex with anyone, but me?"

"Master, you have never had sex with me, apart from a blow job. But you have a very sexy body. I love your cock and want it inside me, so I don't think I would mind too much."

I dropped my eyes as I said it and smiled.

"It's OK, Charlie. I'm not planning to do that. You may not have been used very much yet, but you are very good for staff morale. They love having a white slave in the house. So let's shower."

We soaped each other down, and I took a long time making sure the Master's genital area was exceptionally clean. I wondered about putting my finger up his ass, but it was OK, as he loved it, but he wouldn't let either of us cum.

"I want you to take my first load in your ass, Charlie, and your first load in mine."

"But Master, mine will hurt you so much. There is nothing I can do to stop it."

"I know that, Charlie, but my boyfriend in New York is nearly as big as you, and I manage being a bottom with him."

"Have you many boyfriends, Master?"

"Yes, Charlie, I like to have sex with more than one guy, frequently at the same time. We will have members of staff in from time to time to make up threesomes. I think it will be fun to see how they handle you when I am here as well. If you are making love regularly to one particular staff member, you must tell me when we are going to have a threesome. I would not embarrass you in front of your lover."

"Thank you, Master, that is more than I deserve."

"Probably, Charlie, but come and make it less so. Pleasure me until I am ready to fuck you."

He positioned himself in the middle of the huge bed and pulled me down on top of him, kissing me gently all over my face. He said to me, "Charlie, you are so cute. I find it difficult to believe you are 20. Now you take control and pleasure me, treat me as your slave for a little while."

It was wonderful. I had him change his position on the bed purely for my enjoyment. He really was incredibly sexy. I loved licking his chest until the hair on it was really wet. His nipples took a lot of action, and I had him gasping with the sensitivity of it. His cock was beautiful, with a neat package hanging underneath. Sucking on his ball sac, I made them drop a little more so that I could grasp them as I played with him, maintaining control of his orgasm. I didn't want him to cum for a long time, so I just pulled his balls down and squeezed them hard every time he came close.

"Oh, Charlie, that is killing me, let me cum, you know I will be ready for you again in no time."

"No Master, I am not ready for you to cum yet, and you told me the first time you do it will be inside me." I pleasured his cock head again as soon as I had spoken.

He was a delight to play with, just one big bundle of sensitivity. Eventually, I lubed up his cock and my ass and straddling him took all of him inside me in one smooth motion. As soon as I bottomed out, I attacked his nipples with my teeth biting them quite hard before starting to ride his cock with long strokes, rotating my hips as I did so.

"Oh my God, Charlie, that is amazing."

I increased the speed trying desperately not to cum, and fortunately, I achieved it. His orgasm was stupendous, and I kept riding him long after I had milked him dry.

"Oh God, Charlie, stop, get off me, that is so sensitive, stop Charlie please stop you are killing me."

I pulled off him and immediately went to work stretching him ready to take me. He was rock hard again and gasping as I kept hitting his prostate. The precum was oozing, and I just had to lick it off even though he had been inside me. When I was sure he was completely relaxed again, I lubed us both up and entered him, very gently easing over his sphincter. He still screamed and gasped but told me to remain in him. I slowly fed him all of it, and as I hit his ass with my pubes, he sighed and said, "Now fuck me violently, Charlie, hurt me and make me your slave."

Amazing, but I did, I powered into him so hard I thought I would kill him. I know I was hurting him by the screams every time I powered in. Using long strokes, I kept going for a far greater time than I thought possible, but eventually I could last no longer and my orgasm burst inside him like an explosion. I gasped with the intensity of it, and he came at the same time, an enormous quantity of jism accompanied with another scream, only this was of pleasure not pain. I remained deep inside him and fell forward onto his chest. He started stroking my hair as he recovered and said, "Charlie, that was amazing. My New York lover has an incredible act to follow next week."

I laughed and replied, "Thank you, Master, but that was only a warm-up. Are you ready for the main event now that I know your body?"

He lifted my head off his chest so that he could look into my eyes.

"You are joking aren't you, Charlie?" He looked serious.

"No, Master, I know I can do better than that." I was laughing as I said it but then went all serious and said, "I really can."

My reward for that was a loving kiss and the assertion that he would find out later.

Another shower during which I de-spunked him again and I was off for my other duties.

Life was getting better. I was getting plenty of good sex, and it was becoming more frequent and varied all the time.

I was experimenting and producing better meals. David even flew me to New York for a couple of days to explore the markets for ingredients. He had his tailor and cobbler produce some exquisite clothes for me. It felt funny wearing a complete ensemble again; I had become so used to my little white shorts or nothing at all and liked it.

My first night in New York, David sent for me after supper. The message was to wear my white shorts and nothing else. When I arrived in the drawing room, David was with four other men all dressed like him in Jeans and cowboy shirts and all about his age. There were also two young guys about my own age dressed in white shorts like mine.

"Come in, Charlie, we are all bored and thought you might furnish some entertainment for us. My friends don't believe you are a slave, so I am going to prove to them you are. I have the paddle here, Charlie, you know the position."

"Yes, Master," was my reply.

I took my shorts off and stood legs astride bent over gripping my ankles where David pointed.

"Just five tonight, Charlie, because I think you will be receiving more later."

"One, thank you Master."

Painful.

"Two, thank you Master."

That one really hurt.

"Three, thank you Master."

Why was he hurting me? I had not done anything wrong.

"Four, thank you Master, why are you hurting me, Master?"

The fifth one never arrived.

"Stay where you are, Charlie."

What new devilment or humiliation did he have in store for me? When we were alone, he was loving and caring. Why was he being such a beast to me in company?

"These other two young men are Ivan and Petrov. They don't like English boys, so they are going to entertain us at your expense. Ivan come and stretch Charlie ready to take Petrov's present."

Ivan finger fucked me, opening me up wide. Then Petrov slid a very large, very long dildo into me. I screamed as he went in and continued screaming as he buried it deep in my guts. I was panting as I tried to adjust to this massive intrusion in my anus and the incredible pain. I thought it must be bigger than my monster because Darren had not caused this amount of trauma when he fucked me.

"Well done, Charlie, now walk round the room and show all my guests a close up of your ass. When they are finished with you, I want you on all fours in the centre of the room."

The first one told me to stand sideways in front of him, and slicking up one hand he started to play with my cock and balls and wiggle the dildo about, painfully. I had a dildo fucking me and a hard penis, which he made shrink again very quickly by hitting it quite hard. I yelped and jumped. The others laughed.

"Not very nice, Gregg, I hope you don't treat your boyfriends like that."

The other man laughed as he said it but then used the dildo like a prick and fucked me with it. Again, I jumped away from him a little, so he smacked my ass hard with his bare hand and sent me to the next one.

"We need to look after this, Charlie, it is something special." Caressing my cock and balls as he said it and returning it to hard. Number three.

"David, this really is an amazing piece of kit. Any chance I can have him tonight after we have finished playing?" Number four and he didn't touch me.

"No problem, Tom. OK, Charlie, you will be sleeping with Mr. Tom tonight."

"Very well, Master."

I went to the Master next, and he just pointed to the centre and nodded to the two boys. At the same time, the lights got very bright.

In very heavily accented English, Ivan said, "Now English slut take my shorts off and suck my cock."

I pulled his shorts down, and he sank to his knees. I started to suck him and resting on my elbows used my hands to play with him.

Petrov walked around behind me and kicked my legs further apart before curling up on the floor and abusing my ass. He pulled the dildo out and then pulled my cheeks apart until it hurt and tried to fist me.

"He is not very good, Petrov, I think he is going to sleep."

Ivan was getting first class service, so he was just being a bastard.

Petrov used his bare hand and delivered two very hard slaps on my bare ass. I gasped and doubled my effort on Ivan.

"I think perhaps his ass will be better for my dick, Petrov, you come and try him."

They changed places, and Ivan delivered two more stinging blows to my buttocks while Petrov rammed the whole of his eight inches straight down my throat. Ivan shoved his cock up my ass and both of them fucked me for a little while. All the time, I could see the Master's guests watching the action. This was a new humiliation for me. After a while, the boys turned me over and squatting either side of me pulled my legs over my head and pinned them to the floor either side of my shoulders. With my butt pulled well into the air they proceeded to spank me for about five minutes making sure that my balls took many of the smacks. I was soon pleading and begging them to stop.

When I thought I could take no more, Tom said, “David.” And David stopped the punishment. They put two fingers each into my rectum and tried to pull them apart when once again Tom called to David.

I don’t know how long this had been going on, obviously some time because David said, “OK, guys, fuck him as hard as you can, and when you have cum you can go.”

They set out to hurt me, holding me in the same position, one of them fucking me, the other holding my legs and then reversing the role. They both came all over my face and chest. After they left, I could not get up my lower part hurt so much. My ass was on fire, and my balls felt badly bruised.

“Tom, if you want him for the night you had better remove him to your room.”

Tom picked me up gently and after saying goodnight to the others carried me to his room. He was so tender and caring, cleaning me up and tending to my bruised balls and ass.

“I was hoping to enjoy your body tonight, Charlie. I have never known David to be cruel before. He must hate you a lot. I don’t understand him. He told me you are a wonderful chef, and I can see you are a beautiful boy. I would treasure you if you were mine.”

“Thank you, Tom, you are very kind. I’m sorry I am not any good for you. I could manage a blowjob if you would like one.”

“No Charlie, I would like you to cuddle up to me though. You feel so good to touch.”

I fell asleep with my head on his chest and one leg curled over him. He was so nice to hold. The next morning I was still very sore and bruised. I managed to order in the goods I wanted to take back to the island and was ready to leave after lunch. David would not see me. He just approved my request to leave via his butler. So I flew back by myself with boxes of new ingredients to play with.

The staff loved me because I tried out new dishes on them. The best-fed house servants in the world I told them, and the best serviced I said grinning like a Cheshire Cat. Some of them looked quite embarrassed but were soon fine when I planted a kiss on the odd cheek and told them it was OK. I enjoyed our little dalliances immensely. The staff restaurant was always vibrant during meals. I loved walking round and talking to everyone, asking them what they thought of the food. They were always fulsome in their praise and the cheekier ones would pat my ass or tweak my dick as I talked to them. I usually had a stock phrase for them when they did either of those.

“Naughty boy, I’m the chef for another hour, you have to book the slave if you want to do that.”

When David came back from New York next, he brought with him most of the staff from his home there. At the end of the staff wing was a dormitory, and I found out what it was for. Regardless of status, all his New York people were accommodated there.

"Charlie, we are going to have a summer party, and there will be about a hundred guests each day for four days. My chef from NY has done this before, as have most of the kitchen staff. They are here to help you, but you are still in charge. Here are the menus for each day, and the notes will tell you what is to be available and at what times. If you want to vary the menus you are free to do so of course. Off you go, and don't let me down. I have been singing your praises to all my friends."

He never mentioned my last night in New York, nor did I.

We all worked very hard to get everything ready, but I knew I had ruffled many feathers among the NY guys, some black, some white. They were aware of my weird status, showing varying amounts of surprise and annoyance. It was obvious that the ones who had treated me like a guest when I was in NY with Master were seething about it. The NY chef was called Raymond and came from Haiti.

"Charlie, we have really broken the back of this work today. What time are you planning to let us go and relax?"

"About another half hour should see it through, Raymond, and then your boys will be free until after breakfast in the morning. My own staff will handle staff meals, and the Master is off island rounding up his guests, so I have no other duties to worry about."

"OK, Charlie. When we finish will you bring the chores and punishment book to our dormitory. Some of my boys have things for you to do."

The smirk on his face told me I was in for an interesting afternoon.

I handed the book to Raymond as I entered the dormitory, dressed as always in my little white shorts. All of the NY staff were there, ten in all. They stood around at the end of the dormitory with a bed pulled out into the centre and an armchair off to one side. Raymond walked me through to meet them all. After introducing me to the ones I didn't know, he said, "The boys would like you to take their clothes off them, Charlie, and hang them in their proper place. I will take your belt and your shorts."

I felt very embarrassed stripping in front of these strangers, all of whom were junior to me in work status.

One of the boys stood in front of me to be undressed. Trousers and shirt came off, and I looked for the correct place to put them, but naturally, I chose incorrectly. The boy who was one of the kitchen staff smirked as he told me I was wrong and had to be punished.

"Take my boxers off, Charlie, and then bend over the chair pushing as far forward as you can. Spread your legs wide. I'll support you from the front."

He moved round in front of me and held my shoulders, making sure that his cock was only an inch or so from my mouth. If he got hard, I would be able to swallow most of it without moving.

Raymond stood up behind me and used the whip to give me three quite hard strokes, each one made me move forward so that I kissed the cock in front of me. It was hard by the second one, and the boy told me to take it in my mouth. He face fucked me for a couple of minutes while I calmed down from the beating.

"Stand up, Charlie, and try to get it correct with your next one."

Of course I didn't, and I had received 12 strokes and got four boys erect when the system changed. I was very sore, but they had obviously been briefed about limits, so I was not incapacitated.

"You aren't learning, Charlie, so while another member of our staff does your job, you can do his. He is our fuck bunny, so for the next hour or so that is what you will be. Turn around, Charlie, spread you legs wide and bend over, use you hands to pull your cheeks apart." Raymond was obviously enjoying this.

They all stood behind me staring at my asshole, making ribald comments and occasionally slapping the bottom of my buttocks where they joined my legs. They must have known how sensitive that would be, and how painful. It was also very humiliating having ten complete strangers looking at my hole, slapping around it and at odd times lubing a finger and sticking it up me. They occasionally hit my prostate so despite myself I had an erection on which drew a few gasps and a lot of jealousy.

"Look at that shitty big dick on that little slut. It's obscene."

I was told to lie on the bed on my back. Two of the boys grabbed my legs and pulled them right back securing them with their belts to the edges of the sprung portion of the bed frame at maximum width. With no head or foot boards they could all move around me unimpeded.

With one on either side of me, my ass cheeks were pulled apart as far as they would spread, and they took turns finger fucking me, sometimes two or three of them together. Another one would be face fucking me and others were playing with my cock and balls. It was humiliating in the extreme because there were always ten pairs of eyes watching my ass being abused. The two pulling my cheeks apart were stretching my anus until it hurt and then one of them entered me. None too gently but at least they had lubed me. He grabbed my cock as he rammed all the way home and yelled, "Hey, guys this is like riding a rodeo horse. I even have a pommel to hang onto so that I don't fall off."

He fucked me for a little while and then swapped places with the guy whose cock was in my mouth. They all watched as I had to lick him clean. It was disgusting.

Raymond stepped in again.

"I know how horny all you guys are, so why don't we make sure we can fuck him for a long time by unloading a quick one first. We can check how good a shot you all are at the same time. Gather round and wank yourselves off. A bull's eye is straight in Charlie's mouth. Let's see how many of you can make it. Open your mouth, Charlie, and everything that goes in you have to swallow. Don't close your mouth though until it is full. I wouldn't want you to miss a load while you are swallowing."

Looking round I could see ten big dicks all being jacked furiously. As they started to shoot, my mouth filled up and the rest of my face became covered in copious amounts of cum. I had to close my eyes because they were becoming gluey. I eventually had to swallow and in the process missed one lot of cum.

"He's cost you a bulls eye, Joey, by closing his mouth. Give him a good hiding for it.

Joey grabbed my whip and laid into me with it. Oh God it hurt. I was screaming and begging for mercy, choking on cum. I could not believe how they were treating me. They appeared totally oblivious to my pain and suffering. The humiliation was unbelievable. When the beating finally ended, they just resumed their previous programme.

After I had taken most of their cocks up my ass and sucked many of them off, they got bored. A few of them wanked over me again leaving pools of cum all over my face and hair, chest and belly. I had even added to it myself to great hoots from the audience, until someone said. "How about Master Cock, he obviously gets off on cock. I reckon he could take that now he is so slack."

Master Cock turned out to be the biggest dildo I had ever seen.

"You'll like this, Charlie. It is 18 inches long and nine inches round. I am going to fist fuck you first and see how far up your ass I can get my arm and then you can take this. Say thank you, Charlie, or I shall have to beat you again, be fulsome in your thanks."

"Thank you, Raymond, for being so considerate as to fist and arm fuck me before giving me that dildo, which would otherwise have killed me I am sure."

They all cheered and the degradation continued. I screamed when Raymond's knuckles went over my sphincter and the tremendous pain as he pushed further into my rectum had me gasping and sobbing with the pain level.

"Measure my arm where it enters his body, Al. I reckon we have him stretched for the nine inches."

They were all looking closely at my anus with an arm sticking out of it. Al measured around Raymond's arm and said, "The boy done well. He has 91/2 inches round stuck up that cute ass."

He slapped me as he moved away, and Raymond pulled out.

The dildo went in next. The pain was intense, and I was still sobbing.

"Well, Charlie, you have 12 inches, that is the same as being fucked by your own cock, except of course this one is thicker. Tell me you love it, Charlie, and want more."

I couldn't speak because the pain was unbelievable.

"I'll punish you if you don't talk to me, Charlie."

I still couldn't speak until he thrashed my ass with my whip.

"Give me more," I screamed at the top of my voice.

"You have it, boy. That is 14. You really are a fuck slut. I reckon the last four should be no problem."

He pushed again, and I screamed deep from within my body. I thought that I was going to die.

"Keep the noise down guys," the voice came from the doorway. "Some peo…. Oh my God what are you doing?"

It was Cloud, and he had come to my rescue again.

He looked down on me still with 14 inches of dildo stuck in me. My whole body was smothered in cum and the other material from my ass that I hadn't actually licked up.

"Get that thing out of his ass." He just gaped at it when he realised how much I had in me and how thick it was.

I was barely conscious.

"You guys must be mad. If I tell the Master what I have just seen here, all of you will be looking for new jobs. This boy is a slave not an animal. Charlie, are you OK?"

I managed to say, "I think so, Sir."

I gradually calmed down enough for Cloud to talk to me and get an intelligible reply.

"Charlie, I am going to leave the decision to you. If I tell the Master, they are history. Do I tell him?"

"No Sir, provided they are not allowed to touch me again. They are frightening. I don't want them in my kitchen again either, Sir."

I was able to walk with Cloud's help after about half an hour during which time I heard him take the NY guys apart verbally.

"The Master will realise something is wrong when all of you worthless pieces of shit are serving instead of being in the kitchen. I will leave you to tell him what you like."

We had to work longer and harder than we had ever done, but Cloud's back up crew helped enormously. I was terribly bruised and sore, but I worked through it. We all knew each other and worked well together. The four days of partying were a huge success from the catering side.

The New York crowd went home without another word to me. A thank you, Charlie, for saving our jobs would have been nice!

The next time I was in bed with David, he said, "You did me proud, Charlie. The food was superb and the catering side overall was faultless.

Would you like to tell me why my New York crew were kept out of the kitchen completely?"

"Not really, Master, unless you insist."

"No that's alright. I presume they got a bit rough with the slave did they?"

"A little, Master."

"You're a little guy, Charlie, but you are no wimp are you? You aren't damaged are you?"

"Yes, Master, would you like to send me back to the shop and get a replacement?"

I was laughing as I said it, and he joined in cuddling me tight as he did so.

"I think I am a little in love with you, Charlie. I may well have to send you away if it gets more serious."

"Where would you send me, Master? I like it here."

"I don't know, Charlie. I would probably just have to beat you until you hated me and then our sex would get bad, and I would stop loving you. How does that sound?"

"Not good. I like you loving me, but I don't like to be beaten, and I don't want to go away."

"We will have to see. I will probably be away almost continuously for about six months starting after the big dinner for my bankers in two weeks time. I want the best meal you have ever produced for that one, Charlie, because I am softening them up for a very special loan. I may well send for you to join me occasionally when I am not in New York, so we had better get you a decent worldwide wardrobe."

The next two weeks were a mixture of good and bad.

The good was sleeping with Master every night, playing a lot of sport with him, working out and swimming with him every day. I was incredibly fit and with my all over tan and white gold hair I looked like a Greek god, a little one perhaps, but a Greek god nonetheless.

The down side was that I did not get to sleep with Winston except for an hour or two after dinner most nights, and I was in much more demand from the staff for sex rather than chores.

In all honesty, some of that was fun but one incident wasn't. The two newest and youngest staff were pantry boys. I referred to them as Pinky and Perky after they had shaved me. Winston used to slap me playfully and tell me I was rude and deserved to be punished.

"Oh yes Sir, beat me, beat me for making derogatory remarks about my betters."

He snuggled in closer to me and said, "I could never beat you again, Charlie. I love you far too much."

"I know, Baby, and I love you, too. David is going away in two weeks. I hope I will be able to sleep with you every night then."

Of course, some one let my nicknames for them slip in the presence of Pinky and Perky, and they were pissed off. A few days later, obviously after they had time to plan something, I was asked by one of them to take the punishment and chores book up to their room after lunch. They knew precisely what they were allowed to do and how to write it up. Their actual names were Peter and Paul. They were both 18, and in keeping with David's usual standards, they were drop dead gorgeous. They were the same height as me with the usual beautiful bodies and eye-catching boxes. Both light-skinned Dominican boys, they were waiting for me dressed in white briefs. I gasped as I entered their room. They truly were beautiful.

"Charlie, we understand that you refer to Peter and me as Pinky and Perky. That is rude and derogatory. As a senior member of staff, we feel that you should give us an apology, and as a slave we feel that you should be punished in a way that is humiliating because you have humiliated us."

It was a long speech for this young man, and I knew how much it had cost him to get it all out. He sounded so nervous, but he never dropped his eyes from mine as he said it, and he didn't stumble over his words. I would tell Cloud about him. He was self-assured and would progress in this house.

"Paul, you are right. It was contemptible of me as the chef to use names like Pinky and Perky. I apologise unreservedly. You are both beautiful young men and deserve my respect. As a slave, I prostrate myself before you and accept any punishment and humiliation you wish to heap on me."

With that, I lay on the floor on my tummy head down so that they could not see the smile on my face. I knew I had dumbfounded them, and they were unsure how to proceed.

Peter was the first one to get it together again.

"Stand up, Charlie, and hand me the punishment book. Take off your belt and give it to me. Take off your shorts and stand legs astride hands behind your head."

I was facing the two of them and they stood looking me up and down, particularly my groin area. Paul realised the next rehearsed move was his.

"We are only required to notate punishment administered with the whip and the reason for it. I am writing in ten lashes, Charlie, five from each of us for hurt feelings. We are also going to spank you the way our parents did us when we were naughty as children. You have been childish so that is the reason. To humiliate you, we are going to use your body for our own gratification."

Peter had sat on the bed and after Paul's little speech told me to bend over his knees.

My cock was crushed on his right thigh, and he held me around the waist pulling me further over his knee so that my feet were barely touching the ground. My nuts were now hard up against his thigh as well, I could not move, and it was bloody uncomfortable. Paul pulled up a chair opposite Peter so that he could smack my buttocks as well. They started smacking my ass with their bear hands each striking the buttock furthest away from them. It began to sting very quickly, but initially I found it very erotic and got a boner on. Peter could feel it and made me stand again to show Paul. They both played with it for a few minutes, and that was erotic as my ass was tingling. When I bent over the next time, Paul pulled my cock down so that it was not trapped, and they made me spread my legs. The result was that my balls were sticking back almost as far as my ass cheeks. If either of them took a sideswipe, I could have two very painful balls by the end of this. They both realised it as well, and every third or fourth slap caught my balls. Every time it happened, I grunted. My balls were getting very sore, and my erection subsided. It was also becoming very painful. Their hands were very strong.

"Please, Peter, please, Paul, don't beat me any more. That is so painful. I am truly sorry, but please don't beat me."

They completely ignored my pleas.

"That is 50, Peter, I think it is time for the whip now don't you?"

"Yes, stand up, Charlie."

I stood to let Paul up and was told to get on the bed on all fours, spread my legs wide and lower my head onto the bed and push my ass back. Very clever, it was a position that showed them my asshole that they finger fucked for a little while, both of them going at it together. It also stretched my ass further than almost any other position they could have put me in.

"Peter will administer five, Charlie, followed by my five. You count them loud thanking us for them on each one."

"One, thank you, Peter."

I had been given harder ones, so I only grunted as it landed. The next three were the same. The fifth one was a hum dinger and really made me gasp and squirm.

"Five, thank you, Peter."

Peter passed the whip to Paul, and the punishment started again. Paul was not as gentle as Peter, and I was soon begging him to stop.

"Two, thank you Paul. Oh God, please stop, Paul, you are hurting me so much."

Bad plea, the third one was much harder, and I couldn't speak after it.

"I didn't hear the count on that one, Charlie, so I will administer that one again."

"Three, Paul, I beg you no more."

The next two came so quickly I didn't have time to call them.

"Stand up, Charlie, and face us."

I could just about stand, my ass was on fire, and my whole body was consumed with pain.

They curled up on the bed together and made me stand legs astride hands behind my head only a few inches away from the side of the bed. They started to play with me, but I was in too much pain to react. A hand went around my back and caressed one cheek. It was like fire again. I jumped and let out a sob.

"Keep still, Charlie, or I will have to put you over my knee again."

They were rubbing one cheek each, very gently, but I was gasping the pain was so intense. It did begin to recede though, and I gradually calmed down and started to react to their ministrations.

"OK, Peter, I think it is time he gave us both a blow job before we fuck him in turn and cum in his ass. With luck we will then still have time to cum again all over his face and make him crawl back to his room naked and covered in cum with loads dripping out of his asshole. That should be enough humiliation for one day. We can always do it again if we want to."

They both looked at me and sniggered, "Pinky and Perky are naughty little toys aren't they, Charlie? Now, get down on your knees and take our briefs off."

They were both fully erect and about seven inches. They were delightful to look at, and in other circumstances, this would have been more than a pleasure. I had both cocks in my mouth alternately and both hands thoroughly wetted playing with their balls. They really were gorgeous. When they were both aroused they spit roasted me. Peter fucking my ass, and Paul my mouth. Paul's load covered my face, but Peter I could feel deposited copious quantities of jism in my anus. Then they reversed roles. Neither of them had gone soft, so it was a continuation. I had to suck a cock that was straight from my ass, and to me that was the most degrading and humiliating act anybody could ask me to commit.

They had choreographed it perfectly, and I did return to my room covered in cum and dripping it from my very red bruised ass. Winston was there, which I hadn't expected and was overcome by shock at the state of me. I had cum on my face, and cum was still dripping from my ass, as I headed for the shower. When he saw my ass, he started to cry.

"Charlie, who did this to you?"

"It doesn't matter, Baby. It was my fault for being a smart ass."

"Oh God, those bastards."

I climbed into the shower and washed everything clean. As I was drying the sound of a commotion reached me, and I slipped on shorts before going to see.

Winston was in the corridor going after Peter. I went at the run. Well as near to it as my sore ass would allow. I looked in the door of their room and saw Paul sitting on the bed nursing a very swollen face and hugging himself. I helped get Winston off Peter.

He was crying fit to break and screaming.

"If you ever hurt, Charlie, again I will kill you with my bare hands."

I took him in my arms and stroked his hair and face until he calmed down.

He could see almost all the staff had turned out to watch.

"I will kill anyone that ever hurts Charlie again."

It was said in a tone that made me shudder.

He stood up, and as he turned, he administered a vicious kick to Peter's balls. I thought crikey that boy won't be getting a hard on for some time. His face was a mess as well. I was surprised my Baby had it in him.

"Darren, get those two boys to the nurse, ask him not to say anything until tomorrow after I have had a night with the Master to clear this up."

Chapter 3

Ryan Shows His True Self

As luck would have it, David was in a submissive mood and only wanted me to screw him. He did of course notice my bruised ass.

"Oh crikey, Charlie, what did you do to deserve that, or have we a sadist I need to get rid of?"

"No Master, it was my fault, and the two who administered it are going to look a mess when you see them tomorrow. I'm sorry, but I have a White Knight to protect me now, so I don't think it is going to happen again."

"I won't have a member of staff undermining my instructions, Charlie, just to protect you."

"That won't happen, Master, he has just made it clear that brutality will require retribution. I won't allow him to undermine your instructions in any way."

"Good, Charlie. I think you had better go to your own bed tonight. I am not in the mood for anymore company."

I was shocked when I crept into my room. I could hear sobbing sounds coming from my bed. I turned a bedside light on and found Winston curled up in the faetal position crying like a baby.

"Baby, what is it?"

"I'm sorry, Charlie, I keep thinking about the humiliation and pain you went through this afternoon. I love you so much, when you hurt I hurt, and that was so awful, and your ass is so bruised."

"I'm OK, Baby, I'll recover. Please don't cry anymore. Move over and snuggle up to me."

I had his head on my chest and his arms wrapped round me in a millisecond. I stroked his hair and kissed the top of his head until I could hear the gentle breathing of a sleeping boy. I loved this boy so much, and now he was my champion, but I had to be careful that he did not undermine David.

By breakfast the next morning I had my plan. Winston was still in bed on my instructions, and I got Darren in the kitchen with Ryan and Johnnie.

"You all know the commotion yesterday was because Peter and Paul, the new pantry boys, were a bit over enthusiastic in humiliating me for calling them Pinky and Perky. Winston has threatened to kill anyone else who hurts me. That is nice, but we must not let it undermine the Master's wishes for me as a slave, or Winston will be moved out. Will you guys just let it be known it is business as usual, but Winston will kill them if they send me back to my room in the terrible state I was in yesterday. Tell them I'm a slave not a bloody animal. I hope that will keep everyone happy."

"I know we are on duty, Charlie, and you are the chef not a slave, but would you just drop your shorts for a moment and let me see your bum?"

Shy little Ryan was asking to see my bum in working hours, or out it would have made no difference. I wanted to laugh, but I knew it would devastate him. Darren looked at me to see my reaction. I just turned round and dropped my shorts for Ryan to see my backside. I winked at Darren, and he left the kitchen. He couldn't keep it together.

"That's OK, Charlie. Will you come to my room after lunch? You don't need to bring the punishment book. I am not going to beat you."

I loved the way he said it. I was still struggling to keep a straight face.

"Very well, Ryan, now everyone can we get on with some work.

Darren came back into the kitchen, and I could see he had been crying. He dragged me off to a storeroom and nearly broke down again. He was laughing so hard, the tears were there again, I had to join him.

"Oh, Charlie, I wish I could have that on film. It's a classic. Promise you will tell me what goes on in his room. My imagination isn't good enough for that one."

Then he was off again.

"Darren, piss off until dinner, the rest of us will manage lunch."

All I can say is that Ryan has the kindest heart in the world in my book.

When I got to his room, he said, "Take your belt and your shorts off Charlie and lie on the towel on my bed. He looked away as I did it and only looked back again when I said, "Like this."

He turned round and blushed, "Oh no, Charlie, I meant on your tummy."

I had to take pity on him as he was just too much.

"Ryan, come here."

He did, but he studiously avoided looking at my cock. I told him to sit on the bed patting the place I wanted him. I took his face in my hands and pulled it towards me so that I could kiss him gently on the lips. Still holding his face, I twisted it so that his eyes were directed at my cock.

"Now look at it, Ryan. I'm not embarrassed that you should see it. Most of the staff have done much more than look at it. I don't know what you are planning, but I am sure it will be good. It is OK, to see me naked."

"Oh, Charlie, I shouldn't. You're my boss.

"Fiddlesticks. What would make you comfortable with my nudity?"

"If I were nude, too, Charlie."

"Well, in that case, get nude, but you are one cute guy. I may want to ravage your body if I see it naked."

"Oh, Charlie, would you?"

He was unbelievable, a little boy asking for something special.

"I'm a slave, Ryan. You don't have to ask you can just tell me to."

He stood up and stripped off his uniform. He was cute. They were all cute. That was why my sex life was so fantastic.

"Now, Charlie, will you turn over onto your tummy so that I can do what I invited you for."

He started to rub some cream into my buttocks telling me his mother made it from herbs and fruit on this island. It was fantastic. His hands were soft, and I could almost feel the cream working as he rubbed it in to each buttock in turn. I looked round and saw that he had a steaming hard on. I looked away again quickly so that he would not know I had seen it. When he finished, he tried to walk away from the bed, but I grabbed him, swung him round and pulled him back towards me.

"That was wonderful Ryan, my ass feels better already. Now can I do something good for you?"

"What, Charlie?"

"How about a blow job?" I ran a finger gently down the length of his shaft. He shuddered.

"Oh yes, please, Charlie, but you don't have to."

"I know, but you deserve it, you are very sweet to try looking after me."

I kissed him again gently as I pulled him onto the bed and gave him one of my class one blowjobs. He was delightful. It gave me more pleasure to see him cum than almost any one else I had done it to. When we were finished and he was back with me, he purred and said, "Thank you, Charlie, that was amazing. You need to have the cream again tomorrow, but you don't have to do anything to me."

I gave him a gentle kiss as I was leaving and said, "We'll see."

What was I going to do for six months? I loved Winston, but he accepted that I had sex with any one who wanted it because I was a slave. The problem was I wanted it too and encouraged it. I knew Winston would be devastated if he was aware that I could avoid half the shagging that I got.

Things were about to change though. The special dinner night arrived and I made every effort to impress. I knew the meal was the best I had ever produced.

"David, that is without doubt the most exquisite meal I have ever had. Your chef is truly amazing. Who is he, and where on earth did you find him? Can you summon him before the sweet so that we can congratulate him?"

The Master was entertaining a group of International Bankers who were handling his portfolio. There were no women present, and they were all well aware that their client was not only one of the wealthiest men in the world but also that he was gay.

"I think that can be arranged. Cloud, please ask Charlie if he could join us for a few minutes. Tell him to leave his apron in the kitchen."

A few minutes later, I stood at the side of David dressed as usual in my skimpy white shorts not really hiding anything. I was displaying five or six inches of cock.

"You summoned me, Master."

"Yes, Charlie, these gentlemen have something they wish to say to you. Well here he is, my chef."

"Come along, David, this is some sort of joke, yes? You are trying to kid us that this beautiful young man is your chef. He looks more like one of your sex toys."

Everyone laughed.

"He is both, Colin. Aren't I lucky?"

"We don't believe it. Prove it."

"Charlie, is the dessert ready?"

"Nearly, Master, I have a little more work to do on them as I plate them."

"Gentlemen, let's go down to the kitchen and watch Charlie finish up."

They all followed me to the kitchen and watched as I finished the desserts with the help of my staff and organised the clear up before rejoining the Master in the dining room.

"OK, David, what's the story, and why is he dressed like this when all the rest of your staff are in immaculate uniforms?

"Because Charlie is a slave not an employee."

There were gasps from the guests, and David told them the story.

"Charlie was on track to be one of the finest chefs in the world. Unfortunately, he had an uncontrollable gambling habit. When it reached unmanageable proportions, he was offered the chance to clear his debt by becoming my slave for the next ten years. It is legal. In one package, I now have a superb chef and a sex slave for myself, and when I don't need him, the remainder of my staff have a menial to do the things they don't like doing, and of course Charlie can satisfy their sexual needs as well. When he misbehaves, or is less than perfect at his chores, the staff are allowed to beat him to improve him. That's the means of punishment attached to his belt. Is that all correct, Charlie?"

"Yes, Master."

"A bonus for all the size queens on my staff is that Charlie has the biggest penis I have ever seen. I have very happy staff members in this house."

David said it with a laugh that made me blush, fortunately not easy to see now because of my fantastic tan.

"Are we allowed to see it, David?"

"Yes of course, Charlie is finished in the kitchen now. You can keep him here to play with if you like. You can do anything you like to him and with him, and he will not object. I promise you. Cloud will serve liquors and coffee in here. Please take your fill of this beautiful young man."

The guest the Master called Colin appeared to be the leader of the group. He stood up, moved me to the centre of the floor so that every one at the table could see me and said, "I am going to prove you wrong, David, I am sure. I can't believe that you have that much control over him."

"Be my guest, Colin, would you like to take a wager on it?"

"Oh yes, this will be one of my easier wins. Shall we say a thousand dollars?"

"Accepted."

"OK, Charlie, remove your shorts and play with yourself until you have an erection."

This was the first time the Master had exhibited me like this, different to the New York incident. I was so embarrassed I could not get hard.

Colin was not a happy bunny and told me if I were still not erect in one more minute he would chastise me. Of course I wasn't, so he picked up my whip.

"Turn around, Charlie, spread your legs and bend over to grip your ankles. I don't want you to move from that position until I tell you to. Do you understand?

"Yes Sir," I replied.

He started to beat me then, very steady and very hard. After three, I was gasping, after six I was begging. My body was wracked with pain. There didn't appear to be one square inch that didn't hurt. At ten, I was screaming, begging, and pleading, and I collapsed, curling into a ball to try to protect myself from any further punishment.

"Please Sir, please don't beat me anymore. I beg you. It hurts so much, please stop. Master, please don't let him hurt me anymore. I'm sorry, Master, but please don't let him."

I was sobbing uncontrollably.

"Sir, I am sorry, I can't watch anymore of this I am leaving."

I did not even realise Cloud was here until I heard him say that.

"You will not leave, Cloud, until I tell you to."

"I am sorry Sir, but to damage that gentle boy any more would be a terrible crime. I will not watch it."

"I'm sorry, Colin, my man is right. I have allowed this to go too far. You may not use the whip any more."

"In that case, David, perhaps you would like to send him to my room when he has recovered, and I can see if he really is a sex slave as well. I promise I will not damage him any more."

"That is acceptable, and you can tell me your conclusion in the morning."

"Cloud, attend to Charlie, and when he is recovered, send him to Mr. Colin's room."

The party broke up then. Cloud took me to his quarters and attended to my ass, which was bruised and hurt, but the skin was not broken.

"Not as bad as Winston did Charlie, but you will be very bruised in the morning. Let's get some salve on that and prepare you for the next round."

I was nearly an hour recovering so that when I arrived at Colin's door, he was in a foul mood.

He was lying naked on his bed with a solid erection. His cock was nowhere near as long as mine was but it was monstrously thick, I had never seen anything remotely close to it in thickness. Even the monster dildo the New York boys had used on me paled in insignificance to this. It looked like a huge battering ram. I was sure I would be unable to get it in my mouth, and he would split me if he pushed it into my ass.

"I want you laying sixty-niners with me, Charlie. I am going to open you up ready to take my cock in your ass, and you are going to show me what a great cocksucker you are."

I could not even get the head in my mouth, but I did do a lot of pleasuring in the hope that I could make him cum and save my ass. He was ready for that though and made me leave him alone when he was close to cumming. He did get me very hard though playing with my balls and cock, and left my ass alone except for fingering me. Eventually, he moved around and straddled me with me on my back, legs in the air.

"I am going to use your cock as a lever to help me ease into you, Charlie. I don't want you trying to get away from me." He laughed as he said it, but not a nice laugh.

I felt his head pushing against my sphincter and told him it would never go in.

"Oh yes it will, Charlie," and with that, he shoved as hard as he could and was in. I screamed so loud and so long the whole house woke up. (I was hearing the story for days afterwards.) Cloud shot through the door like a rocket. It appears he had been sitting outside waiting for just this. He pulled Colin off me and threw him on the floor. I was bleeding profusely from the split in my ass, but he still picked me up and carried me down to the dispensary where the nurse was already waiting.

The next thing I knew was David looking at my ass and asking me how I felt.

"Abused like a slave, Master. I just want to die, please let me. I don't want to live with this abuse and degradation. I beg you let me die."

I was in such pain and felt like an animal. I would not stand by and watch a dog treated the way I had been this night. The thought of another nine plus years of this kind of treatment filled me with dread. I would take my own life I knew.

"I want you to personally oversee Charlie's care, Cloud, until he is well."

"Very good, Sir, but I will be leaving your service the day he is fit. I cannot, will not see another human being abused like this boy has been tonight. It was vile and disgusting."

The Master replied in a very low voice. "I know, Cloud, I am ashamed. We will talk when Charlie is well enough."

I was kept under 24-hour observation for three days, not because my injuries were life threatening but because I was suicidally depressed, and David feared I would kill myself.

On the morning of the fourth day, I was summoned to the study.

"Sit down, Charlie, we are waiting for Cloud to join us."

"I would sooner stand, Master."

"Oh, um, yes well that is ok. How is your bum, Charlie?"

"Very sore, Master and I still have quite a lot of pain from the split."

"I'm sorry, Charlie. I had no idea Colin Stevens was a complete sadist. Please forgive me. I will try to make this right for you."

Cloud came in and at David's invitation sat in the chair next to where I was standing.

He put an arm round my waist and said softly.

"How are you feeling, boy?"

"I'm on the mend, Sir, thank you for saving me."

David blushed.

"I must apologise to both of you for my behaviour at the dinner party. Charlie, I swear nothing like this will ever be allowed to happen again. You did not deserve that even if you are a slave. In the future, you will be treated more humanely. I am, however, going to set aside rigid periods when you are to be treated like a slave by the remainder of the staff. That is good for their morale. There will be very strict guidelines issued with regard to punishment, and all slave chores and punishments will be logged. Cloud, I cannot force you to stay, and if you still wish to leave even with Charlie's new guidelines, I will not try to stop you, but I hope you will reconsider. I will do anything in my power to keep you here."

"If Charlie is to be treated like senior staff, Sir, I presume we can resort to first name terms. I would rather like this young man as a friend, and 'Sir' doesn't make that very easy to achieve."

"I think that should be OK. Does that mean you are staying, Cloud?"

"Yes Sir, I still want to look after Charlie."

David blushed again and dismissed us.

"Thank you, Cloud, I don't know what I would do without you."

"You are worth it, Charlie, you are special. Young Winston is a very lucky boy."

I gasped, "Oh my God, does the Master know as well?"

"I don't think so, Charlie. If he finds out, how do you think he will take it?"

"I'm not sure, he says he is not possessive of me, but he is very caring when we are together and tells me he is a little in love with me. After the other night I have to wonder."

"Be careful. I wouldn't want to see you lose each other."

I had plenty to think about now. I was very much in love with Winston. He was the most adorable creature I had ever had a relationship with.

All of those kinds of problems though disappeared a couple of days later. Master sent for me.

"Charlie, a little information. The man who abused you so badly is off my banking team. His bank has axed him for losing such a valuable client. I will be going away for approximately six months to work in New York on this new project. During my absence, I want you to compile a selection of unique meals to publish as a book. The plan is that the only place you will be able to buy the book is in the restaurant where those meals are produced, which will be in New York. We will talk about it when I return. If you need to come to New York, or anywhere else to pick up ingredients, Mac has instructions to accompany you. He will be your Master while I am away. I want you to continue working out swimming and playing Squash. You can do that with my personal trainer. Cloud will control you within the house, but he knows I expect you to spend part of every day being a slave to my staff. Do you understand that, Charlie?"

"Yes, Master."

"I have also instructed Cloud, Lars, my trainer and Mac that you are to be punished once a week by one of them if no other staff has done so. I won't allow you to forget who you are."

"I understand, Master."

Then he was gone.

That night I had my first ever nightmare.

* * * * *

David arrived on the island unannounced with six friends. The whole house was thrown into turmoil getting bedrooms ready for the guests, and in my case, ordering in all the extra food and drink once David had told us how long they were staying.

"Charlie, my friends and I are staying for a week. You will of course be responsible for the food, but you are also going to entertain us in the afternoons and evenings during and after dinner. I will brief you later on what I want."

"Yes Master."

That was all I could say. I was very apprehensive, the only times David had gone for group sex with me I had been left bruised and battered. These new guys were a complete unknown quantity. I had noted that they were all very attractive with athletic looking bodies and substantial packets in their jeans. I assumed, correctly I found out later, that they were all university mates of David and were the epitome of the archetypal college jock.

The remainder of that day was manic in the kitchen, so I was not a happy bunny when David sent for me after dinner. He was alone in his study apart from two houseboys I knew slightly. I had been fucked by both of them but only the once.

"Charlie, you know George and Max."

"Yes Master."

"They have agreed to help you entertain my guests, starting tomorrow evening. I want you to take them away now and spend as much time with them as you can, making sure they can give excellent blowjobs and can use their anal muscles to be good fucks as well. I don't want you opening them up so you will have to orchestrate them fucking each other for practice and watch that they get it right. Check with Housekeeping that they have plenty of white shorts your size because I want them for these two plus Peter and Paul. Cloud will brief those two on their after dinner duties keeping us all supplied with drinks."

"Am I going to be performing with Peter and Paul, witnessing the action as well as George and Max, Master?"

"Yes, Charlie, is that a problem."

"Please Master, not in front of Peter and Paul, that will be so humiliating."

"Don't be silly, Charlie, who else is going to serve drinks, Winston and Ryan."

"Oh no, Master, you wouldn't would you?"

"Peter and Paul, Charlie, or Winston and Ryan, your call."

I hung my head, defeated,

"Peter and Paul, Master."

We went to a large spare bedroom in the staff quarters where I spent a couple of hours with George and Max sucking them and getting them to do the same to me but not allowing anyone to cum. We needed to be hard all the time. I had them fuck each other as well telling them how to work their glutes to give maximum pleasure. I fucked each one for a couple of minutes to make sure they had it right, but I only entered them a few inches. When we had finished practicing, I brought them both to orgasm and had them gasping on the bed.

"Gosh, Charlie, you really are something."

"Thank you, guys, just don't let me down this week, and by the way, why are you doing this, you aren't slaves?"

"No, Charlie, but Mr. David is paying us a large bonus, and we get the chance to fuck you at both ends during the week and give you some gentle paddling as well."

"Ah, I see. Well take it easy with the paddle. You will remember I am human not an animal."

"As long as the Master doesn't make us hurt you, Charlie, we will just tickle that gorgeous butt."

I went back to Winston and told him what I felt he needed to know. He was very unhappy with that and wanted to come with me to protect me from any excesses.

"No, Baby, that would be too embarrassing knowing you were watching me being humiliated."

The next day, David told me I should leave Darren in charge in the kitchen after all the prepping had been done. With George and Max, we were all to have at least three enemas each to make certain we were perfectly clean. I was to ensure I was totally devoid of body hair apart from my head, and we were to use all over, after we had showered, the slightly scented body lotion he gave me.

"George and Max are to go to the lounge, Charlie, in their little shorts just before dinner is finished and wait in slave rest position either side of the fire place. You can show them. I want you to enter the dining room as soon as you can see everybody seated. You will be flanked by Peter and Paul who will be in uniform and stand you next to my chair before resuming their serving duties. You are to be naked."

"Please, Master."

"You will do as you are told, Charlie, or I will punish you in public. After dinner, Peter and Paul are also going to dress in little white shorts with silver belts on which will hang a paddle that they will be using on you, Charlie, but only at my guest's request. They won't be paddling you hard because we have a week of this, and I don't want your ass bruised or damaged in any way, paddling for erotic effect only or for punishment if you are unsatisfactory in any way. Do you understand those instructions, Charlie?"

"Yes, Master." I couldn't look him in the eye because I knew my resentment would show and get me punished.

"Lastly, Charlie, I am considering having Winston witness the proceedings every evening and during the afternoon sessions at the pool."

"Oh please no, Master, not Winston. I will do anything, Master, but please don't let Winston see this."

"Alright, Charlie, but only if you are as good as it is possible to be. I expect you to enter into this enthusiastically. Do you understand?"

"Yes, Master, I will do my best."

I was dreading it. Winston was upset all day, and Darren and crew could almost touch the atmosphere, it was so heavy. I briefed Darren fully because I knew he would be unable to call on me for help after I left the kitchen.

I hated enemas, but George and Max who had never had one were so funny I actually ended up enjoying it. I briefed them thoroughly on what David wanted, and they kindly inspected my body minutely to ensure I had no body hair, getting me a raging hard on as they did so.

"Come on, guys. I am sure you will see plenty of that this week. Let it go down now, will you?"

"Oh OK, Charlie, you are just so damn sexy."

"Thank you, Max." And off we went.

Peter and Paul were in the pantry with Cloud when I arrived.

"Golly, Charlie, you look sexier than I have ever seen you. I am sure I will have a hard-on all through dinner if you are in the dining room with us. You are absolutely awesome."

"Thank you, Peter, I am not looking forward to this, but I guess I will survive the humiliation of being used in front of you two all night and all week I understand."

"Don't worry boy. You know we are all on your side, and I have been very insubordinate to David reminding him that you may be a slave but you are not an animal. Try not to feel humiliated, remember we are your friends, and I understand only Peter and Paul will be using the paddles, so you should be OK, with that. I will be here during dinner, but David has told me he doesn't want me in the lounge afterwards."

Cloud as always was being considerate of my situation

"OK, Charlie, show time."

I walked into the dining room with Peter and Paul on either side of me, but I had my head down. I didn't want to look at David's guests, I knew they were only a few years older than I was, and I was blushing scarlet with embarrassment being naked in front of these strangers. Peter, Paul and Cloud watching being fully clothed as well didn't help. I did find it slightly amusing because I could see Peter and Paul's crotches, and they were both sporting obvious erections. It would be worse later when they were wearing little white shorts. I thought they were likely to be raped they looked so drop dead gorgeous.

Every eye in the room was on me as I stopped by David's chair and Peter and Paul returned to the pantry.

"Charlie, I would like you to meet my guests."

He went around the table, and I tried to remember all of their names. I had to look at each one, still blushing terribly. They nodded as they were introduced except for one who spoke.

"Hello, Charlie, I think you look very cute. I hope we can have some fun this week. Your body is beautiful."

"Thank you, Guy, I will try my best to please you and make your stay at Lara's House most enjoyable."

Everybody clapped.

"Well done, Charlie, that is a very good start," David whispered to me. "While Peter and Paul are filling wine glasses and serving the soup, why don't you go around to each of the guests and make a little small talk about the food. They know you are my chef."

So I did. It gave me a good opportunity to ensure I remembered the names.

"Hello, Conrad, I know Peter and Paul will look after you, and of course, Cloud, but if there is anything I can get you during the week, please ask. I think I am likely to be in your company all the time that I am not preparing your meals."

Conrad took my cock in his hand and started playing with it as I spoke.

"Thank you, Charlie, but I have the feeling all I am going to want from you is this fantastic cock and your ass which is to die for. I hope it is well lubricated for after dinner."

I was fully erect by the time I moved on. Conrad was going to be OK, I thought, but would want a heap of sex.

The others all fondled me front and back until food had been served, and I returned to David's side in slave standing position. My erection subsided amid ribald comments from the guests. No one had tried to penetrate me with their fingers and no one looked mean or sadistic. Cloud was ever present and that reassured me for now.

David played with me during the remainder of dinner, as did Conrad who was on David's right. I wasn't allowed to stay soft but having hands playing with my cock and balls and caressing my butt was never going to get any complaint from me.

"That is a fabulous cock, Charlie, but you can't be a top with it very often can you?"

I was feeling a bit cheeky with everything going so well so I replied, "Oh yes, Scott. I know how to use it, and the only sex partners I have who won't take it tend to be wimps."

He blushed and looked down at his plate. I had the feeling I had gone too far. David thought so, too.

"Charlie, that was an unacceptable reply. You have embarrassed my guest. Move away from the table, turn round and bend over."

I did and received four very hard slaps on my ass with David's bare hand. I now had a very red face again and a backside that was starting to glow. I hoped that I had not started a trend. I didn't want half a dozen fit young men smacking my butt all week.

"I'm sorry, Scott. I had no intention of being rude or embarrassing you."

"Well done, Charlie, be careful though. I don't want you bruised this week, but I won't put up with insubordination."

"No, Master, I'm sorry."

I hoped I had grovelled enough to satisfy everyone.

Dinner finished and David suggested every one reconvene in the lounge when they were dressed in clothing more appropriate for the games.

"Charlie, you come with me."

We went to David's suite where I undressed him and helped him into a pair of leather briefs studded at each side for quick disposal and a leather cross belt with several small whips canes and riding crops attached. There was also a box, which he opened to check contents, and I could see dildos and a string of balls, wrist and ankle restraints and gags that looked like small dildos.

There was also a stack of lube tubes. I was not too happy with this turn of events. The whips would hurt however gently they were used.

"Don't worry, Charlie, the whips are not for you unless you seriously annoy me. Peter and Paul have the paddles for you."

"Thank you, Master."

"Take the box down with you, Charlie. Those toys will be used on you during the course of the evening I would imagine."

The lounge looked quite different to normal. All the sofas and chairs had been moved back so that the centre was like an arena. There was a low, very sturdy coffee table in the centre, which had been covered with a padded cushion the exact size and secured underneath. There was another piece of equipment I had never seen before. David explained it to his guests.

"This is a genuine antique, which I have had recovered but is otherwise authentic. It is an old slave whipping horse. House servants who misbehaved could be punished in the house instead of being taken to the barn like the field hands. You can see the long top is for the slave's chest. His legs are secured to the lowest, widest restraints and his wrists to the ones above. The idea is that his butt is pushed back and stretched for maximum pain when the whip strikes. I'll demonstrate. Charlie, lay along the horse. George and Max, secure Charlie."

I was surprised how comfortable it was when I was secured. David had padded the restraints as well, which I was sure the original hadn't had. I could go to sleep here if left alone.

George and Max returned to slave standing each side of the fireplace leaving me restrained. Just at that moment, Peter and Paul entered. They looked so cute I sprung a serious erection. I was pleased it was not trapped under me.

"Crikey David, are these two gods going to pleasure us as well?"

"No, I'm sorry, John, these two are house staff and are only here to do your bidding with regard to punishing, Charlie."

"God, that is a pity. They are instant erection material. Look at Charlie for proof."

They all did.

"Paul, stand by the side of Charlie in position to beat him, good, now paddle him. Long sweeping strokes, ten should suffice."

Paul did, but he had obviously been briefed because he didn't look at all worried and I soon knew why. The touch of the paddle was so erotic my erection got even harder.

"Well done, Paul, now release Charlie, and you and Peter can take drink orders for everyone."

The other guests all slumped in chairs and on sofas. I noticed they were all dressed like David but without the additions. Every one of them now sporting erections and every one of them looked impressive. The longest I guessed was about ten inches, and the shortest about eight. I was in for some serious fucking I was sure. I just hoped there were no sadists amongst them.

Drinks orders taken, David explained the SP for the night.

"OK, Max and George are here for your sexual pleasure. They will give you blowjobs, fuck or be fucked, whatever is your pleasure. No rough stuff with them, and you can only get kinky with their permission. With Charlie, there are no such restraints. He will do anything you ask, and you can do anything you like to him apart from mark him permanently or incapacitate him. Peter and Paul will keep you supplied with drinks and food if you want anymore, and they will punish Charlie if you ask them to do so. The toy box is here for use on Charlie without restraint. If you have no questions, go for it."

Tony, who had sat quietly through dinner retrieved a large dildo from the box and said, "Charlie, lie on the table, swing your legs over your shoulders and spread them as wide as you can."

I did and after lubing the dildo, he fed it to me slowly. The other guys were clapping and urging him on. I could see Peter and Paul watching and once again, I blushed profusely. This was so embarrassing. The dildo was very long, but thankfully not too thick. By the time he had inserted 12 inches, I was uncomfortable. Every millimetre after that had me screaming with the pain.

"I don't want to hear this, Max, secure this gag in his mouth."

As Max approached, I pleaded, "Please Master, don't remove my vocal cords."

"Sorry, Charlie, you are becoming too vocal, I agree to gagging you."

Max secured the gag in my mouth. All I could do now was suck on a four-inch dildo instead of scream. Tony continued to feed me the dildo. The pain was unbelievable, only easing when I had it all.

"Well done, Charlie, that is 15 inches long. I never intended you to take it all."

Tony then started to fuck me with it. Erotic or what. Despite myself, I started orgasming all over the place. Guy jumped in and took the gag out to feed me his beautiful eight inches. Certainly the sexiest cock there, but not the longest. I sucked on it happily and used my hands to play with his ball sac and his perineum and hole. He pulled out to orgasm on me filling my mouth, eyes nose and face with monstrous amounts of cum.

"Oh God, Charlie, that was fantastic. Never mind the dildo, David, I want my cock up his ass."

"No problem, Tony, go for it."

Inside me, Tony's cock was fantastic. Yes, I was embarrassed with P&P watching, but the sex was amazing.

After he came, Tony said to David, "Not brilliant, David, do I have some recourse to punishment?"

"Of course, Tony, tell Peter or Paul how many strokes of the paddle, and degree of hardness he should receive, and they will secure him to the horse to administer it."

"Good, I think ten medium hard would be just."

I was amazed. I knew he had a fuck and a suck as good as they come.

Peter and Paul secured me to the horse and Peter whispered to me, "Sorry, Charlie, this will have to hurt enough to show."

I handled the first five with just a series of grunts, but the other five were horrific because I could not scream, having had the gag replaced. When he released me, he could see in my eyes how painful it had been.

"I'm sorry, Mr. David, I did not realise how much this was hurting Charlie because he still has his gag in."

"Take it out then, Peter."

David approached me and saw my distress. I was sobbing with the pain.

"Stand up, Charlie, slave rest in front of the fireplace. Paul, feed Charlie the largest of the butt plugs, and we will leave him there to recover. George and Max only for the next half hour guys before you can return to Charlie."

Paul fed me the butt plug. Boy was it big, and did it hurt.

"Sorry Charlie, I would much rather it was my dick."

"So would I, Paul. That would be so exciting."

David heard.

"You can remove the plug, Paul, but you have to remove your shorts, let Charlie blow you but cum in his ass."

Paul looked at me.

"Whatever you want, anything has to be better than this plug, Paul. It hurts so much."

"I would love to fuck you, Charlie."

"Go ahead then, no complaint from me. You already know you are special."

Over the coffee table, Paul arranged me, removed the butt plug and his shorts showing his wondrous erect penis and slowly fed me it. Oh God, it felt so good. It must have to Paul as well because he fucked me slowly and sensuously getting three obvious orgasms from me before depositing a load inside me.

"Paul that was incredible, I love you."

"I love you, too, Charlie, I wish we could do this all night."

"Mmm, me, too."

No such luck.

"David, I think we should have a fuck fest round robin. Charlie, Max and George, get doggy position and the rest of us fuck them for about five minutes each before moving round, keeping it going until we have all cum and been satisfied."

"Sounds good to me, Conrad," was David's reply and for the next hour or so I had multiple cocks up my ass. It was getting so sore before the last one had shot his load. All three of us rolled over on the floor gasping.

"David, Charlie is definitely flagging. Can I please use my barehand to liven him up?"

"I think that might be a good idea, Scott."

I realised Scott was going to get his own back for me embarrassing him.

"On your back on the table, Charlie, Peter and Paul, come and hold Charlie's legs high and wide. Pull his legs down further, guys. I want his ass pointing to the ceiling."

Scott knelt close to my ass and then played my cheeks like a tom tom. From the first stroke, I knew it was going to be unbelievably painful. My ass was facing the ceiling, and Peter and Paul had my legs as wide as they could stretch them. Scott started a rhythmic staccato on each cheek. After about ten, I was consumed with the pain.

"Please, Master, don't let him hurt me anymore. This is so painful. Please make him stop."

David looked round the room and noticed that everyone was rock hard. Even Peter and Paul who were my friends were sporting very obvious erections.

"Peter, Paul, George and Max, as soon as you have cum in Charlie's mouth, Scott will stop spanking him."

Peter and Paul immediately dropped their shorts and all four of them wanked furiously over me. Scott was equally enthusiastic in upping the pace of the spanking.

By the time I had a mouthful of cum and my face was covered in it as well, I was screaming from Scott's vicious attack on my ass. David felt he would be letting his friends down if he wrapped it up there, so he asked them what they would like to do now.

"Can we spit roast Charlie in pairs, David, and culminate in George and Max double fucking him? I will volunteer to open him up enough to take two cocks at once."

"Mmm, sounds interesting, but we have not used many of the toys. At least let us see how many of the string of balls he can take then you can go for it, Tony. Peter and Paul, keep Charlie splayed while George feeds him the string of balls. There are ten of them. If you give him all ten, I will double your bonus.

George started pushing them into me. I wanted to die. Peter and Paul were only inches away from my ass watching the action. I took all ten, but for the last three I was screaming continuously. It was only encouragement from David that kept George going.

"Now pull them out in one quick movement, George."

My scream was so loud Cloud came running.

"What on earth are you doing to Charlie, Sir? It sounds as though he is being killed."

"No Cloud, but we are almost ready to wrap it up for the night, would you like to be first fucking him in our final round robin of spit roasting him?"

"Well thank you, Sir, yes I would like that."

Cloud had a dick bigger even than mine and rammed it home with very little hesitation. I screamed and Cloud started to long stroke me. I couldn't scream any more because David was face fucking me.

"I am going first, Charlie, because when everyone else has finished, I want another blowjob from you."

Being face fucked and butt fucked at the same time would normally please me, but I was so sore and George and Max were the final straw. They were so big, I screamed from the moment they entered me until they came inside me and pulled out splashing the last of their orgasm over my face.

All of David's guests cheered. George and Max looked desolate and Peter and Paul were crying.

"Charlie, you can give me a blow job and then I think that ought to be a wrap for tonight. We can repeat this by the pool at lunchtime tomorrow."

They all watched as I crawled over to David and sucked him off. I was in so much pain I did it like an automaton.

Breakfast the next morning was a nightmare for me. My ass was as sore as it had ever been inside but outside there was very little bruising despite the fact it hurt so much. David as always was up early and walked into the kitchen to watch me work.

"Charlie, you are moving badly. After breakfast has finished leave Darren to do lunches, shed your shorts and go to the pool. I think some of our guests are going to want a morning blowjob or fuck. You had better take lots of lube. Darren, Johnnie and Ryan blushed and turned away from me.

Winston said very boldly, "Why are you hurting Charlie so much, Sir? He is such a wonderful person."

David looked at him and said, "You are an insubordinate little shit, Winston, pack your bags, you are fired."

Winston burst into tears.

"Oh no, please, Sir, don't separate me from Charlie."

"You should have thought of that before you opened your mouth. You are going, today."

He left then and I followed him.

"David, you can beat me to death, but if you take Winston away from me, I will never again do anything for you. Nothing."

"We will see, Charlie"

I went to my room and consoled Winston as best I could, but he was inconsolable, as was I.

It was about an hour later that two of the estate security guys came and frog marched me down to the pool. I was strung up to the arbour with my arms wide apart and my legs the same. George and Max were there with Peter and Paul, each of them had a paddle.

"You four are to give Charlie ten very hard licks with a paddle. You first, Paul."

All four of them were upset after the first ten because I was screaming for them to stop.

"Oh God, Peter, please no more that hurts so much!"

"Keep going, Peter, the full ten. Charlie, it will stop as soon as you tell me you will obey me."

"I promise to obey every command, Master, but only if Winston is allowed to stay."

"No conditions, Charlie, continue Peter."

Max was next, but I was past caring by then. I was screaming with each stroke, but I said not one more word. George finished the first 40 with me barely conscious.

"Paul, you again, ten more and put a bit more weight behind them. I want to see Charlie almost jumping at me."

I couldn't believe Paul had that much power in his arm. The first of his new ones made my brain explode in a million stars. Each one after that was worse, and I lost consciousness. When I showed signs of life again, David told Paul to continue. By the time Peter had completed his second set, I was losing consciousness after each stroke. I knew I was damaged, but David could kill me because life without Winston was no life. Peter told me that David gave up at 118 because the gaps between me gaining consciousness had got so long.

I was over a week in my bed, and Winston was gone. I cried almost continuously once I found out. When I was fit enough to get up David, sent for me and continued his tirade in his study.

"Am I going to continue punishing you, Charlie, or are you going to do as you are told?"

"Without Winston, Master, you can kill me. I don't want to live without him."

"Alright, drop your shorts, lie over the desk. Let us see if a whip is more effective than a paddle. When you are ready to obey me, say so and I will stop."

The whip was unbelievable. I thought I was used to it, but no one had ever laid it on with such force. I could feel the blood flowing after the first one. The amazing thing was that the pain was almost like an anaesthetic. I hardly felt the following ones. Yes, I knew they were raining down on me and I could feel the blood flowing down my legs, but I stopped screaming. David stopped eventually and sent for the nurse.

After a close inspection of my body the nurse said to David, "Sir, Charlie will quite possibly never recover from this. We need to fly him to New York to a specialist unit. His muscles and nerves in his buttocks have been almost totally destroyed. I doubt he will ever walk again, and we will be lucky if he even lives. Your whipping has penetrated his flesh right through to the bone. What is left of his flesh is without structure. I could not have done a more thorough job if I had cut the flesh off, put it on a meat board and used a tenderising hammer on it. If he lives, I will press the authorities to charge you with grievous bodily harm and if he dies, with murder. I am now leaving your employ."

* * * * *

That was when I woke up screaming. Winston was cuddling me so tight I could hardly breathe.

"It's OK, Charlie, it was just a bad dream."

I was shaking uncontrollably.

Would I really have taken all that punishment for my baby? Yes, I knew I would, I loved him so much.

"Charlie?"

"Hello Cloud, how are you?"

"Not happy, Charlie. The master has told me that you are to be punished once a week regardless of whether you deserve it, and I may have to administer it. I don't like the idea at all. I have drawn up a roster. Lars, Mac and me, when we are duty we will check the punishment book and administer ten if nobody else has that week. We have to be vigilant that you don't pull any fast ones, and if you do we have to quadruple the punishment over a four day period."

"Cloud, please don't worry. I know you will only do what you have to and will not be vicious. I can't expect better than that. You are a true friend. I will never condemn you for beating me."

I felt I was in safe hands. Lars was my first rostered administrator and we got on well. I worked hard in the gym, which pleased him and beat him at Squash, which didn't. Mac was next and he was great, Scottish to his toes and like a little boy when dealing with me. Cloud would take the third week, and he was my best friend on the island.

One member of the staff, sometimes two, used me most days for sex. I gave Ryan another couple of blowjobs before he went for the big one and fucked me. He was adorable. I really did love him but not in the same way as Winston, who monitored my slave time and used to get antsy if I went with Ryan. Johnnie was the last of my crew to take me and he was delightful as well.

"I love sex, Charlie, but I have never been with a white man before. You don't mind me fucking you, do you?"

It was almost a plea. I knew he had a regular lover who was a houseboy so this was a one off for experimentation purposes.

"Johnnie, it's OK. I want you to be part of the team in every way, and this is one of the ways."

It was good. Winston was pissed off but calmed down as soon as I cuddled him.

"It's only sex, Baby, what we have is so much more than that."

The last day of the first week, and I had just beaten Lars at Squash for the fourth straight time.

"Charlie, will you bring the punishment book down for me to inspect tomorrow on your gym session."

"Of course, Lars. No one has chastised me this week. I guess I am becoming a good slave. Master has told me I have to be reminded once a week by receiving ten. I can't pretend I like it, and this whip really hurts, but I fucked up."

I was not particularly worried the next day when I trotted down to the gym after showering from lunch. I had the punishment book in my hand and passed it to Lars as I entered the gym office.

"OK, Charlie, if you would like to leave your belt and your shorts here, you can go out and start your warm up exercises."

Weird, Lars always made me bring spare shorts and a towel so that I could shower and put on clean shorts before going back to the house. I always exercised clothed.

I had completed my warm up and had watched Lars lock the doors to the gym so that we could not receive company.

"Charlie, just giving you ten with this thing seems a bit pointless." He was waving my whip about. "I know you like a challenge, so what we are going to do is this. Ten exercises. At the end of each one, I will assess it on a scale of one to ten. One is bad and will earn you as hard a stroke as I think I can administer without breaking the skin on your butt. Ten is so good you will barely feel it at all. Want to play?"

"That is brilliant, Lars. You know I always work hard for you. I should be a happy bunny when I leave here,"

"Don't be too sure, Charlie, we are going to do ten new exercises today."

The first one was really quite complicated, and I got it very wrong.

"I'm sorry, Charlie, that was piss poor. I hope you have not got complacent with our regular programme. I can only give you a two for that. There is a bench pushed up to the vaulting horse. Stand on it with yours legs spread and bend over the horse.

Lars stood alongside me and brought the whip down in a clean sweep to make contact with the lower part of my ass. I screamed. It was the hardest I had ever had apart from the two on my first day.

I held back the tears just as I stood up and said to Lars, "Please, Lars, that was the hardest stroke I have had to take since my first day. Am I really that bad?"

"That was, Charlie, hopefully it will spur you on to do better."

The next exercise was slightly easier, but he still only gave me a four.

"Same position, Charlie."

The pain was almost as bad and I cried out.

I did not warrant better than a five on any of the first five exercises getting a 2, 4, 3, 5 and 2. I broke on the fifth.

"Please, Lars, you are hurting me so much. Why do you hate me today? I thought we were friends."

"We are, Charlie. I thought you would have an easy time with this plan. You are just not very good."

The second set of exercises I was worse because I was stiffening up from the punishment and the pain. By seven, I was almost collapsing with the pain and earned only a one. The last three exercises the same. Lars had to position me over the horse for 8, 9 and 10. He was merciless. I could not stand, so he unlocked the doors and made me crawl back to the house. Darren had to handle dinner that night. I was unable to stand. Ryan came in after dinner and worked his magic with Mum's cream, but it was two days before I could return to work. Winston would not stop crying, and Cloud would not stop fussing. I wouldn't tell him why I could not get out of bed. Lars did not come near me even though I missed two sessions with him.

On the third day, I was back in the gym telling Lars I would only be able to carry out a gentle work out because I was still very stiff and in pain. It was carried out naked again much to the surprise of other guys who were used to seeing me clothed for exercise. On the fourth day, Lars brought a paddle in with him. I had seen them before so I knew what to expect.

"I think you are shirking, Charlie, so I have brought this in to ginger you up a little."

I missed another two days of work, but Cloud heard why this time because all the staff in the gym had talked about nothing else.

He came into my room and ordered me to turn over and he pulled my sheet off. My ass was literally black and blue. The ten stripes from the whip were clear black streaks across my buttocks and the gaps were a bluey purple from the paddle. Cloud took photos and emailed them to David. Lars was off the island the next day, and I came back to health. What was it about my ass that made people want to damage it?

At the end of the next week, I found out. I took the punishment book down to Mac at the pool.

"Charlie, I was really sorry to hear what Lars did last week. I can understand it though. You have either to fuck that cute butt or fuck it up.

"In that case, Mac, will you fuck it?"

"Are you serious, Charlie?"

"If the alternative is more of last week's pain absolutely."

"Oh well, Charlie, nice thought, but just bend over the pool wall will you."

The first time any one beat me with my shorts on and the strokes were so soft I hardly felt them. Mac filled in the book gave it back to me and with a quick swot across my ass he was gone. The worst and the best, I wondered what Cloud would do. In the event, nothing. He signed the book and gave it back to me.

"I can't strike you, Charlie. All I have ever wanted to do with you when I have seen you naked is make love to you."

"Wow, Cloud, that is totally awesome. Why don't you then? You could make love to me everyday."

"No Charlie, I could rape you every day. The only person in this house who makes love with you is Winston. You do it with everyone else because they demand it from you. I'm not saying you don't enjoy it with others, but you don't go looking for them."

"No, Cloud, but I might if they didn't." I laughed and kissed him gently on the lips.

"Cloud, I will make love with you any time you like to ask. I mean it, no slavery, no bullshit, I would be happy to pleasure you and satisfy your sexual needs."

And I was gone, back to the boy I really did want to make love to.

I began to get cheeky about places I went for cookery things. Mac and I had three days in Rio while I looked at South American cuisine and ate in the best restaurants. Another three days in New Orleans studying Creole cookery, and again to New York for Asian cookery. I didn't think David would stand for me doing a tour of Korea, Thailand, etc.

I stayed at the New York apartment because David was there. It was made clear to the staff that they were not to touch me. They hated it. If David ever again let them use me as a slave I knew I would be in for some real grief. He never touched me. His boyfriend here must be quite something, but I never saw him.

I was compiling my recipe book with international meals. The staff were over the moon. Almost every meal was an assault on their taste buds. It had been weeks since anyone had used the whip on me except for Mac whose attempts were hardly felt and Cloud who never actually touched me but made the entry in the book.

All good things come to an end, and this one came in a double portion.

David returned to the island unannounced with a new staff fitness trainer. I had been trying on some new clothes the tailor had brought for me and slipped down to the kitchen in them to get drinks for Winston and me without removing them.

David saw me and went ballistic.

"Why are you improperly dressed, Charlie?"

"I'm sorry, Master, I was just trying these on and wanted a drink."

"That is feeble and not acceptable. Neil, I told you about this young man. I can see he needs more discipline when I am away. You may as well witness how we carry it out. Go and get properly dressed Charlie, bring the punishment book to me in the Gym."

I ran into the Gym in my shorts and Neil's jaw dropped momentarily as he looked at me.

"This is how Charlie dresses, Neil, under normal circumstances. When he is training or playing sports with you he will dress, or not, as you see fit and when he is doing slave duties most times the staff make him do them naked. If he is punished with the whip, it is entered in the punishment book with the reason and the number of lashes. We don't break the skin during this punishment regime because I do not want him marked permanently. Other punishment is acceptable from you, Cloud or Mac that does not incapacitate him. He is a sex toy for the staff as well, for which he is more than adequately equipped. I am going to administer ten lashes for daring to wear clothes other than for leaving the estate. Charlie, take your belt and shorts off, give them to me."

I did and the new man got his first look at my package, mouth agape of course.

"I ought to double the punishment, Charlie, I told you to remain hairless below the neck, and I see you have disobeyed me. Bend over the balance beam legs astride. Neil hold his shoulders so that he doesn't move."

The Master was not too heavy handed, but he did break me on six. I was staring straight at Neil's crotch while this was going on and noticed his track trousers tenting as he got a hard on. His jock strap stopped it being too obvious, and I'm sure David didn't see it. As soon as he completed the ten, David threw the whip down.

"Now get dressed, Charlie, and don't be so bloody stupid again. You can stay here with Neil and sort out your programme with him. Tell him what you used to do with Lars."

I put my shorts back on and my belt, went to the washroom to tidy myself up and joined Neil in the gym office looking very sorry for myself and humiliated at this first contact with my new trainer.

"I'm sorry, Neil, not the best way for us to start. I'm not usually stupid."

"I'm pleased to hear that, Charlie, because I believe in corporal punishment as well but only use it when necessary."

We discussed my gym training and the squash and swimming regimen that I had followed with Lars and the Master.

"That is OK, Charlie. Let me have a good look at you to see if there are any sets of muscles we aren't developing properly. Take your shorts off again and join me on the wrestling mats."

"OK, Neil, but I only have another half hour before I need to be back in the kitchen."

"That's OK, Charlie, I shan't need that long."

I stood in front of him with my hands covering my cock.

"Stand with your legs astride and your hands clasped above your head. Tense all your muscles."

He proceeded to run his hands all over my body front and back, checking the muscle texture, but I knew just using it as an excuse to fondle me. He got down on his knees behind me to feel the backs of my legs. Pulled my very sore cheeks apart and took a long look at my asshole, ran a finger down the crack and touched it before coming around to the front. He felt my thigh muscles and ran his hand gently up the inside of my legs until he touched my balls. He weighed them in one hand while he lifted my cock up with the other all very gently, and I started to get hard. He stroked me until I had a full erection.

"We won't need to develop this, Charlie, will we?"

I now had a red face as well as a red ass.

He stood up still playing with my cock, and I could see he was hard.

"Did Lars ever screw you over his desk, Charlie?"

"No, Neil, Lars never screwed me, our relationship was purely professional."

"So will ours be, Charlie, but I'm going to screw you over the desk so that you know your place with me. Let's open you up first."

He pulled me back into the office by my dick.

"Get your legs as far apart as you can, bend over and grip your ankles. He pulled up a chair and sat behind me. Starting with one finger, he gradually opened me up. When he had four in place, he started to finger fuck me, at the same time slapping my left buttock quite hard. My ass was already very sore from the whipping, so this new assault was doubly painful and humiliating. After five hard slaps, he changed hands, finger fucking me with his left hand and slapping my right buttock. He carried out two complete sets by which time I could barely stand.

"In future sessions, Charlie, you will get that to start your training and if you are unsatisfactory another 30 to finish, and of course I shall fuck you. Now take my clothes off, Charlie, and then bend over the desk."

I did as I was told and took his top and trackies off before removing his jock strap to reveal an impressive piece of meat. How on earth did David always find guys with huge cocks to fill his staff positions here? He was rock hard and told me to bend over the desk before ramming it straight in to my anus with no lubricant. I screamed with the pain.

"Oh God, Neil, you'll tear my ass to bits without lubricant," I gasped at him.

He was powering into me now and he said, "No problem, your blood is providing all the lubrication I need."

He came very quickly, but I felt severely damaged.

"You can go now, Charlie, I only need to do that once a week so you should be healed enough for me each time."

I found it difficult to walk back to my room. No one saw me, and I showered and used tissue as a pad so that the blood would not soak through my shorts. Winston was already in the kitchen.

I made excuses for my lack of movement around the kitchen at lunchtime, but my luck was out as we were clearing up. The Master came in and said, "Charlie come with me now, will you."

In his room, he said, "I haven't made love to you for so long, I think we ought to remedy that now, Charlie. I am going to fuck you very slowly to reacquaint you with my dick."

"I'm sorry Master, it might be a little messy for you."

"What do you mean?"

"I'm bleeding quite badly, Master."

He pulled my shorts down, removed the tissues and spread my cheeks. The splits in my rectum started to bleed again and he saw the heavy bruising starting to develop.

"Who the hell did this, Charlie? You look as though you have been butchered?"

"The new Trainer, Master, he fucked me without lubrication."

I broke down then and sobbing hard said, "Why do people like to hurt me, Master. He beat me as well. I'm not a bad person, am I?"

I guess it was a build up of abuse that triggered the crying because I couldn't stop. David cuddled me and tried to soothe me, but I was inconsolable. He called Cloud who was naturally shocked when he explained.

"Is there anyone we can leave this boy with who will look after him?"

"Yes Sir, I'll get him."

He was back in a couple of minutes with Winston, who joined the crying crowd when he saw me and the Master told him to take me to the nurse to be tended.

"Why Winston, Cloud?"

"They are very close, Sir."

I was nearly out the door when I heard the Master say, "You mean they are lovers?"

Nurse did the necessary and sedated me because I would not stop crying.

During the 24 hours I was out of it, a lot happened that I would have loved to see.

* * * * *

David was so angry he got several of the security people. They stripped Neil and secured him to the wall bars in the Gym. The Master then summoned all the staff and addressed them.

"This man has abused Charlie and incapacitated him. He will be off this island as soon as I have punished him. I want you to witness this because if any one of you abuses Charlie outside of the guidelines you have, I will administer this same punishment despite the fact you are all free men."

He then used my whip to beat Neil until he was bleeding and unconscious.

"Now get him out of my sight."

When he had calmed down, he came to see how I was and seeing me asleep told Winston and Cloud to follow him to the study.

"Winston, what is your relationship with Charlie?"

He was too scared to answer and looked at Cloud for guidance.

"It's all right, boy. Tell Mr. David the truth."

"We are lovers, Sir."

"So are most of the staff as far as I can ascertain."

"No Sir, I love Charlie, and he loves me."

"Is this true, Cloud?

"Yes Sir, it is. They are two special young men, and I have done everything I can to protect them within your guidelines for Charlie."

"If this is true, Winston, how do you handle the fact that Charlie has sex with almost all the staff at one time or another?"

"That is only sex, Sir. What Charlie and I have is much more than that, so I don't mind. I know it is his duty to repay his debt to you."

"I see. In that case, I won't need to tell you that when you leave here you are to look after Charlie until he is well again and give him as much love as he deserves. Now off you go."

"Cloud, I think we have a very damaged boy on our hands. He has obviously been receiving abuse that we don't know about in full. Do you know what abuse Charlie received to warrant Winston beating Peter and Paul so badly?"

"No Sir, everybody clammed up on that one because Charlie asked them to. Most of the staff like Charlie a lot, and it appears that he is something special in bed. He enjoys sex more than anyone I have ever met."

"You mean you have never taken advantage of his slave status to find out?"

"No Sir, not that I haven't wanted to."

"You should, Cloud, he is a superb sex toy. How about Mac and our resident medic?"

"Neither of them to my knowledge. Mac said he played with Charlie for a few minutes one day out of curiosity about his dick but has never gone any further. He even allows Charlie to keep his shorts on if he has to give him the ten licks. He thinks a lot of Charlie as well and respects him for the way he handles himself here and abroad. Mac said he was fantastic in Rio and New Orleans, being very imperious towards people to get what he wanted on the culinary front"

"It sounds like I have quite a star under my protection, Cloud. I need to do a better job. What about the New York crowd?"

"Charlie told me I wasn't to tell you. I thought it ought to be his decision. They treated him worse than an animal. The degradation he suffered at their hands was unbelievable. If I hadn't heard his screams, I think they would have maimed him."

"I want details, Cloud, I demand them. Charlie is likely to spend a lot of time in the future in New York. I need to protect him there."

"You won't like this, Sir. They all fucked him at both ends and made him lick their cocks clean after fucking his ass. Raymond fist fucked him and then buried a dildo in his ass that was 18 inches long and nine inches round. I still have it if you would like to see it. They only got 14 inches in, the rest would have done serious internal damage I believe, before that all started they beat him with his whip."

"After all that, Charlie still wanted to protect them. He must have been terrified, no wonder he wouldn't let them near his kitchen again." David was amazed.

"It goes on, Sir, Lars had also been abusing him for some time before we caught him. He had a nice piece of equipment that did not require the punishment book. He could lay Charlie up for days with that. So in only a few months, Charlie has been incapacitated by Winston, your banker, Lars, Peter and Paul, Neil, your New York animals and that is only the ones we know of. He won't rat on any of them, and Winston is forbidden to mention it if he sees Charlie in a state. The boy tries to protect Charlie, but he is only 18 and not much bigger than him."

"Get Winston back in here, Cloud."

* * * * *

Cloud told me all of this later including Winston's second summons.

"He looked terrified, Charlie. If you had been there you would have swept him into your arms, and I wanted to do the same. The Master was angrier than I had ever seen him. He was breathing fire."

* * * * *

"How much do you love, Charlie, boy?" the Master asked.

In a very soft voice that shook with his fear, he replied, "More than anyone or any thing in the world, Sir."

"Good because you are going to have to if you stay in my employ. Whatever Charlie says, if he returns to your room looking as though he has been mistreated you are to tell Cloud. Do you understand?"

"Yes Sir."

"You are also going to travel with Charlie whenever he leaves the island and report to me, or Cloud if anything bad happens when you are anywhere else. Do you understand?"

"Yes Sir."

"If you let me down, Winston, you will never see Charlie again. Now go and look after your lover."

* * * * *

"That is going to cramp my style a little, Cloud, knowing that whenever I have Charlie in my bed I am stealing him from that kid. I can understand why you have not touched Charlie but I still advise you to try him, even if it is only once, he really is an awesome lover."

Case closed, I was back at work after a day, but I had the stuffing kicked out of me and was very fragile of temperament. I cried at the least little thing and seemed to spend half of my shift in tears in Winston's arms. The rest of the kitchen crew were terrific and made sure that the remainder of the staff left me alone as well. I swam a little and worked out by myself a little, but most of my off duty time was spent crying in Winston's arms in our bed. Looking back, I suppose I was having a mild break down. So much had happened to me in such a short space of time.

Cloud was fantastic. He fussed around me like an old mother hen. David called every day from New York where he had returned and sent me a new fitness trainer after about a month. I recovered some of my old zest thanks mainly to Winston and Cloud, and after my first work out with the new trainer, who I christened "Bionic Bob" because he was so fit, I improved rapidly.

The remainder of my routine did not change. Mac and Cloud signed off my punishment every week with David's blessing, but six weeks after his return to New York, I was called to the phone to talk to him.

"How are you, Charlie?"

"I'm fine, Master. I am back in top gear again with my work and my workouts. I like Bob."

"That relationship is going to change, Charlie, because I am reinstating your punishment routine, and I want the staff to understand that you are now to be treated as before. I'm not being vindictive, but you cannot expect to have an easy life when you owe me so much money. I have told Cloud and he will take the necessary action."

"Very good, Master, is that all?"

"Yes, Charlie, I will see you in New York in a few weeks, hopefully with the draft for your recipe book."

Cloud and Mac addressed the whole of the staff at dinner that night.

"The Master has informed me that Charlie is to go back on full duties. That includes his slave time. I want you all to be aware though that if he is abused by any of you in the way that some people have done in the past, your employment here will be terminated instantly. The punishment and chores book will be monitored very carefully and is to be kept meticulously. Is anyone in any doubt of the limits to which they can go with Charlie?"

Everybody shook their heads and life started again.

Bob was the first book monitor and looked very uncomfortable when I took it to him on the last day of his week when I was due a workout. We had been getting on well. He was bringing me back to fitness and was impressed with my work rate. He was another player that could not beat me at squash. It was funny to see how angry he got. Like most competitive people, he hated losing to me.

"Charlie, you are going to have to help me with this. What do I have to do?"

We sat down in the office while I explained everything to him. I finished up with the modus operendi.

"What normally happens, Bob, whoever is going to punish me, is that I am told to strip, maximum embarrassment. I am often played with until I have an erection, sometimes fingered, nice chunk of humiliation. I am then made to stand or squat or whatever in a position that is most degrading. The lashes are applied usually to cause enough pain to make me scream and or cry but not enough to damage me. If I have a senior member of staff like you, Cloud or Mac, I get it easier, but the Master would be pissed off if I got it too easy. Cloud and Mac don't strip me or play with me, but again I don't think the Master would be too pleased with that. He really is pissed off that I owe him so much money, even if I do have great sex with him."

I laughed and finished with, "It really is up to you, Bob, what you do and I don't hold you in less respect because of what you have to do. Cloud and Mac are still my friends, and I hope you will be as well."

"Are you ever punished publicly, Charlie?"

"You mean like with an invited audience?"

"Not exactly, but if there are people working out in the Gym would I still carry out the punishment?"

"No reason that I know of why you shouldn't. It hasn't happened up to now, probably because no one has wanted to humiliate me that much."

"I see. OK, Charlie, if you would like to go out and do your warm up exercises I will think about it. The Gym is empty now, when do people start arriving?"

"In about an hour, usually as I am finishing there is an influx of about five or six. If I have the book with me, they use our passing to book me for chores and whatever else they want."

"Like sex, Charlie."

"Yeah like sex, Bob," I said laughing and shrugging my shoulders.

We had a good session. Bob worked me very hard so that at the end, I really needed the walk down period. I went for a shower forgetting about punishment. When I walked back through the gym to Bob's office, I noticed an unusually large number of staff, far more than normal. Some not even changed for gym.

In his office, Bob was filling in the punishment book.

"Thanks, Bob, that was a terrific work out today. I am obviously not the only one who appreciates you. Have you seen how many customers you have? What do you want to do about my punishment? I see you have signed it off."

"We are going to do it now, Charlie, I guess the guys out there have heard and are here to witness it."

The colour drained from my face and I looked at him.

"Oh no, Bob, you wouldn't would you? Not with all those witnesses, that would be so humiliating."

"Yes, Charlie, I have to do it now."

I started to cry quietly, another sadist for a trainer.

He walked me out to a position in the centre of the gym under the two climbing ropes. There were two wrist loops tied to them at about a foot above head height and six feet apart. The boys were all stood around watching.

"Take your belt off, Charlie, and your shorts."

My wrists were then secured, and he told me to spread my legs. I was still crying gently at this humiliation. He stood up close to me and started to fondle my dick and balls, as I started to react he moved round behind me and finger fucked me making sure every one possible could see what he was doing. When I was completely erect, he picked up the whip and moved round to the side of me. At the same time the gym emptied, every single member of staff walked out the door. Bob looked stunned. He looked at me, shrugged his shoulders and delivered ten of the softest lashes I had ever received, released my wrists and went back into his office. I dressed, opened his door to pick up the punishment book and he was crying his eyes out.

I was amazed, "What is it, Bob?" I moved round his desk and hugged him. "It's OK, I'm alright."

"While I was in New York, Raymond told me that whatever you or any one else said I was to cause you maximum humiliation and pain and let the staff know what I was going to do so that they could witness it. That everybody really hated you, and I would be popular overnight if I did this. I didn't want to, Charlie, how can you ever forgive me, the staff obviously love you."

"Shit happens, Bob, forget it. I will see you at dinner. Now, I must go."

When I walked into the staff restaurant that night, Bob was seated by himself with a wide circle of empty tables round him. The other staff had crowded uncomfortably round tables as far as possible from him. He looked devastated.

"Hey guys, this is no way to treat a new staff member who doesn't know the ropes yet. You all remember Raymond and his little crowd from New York. Well they have done a great snow job on Bob. They told him he had to do to me what you all walked out on this afternoon."

I turned and dropped my shorts showing them all my ass.

"Look, he didn't even mark me when he realised the score." I pulled my shorts back up turned to them and said. "Let's give him another chance shall we." And another crisis was averted.

I patted Bob on the back as I passed him on my way back to the kitchen.

"What was all that about, Charlie?"

Cloud had followed me out. So I told him.

"That is the last straw, the Master is going to be told about this. Nothing you can say, Charlie, will change my mind so save your breath."

"Thank you, Cloud, I wasn't going to try. This big brave chef is beginning to run short of courage after so many kicks."

He gave me a soft kiss on the cheek as he left.

"Don't worry, Charlie, there are a lot of people looking out for you now."

The next lunchtime just as I was about to leave, I picked up the punishment and chore book. I hadn't seen any one put anything in, so I was anticipating a lazy afternoon with Winston before my swim. But when I opened the book, I was a bit shocked to see Peter and Paul's names and a time five minutes from now. More trouble I thought, it never stopped.

I had a very quick shower. I hated going to any of these things smelling of the kitchen, and knocked on their door with still damp hair.

"Come in."

I hadn't spoken to either of them since the incident but I had seen them and still thought they were very cute and sexy. They didn't do anything to dispel that feeling either. They were both on the one bed in the same sexy little white briefs. I could have eaten them.

Peter stood in front of me, took the punishment book and dropped it on the bed. He then asked for my whip, which he uncurled and gave back to me.

"Charlie, Paul and I have heard about some of the horrendous abuse and humiliation you have tolerated since you came here, never complaining or holding a grudge. We weren't the worst, but we still went over the top, particularly as you apologised so sincerely in both your roles. We also know that you had a good word to say for us with Cloud. We are both very sorry and wish that you would do to us exactly as we did to you as atonement for our behaviour.

"Not a chance, Peter, I don't beat beautiful boys like you two, and I won't shag you either because my monster will hurt you too much."

"We appreciate your sentiment, Charlie, but we are not asking. You are a slave and will do as you are told."

He picked up the whip and gave it back to me. He pulled down his briefs and bent over the chair spreading his legs wide. He had a gorgeous little butt. I would certainly enjoy fucking it, but I didn't want to beat it.

"Beat me, Charlie. Ten good hard ones and if you don't, then Paul will."

I gave him ten at the end of which I lifted him into my arms and kissed him. He had not cried out, but I knew I had hurt him. I laid him on the bed still kissing him all over his face. He calmed down gradually and even started to get an erection from all my ministrations.

I turned to Paul who had watched everything.

"You don't really want me to do this to you as well do you, Paul? It is so painful for both of us. I gained no pleasure from that at all."

"You have to, Charlie. You can strip me first and beat me in any position you like."

"I will do it exactly the same as your brother."

So another cute bottom was offered up to me, and again after ten lashes, I had a very tearful boy to console.

"Peter, Paul, please, this is ridiculous. It is very painful for me to hurt you. You are punishing me again by making me do this."

"Charlie, let us satisfy you then at the very least."

"That's a deal. Where do you want me and what do you want to do?"

"We would like to give you the best blow job our combined abilities will allow."

"OK, no arguments from me as long as you do it sixty-niners so that I can play with both of you as well."

They looked at each other and grinned. It was a fun half-hour. They did a good job making me orgasm heavily twice. I played with two beautiful cocks and two lovely ball sacs. They were delightful. I would have to engineer a session with them one at a time.

"Oh, guys, that was great. I would like to make love to you individually sometime. You are both so gorgeous."

"Thank you, Charlie, we'll never hurt you again."

"I know, it's all right."

I gave Winston an edited version when I got back to our room so that fences could be mended all round.

Cloud told me a few days later that Raymond and his band of sadists had all been fired and the Master had a new crew. I was to fly to New York with Winston to help the new chef settle in.

Chapter 4

Winston was like a little boy with a new toy as we headed for New York. David had sent the helicopter to take us to the airport and then his private jet to take us the remainder of the way, culminating in a limo ride to the apartment. Winston wouldn't sit still for a minute; he was just so adorable to watch. It was, "Charlie look at this, Charlie look at that." The highlight of the trip for him was when the captain invited us up to the flight deck and let Winston sit in the co-pilot's seat. He was very quiet, absorbing everything he was told, but when we returned to our seats, he was unbelievable, enough enthusiasm from his experience to brand any other kid as being dull and unenthusiastic. I loved him so much. I hoped he would never grow up.

David laughed with me when we sat in his study after arrival, and I recounted our trip.

"You love him very much don't you Charlie?"

"Yes, Master, he is my whole life now. I think I would die without him."

"Alright, Charlie, while you are here you will address me as Mr. David. Michael is the only one who knows you are a slave. He is staying at the moment. I will introduce you to him at dinner. I want you and Winston to work with my new kitchen staff for a few days to get them into my way of things. Be gentle with the chef. He is old enough to be your father, but he comes very well recommended. James is my new butler. You have already met him. I cleared the other lot out en masse, so everyone you meet here is new. How are the recipes going, Charlie?"

"I have brought them with me, Mr. David, but if we have the time, I would like to add about half a dozen more."

"We go to press in six weeks, Charlie. As long as they are with me a week before that, I am sure we can add them. Now, off you go and sort chef out."

Life was easy here. The only meal I had to really take care of was dinner. That night, David sent for me to introduce me to Michael.

"Michael, this is Charlie, how would you like him to address you?"

I guessed Michael to be about two years older than I, and powerfully built, not at all what I expected.

"Sir, should do, David, considering what he is."

No love lost here I guessed. I wasn't a threat to him, so I found it difficult to understand the obvious animosity.

"Thank you, Charlie. I won't need you at all tomorrow until I return probably quite late. We will need to talk then about the restaurant."

"Very well, Mr. David, I will have a siesta in the afternoon so that I am fresh for our discussion. Goodnight and goodnight, Sir."

Goodnight from David nothing from Michael.

I had sorted breakfast the first day. I helped in the kitchen really to justify my existence. I made sure that Winston was sent on errands around

New York, with an escort of course, so that he could see the city. It was during one of these mornings away, that I was summoned to see Michael. He had been quite obvious in his dislike of me at dinner the previous evening, so I was not surprised.

"Charlie, how do you dress when you are at Lara's house?"

"I just wear shorts, Sir."

"Have you any with you?"

"Yes Sir."

"Good, go and fetch a pair for me."

When I returned, he sent me to his bathroom to change.

"I like that. You are a very cute slave, Charlie. I can understand why David is so enamoured with you. What punishment do you think is appropriate for sleeping with someone else's boyfriend?"

"I don't know, Sir. You would have to ask, David. I only do what I am told."

"You are quite the little smart ass, Charlie, aren't you?"

"I hope not, Sir. I believe I am a realist. David owns me. I only do what he tells me or allows me."

"I don't believe that. You offend me, so I am going to punish you. Do you know what this is?"

"Yes Sir, it's a riding crop. I have seen them in use on horses in London."

"Well I am going to use it on you, but not before I have had some fun. Undress me Charlie and let me see how good that pretty mouth can be in exciting me."

So I did. He was climbing the wall after only a few minutes. I didn't like him, and I was going to make sure that he realised I could satisfy David far better than he ever would.

"Stop, Charlie, you have to be a slut to be that good. Take your shorts off and get doggy fashion on the floor."

I did, and he showed me a dildo, about the same size as my cock.

"I am going to fuck you with this for a while Charlie before reaming you out with my own cock."

He was a pig. He set out to hurt me and succeeded. I was crying with pain after a few minutes. I had all 12 inches on every thrust, and he was twisting it round as well as pulling it from side to side. When he eventually replaced it with his own penis, it was heaven. He obviously intended to have a great orgasm because he was exploring my insides with careful precision. I was turned onto my back and fucked missionary style. He could see how excited I was by the number of times I orgasmed before he did. It was bloody fantastic. When he pulled out of me and lay along side me, he gasped,

"Now, slut, I am going to beat you."

"Oh come on, Michael, that was a great fuck. Why spoil it now by being sadistic."

"Because, Charlie, that was for my pleasure not yours, and I am going to spoil it because you make my life a misery every time David goes to Lara's, and I know he is fucking you or taking your monster up his ass. Now bend over the arm chair and don't you dare move."

The riding crop was a monster chastiser, far worse than either the whip or a cane. I screamed after the first one and threw myself into a corner to avoid any more. The pain was unbelievable. I was screaming, no probably squealing in terror would describe what I was doing more accurately. Michael went to a box and came back with leg and wrists restraints that he fixed to me before dragging me to the chair again and securing me to each corner of it. I was begging him not to use the crop again and shaking uncontrollably. I was terrified. I had never been afraid of punishment, but I was now.

When the second one landed, my vision exploded into a million stars, and I screamed. I had never known pain like it. I don't know how long he kept going or how many I received after I was unconscious. When I came to, the pain was unbelievable. I was curled up in a ball on the floor, and Michael was seated on the banquette at the window watching me.

"I have been charitable today, slut. You only took 15. We will have to see how many you can take each day before you leave. Twenty tomorrow I think and five more each day thereafter. Now fuck off back to your room."

I couldn't stand. So I crawled. No one saw me, and I curled up in bed wondering how I was going to keep this from Winston. He would be devastated if he saw me in this state. David wanted to see me when he came in from work as well, and if he witnessed me in my present state, I didn't know what would happen. There was only Michael for dinner, so I stayed in bed and told Winston I was just too tired to eat. I would probably have a snack with David when he came in. It worked, and I was off the hook until about ten when David sent for me.

I walked badly to David's study.

"Hello, Charlie, what have you been up to today? You don't look very well, and you are walking badly. Have you had a fall?"

"I'm sorry, Master, I am hurting. Please don't leave me alone here anymore."

I was terrified at the thought of Michael's activities the next day. I was sobbing uncontrollably. I had never been this afraid in my life. Michael beat me while I was unconscious, which registered as a recipe for me being maimed while out of it.

"Stand up, Charlie, and take your trackies off."

I did, and David gasped at the sight of my ass.

"Oh no, Charlie, who did this?"

I wouldn't answer.

"Oh no, this has to be Michael."

He ran from the study returning a few minutes later dragging Michael naked by his hair.

"Look at Charlie's ass, Michael, look. I thought I loved you, but this? You're an animal. Get out of this apartment and get out of New York. I am going to set the hounds on you tomorrow if you are anywhere near here. You disgust me."

David literally kicked Michael out of the study before taking me in his arms and stroking me gently.

"I am so sorry, Charlie, please forgive me."

He carried me back to my bed and left me in Winston's care.

"Look after him, Winston. He is hurt badly."

We were both emotionally shattered. David allowed us to go back to Lara's House a couple of days later when I could walk almost properly. There was certainly no argument from me. I was feeling very fragile, and my ass was a mess.

We had been back at Lara's House for a month before the bruising disappeared. I had completed the other six recipes and sent them off to David. Bob was working me gently in the gym because of the stiffness from the beating. I had no slave duties, so apart from cooking for the staff, my life was very easy. Winston fussed over me worse than Cloud, so I was relieved when I was able to carry out my first full session in the gym. It heralded a return to normal.

I talked with David often concerning the restaurant and eventually concerning my health.

"Back to normal slave duties I think, Charlie. I will set the parameters with Cloud, but I think whippings will have to go."

"Thank you, Master." And I meant it. My ass was not meant to take the kind of punishment it had for the previous several months.

Sex became fun again because I was indulging in it with all the staff, just about. Usually one on one, but occasionally two together, which got me a spit roasting – lovely – a cock in both ends was best of all for this greedy slut.

David flew me back to New York two months after I had been back at Lara's.

"Charlie, I want you to have a look at the premises I have bought for the restaurant and make suggestions to the architect for the way you would have the kitchen set up."

This was fun, organising the construction of a kitchen totally from scratch to suit me. Only, another chef would be using it, I thought.

"Mr. David, when you have the chef for this place am I going to be allowed to train him to my methods with the recipes from my book?"

"No, Charlie, you are going to be the chef."

I could hardly believe it.

"You mean I am going to move to New York permanently?"

"Yes, Charlie, is that alright?"

He was smiling as he said it, as if I had any choice.

"What about my slave status?"

"We will have to adapt that, Charlie. I will think about it when the time comes."

"Mr. David, what about Winston?"

"What about Winston?"

"Please Master, don't part us. I promise I will be the most obedient slave you could wish for, but please don't separate us. I would die without him."

I was holding back the tears. I really would die without him.

David laughed.

"Don't worry, Charlie. I have no intention of separating you. I expect you to choose all your own staff when the time comes, and I have no doubt Winston will be one of them. I am going to set up a video link for you with the architect so that you can oversee the kitchen construction from Lara's House."

"Thank you, Master. When do you expect the restaurant to open?"

"I hope in about six months. Until then you are to return to full slave duties at Lara's. I will inform Mac and Cloud of the routine I expect you to follow particularly with regard to punishment."

"Yes, Master." That was all I could think of to say under the circumstances.

Punishment was going back into my slave routine. No whip, but the paddle could be very painful. There were no new staff for a while, so I coasted along pleasantly with plenty of sex but no pain.

There were problems with the restaurant in New York to the point where David put it on hold. I wasn't worried. I loved Lara's House, and provided no one got heavy with me, the sex was incredible.

As always with me, good things come to an end. This time it was an influx of new staff to do some building and landscaping that would require extra kitchen and house staff. The new workers were accommodated in the dormitory but not before a quick conversion had been carried out adding bathrooms and turning the wing into four bedded rooms.

The two new kitchen staff were the same age as Cloud and had been headhunted from a hotel in St. Lucia. They were fully trained chefs, so my life looked to be getting even easier despite the extra 20 workers.

Cloud introduced them after lunch.

"Matthew and Mark, welcome to Lara's House. I hope you will be happy here. I have your CVs, and they look impressive. I hope you really are as good as they indicate. Come through to the restaurant, and we can talk about your routine."

They listened dutifully and asked intelligent questions, so I felt comfortable with them.

"Charlie, why do you wear those little shorts when everyone else is in uniform?"

I explained fully, and they were disbelieving until I showed them the chores and punishment book and the paddle. They clarified my position fully before looking at each other and grinning. A couple of days later, I found out why.

Matt and Mark approached me after lunch on their third day on the job.

"Charlie, if we wanted to take advantage of your slave status for a bit of fun, where could we do it? Our bedroom is shared with two others and is too small for games."

"The only place I can think of Matt is the barn on the hillock overlooking the house. I know Mac has it kept neat and tidy because I pass it on my runs sometimes. He keeps a lot of farm equipment in there, but there is still plenty of space."

They put their names in the book for the next day and told me to meet them at the barn half an hour after we finished lunches.

"Make sure you clear it with Mac, before we use it, OK."

The next lunchtime, I showered and put on clean shorts. I told Winston where I was going and with whom. He didn't like it, but I had no indication of what he planned to do.

When I arrived at the barn, Matthew and Mark were already there lounging on a couple of hay bales.

"Come in, Charlie, I'll take your book and paddle."

I gave the two articles to Matt and was told to stand in front of Mark and undress. Matt walked round me first stroking my body.

"Stand with your legs wider apart Charlie and grip your hands behind your head. Mark, slip the chain on the door to stop us being disturbed."

As he brought me to full erection he commented on the size of my cock before slicking up some fingers and finger fucking me.

"Bend over that hay bale, Charlie, for support and open your legs as wide as you can. Mark, come and pull his cheeks as far apart as you can."

I was being stretched uncomfortably wide as Matt pushed more fingers in me. I felt humiliated. These two were new to my staff and already abusing me.

"You're pretty slack, Charlie. I bet you could take my fist."

I didn't say anything. What was there to say?

"I think we'll try, Charlie."

With that, he increased the pressure until I screamed out.

"Oh Christ, Matt, please stop! That is so painful. Your fist is too big."

He pulled out and slapped me very hard on each cheek five or six times.

"Be quiet, Charlie, you're a slave remember. We can do anything we like with you. Now on your back I am going to try that again."

I was stretched wide again and finger fucked roughly for a while before Matt gave up trying to fist me. I was crying with the pain, and he made it worse by slapping my ass hard again ten times.

"Let's see if you are any good at sucking then, Charlie. Take Mark in your mouth and suck him to orgasm. Until he has cum, I am going to continue punishing your ass, but with your paddle. I can't think of a good reason to keep hurting my hand."

"Why are you hurting me so much, Matt? I haven't done anything to you."

"I know, Charlie, but you are so sexy and a slave to boot. It is great being able to abuse you. Now suck."

I counted over 30 with the paddle before Matt broke down laughing like a banshee. Mark didn't appear to be any closer to cumming than he had done at the start despite me playing with his balls as well as sucking him.

"You could do that all day, Charlie, and he wouldn't cum. Mark is all fucked up inside. Never mind, consolation prize, you can take my cum in your ass and then another ten or so with the paddle."

He fucked me hard cumming in great jets all over my body before picking up the paddle and powering into me until I was screaming with pain. He dropped the paddle. They got dressed and opened the door to leave.

As the door opened, Winston and Ryan ran to me and several of Mac's estate workers grabbed Matt and Mark dragging them back into the barn and securing them to bailing hooks hung from the two large pulleys used for lifting bales into the loft. I was only semi aware of this until Mac stood in front of me and asked how many whacks on the bottom I had received.

"About 40 with the paddle, Mac, and about 20 with the bare hand. I hurt so much, Mac. I didn't do anything wrong."

I watched in amazement as Keithroy, the biggest of the estate workers powered in with 50 strokes of the paddle to each ass. They were both unconscious when he had finished.

"I am not sacking them, Charlie. When they are fit, they can come back to work for you, but the tale they have to tell should make this the last sadistic punishment you take. Now let them down and take them to the nurse."

I was off for a couple of days, and Matt and Mark were off for a week. I offered them the opportunity to leave or stay and continue working for me. They remained and were extremely cooperative.

Life once again returned to normal, but not for long. David heard about the M&M incident and flew down for a few days breathing fire. I was sent for, along with Mac, Cloud, Bob and Darren.

"Charlie, I am beginning to think you are more trouble than you are worth. I am going to suspend the punishment book and have senior staff organise a weekly reminder of your position. Mac, Cloud, Bob and Darren, you four will oversee punishment once a week in rotation in front of all your staff. One member of staff will administer ten strokes of the paddle in front of the others, and you can rotate the staff member. I want this notice read out before each session. I will administer the first ten in front of you here to show you what I want. Take your shorts off, Charlie, and bend over my desk legs astride."

David was a strong man and let me know it. I was screaming with pain before he was halfway through.

"That is how I want the punishment carried out. Bob, your witnesses will be made up of the gardeners and the 20 temporary staff. The remainder of the staff are in obvious groups."

That was it. David flew back to New York, and I had a week to worry about my intended punishment and humiliation.

The house staff were first. Cloud called me on the internal phone.

"Charlie, I'm sorry, but will you come to the dining room."

All of the house staff were in a semi circle round Cloud and Peter.

"Charlie, stand here," Cloud said pointing to a spot in the centre. He then read from a card.

"Charlie and most of you appear to have forgotten that he is a slave, or you go over the top and incapacitate him. From today onwards at intervals, you will all have the opportunity to remind Charlie of his position in this house."

He then gave Peter the paddle.

"Turn round, Charlie, drop your shorts and bend over. Peter, give Charlie ten good licks with the paddle."

Peter dropped the paddle and burst into tears.

"I can't, Sir. I hurt Charlie once. I can't do it again. Please don't make me."

"Peter, do it or your employment in this house is terminated."

I stood up and hugged Peter to me.

"Do it, Peter. I don't want to lose you. Please."

I resumed my position, and Peter gave me ten not very hard strokes. The paddling didn't matter – it was the humiliation. I kissed Peter, telling him it was OK, but I couldn't look at anybody else as I left.

I felt so ashamed that I didn't speak to Cloud for the whole of the next week. Then it was Mac's turn. I was summoned to the barn for that and Keithroy was to administer it. He was very strong, and I had witnessed him paddling M&M. I hoped he would be gentler with me. Same routine as before. Mac read from the card. I dropped my shorts and bent over a hay bale. Keithroy spread my legs very wide and played with me a little pretending to adjust my position.

"That's enough, Keithroy, just administer the ten strokes."

Mac sounded uncomfortable with what was happening. I got my ten, and they were nearly as hard as David's. I was screaming by the end, and Mac had me carried back to the house because I couldn't walk. I was in bed for two days recovering from that and the bombshell Cloud brought me the morning after the beating. I still couldn't look him in the eyes or chat to him like the best friend he had been for nearly a year. It was a letter from Mac.

My Dearest Charlie,

For eight months I have watched you receive untold abuse and bounce back from it, never holding a grudge or blaming anyone.

I have loved you almost from the first time I set eyes on you, but I cannot remain here and watch this new abuse and punishment. I certainly won't be able to look you in the eyes again knowing that every four weeks, I have to organise and witness what I did yesterday.

I will never forget you and pray that you will survive this period of your life without any lasting damage.

I love you Charlie. Goodbye.

Mac

I cried for so long I thought I would never be able to stop. Winston told me Mac had left that morning after delivering the letter to Cloud.

The next week, it was Bob's turn in the gym.

"I am going to do this myself, Charlie. None of these boys is close to you, and I don't want any of them hurting you."

Ten strokes that I hardly felt, but the humiliation in front of mainly casual staff was awful. I was descending into a deep depression.

The last of the four groups were my own staff. Darren came for me and very embarrassed asked me to follow him to the staff restaurant. He picked up my paddle, and we went. I don't think I really cared anymore. This was the worst humiliation of all. M&M were smirking, Ryan and Winston were sobbing, and the others were stony faced as Darren read from the card.

"Take your shorts off, Charlie, and turn round."

I did and noticed Cloud for the first time. He must have followed us in.

"He has to feel them, Darren, so don't be too gentle. I'm sorry, Charlie, but David is very insistent that your own staff are not soft on you."

Cloud was obviously embarrassed, but I didn't care. Darren gave me ten that hurt, but not a lot. I just picked my shorts up and went back to my bed.

Chapter 5

When I woke, I was definitely not in Lara's House. It was very sterile. It was a small room with a big bed, everything white and a mass of equipment that I was hitched up to. Hospital. I had never been in one in my life. There was blue sky outside and that was all I registered before I went back to sleep. When I woke again, it was dark, and I was thirsty as hell. I saw a red button on a cable and pressed it. A pretty nurse came in, and I smiled and said, "I'm awfully thirsty, could I have a drink please."

The door opened again, and Mac came in carrying my glass of water. He should have bought the empty glass. I could have filled it from my tears.

"Oh, Mac, how wonderful to see you. How are you? You look older. Have you not been looking after yourself?"

"One question at a time, Charlie," he was crying I noticed through my own tears,

"As of a few seconds ago, I am fine. You have aged me 20 years this last six months, but I am going to get younger everyday as we nurse you back to health."

"What do you mean the last six months, it's only two weeks since I saw you?"

"No, Charlie, you have been in a coma for six months. I don't know all the fancy terms, but basically you had a massive emotional brain overload. The specialists here were not sure you would ever come out of it. We pieced together most of the story we think. You lost Cloud because of the humiliation of his beating, then me and the final destruction was your own staff, particularly Winston, watching you beaten by Darren. Cloud should be here in a few minutes. He usually comes in to talk to you about seven. Not long to go, and he can fill in more details than I can. You had been here for a couple of weeks by the time he traced me to my home in Scotland."

"I don't understand, Cloud, here, you here. Where are we?"

"New York, Charlie, a private clinic outside the city."

"But Cloud here and you, how long have you been here?"

"Cloud left the island with you and brought you here. He was going to pay for everything. He left David and the island, so he wouldn't ask for anything. David does pay all the bills because as he says you are his property. Cloud works for a family not far from here, and I run an estate not many miles away. I guess we all rather gravitated here. Darren works in the kitchens here at this hospital, as does young Ryan. He says you may need him to rub cream on your ass one day, so he doesn't want to be far away. Bob is a personal fitness trainer in the city. He has been in almost everyday to work your limbs so that you will be able to walk almost as soon as you can get out of bed."

"I can't believe you have all sacrificed so much for me. But Mac, you haven't mentioned Winston. Please tell me he is here as well."

Watching a grown man cry is heart wrenching. To watch Mac cry would melt the hardest heart, and Mac was crying. He made me look like a rank amateur. My heart was dying though because I knew why he was crying.

"I'm sorry, Charlie. Winston sat here holding your hand just about 24/7 for nearly four months. David paid a lot of extra money to allow an extra bed in here, and Winston was treated like a patient as well. He slowly slipped away, as he believed you would never rejoin us. He isn't in a coma, Charlie like you were, but he's not with us. He is in your old twilight world, but still conscious. The specialists say that he will never recover. He is in a permanent vegetative state. There is no pain, and he is looked after in the best nursing home money can buy."

I didn't shed a tear.

"I understand, Mac. I am sorry I caused you all so much trouble. I'm not going to stay. I'm going back to look for Winston. He'll be waiting for me. He knows I will look for him for all eternity if that's how long it takes."

I closed my eyes willing myself to go back so that I could start my search.

"Charlie, don't go back yet. Stay to say goodbye to everybody. They have all made great sacrifices for you, and they love you almost as much as I do. You owe them that."

"Alright, Mac, get them here soon. I must start my journey. My baby will be worrying about me."

* * * * *

I learnt this entire story much later.

* * * * *

Mac left my room and hit the telephones. Everybody that had been routing for me was contacted. Mac knew that there was sound monitoring equipment in my room. He got hold of the tapes that had our conversation on them. When Cloud arrived, he briefed him, playing the tapes so that he had all the details straight. Bob was told that I was conscious, but to stay away because he was their ace for Mac's plan. Then he ran. The police car that stopped him for excessive speed escorted him to Winston's nursing home when the officer heard the story. The tapes were put on a loop and played repeatedly to Winston. All the time Mac was telling him he had to wake up and come with him to save Charlie.

* * * * *

Back with me, and Cloud was at my bedside.

"Hello, Charlie, are you never going to stop making me worry about you? Don't you think you have gone over the top to get me to show you how much I love you this time?"

I smiled, or at least that was what I meant to do.

"I'm sorry, Cloud. I guess the humiliation of that last system was just too much for my tired old brain and my much abused body. I was too ashamed to talk to you or Mac after the public beatings and the one in front of Winston with my own staff as witnesses I realize was just one humiliation too many. I felt too ashamed after Darren beat me to even say goodbye to my baby. But Mac says he is in the world I have just returned from. I'm going back, Cloud, he's waiting for me, and he's by himself. He will be so frightened. I have to go soon. He needs me. I am going to search for him for all eternity if I have to. I don't want to live here without him."

"I know, Charlie, just wait a little while so that you can say goodbye to everyone who has helped you."

"Alright, Cloud, but tell them to hurry, please. I'm so afraid I might miss him."

David had listened to this conversation on the monitoring system. When he had washed and made himself look presentable, he came into my room.

"Hello, Charlie, it's good to see you back with us."

"Hello, David. I'm not staying. I'm going back to find Winston."

"I would like you stay and open our restaurant together, Charlie."

"No, David, you took my baby away. I don't want to be with you. You take all my friends away. You are much too clever for me. You find ways to hurt me even when you are a long way away. You took Cloud first, then you took Mac and Bob and worst of all you took Winston. I made a mistake. I told you I loved him more than anyone else in the world, so you took him. You have taken every person I love, David. Why do you hate me so much? I loved you as much as I could, but it wasn't enough was it? I didn't ask to fall in love with Winston, you know. He was just too perfect not to. I didn't want you to make him go to that other world, but I'm going to find him, David. I'm never going to stop looking for him."

"Charlie, don't go yet. Mac is looking for someone to go with you who may know where to look."

"I don't believe that, David, but I will wait. I want to tell Darren I forgive him, and I want to tell Ryan I won't need his bum cream any more because no one is going to beat me again. My other world was peaceful. Nobody hurt anybody there. I need to tell Bob I am sorry. I was crap my last week with him, and before that, I beat the crap out of him at Squash. I'd like to tell him I will teach him to win against me, but I don't have time. I have to find Winston."

I noticed Cloud was crying quietly on the other side of my bed.

"Don't cry, Cloud. It's alright. I'll find him. We'll be together, and then it won't matter where we are."

David left to talk to the doctors that were monitoring the conversation.

* * * * *

"What do you think?"

"The truth, Mr. David, is that he is right on the edge of sliding back into a coma. He is just in touch with reality, but it is so fragile, which is why we are staying out of it for the moment. He is with friends whom he loves, so although the urge to go back for Winston is strong, his love for these other people is keeping him here temporarily. If he does slide back, I can promise you we will have lost him forever. He fought his way back this time for that other boy. Now that he is gone, he has nothing to come back for next time. All that will be left to do is switch off the machines and the lights and go home."

David was given a sedative and a bed with the promise that he would be notified of any change as it happened.

* * * * *

Darren was the first of the two boys to come and see me. He looked so ashamed and wouldn't look me in the eye.

"I'm sorry, Charlie, that is the worst thing I have ever done in my life, even worse than with the first Winston."

"You did what you were told to do. It's OK. I don't mind. It wasn't your fault. We were a good team weren't we? When the New York restaurant opened, you were coming with me, now you are here any way. Darren, look after Ryan, he's another Winston. He is very special. You know I love him, too. Winston used to get cross with me when I went to Ryan to give him a little pleasuring, but he would be alright once I had cuddled him"

I smiled at Darren and said, "I'm very tired. I must start my journey soon. Is Ryan going to be long?"

"No, Charlie, not long. What journey?"

"I'm going to look for Winston. Mac says he's in the world I have just come from, so I'm going back to look for him. I'll find him, Darren. I have all eternity, and I'll find him because I love him so much."

Darren left to find Ryan and hide his distress.

Cloud was still there, and I reached for his hand.

"I'm so tired, Cloud. I have to start my journey soon."

"I know, boy, just a little more time. We have all missed you so much. Stay just a little longer."

"All right, Cloud, but I am so worried about my baby."

I guess I really was tired because I closed my eyes and slept. It was my promise to Cloud to wait a little while that kept me from slipping back into the coma.

* * * * *

As soon as I was asleep, the doctors were in checking all the monitors in my brain.

"It's alright. You've exhausted him, and it is a natural sleep. He should be stronger when he wakes up, which will hopefully make it easier to keep him with us. I promise you we have a very long road to travel before that boy is safe. If Winston were here, I could go home and sleep the sleep of the dead."

"Couldn't we all."

I slept peacefully through the night, and Mac didn't. The hospital rushed more tapes of my voice over to the nursing home to be played to Winston. The doctors all said the chances of success were zero, but Mac would not give up. As dawn approached, he picked Winston up and shook him.

"Listen to me, boy. Charlie is awake. He keeps asking for you. If you don't go to see him, he is going back to that other world he has lived in for months. Winston, Charlie needs you. You are supposed to protect him. Now wake up."

Mac was screaming at Winston shaking him like a rag doll. Security had to pull him off and hold him down in a chair while he calmed down. He was crying, but through his sobs he called to Winston again.

"Please, Winston, wake up, Charlie needs you so badly."

"Charlie needs me? Charlie, I love you, and I'm coming."

Mac had him wrapped in a blanket and in his car in record time. The nursing home staff helped, knowing the story of their young charge, and the policeman had slept in his car ready to escort Mac back to the hospital if the miracle happened.

It was past dawn, and Charlie had woken up again. Cloud and Darren were at each side of the bed, and Ryan stood at the foot.

"Hello, Ryan, thank you for coming. I don't have very long now. I have to go back to look for Winston. He's lost like I was."

Ryan started to cry quietly. "Don't go, Charlie, stay here with us. We have all missed you so much."

"I'm sorry, Ryan, I have to find Winston. I love him so much, and I miss him."

* * * * *

David had been up for hours and had listened to all the tapes. He felt shame and guilt and overwhelming love for that gentle boy who, in less than a year, had taken some terrible punishment and humiliation and blamed only him, but even that not rancorously. More as surprise, Charlie really believed that he hated him. He had spent six months in a coma after a complete emotional and mental break down and was now on the brink of returning to his coma.

The police radio was calling the hospital telling them to keep Charlie awake as they had a very conscious and very worried Winston with them. The wheelchair was waiting for Winston as Mac pulled up to the entrance. He didn't even switch his engine off before jumping out, grabbing the wheelchair handles and almost flying through the hospital to Charlie's room. They almost took the door down getting in.

Charlie took one look at the boy in the wheelchair and broke down completely as did the boy in the wheelchair who threw himself into Charlie's arms. There were so many people crying in the room that it almost warranted a flood warning. The release of tension was almost a physical reality it was so strong.

After about an hour of tears, the doctors threw everyone out of Charlie's room except for Winston so that they could check out these two boys who had climbed out of the abyss against all the odds to be with each other.

The others all went to the restaurant for breakfast, and David started the conversation off.

"You all have every right to hate my guts for what I did to Charlie. I swear it was not vindictive. I was just blind to how sensitive and how special he really is. I don't think I will ever be able to make it up to those two boys back there. If I am to stand any chance at all though, I will need the help of five very special people. In the Caribbean there is an island with a large estate on it. There is every possible facility on the estate, but a skeleton staff is running it. If I could persuade Charlie and Winston to accept my hospitality, I would like them to have it, for as long as they need to convalesce. If they do accept, I will need those five people whom I know Charlie loves dearly to go with him as extra staff. Of course, those five people would go back on enhanced salaries because of the special task they would have. If Charlie accepts, I will promise him and you that although it is my estate, I will not step foot on it without an invitation while he is there and further, my helicopter and private jet will be available to take them anywhere they want to go. I think you may need to talk to Bob as well, so I will leave you while I go and try to build some bridges. Cloud, if those boys turn me down, we will still need to convalesce them somewhere. I will leave that in your more than capable hands, but with my cheque book available if you need it."

David left the four speechless.

* * * * *

It was lunchtime before the doctors would allow David back in to see me. Naturally, Winston was wrapped round me looking like he may never let go.

"Charlie, I know I have been reckless in the way I have handled you since you became my slave. I promise that is at an end. I know you and Winston have a lot of convalescing to do. I want to offer you Lara's House for as long as you want it. Not as staff but as guests. I will have it fully opened up again and further, I will not step foot on the island without your specific invitation. I hope you will accept my offer. We will not discuss your future until you are 100% ready."

"Thank you, David, but we have five very special friends here in New York, somehow or other we want to stay in contact with them. We know that will mean going straight back to work, but they are very special. I also know that I am still your slave, and I guess we are going to have to settle that. I don't know how, but as I grow stronger again, I will have to address that with you."

"If those five special friends happened to return to the staff of Lara's House, do you think you might accept my offer then?"

"Are you serious, David?"

"Of course."

"But I thought you hated me."

"No, Charlie, I have loved you for almost as long as I have known you. I just had a very bad way of showing it. I needed to let you know that you were a slave and went over the top showing my staff how powerful I was. You don't have to make a decision now. Talk to your friends, when you have all decided, please let me know."

The doctors were still monitoring audio, and after David left one came in to see me.

"Charlie, we are sorry we were still eavesdropping on conversations in this room, but I am pleased in this case that we had. You and Winston are going to need a long period of convalescence. There is no question of you returning to any meaningful employment for at least six months. If you do, it could do irreparable damage to your very fragile neurological systems and put you back into comas. Whatever you think of Mr. David, I would take his offer for purely selfish reasons. Give yourselves a chance for a happy life together. You have both gone through so much to find each other. Don't throw it away for a spot of principal."

With that, he left to be replaced by the gang of five. Bob was as pleased as punch. He made me wiggle my toes move my legs all over the place, grip things, wave my arms about, everything except get out of bed. Of course, he had to untangle Winston first. That was fun.

We discussed Lara's House.

"David was a good employer before he started fucking with Charlie's brain. I would be happy to go back to the job that I loved." That from Cloud.

"If we can be with Charlie we'll go any where in the world and work for anyone." That from Darren encompassing Ryan.

"I need to beat a certain little bombshell at squash, so I'll happily go back." Bob grinned at me as he said it.

"Yeah you might be able to beat me now that I'm an invalid, but that won't last."

"We hope not, Charlie, you have given us a little bit of worry this last six months. So I suppose I had better come as well to look after the lot of you. Besides I can't wait to see that little bombshell naked by my pool," Mac winked at me as he said it.

Life was on the upturn again, but I was wary this time. I had thought it was good a few times before and ended up with a kick in the teeth. I didn't want it any more. I was nearly 22 and felt 92. I had a 20-year-old baby that I would die for and nearly had. I needed some balance in my life for longer than 48 hours.

They all gave notice at their jobs to coincide with Winston's and my being released from hospital. We were both champing at the bit at all the tests and all the physiotherapy. We thought we could do it all just as happily at Lara's House.

David came to see us a couple of times. Once to talk about the restaurant that had finally opened with a halfway decent chef. My book had immediately taken off and was selling in bookshops nationwide. He admitted he had played on my coma outrageously to launch it and tell the media that one day he hoped that the book's compiler would be at the helm in "Cloud's" restaurant.

"That's what we have called it, Charlie, I hope you approve. We did think about calling it Winston's, but there is one already."

Profits from the sale of the book are over £75,000, Charlie. I will remit one year of your slavery for each £25,000 of profits from your book. That means you have only about six years left to serve me. By the time you finish your convalescence, you may well be in profit. I swear that whatever happens, I will be very cognisant of your sensitive character and the love that people have for you very soon after they meet you. I will never risk you being abused and humiliated like you were before."

The second time was to tell me details of the arrangements in place for our stay.

"Cloud thinks you will not want to use my bedroom because of past memories, but you are welcome to stay in any of them. He also tells me that you don't want me to get you a new chef as you are happy with Darren."

"Yes, David, we are going to cook up a storm between us. I will take it easy though."

"Please do, Charlie. I came very close to losing you completely once because of stupidity. I don't want to risk that again. I have realised how precious you are to me."

I didn't know what to say to that so I said nothing.

When we eventually departed for Lara's House, David went completely over the top. We had an ambulance to the airport. Full size beds had been installed in the jet for us and special armchair seats had been installed in the chopper to lessen the vibration. When we arrived, we were as fresh as when we had left the hospital.

Many of the old staff had gone, but as we walked into the house, the remainder were there to greet us. I saw Peter and Paul standing together almost hidden. They looked so nervous and so cute. Peter was crying, so I had to go and give him a big hug that turned into a cuddle with a big sloppy kiss. I grabbed Paul's hand and kissed the palm.

"I am so pleased you two are still here. Are you going to look after us in the dining room?"

Peter was hopeless as he was trying to apologise for the beating Cloud had made him give me.

"Paul, take this young man away before I do myself an injury trying to carry him off to bed to show him everything is OK."

I said it with a wicked twinkle in my eye and got a small smile from Peter through his tears.

Johnnie was there, and I grabbed him and danced him round the entrance hall.

"I'm so pleased to see you. The whole kitchen crew is together again. We are going to cook up some storms for you guys. We don't have a boss to worry about now."

They all laughed. It was wonderful to be home. So many good times, so few really awful ones, but they had done so much damage. Now I hoped the good ones were here to stay – at least until I am strong again I prayed.

We did take the master suite. It was so sumptuous, and Winston would not have worried if I had slept in it with the whole of the American Army as long as I only shared with him now.

"Charlie, will I ever have to share you again with people?"

"You've never shared me, Baby. I've always been yours."

"I mean physically, Charlie."

"I don't know the answer to that. We both love sex, we both know I still owe David six years of slavery, and we have a few special friends that giving ourselves to them for a brief period brings out their love for us and shows our love for them. I can't say it is never going to happen. I can say that nothing will ever break my love for you. We have both been to the brink for our love. Nothing will ever do more to cement it than that."

"In that case, will you just kiss me and convince me all over again that you love me?"

It was over an hour later that we returned to the land of mere mortals. Well you can't really say no to a request like that from someone you would die for can you?

We were both very fragile. The nurse monitored us very carefully. His name was Ronald, so naturally, we christened him Ronald Macdonald. He had been recruited for his intensive care skills. Like the rest of the staff, he was young. He also had a wicked sense of humour. Every day he came to check basic functions and made us lay on the bed side by side while he did so. We were usually in shorts or briefs and had to keep away from each other.

"Every time you two touch each other, your pulse rate doubles, so no touching until I am finished."

Once a week, we had to go to the temporary clinic he had set up for a more comprehensive physical, separately. The first time was a bit of a surprise.

"Hello, Charlie, slip your clothes off and sit up on the examination table, will you?"

All the times I had been naked with staff in this house, you would have thought that it would be easy for professional purposes, but I actually blushed as I pulled my shorts off and sat up on the table.

"You don't have to be embarrassed, Charlie, I have seen it all before."

He gently stroked the end of my prick as he continued, "But may be not as much as this."

He checked all the usual things and made me roll over on my side so that he could stick a thermometer up my bum. He pulled one cheek up so that he could see my hole to get it in. Of course, I started to get an erection. I was still such a slut, a bit of a weak slut but!

When he slid it out, I had to roll on to my back again, and he checked the glands in my groin, of course that finished me off. My erect cock sat up tight under my rib cage.

"My God, Charlie, that is amazing. Do you mind if I touch it?"

"No, Ron, I don't mind what you do with it, but you don't tell Winston, and you don't lay a finger on him unnecessarily."

With that, he gently jacked me and played with my balls. It was very pleasant, and I came quickly. I was not getting anything like the amount of sex I needed. Winston and I were both still too weak for anything too energetic or too often. Ronald lapped up all my cum before wiping me down with a cloth.

"You taste as sweet as you look, Charlie. I'll see Winston now."

"Be very gentle and considerate with him, Ron. He is the most special person in my world. I would kill anyone who hurt him."

We started to workout gently with Bob, and we spent a lot of time at the pool. Nothing too energetic. I sunbathed naked, taking it easy to start with because I had not seen sun for six months. Winston remained in the shade when we were out of the water because he said he liked his light coffee colour and didn't want to be any blacker. No argument from me. It was wonderful to watch him fill out again. His body gradually taking on the beautiful definition it had before.

About a month after we arrived, Bob, with Ron's approval, upped our exercise programme. He was beginning to make us sweat.

"Charlie, when you were a slave, you exercised in your shorts the same as you are doing now. I would have preferred you to exercise naked, but I knew that was embarrassing for you having no choice, so I didn't ask you. Now you are free to say no. I am going to ask you to do it. With absolutely no restriction, I believe the feeling of freedom you get will be very beneficial to you. Winston, I would like you to do the same, but it isn't quite as important for you because you are not the jock Charlie is."

"No problem for me, Bob, but if Winston does it, we will have my hard cock getting in the way all the time. I'll leave the decision to Winston. If he does, I will, and if he doesn't I still will. What about it, Lover?"

"Oh yes," he said laughing. "Watching you exercise with a hard on will be fun. Can we lock the doors though, Bob, I don't want Charlie to have an audience."

The exercise programme became a hoot. Bob took every opportunity when he was spotting me on an exercise to touch my cock so that it stayed erect, and Winston would blatantly play with it when I was on the weight bench or doing sit ups.

About another month of this and both of us were looking good. We started wandering everywhere with just sexy little shorts on like I used to as a slave.

Mac used to come to the pool occasionally to talk.

"I can't do this very often, Charlie, seeing one beautiful naked boy was almost brain overload for me, but now that there are two of you, it's too much."

"It doesn't have to be, Mac, my offer is still open, and Winston approves."

"Maybe one day, Charlie. For now, I will just enjoy the scenery."

We were all in the kitchen one day, the old team complete and cooking up a very special meal. The atmosphere was great. It was Winston's 20th birthday, and the whole staff was going to eat with us in the main dining room.

Darren said, "You know, Charlie, I think you look sexier now than you ever have. I would give my right arm to make love to you two guys together."

The others looked surprised. I laughed and said jokingly, "Hell, we are all such close friends, why don't we have a kitchen staff fuck fest with Winston as the centre of attention for a late birthday present after the dinner sometime?"

Winston was almost in shock, "Charlie!"

I laughed. The others looked at each other before Johnnie said seriously, "You shouldn't jest about that, Charlie, have you any idea how much we really would like to do that. You two are the sexiest things on two legs. Every member of the staff jacks off thinking about you both."

That sobered me up. "Sorry guys."

When we were back in our room, Winston said, "Were you serious, Charlie?"

"I wasn't when I said it, Lover, but after Johnnie's revelation, I did think about it."

"You know I have never had anyone else touch my body for sex, Charlie. I can't imagine what it is like."

"Are you curious, Baby? Would you like to find out with other friends?"

"I don't know, Charlie, I want to think about that."

I did some thinking as well, which took me to the clinic.

"Ron, you do the same examination on Winston you do on me, don't you?"

"Yes, Charlie, except that I am very careful not to do anything at all erotic when I carry out the checks. Temperature, which I do under the arm, not quite as good, but adequate, and glands, to the point that if his cock is lying across one of his glands, I ask him to move it. He has never got hard during an examination."

"I want you to change all that for your next examination. Don't ask questions because I can't answer them, but this is what I want you to do. If you were to move the examination table so that you could work the other side of it someone in that cupboard with the louvers at the right angle would be able to see all the action on the table, wouldn't they?"

"Yes, why, are you looking to be a voyeur then?"

"Yes, but for a specific purpose. I want you to tell him that the hospital wants some extra checks on his next examination. You are to do the proper temperature check. I also want you to do a prostate check, and when he starts to get hard, which I am sure he will, carry out a testicle check. Complete the examination by telling him you have to take a sperm sample as well and give him a thorough de spunking."

"Christ, Charlie, are you sure about this?"

"Yes, Ron, I can't tell you why I want it done, just know that my love for him is as strong as ever, and this is designed as part of a plan to make his life even more fun than it is now."

"OK, Charlie, my orders make you the boss, and you get what you want. He is due tomorrow. Do you want it done then?"

"Yes, I will be here five minutes before him to hide."

The party was terrific. My baby never touched alcohol but still managed to have a good time. I didn't touch it either. I think Ron would have killed me if I had.

The best part for me was seeing how happy Winston was and how well he looked. The next best part was watching how contented Cloud, Mac and Bob looked. I was still telling Mac and Cloud they could have my body any time they wanted it.

Winston knew that I wanted to satisfy those two and understood. Bob was the last one, and he was having so much fun playing with me during workouts, collaborating with Winston in making sure I stayed hard for most of the time. Going the extra mile with him was not something I thought about seriously. We fooled around in the showers after squash sometimes, and I had sucked him off one day when he was very horny. The whole sex thing on this island was just so much fun I wanted Winston in it.

The next day was the examination. I told Winston I was going for a walk and not to be late for his appointment. I was in the cupboard with the louvers set when he walked in.

"Hello, Winston, come in and sit down. I want to discuss today's examination before we start. The hospital wants some extra things checked today. It means I am going to be invading your body privacy a lot. I will be gentle, I definitely won't hurt you, and I will tell you everything I am doing OK?"

"That's OK, Ron, I don't have any problems with you, just go ahead."

My big brave boy, he was all grown up when he was away from me.

"Take all your clothes off, Winston, and lay on the table. Temperature today has to be in the correct place for accuracy. Over on your left side and crook your right leg. I'm going to put a little lube at the entrance to your anus so that the thermometer slides in easy."

I watched Ron lube a finger and work it gently round the entrance to Winston's anus before just entering to the first knuckle. I would be surprised if that had not started the process of erection. I knew how sensitive his ass was. Ron slid the thermometer in as far as he could, massaging Winston's cheeks near his hole as he did.

"Is that OK, Winston?"

"Mmm that's fine, Ron. It feels very sexy."

They both laughed.

After a couple of minutes, he withdrew it, checked it and put it away. He donned a surgical glove and lubricated a couple of fingers on it.

"Winston, I need you to come up on your knees with your legs as wide as the table will allow. I have to check your prostate to make sure it is functioning. I will probably have to put two fingers inside you, but again, I will not hurt you."

I could see my baby's cock dangling down in front of his balls and as Ron entered him I watched it elongate. Crikey, that was sexy. Ron was stroking his cheeks with one hand as he pushed his middle finger all the way in, slowly removing it and adding the second finger.

"I'm just going to check the reaction, Winston."

Ron reached round in front took Winston's cock gently in his hand and felt the length. It had grown considerably, and I heard Winston gasp. Ron pulled his fingers out and said, "That is fine, Winston, roll over onto your back, and we'll finish up."

My baby was about three-quarters erect and blushing, and I was nursing an erection so hard it hurt.

Ron checked the glands as normal and then told Winston what he was going to do next.

"I have to check that you have no unusual growth on your testicles, and then I must have a sperm sample. I know that is embarrassing, but I need to have it totally fresh, so I can't let you go off and do it in private."

Winston looked alarmed, but Ron stroked his face and said, "It's OK, youngster. I'll be as gentle and as quick as I can."

He looked up at me before relubing the gloved hand, which he used to roll Winston's balls around and then with an erect penis in front of him started to wank Winston, playing with his balls and running the hand back to occasionally slide a finger back inside him. It was so erotic and it was lovely to watch my baby gradually lose it as Ron did a superb job of getting him gasping with pleasure. There was no attempt on Ron's part to prolong the wank, and he allowed Winston to cum very quickly. He scooped up some of the cum on a microscope glass and slid it under the lens for a quick look. He was making it all look very professional. He cleaned Winston up and told him to get dressed. Seated in the chair by Ron's desk, he looked like a little boy who had been to wonderland. I don't think I had ever seen him looking so young.

He looked up at Ron through his beautiful long lashes and very softly said, "Am I alright then, Ron?"

I wanted to jump out of the cupboard and take him in my arms.

"You're better than alright youngster, you're sensational. I would like to do that every time I see you."

He laughed and said, "I don't think Charlie would like that."

"I'm sure he wouldn't, off you go, see you next week. Back to normal, I guess."

"Well, Charlie, did you get what you wanted out of that?"

"Yes, you were perfect, Ron, and so was his reaction."

"Charlie, that boy is unbelievable. I wanted to cry watching him respond to my touch. You have to be the luckiest fucker in the world if you'll excuse my language. I have never come across such a totally adorable creature in my life. Be careful what you are planning. You could hurt him very easily."

"I know Ron. I'm off. I think I need to get rid of this," holding my over stretched cock."

"Hmm, I would be delighted to oblige, purely in the interests of medicine of course."

We both laughed, and I went to find a certain boy that I badly wanted to sink my cock into.

When I walked into our bedroom, he was sitting on the couch looking very pensive.

"Hello, Baby, you look worried. Everything OK, at your medical?"

"Yes, Charlie." Then he started to cry, very soft little sobs, lots of tears.

I had him in my arms in a second.

"“What is it, Baby? Tell me."

"Promise you won't hate me, Charlie, promise."

"I could never hate you. I would die first. What is it, please tell me."

"I have just let another man put fingers inside me and play with me and make me cum."

"I thought you went for a medical."

"I did. It happened there."

"I see. That is I don't see. Did Ron finger fuck you and play with your cock?"

"Yes."

"Did you enjoy it?"

Lots more tears. "Yes, Charlie, it was exciting, and he was very gentle like you. Please don't hate me, Charlie."

"Did you ask him to do it?"

"No, Charlie, he said he had to for tests."

"Do you love Ron, Winston?"

"Oh no, Charlie, I only love you."

"So you have just had a sexual encounter with another man whom you don't love and who did what he did for medical purposes. Correct?"

"Yes, Charlie."

"So why would I hate you, why would I be upset, and why are you upset?"

"Because I thought it was exciting, and I enjoyed it.

"When I had sex with Darren or Ryan, or Johnnie, or any of the others do you think I found it exciting? Do you think I enjoyed it?"

"Yes, Charlie, I know you did."

"Do you hate me for doing it?"

"No, Charlie, but you were a slave."

"And if I go to bed with Cloud or Mac now, or have a romp in the showers with Bob after squash, do you hate me for that?"

"No, Charlie, I love you."

"Well, don't be silly then. Sex is fun, you have just found out it is also exciting even when it isn't with me. This is what I meant about the romp with the kitchen guys. They are friends, if they put their fingers inside you, or even their cocks and they play with your cock and make you cum, do you think it might be exciting and fun as well?"

"Yes probably, Charlie. It would definitely be exciting to watch you put your cock in someone else."

I laughed. I reckoned we were almost on for a kitchen fuck fest.

I enlisted Bob's help. I had to tell him more than I had told Ron, but that was no problem.

"If this works, Charlie, can I join the team. An orgy with all your crew would give me enough jack-off material to take me into old age, and you say you have had all of them, you lucky bastard."

The next gym session Plan A came into effect. Winston and I were naked as usual, and Bob said, "I'm not being fair to you guys. I should be naked, too." And he promptly peeled his shorts off.

I noticed Winston immediately looked at Bob's crotch. Good.

Bob, with Winston's usual support kept me hard. Winston never actually got erect, and that was what we were going to address today. We completed a set, and Bob told us we were going to do some wrestling to test the worth of our fitness training.

"There are no formal moves. What we are going to do is have a three way wrestle. How that works is we all wrestle each other until two of us realise one is easier and gang up on him incapacitating him with holds."

Winston was easy. Bob and I had him pinned in no time. Bob moved round in such a way that his elbow was in Winston's groin. Some deft movements and Winston was sporting a fine hard on. Bob attacked it then with a hand, playing fast and loose with the whole of his abdomen.

"Please, Charlie, make him stop."

"No, sorry, he's my partner until we have vanquished you, and then we will become enemies."

"I think he should be despunked as a sign that he is vanquished," Bob said.

"I do, too, but you have to do it with your mouth if you are the one nearest the cock, and I will stop his screams of pleasure by filling his mouth with my cock."

Bob started to work with his mouth, and as I saw Winston relaxing, I tempted him with my cock close to his mouth. He took the bait. I pulled clear in time to watch him have a perfect little orgasm that I sealed with a kiss. Bob rolled away and watched me as I cuddled my Baby and whispered, "Did you enjoy that, Lover?"

He looked lovingly at me and said, "Yes, Charlie, that was nice with you here."

"Now that Bob has satisfied you would you like to watch him satisfy me by fucking me?"

He looked at Bob's erection and back at me, "Won't that hurt, Charlie?"

"No lover, not if you are kissing me as he enters me."

"I'm not sure, Charlie. Would you like Bob to fuck you?"

"Yes, why not, his reward for pleasuring you."

"OK."

"Come on then muscle man. Let's see if that rod works."

Bob was good, he opened me up nicely, and Winston looked on with fascination. When he had his cock poised to penetrate me, Winston gave me a long loving kiss but kept his eyes on the action. I was smiling. We had cracked it. I enjoyed being screwed by Bob, and Winston played with me watching Bob all the time. We both had good orgasms, but not together. Winston loved it.

He bounced around the gym shouting, "That was fantastic, Charlie, that was so exciting, I loved watching you being screwed. That was so much fun. Thank you, Bob. Can we do that again, Charlie?"

I was laughing fit to bust. This boy never ceased to surprise and amaze me. I whispered to Bob lying on the mat next to me, "You are on for the orgy. Thanks, pal."

What a great workout.

Winston and I curled up on the couch in the lounge after dinner to watch a movie, but we never actually turned it on. Winston was full of questions.

"Charlie, our threesome this afternoon was fun. You aren't cross with me for enjoying it are you?"

"I thought it was great, Baby. Do you understand now why when I had slave sex with the other staff I used to enjoy it?"

"Yes I think so. I liked watching you being shagged as well. Is that alright to?"

"Of course it is. Sex is supposed to be fun. We are supposed to enjoy it with other people, particularly if we love those other people. The sex we have is different because ours evolves purely from our love for each other. You know the reason everyone wants to have sex with us isn't just because we have sexy bodies, it's because we radiate love all the time, and the others can take a piece of that love. Would you like to share some more of our love with our kitchen crew, and let them show you how much love they have to offer you."

"I think I would, Charlie. I would love to see you shag Ryan. I know he has always wanted you to, and Darren and Johnnie would both like to shag you. I'm not sure about that."

"Why don't we let one of them shag me and the other shag you at the same time so that we can watch each other enjoying it."

"You're kinky, Charlie, won't you mind someone else putting their cock in me? You know only you have."

"No, Baby, not if it gives you pleasure."

"Can Bob come, too? He is fun."

"Of course, would you like me to organise it as a late birthday present to you?"

"Charlie, you are funny. Yes I would like that."

The next day, Winston went to the pool after breakfast, and I called Bob up from the Gym to join our organising party.

"OK, guys, were you really all serious about wanting to join in a fuck fest with Winston and me?"

Of course they were.

"Right, well it's going to happen then tomorrow night. I will get the second bedroom furnished with a couple of extra beds, and I will put lots of lube in there. The party is for Winston. Rules and set pieces. Any of you that touch Winston will be gentle. I don't want to see him with someone's fist up his ass or hear him scream because there are too many fingers tearing his ass out, that kind of thing. Winston wants to see me fuck you, Ryan, so I will if it is OK, with you."

"Yes please, Charlie," he said quietly, blushing.

I kissed him gently and said, "I've wanted to for a long time. Now, it's going to happen. Darren, you and Johnnie are going to fuck Winston and me. You had better decide who gets whose ass and one of you choreographs the whole operation. You can use any of the others you like to make the pleasure greater for Winston. Try to make it different and exciting. You can all enjoy each other, and the party ends when the last guy with a hard on calls enough."

"Charlie, you are real piece of work," Darren said with a grin from ear to ear.

"Clear up from dinner, shower and the second bedroom at eight."

Cloud was a little surprised at my request for an extra bed but didn't ask any questions.

I gave both Winston and me an enema before we went to shower. Winston was so keyed up.

"We can stop this now if you want to, Baby."

I was soaping his back paying more attention to his ass than I needed to.

"No Charlie, I'm just a little worried I might let you down."

I laughed, "That isn't going to happen in a million years. When the boys arrive, you can just let them take charge, which is what I am going to do, or you can ask any of them, including me, to do anything you want. This is your present from all of us."

At eight, Winston and I were stretched out on the biggest bed in the second bedroom in our sexiest shorts when the boys came in.

They all looked a little lost, one on one with me they were used to, but now I wasn't their slave.

"Guys, hello. You all look so worried. You don't have to be, if you want to go you can. If you are worried about what to do, let's role-play. I am the slave again, so is Winston. The only difference tonight is that if Winston wants something he can change from slave to slave master, but not me, whoever is slave master controls me until this is over. Darren, you are the senior apart from Bob who is new to this, so you start the party. You be the slave master. I am not going to give you my whip, but you can have this and you can use it."

I gave him the paddle Lars had used to devastating effect on my buttocks. I bet Darren wouldn't. I hopped off the bed and prostrated myself in front of him.

"Please Master, use me and abuse me, make me your slave."

"Take your shorts off, Charlie, then go and take Winston's off. Bob, you and Johnnie are to pleasure Winston. Don't let him cum. Charlie, I want you to make Ryan squeal with pleasure, but again you don't let him cum."

I positioned Ryan so that I could see what was happening to Winston while I worked on him. It was wonderful. Bob and Johnnie were so gentle and considerate in the way they handled him. With two mouths and four hands working on him, he was very quickly off in another world. How do you tell someone what it is like to watch a truly beautiful young man being pleasured by two, also cute guys, one black one white, and being driven off to a different world? I was doing the same thing to Ryan. He was almost as adorable as Winston was, and I loved watching him drift away into his own world as I pleasured him.

The little purring sounds and the quietly spoken words drove me crazy.

"I love you, Charlie, I've always loved you. This is wonderful, please fuck me, Charlie. I want you inside me."

I'd swear he wasn't 20. He was a little boy, over the moon because his Daddy had bought him his favourite lollipop. I had always loved him and knowing what I was about to do with him I loved him more.

Darren was the only party to this because he was playing with me, opening me up ready to fuck me, which I knew he was going to do.

He pulled away from me and watched us. I heard the sharp intake of breath, and Darren saying quietly, "Charlie, I love him, too. Why do you have his love and not me?"

I pulled Darren to me and kissed him gently.

"Give it time, it will happen. He is such a beautiful person, Darren, he is worth waiting a lifetime for. I am going to fuck him now. I am going to hurt him. When I am finished you are going to make him better and then you are going to fuck me hard as revenge for hurting your baby, do you understand?"

"Yes, Charlie, but I love you, too."

"I know, but show me how much you love me by doing what I ask. Let Bob and Johnnie satisfy Winston, he wants to watch me fuck Ryan. He knows I love Ryan as well and that Ryan wants this."

I kept Ryan off in his other world as I watched Bob and Johnnie bring Winston to a climax. It was beautiful. He thrashed about on the bed and squealed with delight as his cock started pumping into Bob's mouth while four hands were attacking all the erogenous areas they could find. When they had drained him, he lay back panting and sucking in air like he had been starved of it for a week. I watched him recover as I started to open up Ryan for my final assault. His rectum was a delight to play with, so soft, so receptive. I pushed so much lube into him and on to my own cock that I thought any sensitivity would be nonexistent.

My glans passed over his sphincter, and despite how relaxed he was, he screamed. Worse, he shed tears of pain.

"Charlie, that hurts so much, please take it out, no don't, I want you Charlie. I want your monster to take me, break me, make me your slave."

As gently as I possibly could, I fed this wonderful boy my 12 inches. When I bottomed out, I stayed still.

"Charlie, I love you, please fuck me. Plant your seed in me."

In the last two years nearly, more people than I could count had expressed their love for me. More people than I could count had become so dear to me that the thought of life without them made me sad, and they were nearly all here in this place. I didn't want to become a slave again. I didn't want to be an international chef. I wanted to remain here and love all these beautiful people.

"I'm ready, Charlie, fuck me, I can feel you inside me, now please fuck me."

I powered into him at the same time running my hands over his body. I was pinching his nipples, pulling my hands down to caress his cock and play with his balls. They were everywhere. Nobody else moved. They were transfixed watching Ryan completely lose it. He was writhing and squirming, screaming and gasping as I assaulted every erogenous region I had found while playing with him, all the time powering into him with 12 inches of lust and love. His orgasm was frightening in its intensity. Mine followed in seconds, controlled but still hugely intense. I eased his legs off my shoulders, fell forward and supporting myself on my arms gently kissed his face, his eyes, nose, lips, chin, neck, everything. I whispered inconsequential words of affection to him as he returned to us. The only other sound I could hear was Darren, quietly crying, curled up on the bed close to us.

"Why you, Charlie, why does he love you so much? I'm going to hurt you, Charlie, I love you, too, but I'm going to hurt you."

Everyone else heard it and gasped. I looked at Winston and shook my head. He understood.

Ryan came back to us, and I slid out of him moving back on my haunches. He opened his eyes and looking straight at me said, with a little smile playing across his lips, "That was worth waiting for, Charlie, now I know why I love you."

He rolled over and cuddled Darren, "I love you, too, because you are special."

This should have been the finale to the evening, not the beginning. Nothing else was going to match this was it?

Darren looked from Ryan to me and then moved to position himself for me to suck him.

"Charlie, get me excited. Bob come and open Charlie up ready to take me."

Once again, I was the centre of the action. Darren had the biggest cock on the staff apart from me, and it was lovely to suck. My tongue worked overtime on his glans and his balls, and my hands played havoc with his senses on his shaft and his hole. I kissed him and nibbled his nipples, my mouth and tongue were everywhere while Bob finger fucked me and played with my cock and balls. When Darren could take no more, he swung into position to fuck me doggy fashion and simply powered in. I screamed with the pain. Darren's orgasm was awesome. I could feel jet after jet of spunk sinking into me before he fell forward crushing me into the bed.

Bob and Johnnie both had dicks dripping with cum from their own orgasms, but my baby was soft. Watching me being punished by Darren's cock had made his own shrivel up. I looked at him and said, "Baby, it's OK, that was an incredible shag." And I smiled. He did as well and lay back on the bed.

When Darren rolled off me he looked in to my eyes and said, "I'm sorry, Charlie. I'm so sorry."

I laughed and slid on top of him. Kissing him passionately, I said, "No you aren't because that was a fucking awesome shag, you big lug."

We were both laughing, and I whispered in his ear, "Now do the best bit of sexual choreography you have ever done. Get everyone except me working on Winston and finish it with Johnnie fucking him."

Darren was good, eight hands, and four mouths all managing to work on Winston together. He was in heaven. I just watched his face. An occasional kiss to let him know everything was OK, and apart from that, I didn't touch him.

I pride myself in being able to more than satisfy Winston, but his orgasm produced so much cum I thought we were all going to drown in it. Johnnie stopped breathing with his, and we literally had to thump him to get him working again.

It must have been ten to 15 minutes before people started to react normally. Bob was curled up next to me as I cuddled my baby and said to me.

"Charlie, if I live to be a hundred years old, I swear I will never have such an erotic experience as this again."

"Bob, we've only just begun. Darren, what do you think all you black boys could do for this white boy here. I'm sure his cock and ass need some attention."

Darren smiled at me and said, "Charlie, I was thinking that both you white boys need some attention. We've been practising on Winston. I reckon we ought to be able to sort you two now. However, before we do. Bob, you made a big mistake with our Charlie when you first came here and Charlie got you off the hook. We all think you should have been punished for that piece of humiliation, so tonight before we fuck you we are going to punish you."

I was stunned, "I swear I had no idea, Bob."

"It's OK, Charlie. I'll take my punishment like a man if it pleases these guys."

Johnnie and Ryan spread eagled Bob across a chair, and I dragged Darren out of earshot.

"Don't you dare hurt him. This is an evening of pleasure not pain."

"Charlie, just watch."

Darren applied the paddle in strokes that just tingled, after each one Ryan and Johnnie alternated sucking Bob's cock or his balls for a minute before Darren paddled him again. This went on for about ten minutes, and Bob was orgasming almost continuously. I had never seen anything like it. Darren changed tactics then and started finger fucking him instead of paddling him, and then he entered him. Bob screamed at first, but the cries of pain very quickly changed to pleas for Darren to fuck him harder. It has to be just about the most awesome sex I have ever witnessed.

The culmination was Bob being fucked alternately by Darren and Johnnie while giving Ryan a blowjob.

When they all recovered, I said to Darren, "Do I get that as well?"

"No, Charlie, we are all going to bed now. If you want any more loving tonight, you are going to get it there," pointing to Winston as he said it.

Ryan was the first to go. He gave Winston a little kiss and said, "Happy birthday, Winston. I hope we pleased you with our present." And to me, "Thank you, Charlie, I will never forget that, and I'll remember to tell Darren that I love him as well."

Johnnie was next, kissing Winston first and saying to me, "Now, I know why you love him."

Bob was still staggering as he kissed us both and said, "You ought to do this professionally. You would make a fortune."

We all laughed.

Darren still had tears in his eyes as he hugged us and said, "I will love you two guys forever."

We walked back to our bedroom and showered without a word. When we were lying in bed cuddling, I said to Winston, "Was that OK, Baby?"

"Charlie, that was better than OK. Those guys were fantastic. But I know that I only want to do that for a bit of fun occasionally. When I want loving, I want it just from you."

Chapter 6

Ron asked us both to go to see him one morning after breakfast.

When we walked in, he was sitting with two sets of papers on his desk.

"Charlie, you and Winston are probably going to New York next week."

"Why, Ron, problems?"

"No, Charlie, the specialists are so pleased with all my reports, they want to run the final set of tests before giving you both a clean bill of health. I can't remember a happier six months in my life than this. I shall be sorry to leave."

It did not seem possible, we had been convalescing for six months, and then I looked at Winston and saw the boy I had originally fallen in love with, instead of the shadow that had returned to the island with me.

"I have to carry out a final physical and take all your measurements again for comparison."

We were definitely destined to be the little people. Winston was now full grown, and Ron clocked him at 5ft. 9ins. tall and 150 lbs. but the body was perfectly proportioned and beautiful. He had stripped for Ron to take all his measurements, as had I. The big difference with me was that I sported a massive erection looking at my man.

"Does that thing ever lay down, Charlie. I think I have only seen it soft once in this room."

"With Winston here it won't, that is for sure."

I was 5ft.7ins. and 145 lbs., I had a lovely golden all over tan against Winston's light coffee. We were at the peek of our physical fitness and glowed with health.

It was a sad time. David had called to talk to me and said to bring all our personal gear in case we didn't return to the island.

As we waited for the Helicopter, Cloud and Mac told us we had to swear to keep them informed what was happening, under pain of death.

We were taken straight to the clinic where we had spent so much time, put into a private room and immediately linked up to a mass of machines.

"Hello, Charlie, I am pleased you took my advice. You both look incredible."

It was the doctor who had advised me to take David's offer of Lara's House.

"We will probably take 24 hours to run all the tests we need. If you both look as good on the inside as you do on the outside, you will be out of here the day after."

We did and we were.

David's limo picked us up and took us to the apartment. I have to admit I was very apprehensive. I was now back into slavery because I had been declared fit. What had David planned for me?

"Hello, Charlie, hello, Winston. My God, you two look totally stunning. We won't be able to let you out of here without a bodyguard. You'll be mobbed. It would be silly to ask how you are."

His laugh was nervous. It looked as though we were both a bit apprehensive.

"Hello, Sir," from Winston.

"Hello, David, or should I say Master again now?" that was ignored.

"James, show Winston their room and then the drawing room or TV room whichever he wants. Winston, Charlie and I have a lot to talk about, so we may be a while."

He started walking towards the study, and I naturally followed.

"Sit down, Charlie. These papers are for you. We'll go through them together.

"The first sheet details your book sales. I have taken £100,000 leaving about £10,000. Sales have slowed of course, and the publishers don't now think we will make another £25,000. You have paid off four years of your ten, which is very good. The balance, whatever it is will go into your personal account here in New York for when you are free.

"The second sheet shows the break down of our contract. The original date was 20 months ago. Because of my stupidity you have lost six months of your life and me a full year of your services. That leaves four years and four months of your contract remaining. Do you agree?"

"Yes, David," and my heart sank. What plans had he for me now? Another four years with no control of my life.

"The next block of papers you can read later at your leisure, Charlie, and sign the contract when you are happy with it. You can have it checked by an attorney if you have any doubts about its contents.

"Briefly, it gives you 49% of Cloud's Restaurant. The other 51% is mine. All profits from it will be split in that proportion and in your case join your book money in your account. The accounts for the nine months that it has already been operating will give you an idea of its profitability. At present rates, you should be quite a wealthy man when your contract to me ends.

"Your routine for the near future is laid out in the last page. Basically, Cloud's is open for seven months of the year. During that time, you will live in your own apartment above the restaurant, presumably with Winston who will be employed in the restaurant. You will be the premier chef. Your salary will be $50,000 per year from which all your living expenses will be paid. You will take one month's holiday, which the two of you can spend anywhere in the world. I don't imagine money will be a problem for you.

"The final four months of the year, Charlie, you will return to Lara's House to resume your slave status. You will also continue as chef. There is no possibility, however, of a return to any kind of punishment routine. You will be available to perform the duties you did before, and you will sleep with me whenever I am on the island. In New York, you will still be my slave, but you will call me David. I don't propose to use you very much here, but I want you to know that I can. If you deserve any punishment, which on past performance is unlikely, only senior staff or I will be permitted to administer it.

"Is that all clear, Charlie?"

"Yes, David, perfectly. You are very generous. What you are offering is far more than I expected or deserve. I presume I am not allowed to use money from my account to buy out my slavery contract."

"No, you aren't. I am going to enjoy your body for a few more years, Charlie. That was the main reason for instigating the contract in the first place. You are still delightful to look at, and I intend to take advantage of my position. I will not take you away from Winston while you are in New York except for the odd dalliance.

"Finally, when the restaurant is open and you are my partner, you may address me as David. When the restaurant closes, and you revert to slave status on the island, I will be Master again. The restaurant is closed now but will reopen in one month. You can have a couple more days here to look it over and put your mark on your apartment if you wish. Your luggage is already there, and all services are on. All your banking needs are in a package in your room. You will need to go into the bank tomorrow to activate the account.

"If you have no more questions then, Charlie, that's it."

"Just one, Master. What did you mean when you said wanting my body was the original reason for instigating my contract?"

"Charlie, I saw you on the monitors at the casino one day. The manager told me you were running a large debt, and he was going to close you down. I think it stood at about £10,000. You could have sorted that, so I told him to let it carry on. The idea of this contract was already forming."

"I see, once again my body proved my down fall. Thank you, Master."

I joined Winston in the drawing room. He looked worried. As I entered, he shot out of the chair he had been seated in and grabbed me in a bear hug.

"Is everything going to be alright, Charlie? He isn't going to take you away from me, is he?"

"No, Baby, not unless living in New York isn't what you want."

"You aren't serious. We are going to live here? Oh, Charlie, that is fantastic. Are you free?"

"No, Baby, it's all a little complicated, but the important thing is we are going to be together all the time. I am still a slave and will have to perform sexual duties for David and staff at Lara's House. Here as well, but only occasionally. In four years time, when I am free, I shall also be a rich man."

"I don't care about the sex thing, Charlie. I know for you it's fun. As long as you only love me, you can have sex with the whole of New York."

He was laughing and crying. He told me later that he had been terrified David would take me away from him.

Life was still good. It would be interesting to go back to Lara's House as a slave again. It might be fun. The last six months had developed into an interesting finale with the kitchen fuck fest. The chances were all the staff knew about that now, and the scene would be set for more of the same with a wider list of participants. I wouldn't instigate anymore though. That would be up to all the potential slave masters.

We moved into our own apartment and stayed a week because I told David the kitchen in the restaurant needed some work that I wanted to oversee. Winston became the little housewife keeping the apartment immaculate. We did the sightseeing bit in New York, and I told Winston we would spend New Year's Eve in Times Square after the restaurant was closed.

David and I had a couple more meetings during which Winston's role was discussed.

"Charlie, you are in charge, but my suggestion is that you train Winston as a waiter. I think he is such a stunning young man we will get almost as many customers to see him as we will to sample your cooking."

I laughed, "David, I think I had better keep an eye on you, or I am going to be losing Winston."

"Huh, I wish. Don't you agree though?"

"I'll talk to Winston about it. I must admit I have been thinking about the waiting staff. I would like them all to wear sexy uniforms if they have the bodies to carry them. Winston in tight blue trousers and white body hugging shirt will have half the men ejaculating and the women swooning. I'll be able to get away with serving sawdust."

We both laughed.

"David, one last request, and I know this will disrupt Lara's immensely, but can we have Darren, Ryan and Johnnie here when Cloud's is open and back at Lara's when we are there."

"Christ, Charlie you do like to push your luck don't you. Supposing I said that the price to say yes would be 20 lashes for each of them."

I looked stunned and said very quietly, "Alright, David, can we spread them over three days. I don't think I could take 60 at once."

"I don't believe you. You nearly died for your lover, and now you are willing to take a thrashing for your friends. I guess I have a lot to learn about love, friendship and loyalty. You've got them. We'll do some temporary transfer from staff here. They will probably love it. The cost of their apartment will come out of your share of the profits though, OK?"

"Thank you, David, you have my whip here. Do you want to give me my first 20 now?"

He walked across the room and took me in his arms.

"Charlie, I'm not going to touch you with a whip again ever. I will see you in two days time to give you paper work for Cloud and Mac. You had better plan to be back here from Lara's in about ten days after that and work with the Maitre D."

I received a very tender kiss before being shown out by James.

I asked David to phone Cloud and tell him to get my old room ready but not to tell him who was going to use it, and to let me carry the written instructions for him and Mac concerning me. Not to tell Cloud anything except that I was in New York for a while.

When the helicopter dropped us at the pad, no one was there to meet us, so we carried our small amount of luggage up to the house. Cloud had sent Peter down to see who was arriving, meeting us halfway to the house.

"Charlie, Winston, this is fantastic."

He gave us both a big hug and wanted to carry my bag.

"No, Peter, I am a slave again. You don't have to wait on me."

He was stunned. "Oh, Charlie, no, Mr. David wouldn't be that cruel. No one should ever be allowed to beat you again."

"Don't worry Peter, they won't. The rules have changed. The new book is just a chores book. My body is only for using and playing with not abusing."

He looked at me whilst thinking about this and then beamed and said, "That means I get to fuck you as often as I want then Charlie." And laughed. "Sorry Winston, I won't do it very often."

He hugged us both again and said, "Charlie, it's so good to have you back."

Cloud thought the same but was less demonstrative until we were inside our room. For the first time ever, he took me in his arms and kissed me hard on the lips. I was so surprised I didn't have time to respond, so I grabbed his face and planted my own kiss.

"It's good to be back, Cloud. I miss my family so much when I am away."

What did I say? Cloud teared up and sort of huffed and puffed and the tears in his eyes were fighting to roll down his cheeks

"You must go and see Mac, Charlie. He has been worried sick what David was going to do with you. There will be no more punishment here even if you are back as a slave, which I presume you are."

"Yes, Cloud, but only temporarily. I have papers for you and Mac concerning my status, and I have so much to tell you all."

Rather than tell the story a dozen times, I told everybody at dinner that night in the canteen. The business of the money I would be worth in four years I only told to Cloud and Mac, who told me I was worth every cent of it.

Darren, Ryan and Johnnie were delighted to be coming to New York to work. When I told them it was only a few weeks away for them, they were jumping for joy.

"Are you planning on taking away all my best people, Charlie, or just these three and Winston?"

"Well, I'm sorry, Cloud, but I might want to take Peter and Paul later if my plans for the waiting staff work, and David agrees."

"I thought you might, and I know they will go with you, even if the restaurant were in Alaska."

Life was good. David phoned to tell me he would bring the New York kitchen staff to Lara's with him next week, and we could fly back together followed by Darren and company the next week.

The chores book was left in the staff canteen, and Cloud made a large notation at the front, "Maximum two entries per day."

I laughed, "Don't want to wear me out in my ten-day stay, Cloud?"

He blushed a little and swotted my butt, as he left, "Don't want to see that overworked, Charlie."

After lunch the next day, I checked the book just as I always used to. Neither of the names in it registered. But they did make my stomach turn, Luke and John. I remembered the puerile joke I made with two new people, Matthew and Mark who had abused me in the barn, but that was a long time ago.

I called Cloud, "Who are Luke and John?"

"They are two of Mac's people, Charlie, they are new."

So I called Mac.

"They are agronomists, Charlie, college people. They live in one of the estate cottages near mine. One white, one Hispanic, both late twenties. I am surprised they are calling for you. I didn't think they even knew about you because they eat in the cottage and don't mix at all. They are doing some soil analysis and will be gone about the same time you return to New York. I imagine it will only be for chores. I don't think they are gay."

Walking down to the cottages in my little shorts again I realised I felt uncomfortable with this. The boys I knew were fun. These were an unknown quantity, and I didn't think I would be able to take any more abuse yet.

"Come in, Charlie, I am Luke, and this is John."

Luke was six feet and some. He looked like a typical American College Jock. Great body, Colgate smile, blond hair.

John was the opposite, nearly. A couple of inches taller than I, much bigger build, but no fat, thick legs, heavily muscled, jet-black wavy hair, both in shorts, both displaying more than adequate boxes.

"David told us about you when we stayed with him in New York."

I sighed with relief.

"Oh that's fine then. I was a bit worried you being strangers. What chores would you like me to do for you?"

"We would like you to clear up this place for a start, Charlie. We never seem to have time."

I looked around, and it was a typical bachelor pad. Clothes and bits and pieces all over the place.

"No problem, guys, but you know housekeeping would do this for you every day if you ask."

"Yes we know, Charlie, but the houseboys don't do it naked, and you are going to. I'll take your shorts."

I blushed. It had been over a year since I had done this.

I started clearing up their reception room, and they sat and watched my every move.

"That's a really cute butt, Charlie. I bet that gets fucked a lot doesn't it?"

"No, Luke, hardly ever."

"Come here, Charlie." That was John. I stood in front of him and he started playing with me, he was good. He pulled my foreskin back and attacked my glans with a wet finger. Good solid erection in no time.

"I don't believe that is used for fucking very much. It's a brave soul who would take that up their ass. So what do you do for sex?"

"Just about everything, John, just no one thing in excess."

They both laughed and Luke said, "Well, we won't change that, Charlie. We will just spit roast you this afternoon so that you get a little fucking and a little sucking. Come and take my shorts off and show me how good a blow job you can give."

I started on him without much enthusiasm. I hadn't done this with a stranger for a year.

"Come on, Charlie, that doesn't feel particularly exciting. Get up on all fours, perhaps John can make you more enthusiastic."

I was on the floor doggy fashion between Luke's legs. John started caressing my butt. He pulled the cheeks apart and licked all down my crack, over my hole and down my perineum to suck on my balls. It was nice. I got a little more enthusiastic with Luke but not much.

"That's still not good enough, Charlie. John show him what we do with poor performers."

The next thing I knew was a sharp slap on my buttocks. I cried out and immediately curled up in a ball screaming and begging them not to hurt me. The slap itself had not hurt that much, but the memories it brought back were terrifying. They were both shocked at my reaction. They were even more shocked a minute later when Mac burst through the door and floored both of them with almighty roundhouse punches. He was magnificent. He dropped onto the floor and took me in his arms caressing me gently to calm me down.

"It's alright, Charlie. No one is going to hurt you now. We all love you here. We'll keep strangers away from you in the future."

The two guys watched this both rubbing very sore jaws.

"We only slapped his ass once, Mac. It's not as if we beat him."

"You fucking morons, this boy was abused so badly by idiots like you that he spent six months in a coma and another six months convalescing. His lover nearly died as well of a broken heart. Pack your things and get off this estate, and I suggest you do it quickly. If the rest of the staff hear of this before you are gone, they are likely to lynch you. They love this beautiful, gentle boy. Half of them would die for him."

Mac picked me up as if I weighed nothing and took me back to his cottage, laying me gently on his bed. He lay down with me so that he could cuddle me close. He felt so safe. I snuggled up to him with my head on his chest, my arm and leg thrown over him. Of course, that put my cock up against a furry thigh. He continued to caress my body, gently running his hands over my back and buttocks, whispering to me that I was safe now and nobody else was going to hurt me. His hand felt so nice, and as I calmed down, I started to get an erection. When Mac realised what was happening, he got very flustered.

"It's alright, Mac, I love you touching me, and I feel so safe. I know you would never hurt me or take advantage of me. But please Mac, please make love to me."

"I can't Charlie, I feel I would be betraying you if I used you."

"I will probably never get the chance to be in your bed again, Mac, so I am not getting out of it until you have fucked me."

Before he could reply, I kissed him on the lips and started to work on him before he could protest anymore. I could feel him growing under my leg, so I slid it off him and used my hand to caress his manhood through his shorts. When I was sure he wouldn't protest anymore, I undid the top button and slid my hand in, lifting the elastic of his boxers. I ran my hand down his shaft and then took a firm hold of it. He sighed and I had won. I took his shorts and boxers off completely before starting some serious pleasuring. This was a work of love and gave me as much joy as it gave him. I swivelled round to the sixty-nine position hoping he would play with me. His mouth was as gentle with my cock as his hands had been with my body. I wasn't sure whether I wanted to laugh or cry. He was being so gentle with me, a piece of priceless porcelain would have been in no danger of damage.

"Stretch my anus, Mac, get me prepared to take your cock."

"I can't Charlie. I have no lube."

"Then use spit Mac, you are going to fuck me. You have waited so long, please do it."

When he had me more than ready, oozing pre-cum and drifting off to Nirvana, he rolled me onto my back, lifted my legs onto his shoulders and gently entered me. I watched him and cried to see the expression on his face. He had wanted to do this for nearly two years but had been too honourable to take advantage of me"

"Oh crikey, Charlie, that beautiful bottom is more wonderful inside than it is on the outside. I didn't think that was possible."

He fucked me with long strokes, but so gently, our orgasms when they came were together and for Mac shattering, his last couple off strokes as his cock grew to twice its previous size, well it felt as though it had, were hard and demanding. I don't think I had ever felt so many jets of spunk from one orgasm. Still in control despite his shattering finale, he dropped my legs back onto the bed and rolled over to lie beside me, folding me into his arms again like before so that he could continue to caress my body and my buttocks. I was still crying softly, to have given Mac so much pleasure was such a joy for me. At last, I had been able to do something to show this big care bear how much I appreciated his caring and how much I loved him.

"Thank you, Charlie, thank you for the most wonderful experience of my life."

When I was fully recovered, I headed back to the house feeling safe enough to go back to the other cottage for my shorts. I needn't have worried. The guys were gone.

I told Winston about Mac, but not about the other two. I couldn't handle the terror I would have seen come back into his life at the thought that I could still be abused.

Mac called David that night and told him the story of Luke and John and how terrified I had been after only one little slap. New directive from David. No casual staff would have access to me. No new staff would have access to me for at least a month and for the first couple of times after that I was to be escorted by Winston although he could wait outside the door where I was called.

The day before David arrived, Peter and Paul had their names in the chores book. Nothing had changed there. They were in their usual position on one bed in little white briefs. It had been so long since I had seen them like that. They were 20 now but still looked cherubic. I kissed them both on the lips as I walked in and gently squeezed their cocks through their briefs.

"And what terrible chores have you got for me today," I said with a broad grin on my face.

"We both want to fuck you today, Charlie, is that ok?"

They looked so worried as Peter said it. It was difficult to realise it had been more than a year since I had been in this position with them. We had come a long way since that first session with Pinky and Perky beating me and humiliating me.

"Of course it's OK. I love you two. It gives me pleasure to satisfy you."

I went down on my knees between them and started to play with them. They were soon erect and quickly out of their briefs. I had forgotten how lovely they were naked. Two almost identical eight-inch cocks stood rigidly to attention. I enjoyed the next half hour pleasuring them but not letting them cum.

"Charlie, no one else in the world can pleasure us like you do. You really are a sex machine. Can we spit roast you?"

Again, the request was made with worried expressions on their faces. What a difference a year makes.

"I would be disappointed if you didn't."

And, we all laughed.

Peter fucked me first while I sucked Paul, and then he sat and watched Paul fuck me.

I came without touching myself, which was pretty well par for the course. Who wouldn't though, sucking two cute guys who then used all their experience to make you enjoy them fucking you?

We cuddled up on the bed together while we recovered our equilibrium.

The only sex I had better than that was with Winston and Ryan. How lucky was I?

David arrived with a small kitchen team from Cloud's. We were introduced, and I settled them in with Darren to show them the ropes. My slave status here would not be a problem because I doubted they would ever work with me. Darren told me they were a very nice trio and briefed him about New York and the operation of Cloud's. Of course, they were curious about me and amazed that I was the author of the cookery book and the new premier chef at Cloud's. None of them believed that I was the staff fuck slut. They thought it was a staff wind up because I looked so cute.

Being cute had nearly cost me my life, but it had also given me so much pleasure.

I discussed my idea about the waiting staff again with David, and we decided to try it out here on Winston. His tailor came in the next day to measure and make up trousers and shirt for Winston that were tight enough to be sexy, loose enough for him to be able to work.

"Take Winston out of the kitchen, Charlie, and we'll give him to Cloud for the rest of his time here to do waiter training."

Two nights later, David, asked me to have dinner with him.

"Dress properly, Charlie, you are going to be served by a Cloud's waiter."

Winston brought in the first course. I hadn't seen him change, so the sky blue trousers and brilliant white shirt with his own name embroidered into the left breast were a revelation to me. I waited until he had served, and stood back from the table before I said anything.

"David, that won't work." Winston looked crestfallen, Cloud looked quizzical and David got stroppy.

"Why not, I think he looks terrific."

"That's why it won't work. Peter, Paul, come in here and stand by Winston. Now David, we put those two in the same kit and a couple of others. What do we have? The most gorgeous waiters in New York, and the sexiest.

Every customer, regardless of gender or orientation, will want to rape them over the tables. They are just too fuckable for words, and Winston will have to wear very tight briefs or a jockstrap to keep that beautiful cock under control as will Peter and Paul."

"Mmm. I see what you mean, Charlie, but it would boost bookings by a good percentage. I'm absolutely certain."

"I agree, but how do we stop these boys being touched up all the time. I'm bloody certain I couldn't keep my hands off them for a full meal."

"I don't know the answer to that, but shall we go ahead with more uniforms like this while we explore the situation?"

"Why not, David, this has also given me another idea. How would you like to own the classiest gay restaurant, bar or club in New York as well, with barmen and waiters dressed the same only the trousers become very short shorts. Do it all Art Deco like the 1920s clubs so that you can justify bright lights. You will have no problem getting gorgeous guys to do the jobs because they will earn a thousand dollars a night in tips."

"Charlie, just how rich do you want to be by the time you are a free man again?"

"I'm not greedy, David. I thought ten million was a nice round figure to aim for."

Everyone gasped, and I looked round the dining room at all of them and said, "I'm not joking."

"When we are back in New York, Charlie, you and I will go clubbing and have a look at what is already on offer. The restaurant opens in two weeks. You and I can fly back tomorrow. Give you plenty of time to do whatever you need to do in the kitchen and us plenty of time to decide if your latest idea is viable. Winston, Peter and Paul, sorry Cloud we are going to take them, can fly up next week with the kitchen crowd giving us a week to get them all in shape. My tailor will do the uniforms for these three, and we will do the remainder in New York."

I looked at Winston and saw his face drop.

"It's alright, Baby, I'll be with Mr. David, nothing is going to happen to me."

Poor Winston, our love making that night was an act of desperation on his part.

"It really will be alright, Baby, I'll stay at the apartment and phone you every night OK?"

He cried himself to sleep, and I cried with him. It was only going to be a week, and probably the last week we would need to spend away from each other.

I said my goodbyes to everyone, whispering to Cloud, "You are the odd man out, Cloud. You will have to take me next time I am here to join the club. I'm sure Mac will tell you it was worth it."

He looked at me his mouth agape. I laughed. Winston of course was crying, but Darren and Ryan were cuddling him, so he was in good hands.

"Charlie, I would like you to stay with me, tonight, you can go back to your own apartment tomorrow, and we'll go clubbing it around gay New York for the next few nights."

"Yes, Master. Do you still not have a boyfriend?"

"No Charlie, no one special any way."

"I'm sorry, Master. I rather spoilt it with Michael didn't I?"

"Yes you did, Charlie. Do you think I should beat you for that?"

I looked at him to see if he was serious and when I realised he wasn't, I grinned and said, "No Master, I think you should fuck me for that. We would both enjoy that much more."

"You are absolutely right, Charlie, that is what I'm going to do."

He did, and it was good.

The next morning, I met Jean Louis who was the Maitre D at Cloud's. We sorted out menus as a first priority and the wines next. We discussed staffing and agreed that I would have two more in the kitchen to compliment my crew and one more chef to slot in between Darren and myself. He had four more waiters and on David's instruction, they were all drop dead gorgeous and white. I told him when the others arrived, we would work out a roster for them all trying to please everybody if we could. The only days off cast in stone were mine and Winston's, the same, and I thought Darren and Ryan the same, the remainder we would sort together.

"Jean Louis, I have never had anything to do with front of house before, so initially, despite my being the boss, I would like us to work as joint managers making our decisions together. On your days off, I will be on duty, and we will have to train the most promising of the waiters to sub for you. Also, if we have the opportunity, I would like one black waiter and one white waiter to be wine trained."

"That arrangement is completely satisfactory to me, Charlie. One of the white waiters already is wine trained, and you can recommend one of yours to be trained along side him."

I phoned Lara's House each night to talk to Winston, and the first night I discussed with Cloud, Peter and Paul's wine knowledge. Peter had done an extensive course so that was another problem solved.

I spent the next few days making sure everything was ready in the kitchen with the help of the New York staff and spent the nights checking out gay bars, restaurants and clubs with David. On each night, he picked someone up, so I was free. The third night quite late we bumped into Tom, the nice man who had stopped David's excesses the night with the two Russian boys.

"Tom, what a pleasure to see you again."

"Thank you, Charlie, but the pleasure is all mine, you look absolutely stunning. What have you been doing with yourself?"

"For the last year, Tom, nothing. Now I am the premier chef at Cloud's, which we open again next week."

"That is wonderful, Charlie. I had no idea that David's little slave was also a massive cooking talent. Do you still see him or has your service to him finished?"

"No, David and I are partners in Cloud's, so I see quite a lot of him. He is here somewhere with tonight's lucky young man."

"Oh, so I suppose you stay at the apartment with him?"

"No Tom, I have my own apartment above Cloud's in that new block."

"That is wonderful, Charlie. I would love to see it. Would you like to show me?"

"Of course, Tom, are you sure it's my apartment you want to see though?"

He blushed and said, "Well no actually, I would like to see if the damaged little boy I took to bed is as gorgeous all over as the bits I can see."

I laughed and told him I thought I would like that. When David returned, I asked him if it was all right if I left now with Tom. He was a little surprised but nodded, "Go ahead, Charlie, I will pick you up tomorrow, same time same place, goodnight. Goodnight, Tom, look after him."

"You know I will, David, goodnight."

Tom loved my apartment, but was surprised to see the bedroom set up for two on an obviously permanent basis.

"I'm sorry, Charlie, you have a lover?"

"Yes Tom, he will be here next week. So make the most of tonight."

"Lucky boy, Charlie. So I am going to have to fuck you as many times as I can to store up for the rest of my life."

We both laughed.

"I guess so, Tom, but every one of them had better be memorable, or I will throw you out."

"Mmm. What a lovely challenge."

He took me in his arms and kissed all over my face leaving my lips till last. He was a beautiful kisser. He knew how to use his tongue like no one else I knew. I was slowly being stripped as he continued to make free use of my mouth. He left me long enough to remove my shoes socks trousers and pants before devouring my mouth again. Then his hands started roving. I swear he had electric wires in each fingertip. The shocks going through me as he touched my nipples and buttocks had my erection so hard it hurt. He left my cock and balls until I almost screamed at him to play with them. I had never been so turned on in my life. He was incredible.

He laid me gently on my bed and went straight at my cock. I couldn't touch him because he was kneeling by my thighs.

"Forget me, Charlie, concentrate on enjoying the feelings."

My whole being was centred on where his hands and his mouth were. I was gasping for breath having trouble controlling anything. I was writhing and wriggling trying to get away from this man who was giving me a sensory overload. I was on the brink of a massive orgasm and everything stopped. I sank into the bed slowly regaining control as I watched Tom taking off his clothes. He was gorgeous, his body like mine was hairless and his cock looked like a rod of iron. It was tight up against his belly as he stood above me with his ball sac hanging nicely, not too slack, just below.

"Where is your lube, Charlie?"

I pointed to the bedside table still unable to speak. He put it handy and climbed onto the bed straddling me and started on me again with that amazing tongue. This time though he attacked my perineum and my hole with it while continuing to use his hands on my cock and balls. I really was going ballistic this time. He had very wet hands playing with my balls and running the other hand over my cock head. When I thought I was going to die of ecstasy, I felt his cock pushing gently against my sphincter. I was so relaxed it slid in without any pain at all. What an amazing feeling. It really did feel like a rod of iron. There was no give in it at all it was so hard. I had taken more cock than most, but this one was truly amazing. He used it like a probe seeming able to put it anywhere in my love chute he chose at the same time moving it in and out in a soft and gentle motion. It wasn't particularly big, but what it lacked in size, it made up for a million times in mobility. My senses won, and I screamed for him to fuck me hard and let me cum. We both did, together, and for both of us it was kaleidoscopic. After we were drained, he rolled off me gasping, and we lay alongside each other caressing each other's bodies.

About ten minutes elapsed before Tom said in a very shaky voice, "My God, Charlie, that is the most amazing orgasm I have ever had."

"Ditto Tom, where did you get that incredible cock? I have never experienced anything like it inside me in my life."

He laughed, "Mmm, it is a bit of a show off isn't it. Being little it feels it has to produce quality fucks."

"I promise you it has done that. Can I do it to you now? You have such a cute butt, and I want to play with that wonderful piece of equipment."

"Charlie, I would love to say yes, but I am sure I will never be able to take yours, it is awesome. I have never seen one anything like it, and it gets so hard."

"Let me try, Tom, you can control the entry and set your own pain level."

We did it. Tom sat over me to control totally the entry. It was still very painful for him and it took him a long time to get it all in, but his ass was as amazing as his cock. We both had incredible orgasms again, and he shot several loads straight into my mouth.

"Mmm. Tom that tastes good, and you are such a good shot."

We both had to work the next day and settled for the two orgasms. Tom was "tres gallant" the next morning after I had fed him OJ and coffee. As he was leaving, he kissed my hand and said, "Charlie, you are the most awesome lover I have ever had. Your boyfriend is the luckiest man on earth. If you ever need a replacement, please let me audition for the part."

He left me his card, and I started thinking about a threesome with him and Winston. It would be incredible to watch my baby react to Tom's ministrations.

The Lara's House crowd arrived. It was terrific. Six people I loved were now in striking distance. I was not interested in money, except for what it could do for me, so I had taken a three-bedroom apartment in the same block as Winston and I to accommodate Darren and the crowd. David of course told me I was being extravagant, but having the boys so close gave me a wonderful feeling of togetherness. It also meant that socialising was easy. When we went out, it was together, safety in numbers. Without blowing my own trumpet, we needed it – Darren, Johnnie, Ryan, Peter, Paul, Winston and I. You would have to go round the world a few times to find seven sexier guys permanently in one package. We couldn't officially drink in the bars, well the others couldn't, so we tended to use the late night cafes on the fringes of the gay area.

We started to be noticed, and one night we nearly had fits when an oldish gentleman came up to us and said, "You are without doubt the seven most beautiful young men in New York. I would consider it an honour if you would join me in my apartment and allow me to make love to you all. I am very generous and am willing to pay you any sum you wish for the privilege."

They all looked at me, and I said, "If we were available the price would be $10,000 per night, but I am sorry, we aren't available for the foreseeable future."

The others looked aghast at me, and the man gave me his card and said, "If you would call me if the situation changes I would be delighted to renew the request." And left us.

"Charlie, you are outrageous, $10,000!"

"Don't you think you are worth that Johnnie?"

"Err, well, I've never thought about sex for money."

"Well think about it. He was correct. You are the sexiest men in New York, Winston, Peter, Paul. How many times per night are you offered a thousand dollars to spend the night with a patron of the restaurant?"

"Lots," was the simultaneous reply.

"I have made love to every one of you and probably a hundred guys before you, and believe me, he is absolutely correct. You all ooze sex like perspiration. Now, you listen to me and you listen really well. If you want to earn an extra $1,000 per night, I don't have a problem with that. But, there are some really evil people out there. You do not, ever, go with an outsider without at least one of us knowing who he is and where he is taking you. Is that understood?"

"Yes, Charlie."

"I'm serious, guys. I nearly lost Winston and vice versa because of physical problems. Neither of us wants to go through that level of grief again. Winston and I love you all too much to want to lose you now that life is so good to us."

I started to get worried. The boys were high profile whenever they left the restaurant, and Peter and Paul all night in the restaurant. I realised our four white waiters were in the same boat, they were gorgeous as well. I decided I had to sort the whole lot somehow to be able to sleep peacefully in my bed.

I telephoned David, "I'm sorry to bother you, David, but I have a potential problem, which I want to nip in the bud. Could you do something for me?"

I explained the problem, and he took in hand the solution I had worked out. The next training session, I had all seven waiters in my office and gave them each identical folders.

"Now, your sole training today is comprised of reading that folder. When you have finished it, call me, and we are going to discuss it."

An hour later, I had the full attention of seven very frightened young men.

"I don't have to ask if you understand what you have read. I can see it on your faces. Frightening isn't it?"

"Yes, Charlie," in unison.

"Now you understand why I am being an old granny with you. Look at each other. Tell me you don't think your fellow waiters are drop dead gorgeous. Then project that thought to a man 20 years or more older than you. You are prime targets to become another of the statistics you have just read details of. Lara's staff, I love you, please don't make me have cause to cry for you. Jason, Ty, Gregg and Julio, you are beautiful young men. I don't know any of you well yet. Nevertheless, to see beauty defiled would make me very sad, and you are all beautiful. If Winston were not so special, I would be trying to bed each one of you. Stay safe, never go off with a stranger whatever he is offering, without safeguards. If you are ever in doubt about the person you are going with, you all have my permission to request a security guard. I will bill you his fee for the night, but if you are accepting $1,000 offers, you can afford it. Are you all quite clear about what you need to do to stay safe?"

"Yes, Charlie."

"Good, last thing. Winston and I are in most nights after the restaurant closes. If being alone is too depressing on the odd night, come and sleep with us. We love to cuddle, and cuddling any one of you would not be a problem. I'm not suggesting group sex, just someone to snuggle up to when you are feeling lonely. We have a big bed. Now, off you go, and stay safe."

"Thank you, Charlie," almost in unison as they filed out of my office.

The next night, Ty asked for a security escort. Five minutes later, he and the escort were back in the restaurant, nobody else had even had time to leave.

"My trick didn't want to know when I turned up escorted, even when I told him the guy would wait in the car."

Everybody listened to this and there were some very pale white and black faces in that room.

"Case proven," I said feeling very worried that it had happened so quickly.

Once the evil ones realised they could not take the boys from the restaurant, they would devise another way. None of these guys was safe, probably including me. I was strong again, as strong as I had ever been and much more able to tolerate punishment and humiliation than I had been two years previously, but I knew I had only experienced the tip of the iceberg of what could be done. It was time for a long talk with David.

There were so many fancy tracking devices available to the public that I asked David if there were any that we could have inserted under the skin. He looked at me as though I were mad until I told him about Ty's experience and my on going worries about the boys.

"Charlie, when are you going to stop surprising me? You are now running just about the most successful restaurant in New York, but you still find time to get involved with and worry about the members of your staff like an old mother hen."

"Thank you, David, but you really shouldn't be surprised. You know how much I love the Lara's House staff, and our new white waiters are such beautiful young men inside and out, I am falling in love with them as well."

David laughed, I guessed to cover up his embarrassment at his next comment.

"You appear to have an almost infinite capacity for loving, Charlie, doesn't that worry Winston?"

"No David, he told me once I could sleep with or have sex with every man in New York if I wanted to because he knew that the real love I have for him transcends any other love I have. And he's right, that's why he has never been upset when you take me, or when I had sex with Tom, which of course I told him about."

"That truly is amazing, Charlie. How was Tom by the way?"

I laughed and said, "You ought to try him, David, he has the most amazing cock."

We both giggled after I said it and David said, "I'd like to, but we are friends, and it wouldn't work."

"I don't see why not, you and I are friends and partners now, but we still fuck occasionally."

"That's different, Charlie, you belong to me."

"What do you think is going to happen in four years time, David, when my slavery contract expires? Don't you think we will occasionally have a romp in the sack?"

"Are you serious, Charlie?"

"Of course, David, I have always enjoyed our sex together, that won't change just because I become a free man. Winston knows and understands that. I just love sex. I still have the odd romp with the Lara's House boys. The only one Winston gets huffy about is Ryan because they are such close friends and so close in age as well. Even Darren understands that I am no threat, and he and Ryan are lovers."

"Charlie, get out of here before you blow my mind and let me have a look at the market in tracking devices."

Chapter 7

"Closed for today only."

All of Cloud's young staff were going for a day trip out of state.

David had come up trumps. Not surprising I suppose. Money talks they say.

All of my beautiful boys were joining me at a private clinic to have tracking devices inserted under their skin. This was like something from a sci-fi film, but I would be one very happy bunny when it was done. It would not stop any of us being abducted, but once someone realised, we would be able to track them hopefully in time to stop any long-term damage. Most of the cases we researched had shown that the victims had been kept alive for weeks after their abduction. They had been abused sexually and physically, but the build-up had been gradual. Unfortunately, only a few of the missing boys had been found, so there was a big question mark over the others. We would just have to pray if it was one of us.

The next day, everything was normal except that I now felt able to relax.

The restaurant was now full every night, and people were booking weeks ahead to get a table. The waiters were making incredible tips. The atmosphere in the restaurant was amazing and was responsible for the level of bookings as much as my culinary skills.

I had learned a very hard lesson in my first year with David that all good things come to an end. For us at Cloud's, it was the abduction of Paul, the gentlest and most shy of the boys from Lara's House.

It started like a nightmare when a half-hour before we were due to open, Peter burst into the kitchen and told me Paul had not returned from an afternoon shopping trip.

I telephoned David immediately and asked for the tracking service to start searching.

The restaurant was open. Another waiter had been called in to replace the missing Paul when David called with bad news.

"I'm sorry, Charlie, we can't get a fix on Paul. The abductors if he has been abducted have him either in a place where radio waves can't be traced, or he is out of state. I am going to order up a helicopter to search out of range of our present equipment. I will be honest with you. If it is the former, we may never find him, and if it is the latter, we will need to be lucky because it is like looking for a needle in a haystack."

I was now seriously worried. Paul was as beautiful as Winston and Peter and as cute as Ryan. All four of them were the same age. Ryan was the oldest by a few months, and Paul was the youngest by a few minutes. After the initial screw up over the Pinky and Perky incident, I had been very protective of these four boys. We were only two years apart in age, but a decade apart in mentality.

David came up to the apartment after we closed and gave us all the story update. The Lara's House staff were all there, Peter permanently in tears, the rest of us worried sick.

"The helicopter got one short spike of Paul's device, long enough to pinpoint the area but not get an exact fix. We have put in a mobile unit that will watch all night, but we think he is in an underground location with lined walls, and the spike was just someone opening the door for a little while. That happened only about half an hour ago. Assuming it is abductors, we are hoping that our assumption is correct, and the door opening was them leaving the room to go to bed. Paul will be safe until morning in that case. I will let you know if there is any more news as soon as I get it."

None of us slept very much that night. The others didn't even go back to their apartment, and the four white waiters joined us when they heard the news. The vigil was a sad little affair. I looked around the room at a collection of the most beautiful boys I had ever seen, knowing that any one of them would have taken Paul's place willingly. He was the baby, and they all felt his loss.

It was nine o'clock in the morning when David called and told me they had an exact location for Paul and were assembling a crew to go get him. The house belonged to a very wealthy New York Banker, so the police didn't want to know without cast iron proof that there was mischief afoot. David's team would be in a huge amount of trouble if they were wrong.

After Paul had been taken to hospital for treatment for his injuries, David came up to the apartment to tell us what he knew.

"A team of six ex-commandos went in quietly until they found the basement, which was a steel lined room fitted out like a dungeon, hence no radio waves. The radio van found the location when a group of men, including the owner went back into the room to continue their games. The team leader told me that when they burst in, there were four men all in there fifties dressed in leather gear. There were also three young men. One of them was already dead, still suspended from the ceiling by chains, a second one was in a pitiful state. He had been raped with an object large enough to rip his anus quite badly. He had also been beaten with a whip that had taken most of the skin off his body so that he looked like a piece of meat. The medics believed there were also internal injuries. At present, we don't know how bad they are. Paul was coherent enough to make a statement to the police before going to hospital. He is very lucky we found him when we did, Charlie. He had only been worked on a little. I have a copy of his statement here, and you can read it when I go. Before my team left the grounds, the police had brought in a full-scale search team believing that the body of the dead boy would be joining other abducted boys. They uncovered the cache of dead bodies quickly and found several of the boys that were mentioned in your folder that I researched for you. The men are all being charged with murder in the first degree and other crimes. The evidence against them is overwhelming. They are ruined and will hopefully spend the rest of their lives behind bars. That's it, Charlie. Paul should be back home tonight but will almost certainly need counseling, so I have no idea when you will have him back for work."

With that, David left, and the boys asked me to read Paul's statement.

"I was walking along Fifth Avenue when several men gradually forced me towards the edge of the sidewalk. I was about to walk in the road when a limousine pulled up in front of me, opened a door, and I was pushed in. Two men held me down as the door was closed, and the car sped away. I was immediately blindfolded and gagged. At our destination, I was bundled out of the car and marched between two strong pairs of hands without trouble into what I now know was this awful place. My blindfold and gag were removed, and I was left with the four men you have just arrested. The one you called Mr. Weston ordered me to take off all my clothes. I did not move until he swung a riding crop at my ass with great force causing me considerable pain. I undressed then very quickly, but felt very embarrassed to be standing in front of these four men completely naked. They moved around me fondling my whole body including my very private parts. I felt humiliated.

"I could not get an erection despite much work on my cock and balls. The men were very angry and strung me up to the ceiling, spread my legs very wide and proceeded to take turns finger fucking me with increasing numbers of fingers. When they touched my prostate, my penis got very hard, and they cheered. They untied me and led me to that bench [witness indicated a sawhorse contraption with leg and wrist restraints] and bent me over it tying my hands over one side and my legs over the other, spread as wide as they could. They then took turns in raping me with their cocks. They were very big, and it hurt terribly. They did not use any lubricant, and I could feel them tearing my insides. I was screaming with the intensity of the pain, but I could hear them laughing. I think I must have passed out at some point because when I regained consciousness, I was again strung up to the ceiling by my wrists. As soon as they realised I was conscious, they started to paddle me. The pain was intense, and they kept rotating the punisher, the other three playing with me. They hurt my nipples by squeezing and twisting very hard. They gripped my balls and squeezed them until I screamed in agony. My penis was very soft, so they beat it with their hands. I must have passed out again because when I woke it was dark, and I could see nothing until they re-entered the dungeon only a half-hour or so before you came in. In that time, they all made me take their cocks in my mouth and face fucked me until they came. They told me if I let any of there cum leave my mouth, they would tear the skin from my hide, so I swallowed frantically every drop from each of them. Just before you entered, they were discussing which of the whips they were going to use to start stripping my skin to make me a mirror image of the boy I could see strung up in front of me. I was terrified and started to beg and plead, but they did not even acknowledge my existence. At that point, you burst into the room, and now I'm here with you. Thank you. Please tell Peter I am safe. He must be so worried."

Paul had signed the statement.

When I looked up, everybody was crying. I was 23 and looking at these boys, only one and two years younger than I. I wept for them. They were so beautiful and so vulnerable. I felt so old. Was there nothing I could do to stop the evil that stalked them all, including, I suppose, even me?

Peter went to the hospital first, closely followed by the remainder of us. I knew I had two very sick young men on my hands, emotionally and psychologically.

I hated to do it. I knew I would miss them tremendously, but I sent them both back to Lara's House when Paul was well. I called Cloud.

"Cloud, hello, I am sending back to you two beautiful boys. Please look after them. They have been terribly damaged emotionally. I will tell you the whole story when I have time. Say hello to Mac for me and tell everyone I miss them. I will talk with you soon."

I have always believed in fate, and it was to prove my ally only a few weeks after Paul and Peter returned to Lara's House. Cloud's was burnt out in a freak electrical accident. The apartments survived because of the speed and efficiency of the New York fire department. The refurbishment would take months, but all wages, loss of earnings and costs of renovation were taken care of by the insurance.

I asked David if we could all go to Lara's House while this was going on.

"If you go to Lara's House, Charlie, you go as a slave the same as normal."

"I should be working, David, and I will have with me the white waiters who know little of my other status. Can we leave the slavery for another time? You can add it to the end of my contract if you like."

"I will think about it, Charlie. You can all go to Lara's for R&R as long as your boys understand that the house servants are not to be used unnecessarily. I am going to send a psychologist with you. Cloud tells me Paul is not coping very well, and I have noticed a change in the atmosphere at Cloud's. I think all of you are feeling down because of the Paul incident."

"I know, David, the others are worried, and I am frustrated. There doesn't appear to be anything we can do to stop evil people getting at these boys. Their beauty is making them wealthy, but the stress involved sometimes doesn't seem worth it. Paul may spend the remainder of his young life being afraid to go anywhere by himself. It doesn't matter what these boys do, they are going to be hit on."

We all went to Lara's, and within hours the peace and tranquillity there was rubbing off on my brood. They started to relax and return to their previously happy state. The following afternoon was a remarkable sight around the pool. All of us were there, all wearing very brief Speedos. Mac came to see me for a chat.

"Oh, Jesus Charlie, where did you find all of these young gods? They are totally awesome in their beauty. No wonder they need protection in New York. I could make love to everyone of them."

"That's the problem, Mac, so could half of New York. Patrons of the restaurant offer the seven waiters as much as $5,000 for just one night, and never less than $1,000. It's frightening. Occasionally one of them will accept, and we let him go with a security escort, but these boys all make at least a $1,000 per night in tips, so they have no need to be whores as well."

"Wow, Charlie, and what about you?"

I actually blushed, Mac would pay me a king's ransom I know to make love to me again, but even when I am on slave duty, he would not take me for free. I had seduced him once, but we both knew it would never happen again. I thought about asking one of my white waiters to seduce him knowing how frustrated he must be, but they would not see him in the same light as I did and therefore not be so enthusiastic and caring in their treatment of him.

"I'm over the hill now, Mac, at 23, I can't compete with these boys."

"Rubbish, Charlie, you are still the most gorgeous guy here, and no one has ever come even close to having a butt as cute as yours."

The twinkle in his eyes made me hop off my lounger and give him a big sloppy kiss. The other boys were goggle-eyed watching it, and Mac blushed crimson. He was gone in a second, and I was left with a dozen young men looking at me in amazement.

"You don't have to stare. Mac, Cloud and I have been through a great deal of joy and sorrow together along with the other Lara's House staff here. The love I have for Mac and Cloud is special because neither of them ever took advantage of my status here."

I had let the cat out of the bag, so I had to explain to Jason, Ty, Glen and Julio what I meant.

"Oh well I suppose you had better hear it from me. I owe David an enormous sum of money. I had no way of paying him back except with my body. Therefore, I sold it to him for a period of years. I am his to command like a slave. Normally at Lara's House, I only wear little white shorts and am at every member of staffs disposal for menial tasks. I was also available for their sexual pleasure. If I was not very good at something, they were allowed to beat me. The latter has been stopped because I was abused so badly that I was lost to David for a whole year. David has not made a decision on my status here this time, but it is quite possible I shall be reverting to slave status any time soon. If you want any of the gory stories and any more details, you can ask any of the other guys who know everything. You don't have to be coy around Winston either, our relationship has grown around my circumstances and my love of sex, so we don't make a big deal about me having sex with others."

Jason was the first to speak, "You're kidding, Charlie, aren't you?"

"No, Jason, that is gospel. Ask any member of staff, not just these guys, and they will confirm it. I have had sex with all of these guys, initially under some duress and not necessarily happily, but now at Lara's we have some wonderful romps when they want my body."

"Crikey, Charlie, what about Winston?"

"He understands my love of sex and my love for him. They are separate and he knows it. We don't have any conflict with that."

A few days later, I was pleased that I had told them because David telephoned from New York telling Cloud he was bringing some friends down for a couple of days before going on to Rio for a proper holiday. He wanted me back in slavery in my old bedroom and back in the kitchen. My Cloud's staff could remain as guests, but three twin rooms were to be made available for his guests.

David sent for the two new pantry boys and me as soon as he arrived.

The boys were almost as cute as Peter and Paul had been at 18.

"Hello, Charlie. Ben and Sean, hello, after supper tonight I would like you in the lounge dressed in these."

These, being two pairs of extremely skimpy white shorts, rape attire I thought.

"Nothing else. You will assist my guests if they need it. If you perform well, there will be a good bonus for you both. That's all."

After they had left, David told me my part in the evening entertainment.

"I want you in my room after you finish in the kitchen, Charlie, give yourself a couple of enemas and shower first. Make certain you have no body hair. I am going to put a collar and lead on you and lead you naked on all fours into the lounge. I want you to act as close as you can to how a dog behaves. When I say sit, do it doggy fashion, when I tell you to rollover, do it, but have your legs and arms half up in the air. Show me."

So I did.

"If I tell you to show a guest how welcome he is, go and lick his feet for a couple of minutes before sitting up straight as though you were begging and just say, 'Welcome to Lara's House, Sir. I hope you enjoy your sex with me tonight and will not feel the need to beat me.' OK, Charlie, any questions?"

"Do the pantry boys have to be there, Master, that is so humiliating?"

"Yes, Charlie, you may need holding in position for some activities, they will relieve my guests of the task. Cloud's staff will still eat as guests tonight. Will you tell them we are dressing the same for dinner as the activities after, so just shorts and T shirt?"

"Are they all going to be there as well, Master?"

"Oh yes, I would think so, they know you are my slave."

"Please, Master, not them. I am their boss in New York. It will be so incredibly embarrassing."

"They probably need reminding more than you do of your status then. That's all, Charlie."

I couldn't hide my resentment, and David noticed.

"I haven't punished you since you returned from convalescence, Charlie, but I am going to now. Take off your shorts and bend over my desk. Call each one and an apology for your attitude."

"One, thank you, Master, I apologise for my attitude."

"Two, thank you, Master, I apologise for my attitude."

Five good solid licks with the paddle had me crying with the humiliation more than the pain. Worse was to come. David got me hard and sent me back to my room, my shorts in my hands held behind my head. I bumped into Ty and Julio on the way. They stared in disbelief but took a long look at my erect penis.

"Don't ask," was all I said in passing, but I knew all of Cloud's people would know in a few minutes. I dreaded what was going to happen after dinner.

Winston of course broke into tears.

"Well I'm not watching, Charlie, unless you want me to."

"No, Baby, that is the last thing I want. I do need you to dry those tears though because I want you to shave all the bits I can't reach. David wants me smooth tonight."

I was such a trial to my love. Why the hell he bothered amazed me.

Cloud told me that when they had completed the meal, David addressed them all.

"Ben and Sean, go and get ready, be in the lounge in 20 minutes stand on either side of the door. Everyone else, Charlie is going to be available for our entertainment in a double roll. Friendly dog and sex slave. If he is less than satisfactory, you can spank him, but not too hard, remember we may want him to entertain us tomorrow as well. Cloud's staff, you are very welcome to join us and join in. There will be no comeback when you return to New York."

The entire ex-Lara's House staff declined, but the white waiters whispered to Winston, "We won't stay if it gets heavy, but we are curious."

So was I in some ways. I prayed it would not be anything like the nightmare I had nearly two years ago, but there was certainly the potential for some good sex. David's beating had changed my attitude, so apart from having to act like a dog to start with and have Cloud's people watching, I felt good. I was sure they would not take part even if invited.

I bounded into the lounge stark naked and blushing like hell. The four white waiters were seated together on one of the large sofas with David's guests round the remainder of the seats. The pantry boys looked incredibly sexy displaying very full pouches. I hoped to see more of them sometime.

Problem now though was I could feel myself getting erect. No way to hide it seated doggy fashion by the side of David.

"Christ, David, your pooch is totally hairless, that is such a turn on, and he is getting excited, David. Is he a randy little sod?"

"Oh yes, Paul, watch this. Roll over, Charlie, there's a good dog. Watch how quickly he grows if I rub his tummy."

Of course I did. I could see the waiters looking stunned and whispering to each other. More blushing on my part.

"Crikey, David, he puts us mere males to shame. I want to hold onto that for a while when I am shagging him."

"Go and show Mr. Paul how pleased you are to hear that, Charlie."

I did and was eternally grateful that Paul had very fresh feet, or I am sure I would have thrown up. Everybody gasped at what I did.

"Pretty damned impressive, David. Now, Charlie, you can undress me and get my little Paul ready to cut you another asshole."

His little Paul wasn't so little. I slicked him up good. Balls very slippery for my hand and his cock for my mouth. I pulled out the stops to make it good. I rolled his balls around in my mouth using my nose to nuzzle the base of his mighty meat. Slowly, I licked up the shaft transferring a hand to play with his balls. When I took his cockhead in my mouth and swirled my tongue around it squeezing his balls gently at the same time, he went ballistic.

"Christ, Charlie, that feels so good, now doggy fashion in the middle of the floor."

I was sideways on to my waiters, so they would have an uninterrupted view of me being fucked. David had lubed me before entering the lounge, thank heavens because Paul entered me in one continuous smooth movement. Laying his body well back, he gave my boys a perfect view of their boss being fucked. He was a long stroking slow fucker that had me rigid. It was such a turn on. A few minutes later, another of David's friends knelt in front of me naked and sporting a rock hard medium length cock, nice looking guy, nice cock.

"A pity to waste that pretty mouth, Charlie, suck on this until Paul is finished, and I can take his place."

A perfect spit roast. I felt so humiliated in front of the boys that I lost focus not doing anything with my ass muscles. Paul pulled out, slapped my ass hard twice making me yelp.

"Pay attention, boy."

Then he plunged back in fucking me hard and cumming quickly.

"He spoilt that for me, David, mind if I punish him after Mike has finished?"

"No, dig out, bud. An early lesson will keep him on his toes."

"OK, Charlie, on your back. David, can those two cuties hold his legs back for me?"

"Sure, Ben, Sean, help Mike."

I don't know if it was by design or accident, but my head was towards the boys so that they would get the best view again off me being entered.

My legs were pulled well back and as wide as they would go with Ben and Sean either side of me close enough to touch my ass. Mike fucked hard fast and came quickly because I had pleasured him very well with my mouth. He pulled my cock vertical and played with it while he powered into me. The two boys were now sporting very hard and obvious erections.

Paul said as Mike pulled out, "Keep him there, boys, in fact pull the legs a little further back and down to the floor. Good, I can punish him better like that."

He sat cross-legged and spanked me hard with each hand alternating on each cheek so that after ten, which he was counting out I had to beg.

"Please, Master, don't let him hurt me anymore."

David said nothing until my four waiters stood up and said, "Excuse us please, David," and left.

By which time I had received another couple and was in considerable distress. Paul was a very strong man.

"That's enough, Paul. Don't spoil him for the rest of us."

Ben and Sean looked shocked at my punishment. They let me go and I curled up in a ball.

I looked directly at David and said. "Why do you hate me and hurt me so much, David?"

He had the good grace to look very embarrassed.

"I don't, Charlie. OK, guys let's have some drinks brought in and give Charlie time to recover. No more punishment tonight. Paul, that was a bit vicious."

"Yeah, perhaps it was, but I bet he stays focussed for the remainder of the night."

They sat chatting and drinking for a while as I recovered.

"David, Charlie looks OK, again. While we finish our drinks, can we watch those two little cuties spit roast him?"

"Sure, Ben, Sean, would you like to take an end each and fill it with your cum?"

They looked at each other before replying, "Yes, please, Mr. David."

They looked at me a little sheepishly until I winked at them. Then they smiled sweet enough to make me want to kiss them. No point in making them unhappy or embarrassed.

"OK, boys, over the coffee table on his back. Play with him and try to make him cum as well."

I thought, well done, David, maximum exposure.

They stripped off their shorts gaining several gasps from the quests.

"Crikey, David, those two are beautiful. Can we have a piece of them as well?"

"Individually and in private only with there consent, so you will need to have some cash ready. They are staff not slaves."

They were a delight. Ben entered my ass first and whispered, "That feels so good, Charlie, is that ok?"

"Mmm, Ben, better than OK. You can remain there all night. You are great."

"Thank you, Charlie."

Sean then slid his equally gorgeous cock into my mouth and commenced to face fuck me. They both played with my body, cock, and balls. When we came, almost simultaneously, I made a real mess, it was great. I had forgotten the others. Now I looked round to see several jaws hanging down, the applause started, and all three of us blushed.

"Very good, Charlie. All of you quick clean up and back in ten minutes."

As soon as we were clear of the lounge, Ben said, "Thank you Charlie, Winston is very lucky, that was great."

Sean agreed, and we returned to the lounge together happy.

I took so much cum over the next two hours, I thought I would explode. My blowjobs were the talk of the evening. I was fucked in a few new positions as well. Apart from the start, I counted it a great night.

Poor Winston, he was awake and worried until he saw how happy I looked.

"It's alright, Baby, a rough start, but then I had a lot of good sex. Ben and Sean had to spit roast me, but they were very good. Now you can cuddle me after I have showered and make love to me if you want to. I am too shagged out to do much more than just lay here."

"That's alright, Charlie, I just want to cuddle you. Are you going to have to do that any more?"

"Probably tomorrow at the pool and again in the evening, but I don't think it will get heavy again."

The best part was at breakfast the next morning when David sent for me. Paul was with him in the study, naked and bent over David's desk.

"Paul realises he went over the top with punishment, Charlie, and wants you to watch me give him ten with your paddle."

It was satisfying to see the tears in his eyes when David finished and he stood to shake my hand.

"I'm sorry about last night, Charlie. I will try to restrain my enthusiasm today."

"Thank you, Sir, I am sure I will enjoy that."

He dressed and left.

"Charlie, I am truly sorry I allowed Paul to go over the top. Please forgive me."

"Fuck it or fuck it up, I can understand, Master, but allowing both hurts me to my soul."

"I know, Charlie. I am sorry."

I hoped he would remember if the sessions were to continue.

Jason and Co came to see me after breakfast.

"We are sorry if we embarrassed you last night, Charlie. We were curious to see if you really were a total slave. The sex looked awesome, you really are fantastic. The beating was horrible. David has gone down greatly in our estimation and for humiliating you by making you behave like a dog."

"Thank you, boys, but I think the worst is over. There might be some more sex sessions around the place, but don't get embarrassed and tell the others the same."

I must have had a premonition. After lunch, I hadn't been summoned, so I went to the gym with Winston, had a good workout before going to the pool. All of Cloud's' people were there, and we joined them. Darren and all the others said how sorry they were about the beating, but we turned the sex thing into a joke.

David's crowd were at the other end of the pool fooling around, so we just ignored them. I had opted for my sexiest Speedos knowing that the guests were likely to be there. No nudity to invite trouble. Thinking about it in retrospect, the Speedos were probably a bigger turn on than nudity. Anyway, I saw the others get in a huddle and keep looking my way.

Here comes trouble I thought just as Winston saw the same thing and said, "Let's go, Charlie, I don't like that lot."

I was about to agree, when Paul called me over.

"Take your Speedos off, Charlie. Can you stand on your head?"

"Yes, of course."

"Good, do it then. No turn around so that your ass is facing your crowd."

"OK, now spread your legs as wide as they will go and drop them 45 degrees. Mike, Tony, support his legs. David gave us his box of toys. I thought it might be fun to see if he could take a cock the same size as his own, but upside down. I'll open him up first. The rest of you can play with him or get him to suck you."

Paul deliberately positioned himself so that my crowd could see what he was doing. He pulled one cheek apart and had my other one pulled apart by someone else and then started feeding me fingers. I was also sucking a cock.

Paul called to the others, "You can join us if you like, guys. Charlie will be so opened up in a few minutes, we will all be able to have a fuck, two at a time probably and with one in his mouth, we will all have time for sloppy seconds."

The others all just stood watching because they didn't want to walk past us to leave.

Paul grabbed the dildo after a suitable time of nearly fist fucking me. As he fed it to me, I could hear Winston crying.

"Paul, please stop what you are doing for a minute and let the others leave. I will let you do any thing you like after that."

He laughed and said, "We can do anything we like anyway, Charlie. So let's put on a show for them."

"Tony, you have the smallest hand. Put a ton of lube on it and see if you can fist fuck him."

He was very gentle, but eventually he had to hurt to get his last knuckles over my sphincter. I screamed with the pain and heard the gasps.

Winston screamed, "Oh please don't hurt Charlie anymore. You can do it to me instead."

"If any of you touch that boy, I will kill you."

I managed to splutter that out with a cock still half in my mouth. That obviously annoyed Paul because I got a hard slap on each cheek. Good old Tony, he didn't hesitate a second working my butt with his fist.

"I think it would be a good idea for you guys to either join in or go."

Darren said to me, "What should we do, Charlie?"

"All of you go, please, Winston, I'll be OK."

They went reluctantly, hardly able to take their eyes off the fist sticking in my ass.

"Good, now perhaps we can have some fun. I really want a fuck like the one that I started last night. Move the fist Tony. Doggy fashion again, Charlie, and see if you can stay focussed long enough to give a great fuck."

I did, rotating my hips and pushing to meet his thrusts. The others watched mesmerised.

"Christ, Charlie, you really are something else."

I didn't know his name, but when I had to blow him and then take his cock up the back, I made sure he got the best. When he had finished he said, "Thank you, Charlie, that is the best sex I have ever had."

I don't know what it was with Paul. Everyone had been more than satisfied, but he still wanted to inflict pain.

"Who wants to punish him today for his little outburst earlier?"

"No volunteers, OK, I'll do it. I have the paddle. How many shall I give him? Ten or 20?"

"How about a couple of soft ones in place of a pat on the back for being a great sex toy?"

I did only get two, but they hurt, sadistic bastard. I collected my Speedos, and as I passed my champion, I said, "I don't know your name, but thank you."

"It's Charlie, Charlie," and he laughed as he patted my butt. "Look after that, it's special."

David must have heard a little of the story because he sent for me in the middle of preparation for dinner.

"What happened at the pool this afternoon, Charlie?"

"Nothing too bad Master, your friend Paul was just emphasising his credentials as resident sadist. Charlie and Tony kept him in check, and Winston shook him a little."

"OK, Charlie, we are leaving for Rio in the morning, and I will be around for this evening's entertainment. Same routine as last night only no pooch. I'll tell you what I want from you when you get here."

"Any clues to prepare me, Master?"

"No, Charlie, a little surprise will keep you sharp."

No doubt, it was a surprise. I had my nasty double enema and shower, clean shorts, and I presented myself for inspection.

David had two of the biggest of the estate workers with him. I knew them vaguely. They were new and looked like serious bodybuilders, but they had massive packages. Natural bodies because steroids would have shrunk their monsters.

"These two are your guards and punishers tonight, Charlie. We are going to the gym where you will be tried for crimes committed against your slave status. Cuff him, Bradley, and march him to the gym after I have gone."

"Any idea what is going to happen, guys?"

"Yes, Charlie, but we can't tell you anything."

I was gob smacked when I was led to a make shift cage and released from my cuffs. The cage was set to one side. There were 12 members of staff sat in tiered seats like a jury, and my lot were facing the bench as an audience. David was the judge, and the other Charlie was my defence attorney with Paul as prosecutor and the others as witnesses.

David started the proceedings.

"Charlie Fellows, you are charged with neglect of duty last night in that you lost focus when being fucked by prosecuting council. In addition, you are charged with insubordination in that you called me, David. Thirdly, this afternoon you threatened to kill any or all of my guests. This is by far the most serious charge and carries a penalty of 50 lashes with a whip, or any such alternative as I may substitute. How do you plead?"

Charlie stood up and replied, "My client pleads not guilty your honour."

Charlie was very good. I found out why later. He actually was an attorney. I also found out that the jury had been instructed to find me guilty on all charges. They were pleaded and voted on separately with punishment going the same way.

"Your punishment on the first charge is to be spit roasted by your guards."

Now I knew why they weren't telling. I was brought to the front of the court, stripped and played with by Bradley and Hector until I was rock hard. I was also being finger fucked and lubricated, and every couple of minutes, I was rotated about 60 degrees so that everyone got a good view of the action front and back. I felt so humiliated again. This was worse than any thing before because there were so many witnesses to my degradation. I then had to strip the other two and using my mouth get them erect. They were huge, and there were gasps as I managed to get a few inches in my mouth at a time. They were definitely going to hurt. I was then spit roasted with both of them cumming over me rather than in me. They were so well hung that everyone in the court gasped. I had definitely lost my position. I screamed when Bradley entered me even though he was gentle. Every couple of minutes again they pulled out and changed my position to give everyone a great view of the action. They both came gallons. Hector all over my face and Bradley over my back. They took me back to my cage leaving me naked and dripping cum while they went off to clean up and dress.

On the second charge, David pontificated saying I should receive at least ten lashes, but he would be generous and allow me a choice of the ten or ten blowjobs instead. I naturally elected the blowjobs.

"Very well, Charlie, everyone in this court room has their name in that box. Your council will draw them one at a time, and you will carry out the action."

The first three were jurors from the estate whom I knew vaguely. The next one was one of David's friends. All of them had shot over my face, so I was quite a mess. I wanted to die, but not nearly as much as I did when the next name was called. It was Winston.

"Oh no, Charlie, I can't."

"Yes you can, Baby. Come on, let's get it done."

He cried all the way through taking a long time to cum even though I was making every effort to impress. I licked very hard under his ball sac and along the underside of his shaft, eventually sucking in his head and swishing my tongue all over the glans. He cried great gut wrenching sobs as he sprayed my face. And it continued until the last one, my Paul, he also cried through it. I was effectively blind now because I was forbidden to remove any cum which was gluing up my eyes.

After I was found guilty on the third charge, David adjourned for 30 minutes to allow everyone, except me to get a drink. When they were all settled, again David started.

"It is the decision of this court that because the last punishment will take some time, work on the estate will not commence until eleven tomorrow morning. Now, to the slave's final degradation for threatening the lives of my guests. This punishment will be carried out one part at a time. First he will be restrained over a whipping bench and every person here present will pass by and finger fuck him for one minute."

There were gasps and a terrible cry from Winston.

The whipping horse was very comfortable but it pushed my butt well back and spread my cheeks wide. I was pleased I was still blind from cum. I never wanted to see my degradation. Of course, Paul was the roughest and let me know it was him. He started with one finger but quickly reached four before his one minute was up.

When it was over, David invited everyone to pass again giving me one slap on the bottom. I was so pleased most were very gentle because the total must have been nearly 40, and the inside of my ass was already sore. Once again, Paul was the hardest making me cry out. I wondered what was coming next.

"For the third part, each department is to elect two of their number as representatives and come forward. Very good, now two each from my guests and Cloud's staff to be drawn from the hat. Mike and Tony from my guests and Darren and Winston from Cloud's."

I heard Winston gasp.

"Each one of you ten is to fuck Charlie's ass. He will be turned over on his back. His guards will hold his legs back and wide. Everyone is to use adequate lubrication, and Winston will go first. Clean Charlie's face so that he can see who is screwing him. You are all to ejaculate inside him at either end."

My baby was crying his heart out mainly because he took so long. Several of them pulled out at the last minute and walked round to finish off in my mouth, not always terribly accurate, so I had more cum around my mouth, which I had to lick off. Everyone else was encouraged to get in close so as not to miss the action.

I did enjoy some of it. I even orgasmed a couple of times without touching myself. I was very sore by the time everyone had finished and hoped that was it. No such luck though.

"Finally, the guards will retain Charlie in that position but will pull his butt cheeks further apart. Everyone on the way out can see how swollen and puffy Charlie's anus is and play with his cock while they examine it or abuse it even more.

I truly wanted to die then. This was the most awful of all. Almost 40 people looked closely at my ass. Some touched it, and all of them wanked me a couple of times or stroked me. I was of course hard as a rock despite my embarrassment. Paul had his final piece of sadism by being last and rubbing my hole while slapping my penis.

"Please leave my ass alone, Paul, it is so sore."

A hard slap and then he was gone.

I wondered if I would ever be able to work happily with David again.

When we were the only two remaining in the gym, I was standing in front of him still naked and looking disgusting with cum everywhere. I could not raise my eyes to look at him.

"That was a harsh lesson, Charlie, because since your convalescence you have forgotten your position and become loose mouthed at the wrong times. You are my slave. Never forget it, or I will devise something worse than this. You can move back to the master suite tomorrow and resume guest status for the time being."

I was amazed but accepted it without a word and went off to console my very distraught lover.

The following day almost everyone who had attended the trial came to apologise if they had hurt me in any way and state that David had gone over the top. Bradley and Hector came to thank me for great sex and the promise that when I was next on slave duty they would be in the book.

I still felt so humiliated that I couldn't look at any of them. Like all bad things, the humiliation and embarrassment faded. Most people respected me more for what I endured, and life resumed. Bob gave me a huge amount of grief, but only in jest.

"A pity I wasn't there, Charlie, I might have got a fuck or a blowjob," said with a big grin all over his face, but I knew how much he really wanted to.

"You can have either or both, Bob, any time Winston isn't with me."

He blushed and walked away. I laughed. He spun round and said quite angrily, "OK, Charlie, after this session, I'll take both in my office."

Me and my big mouth.

We had a good workout, and after my shower, I felt good.

Bob looked uncomfortable when I walked back into his office.

"You don't have to do this, Charlie. You aren't a slave at the moment."

"I know, Bob, but for your purposes, you can treat me as one because I opened my mouth without thinking again. I deserve anything I get. David was correct. I keep heaping grief on myself because I have forgotten how to control my tongue. Don't be coy about this at all. I know you were angry at my attitude, and I need to change that, so you will be helping me in the end."

"OK, Charlie, you asked for it. Take your shorts off and stand with your legs astride and hands grasped behind your head."

I did and he started fondling me. He played with my balls as well and had me very hard in no time. Moving round behind my back, he started to play with my butt cheeks, eventually sliding his fingers down my crack passed my hole to my perineum and back up, lingering over the entry to my love tunnel. He lubed up a pair of fingers and inserted one and then both inside me twisting them as he did it. He finger fucked me for a while adding just one more finger. His other hand continued playing with my cock and balls. I loved it.

"I could do this all day, Charlie. You have a great ass and a package to die for, but I think you should be looking after my package."

After I had removed his shorts, he sat in his chair legs spread wide while I pleasured him. While I was sucking and licking all over his groin area, my hands were roving over his upper body pinching his nipples and rubbing his tummy. He was almost purring when he eventually stopped me.

"If I let you do that to me much more, Charlie, I shan't be able to fuck you for very long without cumming, so up you get and bend over my desk legs as wide as you can get them."

He used his tongue on me then pushing inside me as far as he could. It was fantastic. He deposited lots of spit in me, so I knew he was not going to use lubricant.

"I want you to know you are getting this cock, Charlie. That is why I am only using spit."

He entered me slowly, but it still hurt, and I whimpered. When I had calmed down, he went in until his pubic hair was rubbing my butt. My ass was still sore from the punishment night, and he was the first one to fuck me since then as well. I was given time to settle, and Bob then powered into me until I could feel his cock swelling ready to shoot. He stopped then and pulled out.

"Turn over, Charlie, legs way back and wide spread."

When he entered me again, he was very slow with long strokes.

"I am going to make this last, Charlie."

He was playing with my cock and balls all the time until I could feel him swell again, and then he pushed my legs further down and powered in for a few seconds before forcing himself as deep as he could and depositing his love juice deep inside me.

He fell forward onto me and kissed my lips.

"Charlie, that was incredible. I don't think I shall be so reticent about using you when you are a slave again. I love sex with you. It's bloody fantastic."

"Thanks, Bob, is there anything else I can do for you before I go for a swim?"

"Yes there is, you said your bad attitude was getting you into trouble. Well as part of your lesson to improve your attitude, I am going to paddle you. I still have my predecessor's old one. Bend over the desk again, Charlie."

I was shocked. Ever since his first punishment session, Bob had been very reluctant to have anything to do with paddling me. He gave me ten, just hard enough to make me squirm. When he had finished, he took some body lotion and rubbed it gently into each cheek. The feeling was so incredibly erotic that my still erect penis was throbbing and hurting it was so hard. When he had finished, Bob turned me round and went down on me sucking me dry in less than two minutes.

"Mmm, you taste good as well, Charlie. Now, a good swim should finish off your sporting activity nicely."

"Christ, Bob, if that is what you call punishment, I am definitely going to keep having a bad attitude with you."

"I wouldn't, Charlie, I might not always be as gentle."

Life was good again, and another few weeks of bliss passed very quickly before David returned to the estate.

"You will resume your slave and chef status, Charlie."

"Yes, Master," was all I felt inclined to say. I was still very resentful of what he had put me through just to entertain his friends.

I really didn't have a problem with returning to my old status. I know it must appear weird, but being a slave with people that all loved me was so much fun. I still had plenty of time to work out and swim. David and I played a lot of squash again, which was good because in New York I had gotten rusty. Even Bob was beating me, which pleased him to no end. The four white boys did a lot of Mickey taking when they realised I didn't have a sense of humour failure. The whole of Cloud's staff started eating in the staff restaurant because like me they resented what David had done. David was very pissed off with me. The atmosphere at the dining table his first night was electric. The boys were in fine form, and even Cloud found it difficult to maintain his normal reserve, so David felt the coldness the next night when he ate alone.

He was decidedly chilly towards me for a few days before commenting, "I have a good mind to paddle you again, Charlie, in front of all my staff and yours. They need to show some loyalty and appreciation toward me. You do as well. I am turning you into a multimillionaire despite your slave status, and everybody gravitates to you."

I nearly laughed outright. Here was this multibillionaire able to get anything in the world that money could buy, and he was jealous of the affection a bunch of pretty boys had for me. I couldn't keep my mouth completely closed though could I?

"David, shame on you," I said in as light a manner as possible, "You aren't jealous of your slave are you?"

Wrong thing to say – I had forgotten how volatile he could be.

"I'll show you jealous, Charlie. Do you remember your first introduction to my staff? I think we should have a repeat to remind you of your place here. You are becoming far too cocky. All this love and affection crap is going to your head. Your Cloud's staff should realise how much your position relies on my good graces as well. I think the gym would be the best place, where I can have you under restraint, and Bob can spell me when I get tired of beating you. I think 50 would be a good number to start with, now get out of my sight while I think about how to humiliate you as well as beat you."

I was shattered and very worried. Not for myself, but for Winston. I couldn't let him watch it, and if possible, I had to make sure he did not even know about it. He would be terrified. The only way to do that was to get him off the island.

"Cloud, have you anyone leaving the island in the near future?"

"Yes, Charlie, Eric from the gardens is going home to New York for a holiday in a couple of days. Why?"

"I want Winston to go with him."

"Why, Charlie?"

So I told him about my conversation with David. "Cloud, he has to go. He will be terrified if he hears about it, and I daren't even consider what it will do to him if he has to witness it. David is planning maximum humiliation and a thrashing to beat anything I have endured before. He is so pissed off with me, and you know how volatile he can be. It's my fault. I have got complacent about my status since recovering from my coma."

"I see, Charlie. Leave it with me. You know David has to sanction all travel requests when he is on the island even if Winston now works for Cloud's."

I had a hard time with Winston the rest of that day. He could tell I was worried about something and was even more upset when I wouldn't tell him. We didn't have secrets, so he had every right to be upset.

Cloud took me aside after dinner and told me he had spoken to David. He would not sanction Winston leaving the island, and there would be no exceptions to everybody on the estate witnessing my humiliation and my punishment.

I asked Cloud to get me in to see David who had ignored me completely since his outburst. I was granted an appointment for ten the next morning.

In my skimpy little white shorts, I knocked at the door of the study at exactly ten.

"Come," was the very abrupt response.

I walked in and stood in front of David legs astride and hands behind my back until he looked up from the papers he was reading.

"Yes, Charlie, what do you want?"

"Master, I beg you, allow Winston to leave the island before you punish me. I will do anything you want, sign anything you want me to, but please don't humiliate me or beat me in front of him." I fell to my knees in front of him as I said it. "He will be absolutely terrified. Please don't do this to him. I beg you."

"Don't do this to him, Charlie, don't you mean don't do this to you? You don't want the shame of him seeing you treated like an animal again is what you really mean isn't it?"

"No, Master, I swear I am so afraid of what this will do to him. I can't bear the thought of him leaving me for that other state again. He isn't as strong as me."

"I don't believe you, Charlie. I am going to punish you this afternoon. You are going to be stuffed with a 12-inch dildo to remind you how much you like cock and then receive 50 strokes of the paddle to remind you that your sexual popularity is no defence for a slave. It will take place in the gym where you will be restrained. If you lose consciousness, we will resume when you recover. After your 50, you will be left there and every member of staff will be invited to fuck you over the next 24 hours. You will then resume normal slave duties until Cloud's is ready to reopen. Now leave me."

I was sure that defying David would bring me unimaginable pain, but there was no way I was going to let Winston witness this. I told Cloud I was sending Winston away without David's permission.

"Charlie, if you defy him, I won't be able to protect you. He will kill you."

"I don't care, Cloud, sooner me than Winston."

I had a real problem with Winston. He did not understand what was going on but knew it was not good.

"I want you to go to New York to check on Cloud's. Stay at the apartment, and I will have a 24-hour security guard attached to you. You are not to go anywhere without him. Your tickets are waiting for you at the check-in desk, and Cloud's chief security officer, whom you know, will meet you. Now go, and remember I love you more than anyone or anything in the world."

I saw him leave the estate in time for the ferry that would link with his flight, and I relaxed. I could take anything as long as I knew he was safe.

After lunch, I was taken to the gym by Cloud who was looking very apprehensive. All of the staff were there stood in a semi circle round the top two tiers of a vaulting horse. There were restraints on the corners obviously for my wrists and ankles.

"Charlie appears to have forgotten his status as a slave, more importantly, my slave. He is going to be punished and humiliated to remind him who he really is. I am going to stuff his butt with this dildo and then administer 50 licks with this paddle. The dildo is to remind him that sex is no defence for my punishment."

With that, he took a pair of scissors and cut my shorts off me.

Stood there naked made me blush furiously because I noticed David had put the four white waiters front and centre to get the best view. He then took an electric razor and shaved my pubic hair off and the hair under my arms. The only hair left on my body now was on my head.

"I have told you before to keep your body free of hair, Charlie. You will receive another 20 licks when you recover from the present 50. You will not wear anything at all ever again on this estate. All the staff will be issued with paddles and will be encouraged to keep your butt glowing red. Cloud, call everyone's name. I want to make sure there are no absentees."

When Winston's name was called, I waited for the reaction from David, but instead I heard Winston say here. I saw him at that instant and took off toward him.

"Get out of here, Winston, you are not going to watch this, get out, get out!"

I was screaming at him, but he did not move.

"Please, Winston, get out! I don't want you to see this, Baby, please go."

"I can't, Charlie, I have to be here to see you safe after he has finished. I'll be strong for you. I promise."

I walked back to take up my position as before. David took hold of my cock and started to lead me round the row of staff. Telling them as we passed to look at me because I was only a slave, and they were now free to use me and abuse me at will. He released me as I faced the horse and told me to lay over it. Bob pulled my legs apart to shackle them to the corners. It was quite painful because it was nearly a five-foot stretch. My wrists were shackled to the same front corners having the effect of pulling my butt back to make it look as though I was begging to be fucked or beaten. Without warning, David shoved a massive dildo up my ass. I screamed in pain and still heard the gasps of everyone watching.

"I want to hear you count off the strokes, Charlie. If you miss any, then you will receive them as extras."

The first one landed with a crunch making me gasp.

"One, Master."

By six, I was sobbing uncontrollably. By ten, each one made me scream, but still I called them. By 15, I could only feel pain like I had never known before. I didn't realise the paddle could end up hurting more than the whip, but I was sure it did with David not holding back at all. By 20, I could not speak, and David stopped soon after when he realised I was unconscious.

When I came to, David gave the paddle to Bob and said, "You can give him the next ten, and then I will finish off."

Bob gave him the paddle back and said, "No thank you, David, I am resigning, effective immediately," and he walked out of the gym."

"Cloud, take Bob's place."

"No sir. I am also resigning, effective immediately," and he also walked out.

"Mac."

However, Mac was already on his way.

"Please Mac, don't leave. We all need you here. If Cloud goes, who is going to look after us," I managed to get that out in between sobs.

He came back, took my face in his hands and kissed me very gently on the mouth. He was crying as he said, "I would follow you to the end of the earth to keep you safe, Sonny, but I could never lay a hand on you to hurt you. I know I can't do anything to help you here, but I will not be part of it."

Then he left. I was sobbing like a baby for the loss of those three friends that had gone to New York to be with me when I spent my six months in a coma. Now they were leaving here again because of me. I was devastated. All of Mac's staff followed him out of the door, and all of Cloud's staff followed them. The only people left now were my restaurant people and the three boys from New York who had replaced Darren and company. They looked lost. So did David. He threw the paddle down and left the Gym.

Winston was at my side in a second undoing my shackles. Peter and Paul grabbed towels and soaked them with cold water. Darren and company cleared an area on the wrestling mats to lay me down on my tummy. Winston pulled the dildo out of my ass very gently, and I was given a continually changing compress of cold towels on my cheeks. The nurse was soon beside me applying the necessary salves, and in about half an hour I was quite conscious and able to walk, all be it badly, back to the house.

The next morning was almost surreal. The house was like a morgue. There were no staff at all. The grounds were also deserted. When I arrived at the entrance to the staff restaurant and the kitchen, I thought they were all deserted as well but once inside, I could see everyone of my crew and the New York trio sat around looking numb.

Darren was the first one to realise I was there.

"What are we going to do, Charlie?"

They all looked so lost, I could have cried.

Julio said, barely able to hold back the tears, "I don't believe what we witnessed yesterday, Charlie, and if you were not naked, I would think it was just a bad dream. How is your butt?"

I managed to laugh, it seemed such an odd comment, but I swivelled it towards him and said, "Glowing like Rudolph's nose." They all laughed and to keep the ice from freezing over again, added, "I'm fine, guys. You all know I have had worse than this to contend with. Must compare favourably with its colour after you and Paul had finished with me Peter, remember."

"Oh, Charlie, don't. You know we will never forgive ourselves for that, and we would still willingly let you do exactly the same to us again as revenge."

I was beginning to feel a little wicked and could see a way of bonding our New York quartet into our circle even closer.

"Right now, here in front of everyone?"

Peter looked surprised and said in a very shaky voice, "Yes, Charlie, if that is what you want."

"OK, Peter, Paul, stand in front of the table, there," pointing at a table in front of all the rest of the staff. "Winston, get my paddle from the kitchen."

"Charlie, you can't."

"Get it, Winston."

"Peter, take Paul's shoes and socks off. Now his shirt and trousers. Nice Paul, I have always liked taking off your little tighty whities. Now you do the same to Peter."

When they were both in just their briefs, I made them turn round and face the table. I stood between them, stroked their butts through their shorts, and said, "Next to Winston, these are probably the cutest butts on the island, so it would be a pity to mark them with this."

I was holding the paddle, which I then dropped. Told them to turn around again and after planting a big kiss on each of their lips said, "How many times do I have to tell you two that there is no way I am ever going to take my revenge for something you did at 18 for which I was at fault. I love you both too much to ever consider hurting you, but I thought our new friends should see how sexy you truly are."

Everybody laughed then, of course, the way things were going it had to be the wrong time. David walked in the door while everybody was still laughing. If looks could kill, I would have been dead at that moment.

"My study, Charlie, now"

I felt so damn stupid stood in front of him naked, but I should have been used to it.

"What was all that hilarity about?"

"I'm sorry, Master, it was like a morgue when I walked in, so I tried, quite successfully, apparently, to lighten the mood."

"Humph, turn round."

I did and jumped a yard as I was paddled hard.

"Ouch, David, what was that for?" I spun round as I said it and glared at him. "Haven't you done enough damage with that fucking paddle in the last 24 hours?"

I was angrier than I think I had ever been. He could have punished me in private and hurt me as much as he felt necessary without destroying the morale of his household and losing most of them.

"Don't you dare talk to me in that tone of voice! Bend over the desk!"

I must have received ten before I broke. I was so angry with David, I was determined not to let him have the satisfaction of seeing me blubber this time. I didn't want to cry or beg, but I was already very tender, so I did. On the eleventh one, I screamed at him for mercy and started to cry.

"Stand up, Charlie."

He went round behind the desk and slumped in his chair.

"You are ruining my peace and tranquility. You have cost me all of my house staff, and you are going to pay for it for the next four years. I am fed up with you being the centre of attention. Any agreement we have that is not legally binding is rescinded. Wherever we are, I am going to use you as a slave. Winston will think it is a holiday when he gets to sleep with you again. I am going to use you and abuse you as I should have done all along. You will sleep at the bottom of my bed when I have finished using you at night, and if I have a companion for the night, we will both use you and treat you like the sex slut you are before making you sleep on the floor. Now get out of here and start organising your 'oh so loving' staff to run this house until we leave for New York."

I was shattered; my good life was ending again. How long for this time, I wondered.

The psychologist's name was Andre, and he was nice. I knew things were going well in New York, and I started to worry about Paul. Andre told me he was coming on well, beginning to lose his fear of being alone, but once back in the big city things might be different. Short term he would need to be accompanied everywhere he went. That made me sad and showed the air of gloom around Lara's House was palpable. David was morose, I was sad, and Winston was going crazy. We had not made love since David put the new restrictions on me and had not slept together either. Most nights, I slept on the floor in David's bedroom. Our sex was lousy. It had been reduced to me giving him an unsatisfactory blowjob, which got me a paddling or him fucking me without much satisfaction either, so another paddling. I could not remember the last time I had an erection. Everyone in the house knew I was taking regular beatings because they saw my glowing red butt every morning.

I still worked out alone or with David, swam alone, or with David, and played squash less and less often as my joy of life deteriorated. Each squash game I lost got me a paddling, but I had given up caring, even the pain from the beatings had long since failed to make me cry or beg.

Everybody was dreading going back to New York. They guessed the atmosphere in the restaurant would be grim. Eventually, the resignations landed on my desk. All of them. The four white waiters came in first, apologised and said they would leave the island in the morning. Then Darren headed the Lara's House crew.

"We are sorry, Charlie, the atmosphere here is so awful we can't take any more. Our new addresses in New York will be with you as soon we have them. We all love you, Charlie, and will come to work for you the day that monster upstairs is out of your life."

Winston was last, and I started to cry before he said anything. I would die without him.

"I don't know what to do, Charlie. I love you, but I cry myself to sleep every night. I cry all day when I am not working with you. I have forgotten what it is like to cuddle with you and have you make love to me. I want to die. Can we go back to that other place, Charlie? No one hurt us there. We could find each other and be together forever."

I took him in my arms, and we both sobbed our hearts out. I don't know for how long.

David came storming in while we were still holding each other fiercely.

"What on earth is going on in this house? Charlie, what the fuck is the matter with you two?"

"Everybody has left, David, and Winston and I want to try to find that place we both went to last year. We want some peace, David. We want to be able to love each other. I can't watch Winston dying a little each day. I love him too much. We will find some way to be together always."

We were both still sobbing as we walked passed him and went to our room. I think we were just so emotionally exhausted that we just fell onto the bed and slept.

I woke up first a little dazed and feeling drained of all emotion. Winston was wrapped round me in such a way that I could not get out of bed even if I had wanted to. I didn't want to. I had no idea what our future held for us. I cuddled him then as though it would be the last time. I felt the presence as my consciousness improved and turned my head. Andre sat by the window looking at us.

"Hello, Andre, what are you doing here?"

"Hello, Charlie, I was attracted to this aura of peace in a sea of madness."

"I'm sorry, I don't understand."

"This house was a monument to people's joy of living when we came here only a few months ago. Now it is a temple of doom, with the only glimmer of joy being the love that surrounds you two."

"I'm sorry, Andre, it is my fault. I upset David, and he has sought and found appropriate retribution. Winston and I are going to try to find our other world that we lived in last year. I won't let him go this time because I don't want to have to look for him when we get there."

"I understand, Charlie. When are you planning to go?"

"As soon as we know that Darren and the rest of the boys are settled again in New York. We couldn't leave before then."

"OK, Charlie, why don't you wake Winston, put some clothes on and meet me in the restaurant. We ought to start feeding you up for your journey."

I laughed. "That's a good idea, Andre. I do feel hungry, how long have we slept?"

"Quite a long time, Charlie. I guess you were both exhausted."

Andre went straight to David.

* * * * *

"Charlie is awake at last, David. That is three days, quite worrying. They are talking about going to another place for some peace. I think he is on the brink of going into a catatonic state. Do you know what he means about another place where they can love each other?"

"Oh, Christ, no. We'll never get them back if they go together. It was a miracle we saved them last time."

"Slow down, David. Tell me what you mean."

So David told Andre the story of my last period of sustained abuse at his hands.

"David, you are not a stupid man, so whatever possessed you to drive Charlie to the brink again? Don't you realise how far you have gone?"

"No, Andre, I just got angrier with him this time and lost all perspective."

"I don't know if we can save him, David. He is almost there. Once again, I think he is hanging on for his friends. That boy has so much love to give. What a pity you have tried to destroy all that goodness."

Andre walked out in disgust and came back to me. Of course, it was sometime before I got all the tit bits of the action that took place while Winston and I once again started the road to recovery.

* * * * *

We were in the kitchen when Andre found us. I was doing what I did best, cooking. We had a light meal, and Andre made us both drink lots of liquid. I was still naked, and Andre got angry with me.

"Why aren't you dressed, Charlie?"

"The Master has told me I cannot wear clothes here at Lara's, ever again."

"I think you will find that is about to change, so you go and get dressed. Better still, why don't you both get your swim gear, and we will spend some time at the pool. You both look a little peaky."

"I can't, Andre. I must not upset David again. If he beats me too badly I will not be able to look after Winston on our journey."

"OK, but go for a swim together anyway even if it is naked. I promise David will not mind."

"Alright, Andre, if you are sure."

The two of us went naked to the pool. It didn't matter. Andre and David were the only two people on the estate besides us. My Baby looked so adorable lying on a sun bed. I should have been as hard as a rock looking at him, but I think I was just too exhausted.

Andre came and sat with us late in the afternoon.

"David has gone back to New York. He says you are to remain here until papers arrive from his lawyers. When they are signed and returned you, will be free to do as you please, go where you want to when you want to."

"I'm sorry, Andre, I don't understand."

"David is going to release you from your contract. He is also going to offer to buy your share of Cloud's if you want to sell. Finally, if you undertake to bring back joy to this estate, he will sell it to you for one dollar, with certain provisos."

I don't think I fully understood what he meant at that time. I began to a couple of days later when Mac turned up.

"Hello, Charlie. I understand that you are looking for an estate manger to run this place for you."

"Are you mad, Mac? I don't know what you mean."

He showed me a newspaper headline from New York:

David Andrews sells his Caribbean Estate for one dollar

Multibillionaire David Andrews today disclosed that he is selling his Caribbean Estate to his Cloud's partner for one dollar. His reason he says is that Charlie Fellows is the only man he knows that can restore the estate to the glorious and happy place it was when his mother lived. The only provisos in the sale are that he should be able to return anytime he needs an injection of happy powder, and the estate may never be sold without his agreement.

The article went on, but that was the gist of it. I was amazed – what Andre had said gradually registering. The next day, papers arrived for me to sign. I was so pleased Mac was there. They were all too complicated for my tired brain.

"Charlie, let's go through them slowly. This first one is the most important. For a token payment of ten dollars, David will sell you his slave contract. In other words, if you sign this and send it back to David with a cheque for ten dollars in it you will be a free man.

"The second document gives you Lara's House and the whole estate for a further one dollar. The proviso was in the newspaper article. Charlie, we can run Lara's at a profit. You will not need a lot of capitol, so I suggest you sign both of these first two.

"The third document is more complicated. David is offering to buy out your 49% of Cloud's, he says without you and your team, it is not worth very much, but the figure he is offering is very generous considering he gave it to you in the first place. Alternatively, you can retain your 49%, but you have to undertake to re-staff it at least to the old standard and continue as chef.

"If you take the latter option, Charlie, you would have to work with David. I don't know if you could do that again, could you?"

"Mac, I need to rest and love Winston for a few weeks before I make that kind of decision. I will sign the first two documents if you will recruit the staff and get the estate running again."

For the second time in less than a year, Cloud and most of the workers returned to run what was now genuinely my home. Cloud called me Sir on first greeting me, and I nearly died laughing. I was still not well but had regained some of my sexual libido.

"Cloud, do you truly want to work for me?"

"You know I do, Sir. I can think of no person in the world I would rather work for."

"Good, in that case come with me."

When we got to my bedroom, I told him to strip me.

"I can't do that, Sir, you are my employer now."

"Cloud if you don't do as I ask, I won't be your employer. Now undress me."

He did.

"Now undress yourself."

He did, very reluctantly. He was gorgeous. A mature black man in his early thirties with a body that had been looked after inside and out. His cock looked awesome. I wondered if erect it might be bigger than mine.

"Now, Cloud, I want you to make love to me and fuck me like you have wanted to do for more than two years."

"Oh no, Charlie, I can't do that."

"Cloud, I am not a slave. You will not be doing this against my will in any way. Now you can do it because we both want it to happen. Now make love to me."

Wow did I put my foot in it. He was bigger than I was. It was the most awesome cock I had ever seen. I knew it was going to hurt monstrously, and I wondered if I would be able to stop myself from screaming as he entered me. I had to try. It was so important to me that Cloud enjoyed what he had waited so long for.

I succeeded. I bit my lip so hard I drew blood, but Cloud did not see it until he opened his eyes again after his orgasm. He had pleasured me for about an hour making me ejaculate twice awesomely before he entered me. Once I had opened up for him, and the pain had diminished, it was just too amazing for words. His cock was incredible. I had never felt so full, so completely taken. When he came inside me, I cried tears of happiness that my final conquest was my best friend.

We took so long to recover that Winston knocked on the door to ask if we were all right.

"Come in, Lover, we are fine."

He slid onto the bed with me on the other side of Cloud and looked at us both.

"Golly, Charlie, didn't that hurt?"

Cloud looked at me and said, "I don't believe you two. Don't you mind that I have just fucked Charlie almost senseless, Winston?"

"Of course I don't, Sir. Can't you see how much Charlie has enjoyed it?"

He shook his head and said, "Have I just entered the mad house? Winston, how can you not be mad at what I have just done to Charlie?"

"What have you just done? You have made love to him and made him very happy, I can't be upset with you for that. I want people to make Charlie happy. I love him so much, but I can't keep him happy all the time. I would be a wreck."

He laughed at that comment, and I cuddled him closer.

"Cloud, I don't expect you to understand us two, just accept us. You know more than anyone that I would die for this boy and him for me, but sex is fun, we both enjoy it. Mostly together but the odd dalliance just for sex doesn't bother me at all and doesn't bother Winston as long as I am there. We make love to and with people that we love. You happen to be one of them. This brings me to the point of this little seduction, Cloud. You were the last of my friends to make love to me. I have only done it once with you and Mac. I will do it again with you every time you call me, Sir. Therefore, if you call me anything but Charlie, I will know you want to fuck me, and that will be OK. Won't it, Winston?"

"Yes, Charlie, if that is what you want."

"And you, Winston, will stop calling Cloud Sir because you are not an employee any more. If you do call him, Sir, again I will know it is because you would like him to fuck you. I warn you, he is bigger than I am, so tread carefully, OK?"

"Yes, Charlie, but if I do say it by mistake will you be there when I let him fuck me?"

"Of course I will, Lover."

"The use of the word Sir looks like it may have interesting consequences in the future. Cloud, thank you for coming back again to rescue me. You know I will never forget all your kindness."

We all showered and dressed and another piece of my personal jigsaw puzzle was in place. I prayed now that all the other missing pieces would appear and drop into place before we returned to New York. Most of Lara's House pieces did including the New York trio who agreed to remain permanently on the island. We had fewer staff than under David, but I wasn't as rich as he was, and the estate had to at least break even. Mac of course was magic. As estate manger, he paired every expense to the bone. Cloud did the same in the house, only taking on staff that he needed and cutting out as much waste as possible. We had a marketing plan drawn up to let the estate for exclusive holidays. We only needed a few weeks a year of that to put the books into credit and allow us to keep upgrading the house and the estate. It was fun.

Winston and I returned to New York when we heard Cloud's was almost ready, moved back into our apartment and started to look for staff to replace our lost ones. They seemed to have disappeared off the face of the earth, and both Winston and I were sad. I wandered around the boys' apartment the day we were to start interviews and wished things could be as they were. I decided I would contact the realtors that day and let them get rid of it. We would not be spoiling the new staff the way we had the old.

Winston was grinning like a Cheshire cat when he walked into the restaurant, and he asked Jean Pierre and me if we were ready to interview the new batch of waiters.

"Show them in one at a time, Winston, and let us have a look at them."

"There are only six, Charlie. I sent all of the others away."

"Why on earth would you do that?" I looked exasperated and turned to Jean Pierre shrugged and said. "I'm sorry, this could be a waste of time. OK, Winston, show them in."

I could not believe my eyes when in through the door walked Jason, Ty, Glen and Julio, I started to tear up until the last two followed, Peter and Paul, and then I did burst into tears.

"I don't believe this, how?"

Jason told us, "David hunted us down and personally begged us to come back. He told us all the shit was finished with. You were no longer a slave and would truly be our boss. We all love you, Charlie, none of us know why except that you are one awesome dude and the sexiest guy we have ever met."

The last comment was made with a big grin on his face.

"I see, and I suppose a condition of your return is that I make love to you all."

"It isn't, Charlie, but would you?"

Everybody laughed, and I had my waiting staff.

Yes, you guessed, when it was time to interview the remainder of the kitchen staff, there were only three left to see, Darren, Johnnie and Ryan. I was on another roll but even more wary of my happiness this time.

When we reopened, there were no new staff and our opening night was a blast. The only bookings we accepted were from people whom we recognised as regulars from before, and no bill was made out. Our most successful night, and we never took a cent. The waiters took no tips, and the kitchen staff circulated as I could spare them to talk to customers about the food. For a laugh, we had them all decked out in their standard uniform above the waist but sky blue hot pants below the waist with white socks and white trainers, including the kitchen staff who also wore pristine white kitchen aprons. The cheers and clapping all night long and lewd suggestions had every one laughing. The atmosphere was electric.

At the height of the evening, David appeared with what we guessed were all his personal staff carrying silver trays laden with champagne bubbling away in the most glorious crystal flutes. He made me stand on a table and said, "I would like to propose a toast. To the cutest man I know, to the most loving and caring man that I know, to a man I hope will become my friend again, to the finest chef in New York and probably America, Charlie Fellows."

I blushed the deepest red I had ever gone. If I had been made to take my clothes off in front of this audience, I could not have blushed deeper.

"Speech, Charlie."

I looked at David, and knew I would not get off that table until I did.

"Thank you. I don't know what to say. I am so happy to be back with you all. I have to be the luckiest person in the world tonight. My best friends, who I am lucky enough to work with, surround me, and the best customers any chef could wish for. I thrive on your praise and will never cease to try doing better for you all. Thank you for your compliments, David, you never had to ask for my friendship or my love. You always had them, you just didn't realise it."

I hopped down and dove back into the kitchen, so that no one would see me cry. David reached me first and took me in his arms.

"I am so sorry, Charlie, I hope I have made everything up to you properly now. I can only beg you to forgive me one more time. I can't possibly fuck up again because you are now your own man."

"It's OK, David, thank you for your generosity. I will welcome you at Lara's as often as you want to come and so will our staff there."

He kissed me on the lips and left. Winston watched this event unfold and smiling broadly came and hugged me as David left.

"I love you, Charlie."

"I love you, too, Baby, more than you will ever know."

If it were possible, Cloud's was an even bigger success than before the fire. All four of the white waiters accepted customer's offers of $1,000 for a night of pleasuring and built large bank balances before one of them was abused quite badly, then it all stopped. Peter and Paul didn't. Paul would not go out alone even during the day, but no one was sorry about that. He either went with Johnnie or Peter and of course we went out as a crew as often as we could.

David and I grew closer together again as we explored the possibility of adding a gay establishment to our portfolio and another Cloud's Restaurant if we could get another chef good enough to carry the name. I even went to bed with him one afternoon and gave him a blowjob as good as any I had ever given him before, and then I fucked him senseless.

It was only a month before we were due to close again that we found a fabulous place in the Village. It needed a huge amount of work to be done on it, but David and I bought it with the reverse deal to Cloud's. I would own 51% and David 49%. The difference this time was that I had to put up 51% of the capitol. It really was a proper business partnership. I didn't care. I was a rich man from my book that had a new lease of life and the amazing profits Cloud's was generating.

We sorted all the conversion before the restaurant closed, and Winston and I headed for Lara's House. All of the boys wanted to go and see family before joining us there. All except Peter and Paul, they flew down with us.

What is the expression? "My cup runneth over." Something from the bible I think. In my case, it was happiness that was running out of my cup.

Chapter 8

Winston, Peter, Paul and I arrived on the island together to be met by our three best friends, Cloud, Mac and Bob. It was wonderful to see them all, and after lots of big sloppy kisses, we headed for the house.

Lara's House looked beautiful. Mac showed me around the grounds, and Cloud, the house. There had been a lot of work carried out refurbishing it in stages. Mac produced the books and showed me that all of the improvements had been carried out without borrowing money or going into debt in any other way. I was amazed at the efficiency of their housekeeping.

"I have put you and Winston in the master suite, Charlie and Peter and Paul in the one next door. On your instructions, we have accepted no bookings until Cloud's reopens."

"Thank you, Cloud, I hope the remainder of the gang will be joining us in a week or two. As they arrive, just allocate bedrooms in the guest wing. I would like to meet all the new staff later today if you would arrange it."

"That's easy, Charlie, Mac and I have done a hatchet job on staffing levels, so the only ones you don't know are the new pantry boys in the dining room."

"Who are they, Cloud, what are they like?"

"They are both 18, Charlie. I trained them myself here on the estate. Mac's staff thought it was great. The boys served them meals in the main dining room until I was satisfied with the standard. You will see at lunch. I assume Peter and Paul are to be treated like guests and will join you and Winston for lunch."

"Thank you, Cloud, yes."

When the lunch was served, Winston looked at me for my reaction. The two new boys were so beautiful I gasped.

"Oh my God, Cloud, where did you find these two? They are unbelievable."

I looked at Winston. He was smiling that knowing smile, and he nodded.

"Yes, Charlie, they are, aren't they? Jamie, Luke, this is your employer Mr. Fellows."

"Hello, Sir, we are pleased to meet you."

They both had said it in unison and bowed together as well. They were delightful.

"They are from the same village in Dominica as Ryan, Charlie, and as he was the cutest guy we ever took on, present company excepted of course, we thought we would look there again."

"Thank you, Cloud."

Winston almost dragged me to the lounge after lunch and looking very deeply into my eyes said, "I know I don't ever have to share you again, Charlie, because of your job, but you want to try those two boys, don't you?"

I had to break eye contact because Luke and Jamie were not the only ones I wanted to try. I wanted to take each of our white waiters when they arrived and another romp with Darren, Ryan and Johnnie was in my thoughts as well.

"Yes, Winston, and I want to have a romp with all of our Cloud's staff when they arrive. Would you mind terribly?"

He moved into my arms and nuzzled my neck as he said, "No, Charlie, I expected nothing less. That monster between your legs always needs feeding. You won't ever sleep with any of them though will you? It will only be for a romp."

"Yes, Baby, just a romp. I only ever want to sleep with you."

"OK, then, how about a swim?"

He was amazing. He had said that with a bounce in his voice as if I had just given him something he truly wanted. I knew he just needed that little assurance. He was aware that physically he would never have me 100%. My sex drive was way too big for that. He just wanted my love, and he would always have that.

"Mmm, I've missed this. I need to workout with Bob as well and see if I can still beat him at Squash."

I was back to the aux natural look, so no swimming trunks for me. I found it hard not to laugh at the reaction of Jamie. Cloud had sent him down to the pool with ice for the pool bar because he had forgotten it. I was stretched out on my back and having been watching my Baby swimming I was almost erect. Jamie did a double take and even through his dark skin, I could see him blushing. I called him over as he was about to return to the house.

"Hello, Jamie, you don't have to be embarrassed seeing me like this. I am a total exhibitionist when at Lara's and spend most of my time naked or nearly so."

"I'm sorry, Sir," he said trying very hard not to look at my cock. He failed of course.

I swung my legs off the sun bed so that I faced an empty one and told him to come and sit down. It was now almost impossible for him to look at me without looking at my cock.

"This appendage of mine shouldn't cause you any embarrassment, Jamie. You look as though you might compete if you were to get hard."

He was so uncomfortable, I nearly had mercy on him.

"Oh no, Sir, mine is nowhere near as big as yours."

"We'll see. When do you finish your shift?"

"I'm finished now, Sir, Mr. Cloud asked me to bring the ice down and then finish."

The other boys were all naked, so I was not being too wicked with my next thought.

"Do you like to swim, Jamie?"

"Yes Sir, Mac allows staff to use the pool when there are no house guests."

"Well, why don't you join us now? You can leave your clothes in the changing room. When you come back, I want a word with you."

He reluctantly did as I asked and when he walked back out he was covering his genitals with his hands, but I could still see how delightful he was. As he approached me, I stood up, took both of his wrists and gently pulled them away from his cock and balls, and looked him up and down. Very softly, I stroked his cheek and said, "You don't need to do that, Jamie. Like the rest of you, your private parts are perfect."

I then kissed him gently on the lips and told him to sit down.

"I don't like to stand on ceremony here at Lara's, Jamie. I am sure you have heard the stories and know my background. I have been very lucky to own this beautiful estate, but I haven't changed. I expect you to show Cloud the respect that he deserves, but you and Luke are to call the rest of us by our first names. I'm Charlie, that is Winston and the twins are your predecessors and are called Peter and Paul. We all work at my Restaurant in New York and holiday mostly at Lara's House. I love it here, so you will see a lot of me and of course Winston."

He was still quite flustered, but Peter and Paul took charge of him, and they were soon playing like a bunch of kids. Winston came and snuggled up on the same sun bed as me. So my near erection was completed. Nearly four years now, and I still could not touch him or even look at him naked without getting a boner.

"Charlie, he is beautiful isn't he? Even more so than Peter and Paul were when we first came here."

"Yes, he is Baby, probably the most beautiful of all the boys we have around us."

"If you have sex with him, Charlie, you won't fall in love with him will you?"

"Probably, Lover, he looks so adorable I think it would be difficult not to."

"Could I lose you, Charlie?"

That last comment made with so much worry in the words and a look of deep sorrow in his eyes. I kissed him deeply and tilted his face up so that he was looking me straight in the eyes.

"You will never ever lose me, Baby. As long as I live, I will love you the way I do now."

There was a big sigh, and I cuddled him closer and waited for him to relax again.

Jamie had watched this interchange before rejoining the game with Peter and Paul. When they climbed out of the pool, I could see Jamie talking to the other two with frequent glances my way. Peter told me later that Jamie was confused about me until they told him I was a sex machine but loved

Winston. I thought that was funny. Even funnier when they told me that they had informed Jamie he would probably be made love to by me at least once if he wanted it, but there would not be any coercion. Nice of them to break the ice. Tomorrow looked like I might make a new conquest.

We had brought a stack of the latest film releases with us on video, so that night after supper all the staff were invited to join us for a movie. When the Cloud's people arrived, we would have to let the staff view movies the day after us because the cinema was quite small.

Winston and I curled up in a double Pullman seat and everybody else spread out round us. I noticed Jamie and Luke watched us more than the movie, which amused me. Winston always curled up in my lap for movies and therefore watched them 90 degrees out all the time. He said it was worth it because I stroked his body the whole time and played with his hair. He would turn towards me occasionally to get a kiss, and Jamie and Luke could be in no doubt that I loved my man.

The next day, I asked Cloud if the third bedroom was ready for use. He said it was. Who was I expecting?

"No one, Cloud. I might need the use of a bed other than my own for a couple of hours."

His eyes twinkled as he said, "Who's first then, Charlie, Jamie or Luke?

I laughed and replied, "Jamie I think, provided he is willing."

"Oh he'll be willing. I heard him and Luke talking about Jamie's action at the pool yesterday. They both want you to make love to them."

I smiled. This was going to be easier than I thought. No necessity for the chores book after all. I had thought about reinstating it as a bit of fun, just to get sex really. I might still have to do it as a means of easing into the white waiters' beds.

After lunch, I asked Winston if he would mind me staying at the house for a couple of hours while he joined the others at the pool.

"No, Charlie, be gentle with him, don't hurt him with that monster."

"I won't lover, and thank you."

He gave me a big kiss, and with a little smile and shake of the head, he was gone.

I went through to the lounge and asked Cloud to send Jamie to me when he was finished.

A very worried looking young man came into the lounge a few minutes later.

"Mr. Cloud said you wanted to see me, Sir."

"Yes, Jamie, come and sit down here with me. And what do you call me?"

"Oh, Charlie, Sir."

I laughed, "No, Jamie, just Charlie."

He sat next to me and I asked him about himself and his family, about travel and expectations for life. Naturally thinking about the new Cloud's if we were lucky enough to open one. Another bunch of waiters of the same calibre as Peter, Paul and Winston would practically guarantee us success again, and when they were older, the new club as well. I told him about my plans for the second Cloud's and the club, how we had staffed the first one so successfully from here. He was wide eyed by the time I had finished.

"We are one big family at Cloud's, Jamie, and I love them all to the degree that I occasionally go to bed with all of them. Does that shock you?"

"No, Charlie, but I am surprised that Winston doesn't get upset because he is your proper lover, isn't he?"

"Yes he is, Jamie, but Winston also knows that I love sex, just for sex sake, particularly if is with other people that I love. He also knows that he is my life, and if he objected I would not do it, but he understands me. Jamie, I'd like to take you to bed this afternoon and make love to you. Will you let me?"

"Yes, please, Charlie, but I am a virgin. You won't hurt me with that will you?" he said, pointing between my legs.

"No, Jamie, I will let you take control if you want me inside you, but I am just as happy being the bottom if you would prefer it."

"Oh no, Charlie, I couldn't fuck you, you're my boss."

I laughed, "In bed with me for sex, Jamie, there is no boss. We are going to enjoy ourselves, that's all."

I stood up pulling him with me, and we walked up to the third bedroom.

"Would you like to shower before we go to bed, Jamie?"

"Yes, please, Charlie."

I started to undress him, which once again flustered him. I took his socks and shoes off, stood up and kissed his face all over.

"I am going to take charge, Jamie, but anything you want to do to me you can, and if I do something to you that you don't like you stop me. Don't be afraid. I truly want you to enjoy this, OK?"

"Yes, Charlie."

I took his shirt off and dropped his trousers. Like Peter and Paul, he wore the little white tight briefs. He was so gorgeous. He really did take my breath away, sexier to look at now than seeing him naked yesterday.

"Jamie, Winston was worried that I might fall in love with you, now I can see why. You are delightful to look at."

I dropped his briefs and made him step out of them and his trousers before kissing the end of his cock and cupping his balls in my hand. He just stood there very quickly coming to full erection. He looked embarrassed, so I shed my clothes as well. As soon as I was naked, he visibly relaxed and immediately dropped his jaw open as he saw my fully erect penis in all its glory, absolutely rigid and nearly hitting my belly, my balls hanging neatly beneath in their pouch.

"You can do more than just look at it if you want to, Jamie."

It was almost a look of anguish that he gave me. I realised then that I had really jumped the gun with this boy. He didn't know me well enough to feel comfortable with me yet, but here we were as intimate as it was possible to get.

I pulled him into my arms and whispered to him, "I'm sorry, Jamie, I was so eager to make love to your beautiful body I didn't give a thought to your feelings, please forgive me. Let's get dressed again and try to forget this happened. When you feel comfortable with me, please tell me, and I would like to try this again."

"Please, Charlie, this is all so new to me. I have only ever played with Luke, and we have never made love properly. Teach me how."

"I will, Jamie, but not today. Spend some time with us at the pool or in the gym, get used to us, get to know me and then we will try again. Bring Luke with you. My other Cloud's boys should be here in about a week, and they are all young and beautiful as well. They will tell you about me. Peter and Paul will tell you as well, we have been through quite a lot together, particularly when I was David's slave."

"A slave, Charlie, I don't understand."

"Oh it's a long story. Ask Peter to tell you or Winston if you can tear him away from me. Come on let's go for a swim. Or would you like me to get rid of this for you first?"

I took hold of his cock as I said it and he gasped, "Would you, Charlie?"

"Of course, shall we have that shower first though?"

We did. I soaped him down, as I would have done a baby. He just stood there and let me, moving around as I indicated. I took a long time making sure his genitals and his cute butt were clean. With one soapy finger, I caressed his hole, and as he relaxed more, I gently slid it into his love chute up to the first knuckle. My other hand was soaping his cock and balls, and he loved it. I eased into the second knuckle and he still felt relaxed.

"Are you OK, youngster?"

"Oh yes, Charlie, that feels so nice. I don't mind if you want to keep doing that."

I pulled out and just played with his buttocks and the insides of his legs still gently caressing his balls and cock. I went back into his love chute with two fingers, a little resistance initially, but then he wiggled his ass, obviously to get comfortable before pushing back onto them. I hit his prostate this time and started finger fucking him slowly, but making sure I hit his prostate frequently. I started to jack him off as well, and he came very quickly, gasping as he shot several quite strong jets onto the shower tiles. He was gasping, and I pulled him into my arms, gently rinsing the soap from his adorable body until he was gleaming. I did a quick soap job on myself before we exited the shower, and he let me dry him off completely with a big fluffy towel. I patted his butt and told him to go and get dressed while I dried off, but he just turned round and watched me. I of course was still erect, and he couldn't take his eyes off it.

"Charlie, can you really put that inside me without hurting me?"

"No, Jamie, whatever size dick goes into you the first time invariably hurts. For mine, I would stretch you for a long time and ease into you very gently, but I would still hurt you very much to start with. You would have to learn to get over the pain barrier before you could enjoy it."

"Will you do it to me now, Charlie? I like you. You are very kind to me and very gentle. I trust you not to hurt me too much and to stop if I can't take it."

I led him to the bed and made him lay in the centre of it on his back. I moved in alongside him and started to kiss him very softly. I started with his eyes. It was magic to watch each one open again after I had kissed it. The look of wonderment because I was being so gentle with him had me tearing up. The eyes were a beautiful deep green, almost breathtaking to look into, surrounded by long curling lashes. I continued kissing all over his face as my hand roved over his upper body nipping gently on his nipples as I brushed them. I ran my hand down his belly, finally pulling gently on his pubic hairs but not actually touching his cock.

After a while, I worked my way down that gorgeous body with my tongue. His nipples were a delight. I sucked on each one in turn until they were two hard little knobs, almost as hard as his cock, which I attacked with my tongue after sampling his little inny belly button. I licked round the glans before pulling it away from his body and swallowing all of it in one swift movement. He reared up to try to feed me more and nearly choked me. He was another little chap like me, but his cock was enormous. I loved it, straight attractive nine or ten inches with a delightful ball sac neither too tight nor too slack. I came straight back up on it before running my tongue down the underside and taking his ball sac in my mouth sucking on it and making it slimy for my fingers to work on. I returned to his cock with my tongue and worked his balls with my hand. I could feel he was not going to last very long, so I left him completely while I retrieved gel from the table drawer and went back to him to start working his butt. His hole was wondrous to behold. It wasn't at all puckered, just a slightly lighter aureole around the tiny opening. I dived straight in with my tongue licking all round it over it and eventually in it. He was gasping and spreading his legs wider and raising them higher to give me unfettered access. I was almost cumming it was just such an incredibly cute butt. I nibbled and nipped at the cheeks as I slowly fed him fingers. I needed to use every digit on one hand before I felt safe trying my dick. He was so relaxed, I slid back up his body and continued kissing him on the lips traversing his body again with a million kisses before returning to his butt. When I was sure he was relaxed and spread wide enough, I went back to work on his cock with my tongue and lips while I lubed up his love tunnel and my cock.

When I could wait no longer, I pushed the head in past his sphincter and stopped. He screamed. It had been some time since I had taken a virgin ass, and Jamie was quite small, but I was still surprised at the depth of his scream. I pulled out straight away and waited. He started to cry, and I felt like shit. I fell forward resting my weight on my elbows and kissed him all over his face apologising as I did so.

"It's OK, Charlie, I just didn't expect it to hurt that much. Please try again and just keep still once you are inside me. Give me time to adjust."

I thought that was very mature from a first timer, but I did and the scream was milder. I watched his eyes to see what was happening to the pain level. As it eased, I fed him more of my man rammer. With a few inches in him, I started a very slow fucking motion feeding in a little more each time I pushed. It took a long time, and I could feel by how tight it was that he was struggling, but he said nothing and eventually I had all of it inside him.

"You have it all, Jamie, how do you feel?"

He gasped a little and replied.

"That feels amazing, Charlie, you are consuming my body with that cock. I can feel it in my stomach."

"I am going to slow fuck you with it now, Jamie, coming almost all the way out before I push it all the way back in."

I grabbed both pillows and pushed them under him to raise his pelvis so that I could lean back further and watch my cock as it went in between those two perfectly formed little orbs of his butt, and I played with his cock and balls. I watched his eyes, and as the pain finally disappeared, I saw him slide off into another world. He was gasping and obviously having problems evaluating all the new sensations being fucked by my monster were creating. Neither of us lasted very long. I came in great wrenching spurts at the same time as him. Each time he shot, the contraction of his butt muscles made me go ballistic, and I pummelled his ass as the last of my orgasm receded. I would have to do this again and take my time. He was just so adorable this first time my senses were almost overloaded, and I had been unable to control my ejaculation.

"Jamie, that was incredible. I am sorry I came so quickly, you were amazing. I promise to do better next time."

"Thank you, Charlie, I have never had an experience like that. Do you really want to do it again with me?"

"Oh yes, Jamie. I can do much better than that for you, and I have my reputation to think of." I laughed as I made that last comment. Jamie just sighed.

We cleaned up and walked down to the pool. Winston studied Jamie's face carefully and said to me, "You took him off to paradise then, Charlie."

"No, Baby, I offered up a second rate performance. His body was so awesome to look at, I came way too early. I'm disgusted with myself really. You would be cross with me if I could not do better than I did for Jamie this afternoon."

"You had better take him again then, Charlie, soon. I wouldn't want anyone thinking you had lost your touch by being with me."

I kissed him hard and told him, "You are awesome, and I don't even have to be in bed with you to realise it. I love you so much, Winston. Whatever did I do to deserve you?"

"Don't you remember, Charlie? You nearly died for me."

I looked at the love flowing from those huge eyes and felt truly humble.

I took Luke the next day and did a much more professional job. I was ready for the exposure whereas Jamie had been a shock. Although they were not brothers, they were just like Peter and Paul to be with. They had grown up together and were as familiar to each other as brothers were. The difference was that these two had boy sex together, but Peter and Paul had it with me.

I left Jamie for about a week letting him become more familiar with me and then took him again. I managed to last over half an hour inside him this time concentrating on giving him multiple orgasms. After my orgasm, I remained inside him while I went soft and cuddled and caressed him for ages while he calmed down.

"Oh Charlie, that was unbelievable. I don't think I will ever have sex like that again. Winston is so lucky to have you every day. I love you, Charlie. Do you think he will mind?"

"No, Lover, he knows I love you as well, and we both have enough love to share with our friends."

"Thank you, Charlie, can we do this again before you go back to New York?"

"Yes, Jamie, but I would prefer that you and Luke do it together."

"Oh we do, Charlie, but it is good to have an expert to teach us, and then we practice together afterwards."

He was smiling as he said it, and I realised why after making love to either of them they both disappeared for an hour or so.

"Would you like me to teach you both together sometime, Jamie?"

"Gosh, would you, Charlie? I know Luke would like you to."

"OK, I'll arrange it soon."

I thought about it and decided a session like one I had with Peter and Paul might be fun. But I would leave it a week to let them practice on their own. I did leave a large bottle of lube in their room to help.

David and I were talking frequently. The new bar/club/restaurant in Greenwich Village was shaping up better than expected. He was very enthusiastic.

"Charlie, I think you should come back to New York, just for a couple of days to see it and make sure that we aren't making any mistakes."

"OK, David, no time like the present. I'll take tomorrow's flight."

"Winston, I'm going back to New York tomorrow. I will be away a maximum of two days. While I am there, I am going to be working hard all day and probably be in conference with David and the Developers half the night. I will check on the apartments and if possible, I have decided the other waiters should live in our block if there are any vacancies, so I shall be working on that as well. You can come with me if you like, Baby, but I am sure you will be bored, and I will take longer to get everything done if I am worrying about you by yourself all day and half the night."

"That's OK, Charlie, you go, I'll stay here. Try to bring the white guys back with you."

Winston turned to leave me and bumped straight into Cloud.

"I'm sorry, Sir, please forgive me."

I asked him what he said, and he put his hand to his mouth and gasped.

"Sorry, Charlie, I didn't mean it."

"Cloud, when I get back from New York, I think we had better arrange for you to make love to Winston."

Winston looked shocked and said, "You have to be there as well, Charlie, then I won't mind."

I wanted to see this. I could think of nothing more erotic than Cloud using his monstrous tool to satisfy my baby. My return was going to start interesting.

New York was great. I stayed at David's apartment, the first time since I had ceased to be his slave. I stayed in the same room where I had the unpleasant experience with his ex boyfriend. I shuddered remembering it, but it was a lovely suite.

We worked very hard. After I had spent the first morning at the new venue, there were a million things I wanted changed. David and the Developer were amazed at how insightful I was and disagreed with me on only a couple of things. It was going to be fabulous when finished. There were so many mezzanine floors and other different levels. We could run several activities simultaneously if we wanted to.

"Charlie, you had better start thinking about staff. You are going to be responsible for that as you have been at Cloud's. If you repeat that success you are truly going to be a rich man very soon."

"That is a very satisfying thought, David. It won't hurt your fortune either will it?" I said with a broad grin on my face.

"No, Charlie, it won't. I'll get my money back from you in this way won't I?"

I went all serious.

"Yes you will, David, but you don' have to. I will pay you it now if you will accept my cheque."

He moved across the floor rapidly and gathered me up into his arms in front of the Developer and Architect, planted a huge kiss on my lips and whispering.

"You have already more than paid me back, Charlie, by teaching me about love. One day, if I am lucky, I am going to find someone like you to love me the way you love Winston."

I was flattered and whispered back. "You will, David, I could have loved you like that in different circumstances."

"I know, Charlie, I was just a bloody fool. Will you sleep with me tonight?"

"Of course. I would have been hurt if you hadn't asked."

I said that while sniggering like a kid. We both laughed heartily and returned to business.

Everything was going so well. The realtors said the apartment next to the boys would be vacant in a month. It only had two bedrooms, both en-suite, but they were huge. I telephoned Jason and asked him if they would like me to take it and not charge them anymore than they were already paying. He phoned me back within the hour, having talked to the others and jumped at it. They all jumped at the chance to come back with me to Lara's in David's private jet as well.

I slept with David that night, and he made love to me. I had never known him to be so tender. I loved it. I was in heaven.

"Oh God, David, if you had ever made love to me like that when I was your slave, I would probably have signed for another ten years. That was awesome."

He looked down at me lying half underneath him and said with a sad note in his voice.

"Don't say that, Charlie. I don't need reminding about what a bloody fool I have been. There isn't any chance for us is there?"

I was a little shocked and quite sad really. "No, David, I can't even begin to imagine not being in love with Winston. I have nearly died for him twice, and I would go all the way to save him. He really is my life."

"I know, Charlie, but I had to try. I love you, and I have been a million kinds of fool in losing you."

"You haven't lost me, David. You just can't have me all the time that's all."

The boys and I returned to Lara's House together. Winston met us and said to me after burying me in kisses, "What's with you guys?"

"I'll tell you all about it, but basically life is so good."

Winston was so proud of the way I was handling the new club and joined me in my little boy mode when he realised that Jason and company were going to be so close to us in New York.

I told him that David had made love to me and how awesome it had been. He looked at me a little cockeyed but didn't comment.

We all settled in, and there were now eight naked boys round the pool every afternoon some times with the addition of Jamie and Luke. I of course was almost permanently hard. It was incredible. The four white waiters looked as though they were more than adequately hung, and I hungered for a romp with them.

I was having great sex with Winston, but my voyeur side wanted to see Cloud make love to him, so I organised it for after lunch the next day.

We were all undressed in my bedroom. Cloud was a willing participant. As he said, "Next to you, Charlie, Winston is the most desirable boy on this island."

"OK, then, Cloud, you can do anything you like, and so can you, Winston. I am just going to watch unless I get really horny and then you are likely to be taking two dicks, Lover."

He looked a little apprehensive, and got more so when he looked again at Cloud who was already erect.

"Oh gosh, Charlie, I don't know how you took that, but I will try as well."

With Winston on his back, Cloud started to feed him cock, easing over his lips and stopping the penetration as soon as Winston gagged. I watched his eyes watering, but he gradually took more, controlling his gag reflex as he did with me. It looked amazing. I couldn't resist and took Winston's cock in my mouth and started to pleasure him.

Cloud was obviously very turned on watching and feeling Winston's mouth and hands at work because he only lasted a few minutes before asking me to open Winston up for him. Absolutely no problem for me, I started with my tongue penetrating his love tunnel as far as I could by spreading his cheeks wide with my hands. When he was very slick, I lubed my hand and started in again with one finger first making sure I hit his prostate as often as possible. By the time I had all five digits rotating inside him, he was totally relaxed and beginning to space out.

I nodded to Cloud who moved round in between Winston's legs, lifted them over his shoulder and positioned himself ready to enter the most beautiful boy in the world. I kissed my baby's lips very passionately as Cloud pushed his monster glans over Winston's sphincter, causing the minimum of pain. Winston broke our kiss and with tears in his eyes said to me, "That hurts so much, Charlie, please make him stop while the pain eases."

Cloud heard and kept perfectly still, watching my baby's eyes until the pain in them disappeared before slowly feeding him his entire monster. As he started to fuck him with long slow strokes, I watched Winston sliding off to the world of ecstasy I knew so well and added to his enjoyment by taking his beautiful cock in my mouth and bringing it back to full erection. It was a pity we were all so turned on. It would have been wonderful to play for ages, but

Cloud and Winston came together followed closely by me as I watched the emotions on show from the other two. It was so amazing.

Winston told me later that it felt as though Cloud pumped a gallon of cum into him, and Cloud told me he thought the same.

"Charlie, making love to you was an incredible experience, but I have to tell you, Winston was so beautiful to love that I could have cried watching the emotions that his face showed throughout that."

"I know, Cloud, and now you know why I could never stop loving him."

A couple of weeks later, Darren, Johnnie and Ryan turned up. Now we were complete. All my Cloud's boys together. With so many of us, the house staff were working very hard, and I thought this unfair as it would be going on for at least another six weeks. So, one afternoon at the pool, I got all the boys round me and put forward a suggestion.

"Guys, we are putting the Lara's House staff under a lot of pressure. We don't have the numbers to cater to such a large guest compliment. I would like us to reverse rolls with them half the time. Does anyone have any objections to that?"

Darren spoke for all of them after a quick look round. "No, Charlie, we are all on payroll, and this is part of your empire. We should pull our weight. What do you want us to do?"

"That is great guys. How about we release all the house staff three days a week taking over cooking, waiting and cleaning duties? We can let them behave as guests to the point we even wait on them in the main dining room, clean the house and do the laundry and clean our own rooms."

"That is fair enough, Charlie, but do you think I am good enough to cook for you all if we are going to relieve chef as well?"

"Yes you are, Darren, but I am going to join you in the kitchen as well."

So we did it, and it was a hoot. The estate staff joined in as well even though their duties had not been added to. I walked into the dining room the first lunchtime and saw Winston, Peter and Paul waiting tables. The Lara's House staff loved it because they had mostly worked with my Cloud's boys before. It was obvious that Jamie and Luke felt a little awkward until Winston and I walked up behind them and gave them both a cuddle with my comment,

"Enjoy it, boys, we are having fun looking after you."

It was fun as well, everybody thought it was cool, and I got another feather in my cap.

After we had served the Lara's Staff, we all ate in the staff canteen helping ourselves, and that was a laugh as well. I told Ty and company they could wait tomorrow and Winston, Paul and Peter would be washer uppers.

After lunch, I asked Winston if he would mind me resurrecting the chores and punishment book for a laugh on the days we were working and me go back to wearing my sexy white shorts on those days. He initially looked a little taken back, and then he obviously had a wicked thought because he grinned at me and said, "Provided everyone on the estate can take advantage of it solidly from the end of lunch until the beginning of dinner."

I laughed and started to tickle him.

"What are you planning, you minx?"

"You'll find out, Charlie. Are you including the paddle in this little game?"

"If you say I should, I will."

"Good, I'm saying you should."

At dinner that night, Winston told all the Lara's staff and explained his plot, and later when the Cloud's staff were away from me, he told them as well.

I found out after we returned to New York that he had explained what went on with me when he first arrived and that they were to resume that system including paddling me if I failed to do chores to their satisfaction. He also explained about the paddling going over the top. This was to be a fun thing, so the pain was to be kept to an erotic level. They were encouraged to have an audience if they wanted and multiple parties could be involved with the action. Pressing trousers, cleaning shoes and cleaning rooms were where I was weakest if they wanted to get a paddling in. Winston admitted to me that he had allowed a little humiliation in the hope it would deter my sexual excesses in the future. I thought he was very sweet to have this agenda in the hope of getting me for himself.

The next day, Ty and Jason had booked me for two hours, and Jamie and Luke, for the following two hours. I was looking forward to it.

I had seen all of the white boys naked, but never with an erection, so it was something to look forward to. Both of them had seen me humiliated and punished by David before I became the owner of Lara's and had heard from Peter and Paul about spanking me and spit roasting me. It was obvious when I started my two-hour session with them that they had worked out a combination plan to take in all of it.

When I knocked on their door, I was in my little white shorts carrying the sheathed paddle and the book.

"Come in, Charlie."

I walked in and stood before them in the at-ease position with my left hand at my side holding the paddle and book. They were in the same position on one bed as Peter and Paul had been in tighty whities as well. They of course were 20 not 18, but they were still gorgeous and both were half-hard which looked interesting.

Ty said, "Hello, Charlie, I'll take the paddle and book. We would like you to clean those two pairs of shoes as we are waiting staff tonight and have to look our best."

He pointed at the shoes by the desk as he said it. I knew how to do this job perfectly. The first Winston had made that something unforgettable.

So I knew I would have to screw up at least one shoe deliberately if I didn't want to stall this session, but I planned to make it the last shoe just to make them sweat a little. It was so funny watching them go over each shoe and not be able to find fault. They were looking very downcast by the time I gave them the last one to inspect while I put the cleaning gear away. I could hardly miss their grins as they examined the last shoe.

"I'm sorry, Charlie, but this last one is totally unsatisfactory. We are going to have to punish you to make you aware of your failings. Take your shorts off and get up on the bed on all fours with your ass facing us."

I did and dropped my shoulders onto the bed when they told me, making my ass even more accessible.

"Spread your legs now, Charlie, wide."

Jason said it with a snigger in his voice, so I knew they were already enjoying this.

"I think ten on each buttock should suffice, Ty, don't you?"

"Yes very appropriate, Jason, and we can do them simultaneously. If you get an erection, Charlie, we will have to humiliate you by fucking you at both ends with an audience."

They stood either side of me and started slapping my butt, just hard enough for it to tingle and of course, that was erotic, so I had an erection in no time. They stood me up at ten, and looking at their groins, I knew they had found it as erotic as I. They were both very hard.

"You can take my briefs off now, Charlie, and start giving me a blowjob while Ty fetches an audience to watch us spit roast you."

Jason's cock was gorgeous, long and straight, uncut and with a nicely proportioned set of balls. I was in cock heaven when Ty returned with Glen and Julio in tow. They didn't look at all surprised at what they saw, so I knew it was a set up.

Ty took his briefs off got onto the bed and told me to start sucking him positioning myself so that Jason could fuck me. It was great. Jason was a careful lover and really made me enjoy it while I sucked Ty. Glen and Julio were also enjoying it, both had stripped naked and were stroking their cocks gently. I had my wish, all four of my white waiters hard as rocks in my sight. I hoped that I was going to get more than one cock up my ass and in my mouth before this session was finished. I did and it was fantastic. Glen and Julio took Ty and Jason's place after they came, turning me on my back for it so that Ty and Jason could give me a joint blowjob. My orgasm was fantastic. Face fucked, butt fucked and blown all at the same time by four drop dead gorgeous guys.

When they had finished, and we were all crashed on the bed, I got up and gave each of them a loving kiss and said, "I have wanted to make love to each of you from the moment I first set eyes on you. It has taken a long time, but it was worth it. Thank you all. It was great. If you have nothing else, I will be off, Ty, Jason?"

"Yes there is, Charlie. We are supposed to humiliate you a little as well, and I don't think we have done that."

Now, I knew they had been briefed.

"Bend over the chair Charlie with your legs spread. Before we administer ten licks with the paddle, I think Glen and Julio should have the pleasure of giving you a little spanking as well to remind you that by your own authorisation we are to treat you like a slave. They can use their fingers first though to feel how soft you are inside."

I was truly surprised that they were going this far with the humiliation, but I could not back out now without seeming silly.

So I did, spreading my legs wide as instructed and colouring up, Jason and Ty stood either side of me pulling my cheeks apart while Glen and Julio spent a few minutes fingering me.

"Very nice, Charlie, whatever we put up your ass feels incredible you have the most amazing bum."

Julio was laughing as he said it while he and Glen positioned themselves to enthusiastically give me several quite hard slaps on the butt with their bare hands before Jason positioned himself to administer the ten with instructions.

"Count them off, Charlie, in this way. 'One, thank you, Master, may I have another.' Do you understand, Charlie?"

"Yes, Master."

He wasn't very gentle, and I was soon squirming. They hurt, but not enough for me to make them stop. I was feeling humiliated though with three others watching. When Jason finished he was very proper. Ty was filling in the book and putting it away with the paddle, and Jason said, "Stand up, Charlie, put your shorts on, say thank you to Ty and me, and then you can go."

"Thank you, Jason, thank you, Ty."

I was handed the book and I left. However, I had my ear back on the door as soon as it was closed.

"Christ, Jason, don't you think we went a bit far with the spanking and paddling on top of the fucking?"

"No Glen, Winston was very specific, and I have not gone over the top."

I shot off to my next liaison wondering what Jamie and Luke had planned for me and whether Winston had briefed them, too.

The second I saw my next two temporary masters, I knew they had been briefed as well. I was definitely going to get Winston. I would have to plan very carefully because I didn't want him hurt emotionally.

Luke and Jamie were in exactly the same position as Peter and Paul had been, dressed in identical tighty whities.

"Hello Charlie, come and stand in front of us and give me the book and paddle."

I did as I was told and after giving up the objects as asked stood at ease.

Jamie continued talking. "This is correct, Charlie, isn't it? We can treat you totally like a slave paddling you if you displease us, use your body in any way we like, humiliate you and abuse you without any risk to our jobs."

"Yes, the whole idea of this silly game is that my staff should have a heap of fun in the afternoons."

"Good, take your shorts off, Charlie, and until you leave this room you will address Luke and me as Master. If you fail to address either of us correctly you will be paddled, do you understand?"

"Yes of course, Jamie."

"You don't, Charlie, because you have just called me Jamie. I am going to have to paddle you. Bend over the chair, spread your legs wide and grip the legs with your hands."

I did as I was told thinking these boys are being very assertive. Winston had to have done a first class job on them.

"After each stroke, Charlie, I want you to say, 'Thank you, Master, may I have another, please.' Do you understand?"

"Yes, Master."

He delivered the first one quite hard. I gasped and said, "Thank you, Master, may I have another, please."

I received ten and my butt hurt, not enough to want to cry out, but it was very red I was guessing. After the tenth one, Jamie told me no more and to stand up and face Luke. He stood back from me looking at my butt and said, "That is a pretty shade of red, Charlie. You will have to be careful we don't add to it. Now I want you to kneel down, cross your ankles, grasp your hands behind you. Open your mouth and put your tongue out."

I followed the instruction wondering whose imagination was choreographing this.

"Whenever Luke or I say suck boy you are to get in that position. Do you understand, Charlie?"

"Yes, Master."

Luke hopped off the bed, dropped his briefs and put his cockhead on my tongue.

"I want you to lick that to full arousal, Charlie."

"No, problem, Luke, I can do that all day. Oh shit, sorry Master."

"Over the chair, Charlie, resume the position as before."

This was going to hurt, should I stop this now before I broke down or take my punishment for being a sex hound. I decided to let it ride for now, hoping Luke would be gentler than Jamie had been.

"Count them off, Charlie, and then ask me for another after each one."

"One, thank you, Master"

It stung but not too bad. At ten I was gasping, and I was now really hurting. I wondered how much of this was youthful enthusiasm and how much Winston, which was why I had let it continue.

When I stood up this time, there were tears in my eyes and a couple had escaped and were rolling down my cheeks.

Luke and Jamie saw them at the same time and looked shocked.

"We're sorry, Charlie, we didn't mean to hurt you," Luke said.

I grabbed them both and said, "It's OK, my fault for starting it, and you weren't to know how hard you could hit me before it would hurt a lot. Let's forget this one, and you can go in the book for tomorrow, how does that sound?"

"You aren't mad at us then, Charlie?"

"Are you kidding? I could never be mad at you two. You are just to damned gorgeous for that."

I kissed them both, put my shorts on, and with the paddle and book departed.

Winston was surprised to see me back so soon, when I walked into our bedroom. He jumped off the bed where he was reading and said, "What's the matter, Charlie, has something gone wrong?"

"Just a little, Baby. Jamie and Luke got a bit too enthusiastic with the paddle and after 20, I was hurting. I should have stopped it. My fault."

I took my shorts off and showed him my ass, which was very red and showing some bruising already.

Winston burst into tears and sobbing like a baby threw himself into my arms and blubbered.

"Oh, Charlie, that is all my fault. I told them they could use the paddle freely if they wanted to. I even set up the scenario for all of them today. I'm sorry, Charlie. I deserve a beating for being so stupid. I thought it might curb your enthusiasm for group sex. You have to beat me, Charlie, that is only fair."

"Don't be silly. I'm not going to beat you."

"In that case, I am going to organise my own punishment. Don't try to stop me."

I pulled away from him and shook him, "You are going to do no such thing. Now dry those tears and let's go for a swim."

"No Charlie, I don't want to."

"Well I am going to, Baby, with trunks on though to cover my bruised butt. Winston, I forbid you to do any thing silly to punish yourself. I'm not mad at you, just the reverse. You just show me how much you love me when you do something like this, OK?"

"OK, Charlie, enjoy your swim."

I went for a run first so that I had an excuse to be clothed at the pool, which I never normally was. Everybody at the pool had trunks on when I arrived, and Mac was just leaving.

"Ah Charlie, you've heard have you?"

"Heard what, Mac?"

"Oh, I thought the reason you were clothed was because you knew we have government immigration people here checking work permits."

"No I had no idea. Are all the staff legal, Mac?"

"Oh yes, Charlie, and all your Cloud's people are here on visitors visas."

"OK, if you need me I am going to be here for the next hour and then the kitchen."

Luke and Jamie looked at me a little apprehensively, and the four white waiters with a smirk on their faces. I went over to Luke and Jamie gave them both a hug and told them everything was fine. Peter and Paul were with them looking curious.

"OK, you two, we had a bit of fun this afternoon that nearly got out of hand. These two were a little worried that's all."

I guessed Peter and Paul would have all the details by the end of the afternoon, but it couldn't be helped.

When I got back to our room, I immediately noticed that nothing of Winston's was lying around anywhere. I checked his drawers and the wardrobe. He had moved out. I called Cloud.

"Yes Charlie, Winston asked for a room in the staff quarters and I gave him one of the four bedrooms in the extension. Is there a problem?"

"Nothing I can't handle, Cloud."

I found him on a bed crying his eyes out.

"Oh Baby, this is silly, what are you doing here?"

Through his sobs he said, "I won't sleep with you again, Charlie, or be your lover until I have been punished for what happened to you this afternoon."

"You know I won't hit you, Winston. Hell will freeze over before I will do that."

"I know, Charlie, but I have to be publicly punished and humiliated for what I organised with the guys this afternoon."

"No you don't, Baby. I don't want you punished, and you can't possibly want to be humiliated. You have no idea how awful it was for me each time it happened."

"I have to, Charlie, I am responsible for your bruised butt as surely as if I had paddled you myself."

"Winston, I won't allow it, and that's the end of it."

I got up, left, and had a very miserable week. I stopped the punishment book and retired into my shell. Winston would not budge. The atmosphere around the estate was rotten. Everybody knew why and that Winston was living in the staff quarters.

Cloud came to see me.

"Charlie, you are going to have to give in, you are destroying staff morale and Winston has never been as unhappy as he is now. You are doing a David, his obstinacy ruined this estate for a while, don't do the same, none of us would easily forgive you that."

"I can't, Cloud, he wants me to allow a public punishment. I'll die if he is humiliated and hurt in that way."

"You'll die if he keeps this up, and so will he."

"But it's my fault, Cloud, for being such a slut."

"Winston knows what you are and accepts you, but he thought this might curb you a little and be fun as well. It went wrong, and quite correctly, he is blaming himself for choreographing it. You have to let him make his peace with you in his way."

"Oh Christ, Cloud, I'll die if I have to watch it. I'll give in but beg him to let me be elsewhere."

"I doubt he will, Charlie, so be prepared for it, don't make the rift any wider."

The dye was cast, so I went to Winston's room and told him he could organise his punishment. I wanted to know the details, but not be there to watch it.

"You have to be there, Charlie, otherwise it is meaningless."

"Please no, Baby, I will die watching you humiliated."

"Yes, Charlie."

I loved him and missed him so much. He had never defied me before, but I guess he was a big boy now and strong because of our love.

"Alright, Lover, move your things back into our room, so that I can love you after you have done this."

"Alright, Charlie, it will take place in the staff restaurant after supper tonight."

"Who is going to be there, Winston?"

"All of the Cloud's staff plus Jamie and Luke and Cloud of course as head of the house."

I was shocked, I was very unhappy that Jamie and Luke were to be there and all the Cloud's staff was too much, but he wouldn't bend.

"What punishment are you going to take, Baby, and who is going to administer it?"

"You will see later."

I spent the remainder of the day in an agony of apprehension, but at last we were finished with dinner, and everyone required was in the restaurant. Winston had organised the moving of tables and chairs so that the area in front of the small raised dais was clear. We all stood round in a semi circle in the time-honoured fashion so that everybody had a clear view. Cloud and I were front and centre and Jamie, Luke, Jason and Darren stood at the side of the dais. I had a bad feeling.

Winston came in carrying the paddle and dressed in little white shorts like mine. He stood on the dais and read a prepared statement.

"Charlie reintroduced the chores and punishment book to give you all a bit of fun. I screwed it all up with the result that Charlie was hurt. He was punished and humiliated. I deserve to be as well, and I want you all to witness it. Charlie had his cheeks spread while being fingered, he was spit roasted, he was spanked and he was paddled. Jason gave Charlie ten licks, Jamie and Luke, ten each. They are going to give me the same with the same power behind them after Jamie and Luke spread me for Jason to finger me. Finally, however much I cry or beg, Darren is going to complete my punishment with a further ten administered as hard as he can."

"Oh God, no!" I pleaded, "No Winston, that is too much!"

"Charlie, I have dishonoured you. If you don't let this happen, I will leave the island, and you will never see me again."

I knew he meant it. Suddenly, Winston was the strong one. Cloud put his arm round me and held me close, but nothing was going to help.

Darren was master of ceremonies, but I knew that everything he did would be at Winston's behest.

"Winston, remove your shorts and pass them to me."

He did and stood with his hands by his side, legs astride. Darren stood beside him and started playing with him as he told, Winston, "When I have finished this brief, you will turn round and spread your legs wide. You will bend over and grasp your ankles. Luke and Jamie will pull your cheeks apart while Jason fingers you for five minutes. Jamie and Luke will then spank you for a couple of minutes after which the two guys not administering punishment will hold your shoulders to stop you falling over. I am going to finger fuck you before the first set of ten with the paddle. After each set of ten you will stand, turn round and apologise to Charlie for your stupidity before resuming the position for another finger fucking and the next ten. If you fall at any time, we will take a short break for you to recover and then continue. The punishment will not be complete until you have received all 40 strokes. Do you understand?"

"Yes, Darren, please start."

Jason finger fucked Winston for a good five minutes, positioning himself so that everyone could see while Luke and Jamie held his cheeks apart. It was very erotic, and I think everybody in the room had an erection on except me. I was bleeding for my baby. The humiliation was mind blowing. The spanking followed, but Luke and Jamie were noticeably holding back on the power in the slaps.

The first 30 with the paddle were not too bad. Winston didn't cry even when he saw how stricken I was.

Darren did as he was told, delivering the final ten strokes extremely hard. Winston was screaming but didn't collapse until the last one. Ryan was almost quicker than I to reach Winston with his mother's special salve. I cradled my baby in my arms while Ryan administered the treatment and then Darren and Johnnie carried him to our room where he lay on the bed on his tummy.

"Oh, Baby, that was all so unnecessary."

"No it wasn't, Charlie. I love you so much, and I dishonoured you. I had to be punished and humiliated."

"No you didn't, but it's done. I don't ever want to talk about it again, and I won't involve myself in any more sex apart from with you."

"No Charlie, I don't want that really. Maybe not as blatantly, but I know how much you love it, and besides I thought we were going to have a repeat of my birthday romp."

"You really want to do that again?"

I was amazed.

"Oh yes, please, Charlie, that was so much fun."

"Well why on earth did we have this stupidity?"

"I was just annoyed that you were effectively touting for sex, Charlie. I was embarrassed."

Now I understood what a fool I was. Sex with the others was quite acceptable, but to do it as if I were a slave was too much for Winston.

Over the next few days, I explained to everyone involved what it was all about but made it clear if any of them wanted a romp with me as long as they were discrete, Winston wouldn't mind. Also that I was planning a couple of group romps if any of them were interested.

With the time at Lara's running short, I started to work out harder with Bob. We continued to work out naked frequently with an audience, but usually not Winston, so I stayed flaccid much to Bob's amusement.

"Getting too old to get it up nowadays are we, Charlie?" he said laughing on one of our sessions.

"You think so, Bob? Care for a wager?"

"Go on then, what devious little plan have you got for us?"

"Into your office, now. Last one with a solid erection gets fucked over the desk by the other one."

"You are on."

We were both almost hard before we had closed the door, but I won.

"Oh crikey, Charlie, you are going to have to open me up for ages before I can take that."

"Oh goody because I am going to play with you all the time as well. Clear your desk, Bob. I want you on it on your back with your legs round your ears.

"Kinky bugger, Charlie, but I know I am going to enjoy this."

He was grinning from ear to ear.

I fucked him hard, partly out of lust, partly out of frustration. I was so fucked up over the Winston affair. I wanted back in New York, back to normal, hopefully to forget my stupidity and Winston's humiliation. How could I love him so much but still need other sex romps?

I didn't expect the tension to remain when we returned to New York but it did. Jason and company were very unhappy, and I guessed I was going to lose them if I didn't come up with a good solution. Good old Charlie, the rabbit came out of the hat again.

The new venue in Greenwich Village was ready when we returned, and Jason had shown himself to be a good manager of men always organising the waiting staff, so I made him commercial floor manager and transferred him with Ty, Glen and Julio to G.A.Y. Greenwich. Their replacements were equally as gorgeous, so things didn't change. Everything settled down again, and I had time to really get to grips with all the new developments. I got hold of another Brit to be general manager at G.A.Y., and he was terrific. The place was humming from day one. David was ecstatic, so was I.

I promoted Darren to head chef at G.A.Y. and of course had to transfer Ryan with him. Interviewing new staff was boring, but Winston had done all the advertising in the gay press, so we knew all of our interviewees were gay.

Once again, we were so lucky. The waiter replacements were gorgeous, and Darren's replacement was not only gorgeous but a bloody good chef. He was another Frenchman like Jean Louis only this one was named Pierre – Cloud's 2, here we come.

I had the feeling that by the time we closed Cloud's again, I would need my rest time at Lara's.

Chapter 9

Rick Astley took some stick over his name, particularly as he couldn't sing, but as G.M. of G.A.Y. he was brilliant. Darren liked him a lot, and Ryan was jealous. I laughed.

Jason came to see me about a month after the opening.

"Charlie, I think the best things in my life have happened since I met you. I want to do something for you or to you that will show my gratitude, but I don't know what. Would you like to ask me for something so that I can show my gratitude in a material way?"

I thought about it, and Tom came into my mind.

"I can't tell you right at this moment, but would you be prepared to have a foursome with Winston, myself and a third party?"

"Are you kidding, Charlie, for that I will owe you double?"

"OK. Sit on it for now. It's only an idea."

Whenever I could, I spent time at G.A.Y., on my days off and after Cloud's closed in the evening. I was burning the candle at both ends, but I wanted to make sure that the club was operating properly. I usually ate there to check on Darren's cooking, with Winston of course most times, but occasionally he would be too tired after waiting all evening. Whichever waiter I had was sworn not to tell him the order was for me. Difficult to fault the meals that I varied. Occasionally, I would go down to the kitchen after I had finished and praise Darren for his presentation and quality, always loud enough for the remainder of the kitchen staff to hear. I could almost measure how much taller he was after a pat on the back. Rick and I both worked on the principal that happy staff made good staff, and good staff brought in lots of customers. Jason was a good example. Loyal to me above all others and appreciative of what I had done for him.

One night, soon after I arrived, I saw Tom enter the main bar. I had completed a tour of the club and was heading in the same direction. He played right into my hands coming up to the bar next to Winston. As I walked up to the bar on the other side of Winston, I said, "Good evening, Tom, good to see you in a respectable establishment."

"Hello, Charlie, how good to see you. I come here often hoping I will."

Realising he had been talking across a third party, Tom blushed a little, and before I could say anything he looked at Winston, and in a very polite manner said, "I really am terribly sorry to talk across you. I forgot my manners, please let me buy you a drink by way of an apology."

Winston was so surprised, he looked at me and said, "May I, Charlie?"

I kissed him on the nose and replied, "Of course, Baby. Tom, this is Winston, Winston, Tom, remember David's friend?"

Tom looked closely at Winston saying how pleased he was to meet him.

"Jeez, Charlie, no wonder you are not interested in any proposals levelled at you. Winston you are incredibly gorgeous. I'm not surprised Charlie loves you so much."

Winston was blushing like crazy and found it very difficult to get the words of thanks out.

The barman saw me at that moment and hurried down the bar. "Good evening, Sir, Mr. Fellows, what can I get you?"

"Hello, Nick, I'll have my usual and whatever these two gentlemen want."

"Hi, Winston, the usual?"

Winston nodded, and Nick filled Tom's order as well giving me a chit to sign. Stocktaking was a rigorous action here, so my drinks had to be accounted for even if no money changed hands.

"Tom, please join Winston and me for dinner."

"Thanks, Charlie, I would like that."

Dinner was a lively affair. It was obvious that Winston was highly enamoured by Tom's good manners and Old World charm, and Winston besotted Tom. Not often I took a back seat with either of these two, but tonight I could have been somewhere else, which was what I was after the main course. I went to see if Jason was going to be free the same night as my next one off. He was, so when I got back to the table, I asked Winston if he would like Tom to come for dinner at the apartment our next night off along with Jason.

"Yes, I'd like that, Charlie, but why Jason?"

"He is doing a terrific job here, and I would like to reward him. Jason is my commercial floor manager here, Tom, but he started as a waiter at Cloud's when we first opened."

After dinner, Winston went to the little boys' room giving me an opportunity to talk to Tom.

"How would you like to end up in a foursome with Winston, myself and Jason when you come to dinner?"

"You must know the answer to that one, Charlie, without asking. Winston is beautiful, and you are still without doubt the best fuck in New York if you'll excuse the crudity."

"Good, I'll engineer it, but I want you to fuck Winston. I want him to feel that amazing cock of yours."

"Won't he mind?"

"A little, but he will be fine if I am there as well, and he has been in an orgy with some of my other waiters and kitchen staff, so he is not a complete novice. I want him to feel what it is like to be kissed by you and then feel your amazing equipment inside him."

A few nights later, the event took place. I cooked dinner for the four of us, unusual for me. I kept it light because I wanted everybody to be fit for some serious loving before the evening was through. We ate early and afterwards, we played cards, eventually I worked it around to strip poker with forfeits. We had a 75% chance on Tom, Jason or I winning, so I had pre-briefed the other two on what should happen with the forfeits. If things went wrong, it would be fun to see how Winston handled things. I had made it clear that the winner could have up to two hours to take sexual forfeits from everybody else. The plan worked perfectly, Jason won. His brief was that he should have Tom make love to Winston, but for the rest, he could do what he liked.

"I have always wanted to make love to you, Charlie, and to Winston. I achieved it with you at Lara's house, so tonight I think Tom and I should both find out what makes Winston so special for you. I want Tom and I to spend about half an hour exploring Winston's body before opening him up to take me first and then Tom."

That wasn't part of the plan, but I could hardly complain.

"While we are pleasuring Winston, Charlie, I want you to spend equal time between Tom and me keeping us both excited. When I have taken my pleasure with Winston, Tom can enter him and you can shag me. If Winston is still horny after that, Tom and I can watch him shagging you doggy fashion. How does that sound?"

Winston piped up first.

"That sounds like fun. I am sure I will still be horny after Tom has had me, so you won't mind if I shag you with an audience will you, Charlie?"

I hugged him and told him that of course I wouldn't mind.

So it began. Winston was in the centre of our big bed with Tom and Jason either side. Tom kissed Winston on the lips, gently at first and then more passionately. My Baby's eyes popped open to look at me when he realised what a fabulous kisser Tom was.

When Tom allowed him to come up for air, he looked at me and said, "Golly, Charlie, I have never been kissed like that before. You aren't upset that I am enjoying it are you?"

I leant across and kissed him on the nose.

"How could I be upset, Lover, anything that gives you pleasure is more than OK with me. Relax, let Tom and Jason pleasure you."

Jason started at the bottom, licking his way up Winston's legs until his head was buried in his crotch. They had split Winston rather well. Tom was using his hands and lips to attack the top half, especially nipples and lips while Jason paid most attention to the inside of Winston's thighs and his genitals. Very quickly, my baby was gasping, his breathing becoming more ragged as time passed. I started in on Tom's cock swapping every so often to Jason. I was in cock heaven. Tom's was as rock hard as I remembered it. I was licking and kissing it, taking it all down my throat, amazed at its rigidity. I put one of Jason's hands on it to see his reaction.

"Gosh, Charlie, that is like a steel pole."

Tom giggled, "Yes, it does get hard doesn't it."

Kissing Winston again, Tom said to him, “You are so beautiful to look at and to touch, Winston. I think little Tom might be even harder than he was when I shagged Charlie.”

“I like that, Tom, don’t keep me waiting too long for it will you.”

Winston was truly getting into this and I loved it. When we had sex, I just concentrated on letting him see how much I loved him, but tonight I could step back and look at the big picture. He loved sex, and because he was comfortable with both Tom and Jason, he was having a ball feeling the different sensations that a stranger could conjure up. It was magical, incredibly erotic as well of course. Jason eventually started to open him up ready to take his cock. He was being very gentle and using a lot of lube. I did the same with Jason’s cock still using my mouth on his balls and my tongue on his hole.

Tom was pleasuring Winston’s top half as Jason entered him. It was incredible to watch. Tom was kissing Winston’s nipples and nibbling them occasionally as Jason long stroked him. I watched two wonderful young men orgasm very close together having both so obviously enjoyed their parts in the proceedings. When Jason withdrew, I watched them both pleasure Winston back to an erection and then Tom entered him. Winston’s eyes shot open and he looked at me shocked.

“Oh, Charlie, what is he doing to my insides? This is amazing.”

I kissed him passionately on the lips and said, “Yes it is, Lover, and he gets better with practice.”

“Your turn, Charlie, I just want you to open me up and screw me hard. I don’t care whether I have another orgasm or not. I just want to feel that monster raging around my insides,” Jason declared.

“Jason, that will be no problem.”

I opened him up and entered him with no preamble. He struggled to take me at first but soon relaxed and enjoyed it, cumming again very quickly. I hung on because I wanted to cum the same time as Tom and Winston. It worked, but I nearly lost it hearing Winston’s squeal of delight as Tom did amazing things with his cock just before cumming. Jason came again as well because I kept pounding his ass long after everyone else had finished. Winston had orgasmed twice with each of the others, so I thought I was safe. Wrong, he was so turned on he wanted to take me as planned. Tom and Jason could not take their eyes off us as Winston entered me doggy fashion pulling me up against him very early to make sure that I was thoroughly excited, which of course I was. He fucked me very slowly for what seemed hours. God it was wonderful, his cock sliding in and out of me had me cumming all over the place twice before he turned me over onto my back and managed to get me a third orgasm by playing with me before exploding inside me.

We all showered and then sat around drinking and talking for a while.

“You know, Jason, you ought to entice Tom into bed. That phallus of his is the most amazing peace of kit I have ever had inside me.”

Tom looked at Jason and laughing, said, "You won't need to try very hard Jason. You are a delightful young man, and I would consider it an honour to make love to you."

"I agree with Charlie, Jason, Tom is good enough to come back for second helpings if Charlie ever wants to set it up again."

"Whoa, I am going to have to watch you, Tom, or I will be losing my lover and my commercial floor manager."

I had a lap full of lover two seconds after that comment.

"No you won't, Charlie, you will never lose me if you live to be a hundred, but I wouldn't mind another orgy with Tom."

I winked at Tom and laughing said to all of them, "Perhaps it would be nice to do this again only with a bigger crowd of our friends."

Winston jumped up and had us all in fits of laughter bouncing round the room and saying, "Oh yes, please, Charlie, all of our Lara's House friends and Jason's crew. Wouldn't that be fun?"

Winston told me later that because Jason was a good three or four inches shorter than me and not so thick, he was easier to take making it a comfortable shag but not as satisfying as having a real monster inside him. As for Tom, he said no shag in his life had ever been so amazing. Tom's cock was exactly as I had described it, like a rod of metal. He did look a little apprehensive telling me the last bit until I agreed with him.

"I know, Lover, I would quite like to experience it again myself. What amazes me is that Tom does not have a regular boyfriend. I should ask him why sometime."

We didn't have the great orgy Winston suggested, but Jason told us he and Tom had tried another session in private and had enjoyed each other's company enormously. In fact, they were seeing each other regularly now. I was so pleased. They were two wonderful guys, and it gave me pleasure to see them happy.

One evening in G.A.Y. while Jason was working, Tom and I sat at the bar, and I asked him why he had no boyfriends before when I knew him. His reply was a shocker.

"Charlie, I fell in love with you the first time I saw you at David's apartment. Until I met Jason, no one came even close to interesting me. Thank you for introducing me to him. He is not you, but he is a delight to be with, and I think I am falling in love with him."

"Look after him, Tom. He is very special you know. Like all my boys, I would not want to see him hurt emotionally."

"I know, Charlie, I guess your love and concern for them is why all of us are in love with you first and our own boyfriends second. How do you do it? You have so much love it is almost overwhelming."

"Don't say things like that, Tom. I feel really embarrassed when I am flattered. I'm not even that special, I just like sex with all those guys."

"Yeah, right. I could give you a rude answer to that, but that would detract from my previous comment. You are special, do you think David would have released you from four years of a slave contract, given you a half share of the most successful restaurant in New York and sold you a multi-million-dollar estate in the Grenadines for $1 if you weren't special. Oh and for a bonus actually made you a cash millionaire on top of that."

"Can we change the subject, Tom? I can't win this one, and I get antsy when I lose."

Tom laughed and said, "You are a classic, Charlie, no wonder I still love you. By the way, will I be seeing you at David's on Friday?"

"I'm sorry, Tom, I don't think so. I haven't heard anything."

"Oh I'm sure I will. You'll see."

When I arrived home, there was an invitation from David to a cocktail party on Friday evening at his apartment. That meant an intimate gathering. Large ones he hired a venue for. The invitation specified tuxedo, so business more than pleasure. I wondered what it could be.

No one appeared to know anything about it, and I drove Winston mad trying to guess what it could be. However, we found out half an hour after arriving. There were about two dozen people present, mostly businessmen friends of David. Tom and Jason were there, so we had our own little group while we waited for David to join us.

He joined us after about ten minutes accompanied by a man I knew to be his business advisor.

"Charlie, would you join me in my study for a moment?"

When we were seated, he said, "Charlie, I want to make Cloud's into a public company. If you say yes, your holding will drop to about 30%, but you will immediately see that holding valued at approximately $20 million. You will also see cash of $10 million go straight into your bank account. That is triple what you said you wanted to be worth when our contract ended in four years time. You also have a $10 million estate, so I would suggest you are well ahead of the game on my guidance. What do you say?"

"Why, David?"

"So that we can borrow the capitol we need to open three more Cloud's restaurants this year."

"Are you serious, David?"

"Absolutely, Charlie, but only if you would like to revise your worth at the end of our original contract date to about 60 or 70 million."

"I don't know what to say, David. In principle, it sounds terrific, but I would like to look at the details."

"Charlie, I am doing this for you, as an ongoing commitment to show you how much I love you."

"Oh crikey, David, I am beginning to feel depressed at all these declarations of love. But yes, you can go ahead. You want to announce it tonight, don't you?"

"Yes, with one more surprise for you. Come on let's join the guests."

I wondered what else David had up his sleeve, not for long though.

"Ladies and gentlemen, can I have your attention for a few minutes? I would like to announce that Monday morning Cloud's Restaurants will be quoted on the New York Stock Exchange, we have gone public."

There were a lot of stunned faces and a few smiles.

"I would also like to introduce you to Tom Latimer who will be taking over as CEO of the new company. Tom is demonstrating his faith in the company by purchasing the first $1 million worth of shares on public offer."

I was stunned, I had no idea Tom was worth that kind of money or was qualified to take the new company forward.

"Tom, you old devil, I had no idea you were a rich man and a management talent."

"I'm not a rich man, Charlie, but I hope by making you and David richer, I will get that way on your shirt tails."

I laughed, "No, Tom, we will get richer on you shirt tails."

"Charlie, I will need to seek you and David's approval for some of my appointments as the company expands, but I would like to ask a favour of you for one of them now."

"Go ahead, Tom, you know how much I think of you. If it is possible, I will approve it."

"Our next Cloud's will be in Boston, our new corporate HQ will be there as well. If I promise to keep an eye on him in the early days, can I make Jason general manager of the new house?"

"Do you think he is ready for that sort of promotion, Tom?"

"Not at the moment, Charlie, but he will be by the time we open in about nine months time."

"OK, Tom, a leap of faith because I love you both, yes. I will clear it with David. He thinks I have a Midas touch with picking staff, so I don't expect to have any trouble with him."

Winston and I circulated, talking to the other guests whom David told me were going to be big investors.

"I hope the new restaurant's waiters will be as delightful as Winston, Charlie, it wouldn't be Cloud's without that."

"Thank you, I will certainly try."

Winston blushed, and I stood another ten feet tall.

Jason embarrassed me a few minutes after Tom left me. He was crying as he plastered a huge kiss on my lips and said through his tears.

"Charlie, I love you so much, thank you, thank you, thank you."

My baby looked at me in shock and said, "What on earth was that all about?"

"I promised Tom that Jason would be the general manager of the new Cloud's in Boston."

"Charlie, you prove how special you are almost every time you turn around. I love you so much just for being you."

I love happy stories don't you? All the grief I went through to get where I am now almost seems worth it. I could have done without the coma, but the rest doesn't appear that bad in hindsight. After all, what's a little pain if it makes you millions?

"Charlie, I think you had better let your deputy handle tomorrow night in the restaurant. You and I are going to be busy for the foreseeable future starting Monday, so you only have two days to make certain he is up to it."

"OK, David, as long as you understand that he goes to Boston, and I remain here."

"Of course, Charlie, I am not letting you get completely away from me."

My new title was Joint President, in charge of acquisitions, and David was Joint President in charge of finance. Very grandiose, but it meant a considerable amount of hard work and travel. Finding the perfect venue in Boston proved very difficult for both the restaurant and the corporate HQ. We also started putting feelers out in Washington, DC. Our biggest headache though was chefs. I would have to give up doing it full time and that meant finding two more immediately and others later if we continued to expand. I terminated Winston's employment as a waiter immediately and made him my personal assistant. I was going to be out of New York more than in it, and there was no way I was doing that without him.

We soon became regular visitors to Boston and always took a suite at the same hotel. The room staff soon had the whole hotel aware that only one bedroom in our suite was ever used, but Winston could charm the knickers off a virgin if he had wanted to, so we never had any problems. A lot of knowing glances, but my reputation and Winston's charm kept us free of aggravation. Tom had his own apartment with Jason who was at business school and under Tom's guidance, as well as helping with corporate business. I wondered how they ever found time for loving, but they obviously did because both looked so contented.

We had dinner together the day we found the perfect HQ, to celebrate. It was the top two floors of the most prestigious new office building in Boston. Ludicrously expensive, but Tom convinced me that as we expanded we could buy up other leases in the block and enhance our reputation way above the cost.

Dinner was terrific, and I couldn't resist mentioning the last time we had been a foursome. Jason blushed as he said, "Tom and I have made a vow to be monogamous with each other because we love each other very much, Charlie. But we have both agreed that if you ever wanted either of us again we would wave that vow."

Here it was again, I had never, and probably never would understand how perfectly sane intelligent people could be so stupid around me.

I pulled them into a tight embrace and kissed them both hard on the lips before saying, “You two are totally insane. I am over the moon to hear your dedication for each other. I am flattered that you love me enough to wave your vow, but I swear it is never going to happen now, much as I would love to do what we did before with the addition of Tom feeding me that rod of steel that he has between his legs.”

“Thank you, Charlie, we have come a long way in a very short space of time haven’t we? I could never have imagined that three years after you interviewed me for a waiter’s job I would be General Manager Designate of Cloud’s Boston. I love Tom so much for what we have now, but I will never stop loving you for your friendship and the opportunities you have given me.”

I was tearing up. I hadn’t done that for ages.

“Just don’t let me down then.”

The next day we went over the offices, and Tom said, “I doubt you and David will ever be here together, so you are going to share the presidents suite until we have some more income generating outlets. I will, however, put two desks in there just in case.”

“Thank you, Tom. I am pleased to see you are not wasting my money.”

We laughed and continued the unenviable task of finding a new restaurant site.

When we returned to New York, we found Pierre, the chef at Cloud’s, coping very well.

Unless Tom came up with a new venue to look at, I was going to be in New York for a few weeks, so I thought it was opportune for Winston to go off to see his family. He had barely been out of my sight for a couple of years. He went, reluctantly, leaving me to work with David on the new company. G.A.Y. had remained out of the deal and therefore still belonged totally to David and me.

“You are crafty, David, G.A.Y. is hugely profitable, and we still don’t have to share it with anyone.”

“Mmm, I told you I would look after your investments, Charlie.”

“I don’t know what to say, this is amazing, I am worth another couple of million at least because of that move. How can I ever thank you?”

“How about reverting to slave status for an evening to pleasure me and a few friends, Charlie. Everybody sworn to secrecy of course.”

“Are you serious, David?”

“Yes, Charlie. These people know about your previous existence before you became my business partner. We all think you are incredibly cute and would love to pleasure you.”

“How much of a slave would I have to be, David? You know I love sex, but I don’t want anything else to be too heavy.”

"OK, how about limiting it. You set those limits, and I make certain no one exceeds them."

"I can live with that I reckon. I do owe you big time, and you know I like to pay my debts. Besides, for a couple of million dollars, I should not complain if you wanted to do worse than anything that has happened to me before."

"Mmm, I will try not to hold you to that, Charlie, on the night."

I never appear to learn do I? After all the problems I had being a slave and being subject to unbelievably great sex, I forgot how horrible the punishment and humiliation could be.

"Charlie, before you commit to this, I want to talk to you about safe sex."

I wondered what was coming. David knew I romped with anyone I liked who also liked me, always had done, with Winston's tacit agreement of course, after I was a free man and as David's slave whenever he wanted me to before that.

"Most of my guests for the slavery night have multiple sex partners, some of whom are not very careful, so I want them all to wear condoms for penetrative sex. I am aware that you and Winston have unprotected sex with the Lara's House boys and some of your Cloud's boys as well, but you are all in a closed sex community, when they go out of it, they use safe sex practices."

"That will kill the spontaneity a bit won't it, David?"

"Probably, Charlie, but I don't want you to take the risk."

"OK, you're the boss."

"Good, that's settled then. I'll make sure there's a good supply of condoms."

On the night, I only recognised three of the guys present. They were two of David's friends who had been part of the brutal evening with the Russian boys. I was unhappy about that but knew that there were limits this time. The other one was an ex of David's that I recognised. The others were all young as well, which meant I would almost certainly be enjoying the sex – eight plus David.

David had brought me into the room dressed in my little white shorts and carrying the paddle, just like before I became a free man.

"Gentlemen, Charlie has volunteered to become a slave again just for tonight. Instead of pleasuring your palettes at Cloud's, he will indulge your sexual appetites here. He has set limits that you may not break, but in response to you honouring those he will not back out of any thing else, which should give you enormous scope to take pleasure from his body in any way you choose. I hope you will keep the humiliation down to a reasonable level, but he has not set you any limits on that. The only limits tonight therefore are that you may not paddle him so hard, or commit any sex act that incapacitates him in any way, and if you fuck him you must wear a condom. Gregg, you were here when Charlie entertained us once before, perhaps you would like to get the ball rolling."

"Thanks, David, I'd love to. Charlie, to make life easy for us, whoever is commanding you at any particular time can start you off in one of four positions which need no explanation. I will get you into them now so that they can see. The first one, when I say 'slave standing' you stand legs astride about three feet apart hands clasped behind your head and looking at the floor. Second is 'suck slut,' you get on your knees, ankles crossed but knees apart, hands gripped behind your back, head up with your mouth open and your tongue out. Third is 'fuck slut,' on the coffee table on your back, legs pulled back and wide open, your ass just hanging over the end. Fourth is 'spit roast,' you get on all fours, legs wide and head up with your tongue out. Are they all clear, Charlie?"

"Yes, Gregg, very inventive."

"Don't be cheeky, Charlie, or I will have to chastise you. Remember you are a slave. We had better add a fifth one, 'punishment position,' lean over the chair, grip the arms and spread your legs wide. OK, try them as I call them. Slave standing, suck slut, fuck slut, oh yes, I like that one Charlie, naked that will be amazing, spit roast, good. Now take your shorts off Charlie and punishment position."

Gregg picked up the paddle as soon as I was in position and said, "This is for being cheeky, Charlie. Five licks to make you smart a little."

They were just hard enough to sting, so very erotic. When I stood up, I was rock hard.

"Slave standing, Charlie"

He took my hard cock in his hand and looking around the room said to all the others, "Charlie, obviously gets off on a little corporal punishment, so we know how to keep him erect tonight."

His laugh was not nice. I could see I was not going to enjoy Gregg's ministrations.

Next up was a boy really. He was someone I had seen David pick up one night when we were clubbing together. I remembered his name was Sean. I guessed him to be early twenties, probably five years younger than me. He had stripped naked showing off a very tight body, well muscled with a cock in proportion, extremely hard.

"I want a lot of your body tonight, slave, so I am getting in early."

He took my balls in hand and started to play with them, standing to the side, he could attack my butt. Caressing each cheek and slowly running his hand up and down the crack, he stopped at my hole and worried it, wetting his finger to make it slither around easier. Running another wet finger up and down the underside of my monster at the same time as he slid a finger inside my anus, had me gasping, and I nearly came.

"Not yet, Charlie, suck slut."

As soon as I was in position, he said, “Blowjob, slave, to orgasm, take your time though.”

The others sat around in varying stages of undress watching the action. All that is except, Gregg, who went round behind me and started playing with my butt and my cock and balls.

Sean was great, very responsive and with a tidy seven or eight inches, comfortable to suck and easy to deep throat. He loved me taking all of him and playing with his balls as well. Gregg, who was being a little rough spoilt the action, he was opening me up ready for someone to fuck me I guessed.

The boy came in my mouth with the instruction, “Swallow it all, slave, or you are in trouble.”

I couldn’t, there was simply too much of it too quickly, so I let a little of it dribble out of my mouth onto his shaft.

“Lick me clean, Charlie, and then assume fuck slut. I am going to paddle you in that position for disobeying me.”

I assumed the position, but the boy wasn’t happy with that.

“Would two of you take the slave’s legs and pull them back further and wider for me?”

The two who I didn’t know obliged so that my ass was almost facing the ceiling and my spread legs were showing my hole to very good effect. The boy then administered another five licks with the paddle, just a little harder than Gregg, but not enough to have me screaming or crying.

“David, can I be next with our slave?”

“Dig out, Tony, he’s all yours.”

“OK, guys stay on his legs, but let them drop a little so that I can shag him while standing.”

Tony had stripped and now showed me a very thick eight- or nine-inch cock.

“Charlie you can slick this up with your mouth while Gregg opens you up and lubes you and then you can roll on a condom before I fuck you.”

His cock was great, I loved the feel of it as it slid over my lips, and I used my tongue to get a good taste of it as well as pleasure Tony. When he pulled out, I said to him, “I’m sorry I have to cover that beautiful tool, Tony, I would like to feel that powering into me bareback.”

“So would I, Charlie, if even half of what I hear is true, you have the sweetest love tunnel in New York.”

He lubed his cock and entered me in one smooth movement stopping when he had passed over my sphincter to give me a chance to adjust.

“That is nice, Tony, you can go all the way now.”

He did, and continued to fuck me with long slow strokes.

“Oh, crikey, Tony that is beautiful, it feels like heaven.”

“Well thank you kind, Sir, even through this, rubber so do you.”

I looked around at that moment, and everyone was now naked with several of them massaging very erect cocks while they watched. David leant over me and kissed me passionately on the lips.

"Watching someone else make love to you rather than just rape you looks fantastic, Charlie. Can I record this with my cam?"

"Of course, David, provided I can have a copy."

I was laughing, this was turning into a very pleasant orgy for me, Gregg aside.

"Everyone, Charlie says I can record tonight's action. If you allow it there will only be two copies, Charlie's and mine. Anyone have a problem with that?"

No dissenters, so I now have a copy of that night.

Tony continued to shag me for ages, eventually giving us both wonderful orgasms.

Gregg spoilt it of course deciding that the quickest way to get me hard again was to paddle me. It worked, but I was getting sore having now taken nearly 20 licks.

I remained in the same position for ages receiving another four dicks. None as erotic as Tony unfortunately.

Sean was the last of the four.

"Spit roast slave."

Always obedient I rolled off the table onto all fours. Sean was inside me almost before I was settled.

"Whoa, steady cowboy, give me a chance to get comfortable." Wrong thing to say with Gregg at my head.

"You have been out of slavery too long, Charlie, you have forgotten how to behave. After Sean and I have finished fucking both ends, I think I should show you properly your place tonight."

Sean, the boy, did a Tony on me that had me cumming all over the carpet. Gregg was quite rough, which was about what I expected, but he realised that I could give him a fantastic blowjob if he allowed me to and calmed down a little.

When they had both finished, Gregg said, "Suck slut."

When I was in position, he slid his now soft cock into my mouth and said.

"Grip it tight with your mouth, Charlie, and swallow whatever I give you. This should cement your position as a slave."

I didn't know what he meant, but I did as I was told. He took hold of my head so that I could not pull off him and then I felt a warm liquid start flowing into my mouth. I took the first swallow before I realised he was pissing in me. I could not pull away he was holding me too hard, and I had to keep swallowing or choke. David realised what he was doing and pulled him off me, but by then I had swallowed a gallon I'm sure, more of it splashed over my face and chest as he was pulled off me. I fled to the bathroom and threw up. Washed my mouth and throat out with water and then mouthwashed with Corsodyl.

I walked back into the room feeling ashamed and humiliated beyond belief. Everyone showed how sympathetic they were towards my plight and David said we could wrap it up if I wanted to.

"Gregg is history, Charlie, so what we do now is entirely up to you."

Sean was next. "I am really truly sorry, Charlie, I had no idea Gregg planned something like that. Having you as a slave has been fantastic fun and so erotic. You are a great sex machine, please let us carry on."

"David, that was gross. Even as a proper slave, I never had to do that. Provided no one else tries to do anything gross, I don't mind carrying on. After all, you have paid me a lot of money for tonight." I was laughing as I said it and one of the guests who was an obvious voyeur because he had not touched me said, "How much is a lot of money, Charlie?"

I looked at David who nodded at me and I said, "Something over $2 million."

The room went deathly silent. Sean gasped then and said, "You are kidding, Charlie."

"No, it might even be more. David and I haven't valued it accurately."

"Wow, I have just had the most expensive rent boy in history, Charlie."

That was Tony who gave me a very passionate kiss.

"Thank you, Charlie, can I fuck you again?"

"Yeah, I guess so."

He did, doggy fashion this time with David filling the other hole. Crikey, it was good. Tony was better than before because he was playing with me as well, and David's cock in my mouth was like tasting an old friend he was so familiar to me.

I realised when I felt Tony sperm up my inside that he had gone bareback. He did as well when he came down from his high.

"Oh God, I'm sorry, Charlie, but I know I am clean. I'm so sorry."

I looked at David, who said, "Blood tests all round in the morning, I think, and for you, Charlie, another one before Winston returns and every three months for the remainder of this year."

I was devastated. I would have to tell Winston about tonight and not have invasive sex with him for at least six months unless I wore a condom. We wrapped it up after that with Tony still apologising as he went out the door.

"I'm sorry, too, Charlie I never thought about it getting out of hand. Gregg was bad enough, but the possibility of Tony's action being worse is frightening. Not worth $20 million never mind $2 million."

All the blood tests were negative, and Tony swore he had not had unprotected sex for years, so I felt easier, but I still would not touch Winston when he returned. I told him why and he was shocked.

"How could you, Charlie, you have always been a sex slut, so I never thought you would let something this stupid happen to you. What was the point of becoming a free man if you then put yourself back into slavery and risk this new disease?"

I felt ashamed and devastated when Winston moved his gear into the second bedroom.

"Please, Baby, don't do this to me."

"I'm sorry, Charlie, I have to think about what you have done."

For weeks, he would barely talk to me and went back to Cloud's to work as a Waiter.

"I don't want to be your personal assistant, Charlie, not while my brain is trying to register and analyse what your actions mean to our relationship."

I sunk into a depression that would not move. Everything I did was completed like an automaton. After three months, I was a complete wreck, Winston had not budged, he was as unhappy as I was, but he continued to work as a waiter, and I kept swanning off to Boston and Washington. We did find the two new restaurant sites, and I found another chef to understudy Pierre at the New York venue. Life then became even more difficult because I was again working with Winston, and yes, the atmosphere deteriorated.

Three months after my stupidity, the Doctor who had treated both Tony and me said that working on what Tony had said and done there was now no chance of any infection having been passed. I could resume normal activity. I told Winston that night that I was clean and clear.

"I'm pleased for you, Charlie. I have been so worried." There were tears in his eyes as he continued, "I think I want to leave New York now that I know you are safe, Charlie. I have some money saved, so I am going home to start again."

I sat down where I was and bawled my eyes out. After a while, it became gut wrenching sobs through which I tried to talk, "I love you so much, Winston, I will do anything, promise anything you want, but please don't leave me. My life is nothing without you. I'm sorry I have been such a slut. Please don't leave me. I can't live without you, you are my life."

"I have to, Charlie. If you loved me as much as you say, you would never have put yourself at this huge risk. If you had caught anything, I could have spent years watching you die and that would have destroyed me as well. We nearly died for each other once and contemplated it a second time. I can't believe that you would so wantonly destroy us like this."

When I came in from work the next day, he was gone. I left Pierre to look after the new chef, and I told David I was going away for a while. I would not be needed again for several months for anything important. There was no argument. David knew why and felt guilty for his part in my depression.

"Go to Lara's, Charlie." I did.

Mac and Cloud were shocked when they saw me and even more so when they heard the story and realised Winston and I were history. I slid deeper into depression barely looked at Jamie and Luke who would normally have been in my bed very quickly. I could not remember the last time I had an erection.

Six months after that stupid night, I had my first seizure. David sent a medical team to me instead of risking me travelling. I was fed intravenously for some time before being allowed to get up. I took to the pool most days and just lay around doing nothing. Some of the staff came to frolic, but I showed no interest. I lost a huge amount of weight that the doctors decided was going to kill me.

"Charlie, if you have a death wish, we can't help you. At your present rate of decline, you may have another six months to live unless you get yourself out of this depression and start to eat. We can't do anything else for you."

"Thank you, Doc, it doesn't matter."

I saw Cloud that night and asked him to get my lawyer here from New York as soon as possible. I wanted to write my will, and then I decided I was going to end it. Life without Winston was not life it was hell.

Mac disappeared the next day, and I was told he had taken some leave. Mac had taken no leave since I became boss of Lara's, and if I had been well, I would have smelt a rat but I was past caring.

I made my will, made sure that I had thought of everybody and made ready to die.

Chapter 10

"Hello Winston."

"Mac, what are you doing here, how did you find me?"

"Not difficult young man. Your island, a bar called Winston's and the best-looking Barman in the world. You were easy."

"Yeah I guess I didn't hide very well did I? You look ill, Mac, are you here to recuperate?"

"I hope so. You look well, Winston. Is life being good to you?"

"I can't complain, Mac. I am learning to live again without Charlie, it's not easy, but my family loves me and looks after me."

"Lara's people are the only family Charlie has, but that isn't enough, so you are lucky."

"How is Charlie, Mac? Is he well?"

"Charlie is dying, Winston, the doctors give him less than six months to live. I know him, and I give him less than six weeks, but I don't think he will wait that long either. I don't want to watch him die, so I have left the estate for a couple of weeks."

"What is he dying from, Mac? Did he get something from that stupid slave session after all?"

"Not directly, Winston. The doctors don't have a medical term for Charlie's illness. They just say he has lost the will to live. You and I would say he is dying of a broken heart. He truly does love you more than life itself, and I guess in a couple of weeks, I will go to a funeral to prove it."

"You're winding me up, Mac, aren't you? This is a ploy to get me back with Charlie?"

"No, Winston, it is probably too late for that already. Charlie is being fed through a drip and spends most of his time on life support. In fact, it is the doctors who are keeping him alive. I don't know why they don't let him die. He doesn't want to live. They are just prolonging the agony for everyone who loves him. Anyway, it was nice to see you again, Winston. I will come in again before I return to Lara's House. Cloud will call me to let me know when to go back."

If that doesn't work then Charlie is dead, Mac thought as he walked back to his hotel.

Winston was at Lara's House less than 24 hours after talking to Mac, to be met by Cloud.

"Hello Winston, I'm sorry, you may be too late to talk to Charlie. He is nearly gone. You had better go and see him straight away, but be prepared for him not to recognise you, and he probably won't be strong enough to talk to you either."

"He can't die, Cloud. I love him so much. I just didn't think I could live with him again after that stupid thing at David's when I was home with my family."

"I know, youngster, no one is blaming you. Go and see him. He is in the master suite as usual."

Winston was visibly shocked when he saw Charlie. There was nothing of him. He looked as though he only weighed about five stone.

"Charlie, hello, I've come back. I love you so much, I'm sorry. Please get well. I don't want to have to come looking for you if you go to that other place again. We can work this out together, Charlie, but you have to get well for me."

Winston felt a very slight pressure from the hand he was holding.

"I'm sorry, Winston, I'm so tired."

Winston started to cry quietly and through his tears he kept repeating, "I love you, Charlie. Please don't die. I love you so much. I'm sorry. I'll never leave you again. Please, Charlie, don't die, please get well."

The doctors found him weeping over Charlie's lifeless form when they entered the room. They knew who he was and realised there was a very slim chance they could save the life of their patient.

The battle to save Charlie's life was won within a couple of days, but the damage to his body could not be calculated. His heart had almost certainly sustained damage and other organs were unlikely to have escaped unscathed. The truth was that he was almost certainly going to be a partial invalid for the remainder of his life. Winston, as before, never left his side. It was two months before Charlie got out of his wheelchair. His high protein diet and plenty of fresh air and sunshine were working wonders, but regaining all the lost body weight was a major problem. After six months, he was strong enough to talk about light work. With Winston never more than a few feet away from him, Charlie flew to New York for talks with David and then on to Boston to interview the staff for the new restaurant. Winston knocked work on the head the second he thought Charlie was tiring.

* * * * *

"I need to get the staff and the restaurant itself sorted, Winston. You can't keep pulling me off the job after only a couple of hours."

"I can and I will, Charlie, if you don't do as I tell you. I will go home again."

"That is blackmail."

"I know but you have nearly died on me twice. I am not going to give you the chance to make it three."

Tom and Jason were doing a terrific job, so in the end, I agreed to leave Boston to them and concentrate on Washington. That was further behind than Boston and didn't need such heavy work schedules from management.

David put his private jet at my disposal so that the stress of air travel was removed. Bob was brought over from Lara's House to travel with me all the time and start me on a light fitness programme.

The next two years went by very quickly. I suppose it was because I was as busy as my weak state would allow, and there were new Cloud's restaurants opening all along the Eastern Seaboard. As with the first Cloud's, I did much of the planning using video links and stayed at Lara's House. Cloud, Mac and Winston clucked around me like old mother hens. Bob never far from me either continued working on my body. The doctors were still worried about my internal state and much to my pleasure, Ronald Macdonald turned up at Lara's one day with a load of equipment.

"Hello, Charlie, David thought I might be able to keep you in check, so I am now your personal nemesis. I will be monitoring your insides while Bob looks after your outside."

My first session with him was a real hoot. I was wired up to machines that were checking my heart, brain, lungs, liver and God knows what.

"Charlie, you are one very, very lucky man. All of your internal equipment looks to be in a far better state than you have any right to. You nearly kill yourself with neglect, are told you will be an invalid for life, and here you are looking almost as good as when I last saw you. But you are still going to take it easy."

Glands and prostate check were where the hoot started. I remained totally flaccid.

"My God, Charlie, you must be ill. That thing never stays soft during your medicals."

He played with me while laughing about my limp dick. I had to laugh as well. The only person not laughing about my flaccid cock was Winston. He had not had sex with me for longer than I could remember.

Training the chefs to do my recipes was my most important job and picking staff the next priority. Word of mouth brought many beautiful young men for interviews, all willing to relocate if necessary to work in a Cloud's restaurant.

Darren moved into Cloud's New York as premier chef bringing Ryan with him as his deputy. Johnnie became senior chef at G.A.Y. Peter, at 27, became the wine and other beverages manager for the group, based in Boston. Paul was at the Boston Cloud's as Maitre D. They were as delightful as ever and confided in me that they had taken to the habit of threesomes all the time. Whoever picked them up had two beautiful young men instead of one. How lucky was that.

Every one of the original Cloud's staff had moved up within the company on merit, and at intervals told me how much they still loved me and respected me for the lifestyles they now had because of my faith in them.

We opened our tenth Cloud's one-month before my thirtieth birthday. David, Tom and Peter flew in from New York and Boston. Winston and I were already there with Bob, (my faithful minder who had brought me back to shape), and Ronald who wasn't really needed anymore but who was now part of my entourage. I flew Mac and Cloud in from Lara's making a huge fuss of

Cloud who was responsible for the name of the group. The celebration on opening night went on until dawn. It was, after all, Miami's South Beach. Exhausted, I returned to Lara's for a long rest before starting on further expansion.

That last month of my twenties was magical. I was as fit as I was ever going to be again. I looked good, I felt good and I had a lot of my old bounce back. Winston and I were having amazing sex again, so he was one very happy bunny, as was I. My libido was strong, but I didn't touch any of the other boys. I truly wanted to take Jamie and Luke to bed as they had matured into amazingly beautiful young men, but I didn't. I never quite made it to peak again, which meant I never again beat Bob at squash.

"Charlie, I always love to win, but I would give almost anything to see you wipe the floor with me."

"Yes, me, too, Bob, and not to have Ronald slap me on a heart machine after our games would be nice, too."

"Charlie, get used to it. Your heart is the only thing I worry about now. None of the doctors are quite sure how much damage you did to it, so you will have an ECG after squash, every time," thus spoke Ronald.

The day before my birthday, Winston said, "I'm sorry, Charlie. David has called a board meeting for tomorrow in New York. He won't tell me why, but we have to go. We can stay in David's apartment as we will only be there a couple of days, and it seems pointless to open up ours."

The board meeting brought together all our directors and Tom, our CEO. We formulated new policy that included a discussion about going international.

"London and Paris, Charlie, what do you think?"

I told him I was interested but was our financial base sound enough to consider that. I thought maybe a year to see our present ten restaurants running smoothly first.

"I'll have a financial statement for you by this evening, Charlie, but is everybody agreed in principal to expansion abroad?"

All directors said yes, and we left it there.

Once back in David's apartment we sat around chatting.

"What are you going to do for your birthday, Charlie?"

Winston piped up very quickly and said, "I'm taking him to Cloud's, David. The beginning of our good times was there. I think it appropriate that we should."

"Good idea, Winston, that leaves me free to entertain Tom and Peter. I think we will slum it and go clubbing tonight."

Winston made me put on a tuxedo and take David's limo.

I was so disappointed when we pulled up at the restaurant, and it was in darkness. The regular doorman was there and told us they had a total electrical failure and would not be opening at least until tomorrow.

"I'm sorry, Charlie. Shall we go to G.A.Y. instead?"

"We're a little overdressed for that, don't you think?"

"Never mind, you're the boss you can dress how you like."

When we arrived, Rick met us at the door and escorted us inside. It was in total darkness other than the foyer.

"What on earth is going on, Rick? Surely you haven't been hit by problems like Cloud's have you?"

"No, Charlie, come in and let me show you."

We walked towards the main floor, and at the top of the stairs the lights all came on and several hundred voices screamed, "Happy Birthday, Charlie." I looked at the sea of faces and realised that I knew everyone of them. The staff of all ten Cloud's were there plus all of Lara's house staff. David slid up alongside me, mic in hand.

"Gentlemen, please put your hands together for our guest of honour this evening, Charlie Fellows."

The applause nearly brought the roof down. I was flabbergasted.

"Gentlemen, Charlie, I told you at the board meeting today I would give you a financial statement later. Well here is your personal one. Your original contract with me would have expired in about two months. You told us at Lara's when we were about to open our first Cloud's and start on G.A.Y. that you wanted to be worth ten million by today, and we gasped at your cheek. That statement in your hand shows that in cash, stock property and your share of this place, you are in fact worth one hundred million. Congratulations, you deserve every cent of it."

"Here, here," resounded around the room, and I was floored by my worth, I had no idea. Money just didn't mean anything to me anymore as it did when I was a gambler. I had Winston and I had Lara's House, with the biggest bonus of all, a whole load of the most wonderful friends in the world.

David whispered in my ear when everybody started to celebrate, and I had my first glass of Champagne in hand, "You are still the cutest guy I know, and I would love to take you to bed just once more to celebrate the tenth anniversary of our first fuck."

I hadn't had sex with David for three years. I hadn't had sex with anyone other than Winston for about the same period. I was astounded.

"I nearly lost Winston because of my sexual appetite, David. I still have the same appetite, but I will not risk losing my baby again. You will have to ask his permission if you want to get me into bed again."

"I'm going to, Charlie, because I really do want to pleasure you."

"Thank you, David, I am truly flattered, particularly in the present company. There are over 100 beautiful young men here tonight to die for."

"True, but I bet there isn't one of them with a cuter butt than you or a monster between their legs to compare with yours."

"It looks as though those two assets of mine are still able to get me into trouble, David, doesn't it?"

I was laughing as I said it but did wonder how long my ass and cock would remain a lustful thought for people.

The night was a wonder for me. I cried like a baby for half of it as I hugged and kissed all of the original gang – Darren, Johnnie and Ryan, my original kitchen crew; Peter and Paul, the delightful twins who at 18 had taught me a lesson in respect that I never forgot; Jason, Julio, Ty and Glen, Cloud's first white waiters; Tom, the most amazing kisser and the best fuck I had ever received; and Mac, Cloud and Bob who had supported and protected me whenever they could. I was incredibly lucky with the top of that pile being crowned with my mentor who had turned me into a multimillionaire and a lover who was my life.

For our tenth anniversary in a few months, I was going to take him on a world cruise before we started the next major stage of our lives, which was to take Cloud's international and open another G.A.Y.

I was listening and peeking outside the door of the lounge in David's apartment when, the next day, he asked Winston if he could take me to bed as a tenth anniversary reminder of our first fuck. Winston's face was a picture I will carry in my head for the remainder of my life. How I managed not to laugh aloud I will never know.

"I'm sorry, David. I am in shock at that question. I will have to talk to Charlie. I can't farm him out like a slave."

"No you can't, Winston, but it is only because of my generosity that he isn't still a slave, at least for another two months."

"I'm sorry, David. I still have to talk to Charlie."

He did, when we were alone in the apartment that afternoon.

"I don't know what to say to either you or David, Charlie. I should just say no, but he reminded me that you would still be a slave for another two months if it were not for his generosity. What should I say, Charlie?"

"Oh, dear lover, I'm not the best person to ask am I? You know my appetite for sexual variety. I have been a good boy on that front for the past three years for only one reason. I am never going to risk losing you again, Winston. I have loved you more than life for almost ten years. I will never risk that for sexual freedom however much I lust for it."

"You never say anything about it, Charlie, do you really miss romping with our friends like you used to?"

"Honestly, Baby, yes a little. I suppose I will always be a slut. Our sex is still awesome though, and I can more than survive on that. I have never met any one that I would like to have sex with more than you, but our group romps were fun weren't they? It wasn't just me that enjoyed them was it?"

"No, Charlie, they were great, and I am glad you let Tom fuck me. That was truly awesome. No wonder Jason always looks so happy when we see him."

We both laughed at that which lightened the atmosphere.

"Charlie, I will worry about your heart if I let you loose again, but if you promise not to overdo it, you can romp around with some of the other boys, and David probably does deserve to take you once more for all he has done for you. I will try to forget that he was responsible, at least in part for nearly killing you and me."

I took him in my arms and hugged him. "You are so amazing. Thank you. I will be discreet, and I won't overdo it, I promise."

I called David on the internal phone and asked him if he could be free for a couple of hours next day. He guessed what for almost without hesitation.

"Oh crikey, Charlie, yes. But what about Winston?"

"Don't worry, he is going shopping with Jason before he goes back to Boston. Later, David, we had better discuss what I am going to be doing for the next few months until Winston and I take off on our world cruise."

We reversed our plans and three of us sat down to discuss my itinerary.

"Charlie, do you remember that property about three blocks away from Cloud's on South Beach? It looked a bit run down."

"Yes, vaguely."

"I was thinking we could buy it as the second G.A.Y. but a new concept."

"Go on, David."

"Well, it has a basement car park, which would be useful. The ground floor is a mass of small locales, which we could develop as a coffee shop, men's beauty salon, a small gym, a couple of smart boutiques and a reception. The next floor is already one huge room. We could turn that into a club, restaurant, bar, etc. The kitchen could be on the ground floor as well servicing the club using dumb waiters. All the upper floors we could develop as an apartment hotel, small open plan double occupancy suites with cooking facilities."

"It sounds interesting, David. You have obviously been thinking about it."

"I have, Charlie. It also goes hand in glove with my other thought. Cloud's has not taken off the same as the other nine. I wonder if we need to tweak the format a little for the area. You could go and look, purchase the other property and start working with an architect on it."

I laughed, "You are crafty, David, all the expenses of my trip go to Cloud's and we get the opportunity to further develop our joint interests. Yes, I would love to do that. Are you OK, with that, Winston?"

"Yes, Charlie, but David, I won't allow you to push him on this. I still insist he doesn't overdo the work thing."

"I'm cool with that, Winston. You are the boss when you get down there. OK, Charlie?"

"David, haven't you realised yet, Winston is always the boss? He just lets me act as though I am."

I gave my 28-year-old baby a hug and prayed I would always have him.

"We will leave tomorrow if you are happy with that, David? Can I take the jet and go via Lara's House? I need more clothes and things than I have here?"

"Yes, no problem, and I guess that's a wrap for today."

Winston went shopping after lunch, and I called David.

"OK, David, you have your slave back for a couple of hours. Where would you like me and dressed in what?"

"Charlie, do you mean that? You will be my slave this one last time?"

"Yes, David, I think you deserve this. No restrictions, we will pretend my original contract is still in force."

"Do you have any little white shorts with you, Charlie, like you used to wear?"

"No, David, the closest I can come to it are some white hip hugger briefs."

"OK, my study in those, in front of my desk in slave standing position."

When I arrived, I did as instructed and with my head lowered, and I said, "You sent for me, Master."

David got out of his chair walked round his desk and started to fondle me through my briefs. I was very quickly rock hard with several inches showing out of the top of my waistband. David wet a couple of fingers and started pleasuring my cock head and the shaft just behind it. I was gasping in minutes. Leaving my front, he started caressing my butt through the thin material of my briefs and running his hands up and down the inside of my thighs. I was dripping precum at an alarming rate by the time he had been alternating the two actions for a few minutes.

"I must have a touch of the sadist in me, slave, because I have an urge to spank that beautiful butt. Take your shorts off and lie over my desk legs spread wide."

Here we go I thought. My butt was causing the usual problem. You have to fuck it or fuck it up. I hoped David was going to fuck it.

"Slide back a little slave, push your butt out as though you want me to spank it and spread those legs wider."

Fully exposed now, David continued to stroke my butt and reach around the front of me to play with my cock and balls. It was so erotic, and of course, the more precum I drizzled, the more lubrication he had to make me squirm with pleasure. He slapped my butt just hard enough to tingle and said, "Keep still slave, or I will have to seriously chastise you."

Not fair, he was turning me on so much I could no more stay still than fly unaided.

Once he started to finger fuck me using my precum as lube, I really was lost. He kept hitting my prostate, and I jumped every time he did.

"You don't learn, do you slave? I said keep still and you keep defying me. He pulled a chair out and sat down. Over my knee, boy, I am going to spank you."

My cock was so hard that when I pressed it up against David's thigh as I bent over his knees it hurt like hell. I received ten medium hard licks with his bare hands. It was so erotic, I nearly came all over his thigh. I was gasping when he told me to stand in front of him again, not with the pain either. I was squirming with the pleasure. My ass was tingling just enough to be erotic. David took me in his mouth then and started doing incredible things to my glans and that very sensitive area just behind the underside of the head. His own fault, I came almost immediately filling his mouth with my jism.

"Mmm, that tasted as good as I remember, Charlie," he said as he stood up and gave me one of his special long, I love you, kisses.

"You can undress me now and see if you can pleasure me as well as I have just done you."

I did, I gave him a blowjob like the first time when he threatened to beat me with the whip if I didn't let him cum. Was it possible that ten years had elapsed since that day. I did have mercy on him eventually and took a massive load of his cum down my throat.

"Oh God, Charlie, I haven't had a blowjob like that in years. My bedroom now, you are going to have your work cut out getting me hard enough to fuck you."

I smiled up at him and said, "It will be my pleasure to try, Master."

For the following half an hour or so we were sixty-nining, and it was fantastic. Both of us were erect again very quickly despite our massive orgasms, but we kept each other close to the boil again until David said, "On your back, Charlie, I am going to see how long I can remain inside you before I cum."

With my legs in the air spread wide, David attacked my ass with his tongue. He ran it up and down my crack swabbing it thoroughly with his spit. Each time he passed my hole he would swirl his tongue round and round it before pushing it in. When he withdrew, he would suck it before resuming the licking. I was going ballistic. When I didn't think I could take anymore, he slid my legs over his shoulder and with one hand started to open me up sliding increasing numbers of fingers into me until he was almost fist fucking me. The other hand was roaming over my cock and balls with occasional forays to my nipples, which he pinched quite hard.

"Oh God, David please fuck me, this is incredible. I want all of you inside me, now, please."

He did, I felt him slide all the way into me with one smooth movement accompanied by my very audible "Aaaaaaaaaaaah."

I couldn't believe what followed. He remained inside me without cumming for at least a half-hour. He would slow fuck me until he was about to cum and then stay completely immobile, buried in me to the hilt. While he calmed down, he would bring me to the point of orgasm and stop. Eventually he pushed my legs higher and wider before powering into me as hard as I can ever remember. The mess I made on the bed was unbelievable, there were great gobs of my cum everywhere as I went ballistic again. David's orgasm was even more amazing. I thought he was peeing in me the jets of his cum were so powerful and so continuous.

We both took an age to calm down. David stayed inside me as he went completely soft and slid out of me.

"David, that was fabulous, I'm so pleased you remembered that I like you to remain inside me until you are soft. It gives me such a feeling of completeness."

"I know, Charlie, and for me, too. You are truly the most awesome sex machine I have ever been lucky enough to make love to. Those two orgasms are as good as any I have ever had, thank you, a million times over."

"Don't you mean a hundred million times over, David?"

We both laughed uproariously. What a wonderful way to say thank you to him for the culmination of our ten-year relationship.

"I don't suppose this will ever happen again, Charlie, and that makes me very sad. You are still the only guy I have ever truly loved."

"No David, it will happen again. Winston is allowing me to play around again, so we might be able to fit in the odd romp. With you, it is special in a way that it isn't with anyone else, particularly this afternoon. I will be your slave again any time I can as long as we are discreet about it."

"Seriously, Charlie?"

"Seriously, David," I said laughing and planting a very affectionate kiss on his lips.

Winston looked very serious when he returned from shopping.

"Are you OK, Charlie?" Very small voice signifying that he wasn't sure how things had gone.

"Yes, Baby, David had his slave for one last session and beat me and fucked me mercilessly all afternoon."

The shock on Winston's face had me rolling on the floor almost in hysterics.

"It's OK, Baby, he was fantastic. He did spank me, but so gently it was just incredibly erotic."

"Let me see your ass."

I had to laugh as I stripped for him. We had been this route before so many times, him having to look at my seriously abused posterior.

I bent over in front of him, and he very gently stroked my cheeks saying, "It is a little bit red, Charlie, are you sure he didn't hurt you?"

"No, Lover, the whole afternoon was just incredible sex."

"In that case I am going to continue with the same theme. Get on the bed, Charlie, I want to fuck you as well."

I stood for ages my lower jaw just about bouncing on the floor.

"Don't look so surprised. If I am going to allow you to return to your sluttish behaviour, I am going to get my share of it as well. You can be my slave for the next hour while I have some sexual pleasure."

He took me to another planet. No one knew how to pleasure me like Winston. I was swooning with the joy of his loving by the time he had filled my ass with his love juice. What a way to start the second decade of my life with David and Winston. I felt like a teenager again that afternoon.

Miami proved a nightmare. It was obvious the first night in Cloud's that we had it all wrong. The clientele here were completely different to what we had based our thinking. I set about rehashing the menu and the wine list, making the décor less formal. I put the waiters into hotpants like G.A.Y. and introduced a sound system with more upbeat music than we would have in any of the other outlets. A month later, we were hitting targets every week. I promoted Ty from G.A.Y. New York to Maitre D and moved the incumbent one to Boston Cloud's as general manager. Jason accepted a role as general manager of the group checking on all ten outlets. It worked perfectly.

The planned restaurant for the new G.A.Y. on South Beach was down graded to a boulevard type café that worked and didn't conflict with Cloud's. We set up a deal whereby G.A.Y. customers could leave to eat at Cloud's and return without paying entry fees again.

The building we bought for the new G.A.Y. was a mess. It took a lot more capitol to get up and running than we had planned, but it took off so well that David and I were almost ecstatic.

Winston was furious with me that during our world cruise I was on video link at least once a week organising things with the architect and developer.

"Charlie, I am truly sorry to foist this on you while you are on your cruise, but mistakes will be too costly to rectify if we wait until you return. Your flare for getting the venues perfect is your downfall."

"That's OK, David, you will just have to do something special for Winston when we get back."

That was the end of it. The cruise was fabulous. We completely circumnavigated the globe taking three months to do it.

Winston forgave me of course and was very nice to David when we got back to New York.

"You have put up with a lot from me, Winston, not just this last few months but for the last ten years. Please accept this as a measure of my appreciation."

With that, he gave Winston an envelope. When he opened it his eyes nearly popped out of his head. His hands were shaking as he passed it to me.

"Charlie, if that is what I think it is I can't accept it, can I?"

It was a stock certificate for $1 million worth of Cloud's stock.

"David, that is incredibly generous of you, but Winston has my $100 million. He doesn't need this."

"I know that, Charlie, but I don't know any other way to say thank you, besides, the remainder of the board sanctioned it. We all realise that it is Winston's stewardship that has kept you healthy and earning us all unbelievable good fortune.

What a homecoming!

Winston went on the payroll as P.A. to the president of the company. David had stepped down from the joint presidency after we returned from our cruise pleading pressure of work in his other companies. G.A.Y. had always been my baby, so I was now effectively president of two very successful companies. I needed Winston's input more than ever. He missed nothing, kept it all on his PC and kept my appointment diary better organised than I ever could.

We took off for London and Paris looking to open Cloud's Europe. Staffing was going to be a nightmare. People we knew and trusted held all of the senior positions in the States. Europe was going to be so detached, we couldn't have it any different there.

Tom and Jason were the obvious answer. I transferred them both to England, made Tom CEO of Cloud's Europe and Jason general manager with special responsibility for Paris. He spent a month on a total immersion French course, and I based him in Paris with the proviso that he and Tom could be together every weekend in one or other of the cities. Once we had found the venues, and I laid down the plans with the architects and developers. I left it to Tom, setting up the now familiar video link whenever required.

I moved Rick Astley from G.A.Y. New York into Tom's job and Julio into Rick's job. Paul and Glen were now the only original Cloud's people without executive status. I moved Glen to G.A.Y. Miami as GM. He shared a flat with Ty, and they became lovers. Paul to go, but where. In the end, I made Peter and Paul joint GMs in Boston and left Peter with responsibility for wines and beverages as well.

My tired body and mind let me know six months had passed in the blink of an eye. I needed the peace and tranquillity of Lara's House for a while to recharge my batteries.

We had some state of the art communications equipment installed at Lara's House, and I effectively ran the two companies from there for the next three months with hardly a break. Winston would go to New York, Boston or London on short visits if required, as would I, but usually not together and never for more than a few days. We upgraded the company jet to a Gulfstream to allow us to go Trans-Atlantic.

Much to David's pleasure, we had a few terrific sex sessions on my New York visits. We relinquished our apartment in New York that we had only owned for a couple of years. The apartment we had lived in above Cloud's we had purchased as a company flat and used for visitors. Winston and I bought a small estate in Connecticut. If I weren't at Lara's, I would be between our corporate HQ and our flagship outlets in New York. It proved a good investment as I got older and my predicted partial invalidity showed. The old ticker was weak as predicted, and I had to slow down and live as much of my life as possible in unpolluted air. But that was a good many years away.

Our return to Lara's was very emotional. So much had happened to us there. My 18-year-old baby was now a mature executive of 28. Instead of a 20-year-old slave, I was president of two companies with a paper fortune of over $100 million.

Five very important people were at Lara's to meet us at the heli-pad when we landed. Cloud, flanked by Luke and Jamie, (to carry our bags). Mac and Bob just to show their joy at our return.

Cloud looked magnificent, now almost 45. With the first of his salt and pepper hair, he looked sexier than ever. I wanted him to make love to me again. God he was gorgeous.

Mac had aged and added a lot of weight, but he was still the same old care bear who had taken so much emotional flack for loving me.

Bob, no obvious change there. Annoyingly, he didn't look a day older than when he first arrived.

"I hope you are ready to get me fit again, Bob. I am going to be hard work this time."

"Charlie, you have always been hard work. You have far too many ups and downs in your life."

"Busy executive now, Bob," I said, laughing, "can't always find the time to hit the gym, not like all you fit layabouts here."

"Luke and Jamie, you look awesome. Bob has obviously been seeing a lot of you two."

They both blushed and looked down at their feet.

"Thank you, Charlie. It's great to have you back."

Ice broken time to get everybody else settled.

"Cloud and Mac, I would like to see all the staff at tea time, just to say hello."

"Four o'clock, OK, Charlie?"

"Fine. Cloud, send the nurse on extended leave will you? Ronald will be here with me."

We walked up to the house, which as always looked magnificent.

"Mac, you and Cloud keep my home looking so beautiful. I will never be able to thank you enough."

"Charlie, I know I can speak for both of us. You are an amazing boss. You double our pay and put a large sum into our pension funds as well. We never spend any money because you pay for everything here, and we never leave."

"Yes, Mac, so how many weeks holiday do I owe you both?"

"None, Charlie, we live in paradise. We ought to be paying you."

"Thank you, Mac. I don't know what I would have done without the two of you over the years. Is there nothing that either of you want that I could give you to show how much I love and appreciate you."

"No Charlie, just keep coming back here as often as you can. Our reward is having an employer who truly appreciates us."

I asked Jamie and Luke to organise lots of drinks, and the kitchen staff to produce trays of nibbles, and I would meet the staff in the main lounge.

"Cloud, make sure there is enough seating. I would like to chat to as many of the least familiar faces as possible for a little while."

By the time the meeting was over, I had all my staff eating out of my hand. Apart from Jamie and Luke, there were no others that I was close to and I would love to have had the old crew here from when I was a slave. I would just have to try to get to know them all starting from the boss's position instead of the slave's. I told my thoughts to Cloud, and he laughed.

"Mmm, it would be nice, Charlie. I think I could handle being 30 odd again and looking after such delightful individuals as Peter and Paul, and your kitchen crew. Are we likely to see them again?"

"Cloud, it has been so long, and they are spread all over the place now, but there is no reason at all why they should not return here whenever they like. Look, I don't need to keep letting Lara's anymore. Cancel any further bookings. I am going to issue individual invitations to the entire old crowd. Let them know that they are welcome here anytime they have holidays. We won't get them all together, but we should have the pleasure of their company in dribs and drabs. Can you imagine Peter and Paul draped around the pool again or Darren, Johnnie and Ryan playing fast and loose with my butt in the kitchen? Or the four white waiters almost giving Mac a heart attack as they pose round the pool. You know you wouldn't believe how little they have changed. We must have the youngest looking executives of any company in the States."

We both laughed as our individual imaginations took over.

"Cloud, there is one more thing. Jamie and Luke, they are 20 now. I ought to be looking to advance them in some way."

"You mean take them off to the big city to feed your corporate machine, Charlie?"

He wasn't smiling, and I knew losing another two staff to my company would not please him.

"I'm sorry, Cloud, but they really are the most beautiful boys we have ever had on the estate. Cloud's in New York could do with an injection of new waiters, and Jamie is wine qualified, which we again need there."

"I'm not happy with that, Charlie, but if they want to go and you want them, I guess I have no choice."

"Winston is going to Miami tomorrow, Cloud, and we are going to meet in New York next week. I have to see David. I will take Jamie and Luke with me then. You can go staff hunting again for their replacements, and by way of an apology, why don't you come to my room after lunch tomorrow and take your frustration out on me by giving me a good fucking?"

"Are you serious, Charlie?"

"Yes, Cloud. I have never been impaled on anything nearly as impressive as your monster. I would love to feel it inside me again."

"Charlie, I would be delighted."

I have to admit the pain of Cloud penetrating me was terrible. I did scream this time. He was just so enormous. He wanted to pull out, but I wouldn't let him.

"Take it slow, Cloud, but don't pull out."

"Charlie, I can't believe how incredible it feels just having a couple of inches inside you."

"Thank you, Cloud, you can keep coming now, slowly though, your cock is magnificent."

All the time he was feeding me, he was playing with me, it was amazingly erotic. When he bottomed out, I sighed. "Oh, Cloud, that is so wonderful. Fuck me slowly now, but make the strokes long."

I was naughty. I actually timed him. Forty-six minutes from first entry to orgasm. I had cum twice without touching my own cock and with minimal help from Cloud.

"I love you, Charlie, and if you invite me to do that many more times I am going to be in trouble. I will want to worship you and beg you for this everyday. Your ass is like a drug. It could become habit forming."

I laughed to try to lighten the atmosphere and gave him a loving kiss. I did realise though that I shouldn't play fast and loose with his emotions. I knew he loved me, and it had to be hard for him to be around me while I was so besotted with Winston.

When Jamie and Luke had finished clearing from dinner, I had Cloud send them to me in my study. They looked very apprehensive when they came in, and I laughed.

"You both look worried. So what have you been up to?"

"Nothing, Charlie, honestly, it's just that we have never had to meet you in here."

"Sit down. What would you like to drink?"

They looked at each other and then ordered gin and tonic. I was surprised, but made them.

"You are both 20 aren't you?"

"Yes, Charlie."

"I think that you are too old to be pantry boys and house waiters now. It is time you moved on, or more precisely moved up. I don't have any such positions available here at Lara's House, so you should leave here for new pastures."

I was playing with their emotions and regretted it. I didn't realise how dedicated to me they were. They both burst into tears, and Jamie sobbed, "We don't want to leave you, Charlie, what have we done wrong? You know we would do anything for you."

I hugged and kissed them both apologising profusely for being such a stupid prick.

"I don't want you to leave me either. I want you to think about leaving Lara's House and coming to New York with me."

They looked at me, dried their tears, and Luke almost whispered, "Do you mean that, Charlie? You aren't just playing with us are you?"

"No, Luke, I am serious. Cloud's New York needs a new wine waiter and another waiter. Darren and Ryan have a spare bedroom in their company flat that you can stay in. It is above the restaurant, so you wouldn't have far to go to work," I said laughing.

"Oh yes, please, New York, that sounds so exciting."

"You had better go and pack then. We are leaving the day after tomorrow about lunchtime. You are lucky. The company jet is coming for us, so you can have as much luggage as you like."

Jamie got all serious. He walked over to me, knelt in front of me and kissed my hand.

"We love you, Charlie. We'll never let you down."

I made him stand up. "Don't you ever do that again, Jamie. You aren't my slave."

"Yes I am, Charlie, I will always be a slave to your wishes. You can do anything to me, and I will always accept it with joy."

Luke's voice added his assent to that. I sat down again. "So I can thrash you with the paddle until you can't sit down. Fuck you until you bleed, separate you and never let you make love to each other again, and you will still love me?"

"Yes, Charlie, if it pleases you."

I was shocked. "Will you both come and sleep with me tonight?"

"Yes, Charlie. What time would you like us in your bedroom?"

"Eleven. Make sure you have showered and cleaned your teeth. You won't need any bed clothes. I want you naked."

I didn't intend touching them sexually. I just wanted to cuddle them.

That was exactly how it worked. I had one on either side of me draped over me in such a way that their lips were almost touching across my chest and the legs they had draped over me had my cock sandwiched nicely. It was very erotic, and I was hard as hell, but it was lovely being able to run my hands down their very sleek bodies and feel the warmth of them.

When I woke, they were both already awake resting on elbows looking down at my face. I was of course still erect. I received two very passionate kisses and Jamie said, "Good morning, Charlie. Can we pleasure you and make this wonderful appendage go soft?"

He was holding my cock as he said it.

"I think I would like that, Jamie, but I was not engineering this. I just wanted to cuddle you both all night."

"We know, Charlie, it was lovely snuggling up to you. We were surprised that you didn't touch us though. Don't we please you anymore?"

I laughed until I ached. "Oh God, that has to be a classic. You are without any doubt the most beautiful boys I have ever seen in my life. I guarantee that if you wish to prostitutes yourself at Cloud's in New York, you will be able to make between $1,000 and $5,000 per night to sleep with the clientele."

"You aren't serious are you, Charlie?"

"Absolutely. One night when a few of us were out drinking, a man offered us $10,000 for one night of pleasuring, and almost every night people like Winston, Peter and Paul were offered up to $5,000 for a night. You two are unbelievably sexy. If I didn't love Winston so much, I would have you permanently in my company and fuck you both several times everyday."

They were shocked, but I did get an incredible blowjob from their combined efforts.

Chapter 11

I thought I had grown tired of New York, but as soon as we landed, I felt at home. Could my companions have something to do with my newly rekindled joy? I took Luke and Jamie to the apartment first and left them with Darren to settle in. At David's, I asked him for time to sit down and discuss our future, or more precisely my future.

"What is it, Charlie, I sense a change in you. Is this serious?"

"Yes, David, I think it is. I think I might be heading for a personal crisis in my life, and I don't want it to affect either of our companies."

"When do you want a meet then, Charlie?"

"The sooner the better, David."

"Here, 10:00 am tomorrow."

"Thank you, David, that will be fine."

I went back to Darren and Ryan's apartment to talk to Jamie and Luke.

"The first thing we are going to do is get you two tagged."

"What does that mean, Charlie?"

"Every beautiful boy that comes to work for Cloud's or G.A.Y. New York gets an electronic tracker inserted under his skin, Jamie."

"That sounds scary, Charlie, why?"

"If you were to get abducted, the tracker will hopefully end up saving your life. I don't want to go into details now, ask Darren or Ryan, they both have them fitted."

I told them about personal security with the same lecture all of the others received.

"You are such beautiful boys I will never sleep peacefully again unless I know you are observing my rules. Do you understand the importance of this lecture?"

"Yes, Charlie."

"Jamie, Luke, I am more than a little in love with both of you. Please don't ever give me cause to grieve for you. I don't think I could bear it."

"We won't, Charlie, we'll be careful."

I called Darren in and told him on what I had briefed the boys.

"Please, Darren, look after them until they become street wise. I think I would die if the same thing happens to them as happened to Paul."

"We all will, Charlie, you don't have to worry."

I left them with Darren and Ryan, telling them to spend the evening in the restaurant watching, and I would pick them up at lunchtime the next day.

The meeting with David was uncomfortable for me.

"David, I think I have to step back from my commercial life for at least a year. So that our companies don't suffer, I have some proposals."

"This sounds serious, Charlie, can I help?"

"I don't think so, David. I have to sort this one out for myself. I would like to bring Tom back from Europe to head Cloud's. I guess Jason will have to come as well. Rick Astley can go home and be managing director of Cloud's Europe. Initially we will have to let him commute to Paris to run that as well. We can sublet some Cloud's offices in Boston to G.A.Y. and install Jason as managing director. People in whom we have faith will then control both companies. Further expansion may be difficult in that year, but I feel we can afford to do nothing while the managers' fine-tune the operations. I have worked out a bonus scheme that will keep the incentives in place."

"What are you going to do, Charlie?"

"I don't know, David. I'm losing my way. I have to get Winston back here, and then we will probably head for Connecticut to reevaluate my life."

"OK, Charlie, we will hold everything where you think best. Tom must be able to contact you though."

"Of course, David, and thank you."

I took Jamie and Luke for their tracker insertions, brought them back to the apartment and made love to both of them. They were exquisite. I was totally besotted by them. I could have them under any conditions I set, making it totally awesome. David had me as a slave for seven years, and I could now understand the power of it. I could use or abuse Jamie and Luke anyway I wanted without protest. I had never felt the urge to use corporal punishment on anyone, but now I wanted to. I wanted to spank both of these beautiful boys just to see what they would tolerate. In no time at all, I could have them hating me and this obsession could cost me Winston. What was the matter with me? I had never felt like this before. I had known Jamie and Luke for almost four years. Why now did I want to abuse them?"

Winston flew back from Miami, and we left immediately for Connecticut. I cried in his arms the whole trip. I was inconsolable. Winston was going crazy by the time we got home.

"Charlie, please, what is it, what's wrong? Talk to me. I can't help if I don't know what the problem is."

Once in the house, Winston almost carried me straight to bed and called the doctor. As soon as the sedatives had calmed me down, and before I fell into a deep sleep, I managed to tell Winston that I thought I was going mad.

"I have fallen in love with Jamie and Luke, Winston. They want to be my slaves, and I want to do all the things to them that David did to me over the years. I have to be going insane, and I don't know how to stop these thoughts."

I slept for 24 hours. Winston must have realised the level of the crisis and knew he was fighting for our future together. He went back to New York and interrogated Jamie and Luke. He wanted to know everything that had gone on between us. He talked to Cloud and found out we had made love. When he returned he was none the wiser as to why I had flipped, but at least he was aware of the lead up to the reasons for my state of mind.

When I woke, he behaved as though everything was normal.

"I have a light dinner ready for us, Charlie, would you like to eat?"

I did, and over dinner, we talked about inconsequential things before going to bed. Winston bathed me and generally treated me like a kid. I was putty in his hands. He cuddled up to me and caressed me gently until I fell into a deep natural sleep.

When I woke, he was already awake looking at me. He kissed me gently on the lips and said with so much feeling.

"I love you, Charlie, more than my life, I love you. Whatever you want from me, whatever you want me to do, I will do it. You can treat me like a toilet, beat me half to death, tear the skin from my body with whips, fuck me with any object you like, walk all over me, prostitute me to the world. Anything, however vile and cruel and degrading, revolting or disgusting, you can do it to me, but I beg you, don't leave me. Don't throw me out. I will die without your love."

"Oh God, Baby, what have I been saying?"

"I'm not sure, Charlie, but I think you want to leave me for Jamie and Luke. Please don't. I tried to live without you once. I can't do it again. Please don't ask me to"

He was crying so hard that he was wrenching his stomach.

I looked at the boy I had loved for ten years. I thought about the last week without him and the things I had done. I recalled Jamie and Luke's commitment to me and it clicked. Of course, Jamie and Luke were awesome, and Winston had recognised that four years ago. I must have been heading for a minor break down and had let their devotion to me cloud my thinking.

"I'm not going to leave you, Winston. I'm not going to do any of those awful things to you. I don't know what has got into me. Get the doctor back, Baby. I think I am going mad. I need something. I love you. I'll always love you."

I grabbed hold of him and I cried myself to sleep.

The clinic was lovely. The grounds were superb. It was a perfect setting to engender peace and tranquillity into its occupants. Winston spent most of everyday with me. He wheeled me round the grounds, and we talked. He read to me, pampered me and generally made me feel special. As fall approached, he would wrap the blanket round my legs, always worrying about my welfare and comfort. I was there for nearly six months. The analyses were very technically worded but basically overwork after my near death had caused a mental breakdown.

Home seemed strange. I had spent so little time at the Connecticut estate. I had a nurse near me at all times initially until I balked. So, once again David got hold of Ronald. He was better than any psychiatric nurse was. Between them, he and Winston nursed me back to mental health. Almost another year of my life lost. The final test was the exorcism of my demons. I had to see Jamie and Luke again. Winston was frantic as we headed back to New York.

Dinner at Cloud's together, but then Winston went back to David's, and I went to bed with Jamie and Luke. They were wonderful and the sex was amazing. Making love to both of them was exquisitely exciting, my orgasms were almost heart stopping, but at the end, it was Winston who was in my thoughts.

"I needed tonight, boys. The sex was amazing, but I used you two just to prove to myself that I love Winston more than life, but love you two for sex. I apologise to you with all my heart. Just using your bodies for my own gratification was despicable. Please forgive me. I do love you in my way."

"It's OK, Charlie, we know. We still love you, but now, go home to Winston."

I did and curled up in bed with the boy I had loved for too long to stop. He was crying like a baby, as I slid into bed with him, but not for long.

"I've exorcised my demons, Baby, please forgive me. I want you more than ever."

My year out had seen no change at either G.A.Y. or Cloud's. I went to see David, with Winston of course.

"Welcome back, Charlie, what do you want to do now?"

"No idea, David, tell me what is going on and what you would like to see happening to either or both Cloud's and G.A.Y."

"Charlie, a measure of your ability is that both companies are running incredibly well. We have committed to no more expansion, but both are hugely more profitable. We are awash with cash, so you can do whatever you like or nothing if that pleases you."

"David, I think Winston and I could use some time in Spain and Italy. Do you think Cloud's Madrid and Cloud's Rome would look good in the company portfolio?"

"Where did that one come from, Charlie?" Winston looked quite shocked, and I shrugged.

"Are you serious, Charlie?"

"Yes, David, I think we need to get away from the U.S. for a while."

"Well, with your 30% and my 30%, I don't think we even need to call a board meeting for this one. I can tell them any time"

Rome was enchanting, Capri was divine. We started the ball rolling on property search and then vacationed. It was wonderful to have no diversions at all from Winston. The Italian boys were charming and many of them were very seductive, but my life was centred on Winston again, I knew he was 29, but I still thought of him as the 18-year-old I first fell in love with.

After a beautiful day in Capri where we were staying for a while, I wanted to exercise my authority and dominance over Winston by treating him like a slave. I had been ordering him about to see his reaction, silly things like fetch me a soda, move the coffee table a little closer for me, scratch my back, eventually he picked up on it and said, "What am I, Charlie, your slave?"

"You tell me, Winston, are you?"

He looked me in the eyes, saw my expression, and lowering his eyes said, "You know I am, Charlie, forever."

"Good, in that case take all your clothes off and stand in front of me with your hands behind your head and your legs astride."

He looked at me as though I was going mad again, but did what I asked.

As I looked at him closely, naked as the day he was born, I realised how awesome he still was. His body was superb, the butt I had been shagging for 11 years hadn't changed, and it still caused me an immediate erection. I played with his cock and again was awed by the beauty of it. Long and straight, perfectly formed head, colouring to match his skin, low slung ball sac that complimented the appendage in every way. It felt like silk. I ran my hands over his whole body, tweaking his nipples, caressing the cheeks of his ass, running a wet finger down his crack to his hole, which I worried for a while.

"Do you like being my slave, Winston?"

"You know I do, Charlie. You know I will do anything for you, be anything you want me to be."

He was still looking a little bemused at this strange turn of events. I had never used him in this way before.

"Good, now you can undress me and lubricate my cock and balls with your tongue."

This was becoming very erotic, and Winston noticed it as well. He started to smile crouched in front of me sucking my cock and balls and looking up at my face.

"What are you looking at, slave? Keep your eyes on what you are doing."

The "yes Master" didn't carry quite enough subservience in the tone to sound genuine. He looked up at me again, and I just dissolved. He did, too, and we ended up supporting each other laughing ourselves silly.

"I am still going to do to you what I intended, slave, OK?"

"You know you can, Charlie, and I'm sure I shall love it."

"Huh, we'll see. In the bedroom on the bed doggy fashion with your legs spread as wide as you can."

When I followed him into the bedroom, I was greeted by his beautiful ass pushed back towards me.

"I have never spanked that, slave, but I have the urge to do it now." I was stroking his butt as I said it.

"Yes, Master," said very seriously, the doubt at my commitment was there in the voice.

I slapped his butt once, not hard, but he jumped with the surprise of it.

"Keep still, slave, or I will restrain you and use a belt on you."

I slapped him again, and he didn't move. I attacked both cheeks then with my lips and my tongue. My cock was so hard it hurt. I pulled his cheeks apart and spent at least ten minutes licking and kissing his hole, burying my tongue as deep as I could before sucking on it. He was moaning and gasping with the pleasure of it. I pulled back then and gave him two more sharp slaps on the bum. Not hard, but he squirmed, and I could tell from reaching around in front of him to feel his incredibly hard cock that he was enjoying it.

"Roll over onto your back. Close your eyes. Pull your legs up over your head and spread them wide."

I went into overdrive then pleasuring him. His hole, cock and balls received a thorough swabbing with my tongue until he was gasping for breath. Another four slaps on his butt before stroking it again, and he orgasmed. I was amazed.

"Oh crikey, Charlie, that was amazing."

I told him to drop his legs and slid down beside him taking him in my arms. I kissed him gently and watched his eyes. They were full of wonder.

"You little, masochist, you get off on being spanked, and I never realised it."

"Mmm, it was nice, Charlie. I know I don't like punishment type spanking, but that was wonderfully erotic. Will you fuck me now? I want to cum again with you inside me?"

"Oh yes, Baby, that is what I intended, but I want you to fuck me first."

"Gosh, Charlie, whatever has got into you today? It is ages since you wanted me to do that to you."

"I know lover, far to long. I'm going to get you rock hard again, and I want you to just fuck me."

I looked down at his groin and laughed, it was already rigid.

"Hmm, I guess I don't need to work on that."

He laughed. I rolled onto my back swinging my legs into the air and after a quick lubing, he entered me in one smooth movement.

"Oh gosh, Winston, I had forgotten how wonderful you feel inside me. Now fuck me slowly."

Long slow strokes swivelling his body to hit different places inside me. The jolts as he hit my prostate making me orgasm several times before he did the same. We were very messy after we had kissed and cuddled for a little while. In anticipation of shagging him, I was hard again very quickly and entered him gently in the missionary position. His insides felt like silk as I slow fucked him the same as he had done to me.

"I love you, Charlie, I don't know how I could live without this. I can feel your love for me with every thrust."

"I'm pleased. You know I don't deserve your love, Winston. I have led you a merry dance at times throughout our 11 years."

"Mmm, but this always makes it worthwhile."

The twinkle in his eyes made me gasp with the rush of love I felt for this man.

We came together again, and I fell onto his chest kissing him deeply.

"Don't you ever feel that you would like to leave me for someone less volatile and less demanding than me, Winston? Someone who would be faithful to you in body as well as mind?"

"You are silly, Charlie, if I wanted to I could. Remember, I'm a millionaire. I can do what I like. So, why do you think I stay with you, even though you break my heart sometimes?"

"I'm damned if I know, Baby."

"Yes you do. I stay with you because I love you. I love you more than life itself. I left you once for six months, but I died inside. It was only the love of my family that stopped me dying like you nearly did. Before that, when you went into your coma, I nearly died as well. You are clever, Charlie, but sometimes you act really dumb."

He rolled into my arms and kissed me so passionately I nearly stopped breathing.

"I'll always love you. There is nothing you could do to stop me. I could share you, Charlie, if I had to, but I would die if I lost you."

Holiday over, we spent nearly six months commuting between Madrid and Rome until we had another two Cloud's Restaurants up and running. I worked in the kitchens training the chefs to my methods, and Winston trained the waiters. We insisted on bilingual staff, which wasn't difficult. English appeared to be everyone's second language. Rick flew out several times at my request to put his stamp on the operations as managing director.

"You've done it again, Charlie, haven't you? Cloud's New York transported to Rome and Madrid."

"I certainly hope so, Rick. Now all you have to do is produce the same profit figures we do there."

Winston and I took another short holiday and toured in Spain returning to New York in time to see Cloud's reopen after a major refurbishment. I decided to go in as chef for the first month, and Winston took over as Maitre D. We both loved it. Many of the customers remembered us and made us realise how terrific they had been before. The staff were very uncomfortable at first knowing I was the president of the company and Winston was my P.A., but they soon relaxed, particularly after they saw how we treated Jamie and Luke. In front of everyone, I gave them both long kisses to the lips and hugged them tight telling them how much I had missed them. They both blushed but were quite obviously pleased at my greeting. I did the same with Darren and Ryan in the kitchen. Ryan cried, and I had to cuddle him for ages.

"Oh, Charlie, we have missed you so much. Are you really going to be the chef again?"

"If Darren doesn't mind, Ryan, I would like to, just for a few weeks."

Darren hugged me again and said he would be delighted. It really was fun, and over the next month, nearly all of the original staff came in and resumed their old jobs for a few days. Of course, the financial benefit from that piece of PR pleased everyone as well.

"Charlie, we are all so pleased to see you back and obviously in top form. Are you going to fully take over the reins of both companies again?"

"Yes, David, time I stopped being a playboy and earned my salary."

"I'm delighted, and I'm sure Tom and Jason will value your input again."

Winston and I flew up to Boston and spent a couple of weeks with Tom and Jason. I spent a weak with each, going through the books and looking at operating methods. As we expanded, control of the company for standards became increasingly difficult.

"Tom, I think we need a roving manager who can drop in on any of the restaurants unheralded and check standards so that Cloud's anywhere in the world will be the same, with the exception of Miami of course."

"I agree, Charlie, but who is the big block on implementing that one. It has to be someone who knows Cloud's almost as well as you do. I couldn't do it, Jason could, but please, Charlie, don't take him."

"Don't tell me you still love him and can't bear to be away from him."

"Yeah, afraid so. You can't even begin to imagine how much I owe you for bringing us together."

"Yes I can, Tom. Under different circumstances, I would be in Jason's shoes with you, and I know how gorgeous he is as a lover, so there you have it. How about Paul? It will be a senior management position on a par with Peter, but it will take him away a lot. Is he up to it? We can always employ a bodyguard for him if he still has problems."

"No, Charlie, he is fine now. Why don't you eat in the restaurant tonight with Peter and ask Paul then? You see I am learning, Charlie, look after the people, make them feel special. I know your old Lara's House people are special. You ought to send Cloud to Cloud's as the recruiter. He has never produced a dud."

"Tom, you might have given me an idea. Let's go with your idea for Paul first."

Dinner was fantastic. Peter, Paul, Winston and I. We had been through 11 years of joy and sorrow. The three of them had matured into thrusting assertive businessmen working their balls off for me.

"I love you guys. What did I do to deserve anyone of you never mind all three?"

"You made us feel special, Charlie, which meant we had to perform special. We hope you still feel we have."

"No, I am sorry you haven't all performed special. Paul, I am relieving you of your present appointment."

I paused to take in the reaction. Paul at 29 was almost on the point of tears and Peter and Winston were looking at me stunned.

"You have performed above special. Would you like to become a senior manager with responsibility for standards in every Cloud's restaurant in the world?"

Winston hit me hard in the shoulder.

"Don't do that, Charlie, that is so cruel."

"I know, I'm sorry. Paul, I love you. Even if you were crap, I would still employ you. Would you like the new appointment? It will mean a lot of travelling, but you will travel everywhere first class and see Europe while you are doing your job?"

"Peter, are you OK, with that?"

"Of course I am, Little Bro, just make sure you come back here as often as possible."

"Thank you, Charlie, that sounds fantastic."

"Good, meet me in my office tomorrow at ten, and we will discuss pay and conditions and run you through what I want from you."

I loved this part of my job, rewarding the young men that I had loved, promoting new blood who were Cloud's people, feeling the warmth of their affection. I was so lucky, and on top of that, I had a massive fortune.

I thought it was time Winston and I ran down a little, so I suggested to him that we take a month off at Lara's House.

"Oh, Charlie, can we? That would be wonderful. We both need that input of happy powder, and Bob needs to get at both of us, I think."

I told David what we were planning, and he said he would try to get down for a few days as well. I circulated our programme throughout the company and asked anyone on leave during that period to fit in a trip if possible.

Lara's House, how I loved this place. The only down side was very few faces we knew and loved. The house staff all looked incredibly young, and of course, Winston's senses went into overdrive looking for the threat to our relationship. I laughed.

"Stop it, Winston, just enjoy."

"Remember, Charlie, I know you."

"So you know that if I have a romp I will be discreet, but whoever it is will not be a threat to us."

Mac was looking old and that worried me.

"Cloud, Mac doesn't look well. Is there a problem with his health?"

"I think so, Charlie, but he won't see a doctor."

I sorted that in double quick time.

"Mac, I have booked you into a private clinic in New York. My doctor is going to run every test imaginable on you and find out why you look ill. I am not taking no for an answer. What would I do without you here to look after paradise for us?"

"I'm fine, Charlie, I don't need to go to New York."

"Yes, you do. I have sent for the jet, and David will take care of you when you arrive. I am not discussing this, Mac, you will go."

The results were devastating. Mac had the big C. It had riddled his body by being left too long and nothing could be done. I was inconsolable. This wonderful man was dying. He came back to us, and David got hold of Ronald again. What a huge gap was about to be created in my world. We pampered him and despite our best efforts, he spent time with his deputy handing over the estate to him. I sat with him for a few hours each day until he died, like he had lived, without fuss. We flew him to Scotland and buried him on the knoll overlooking the home he had been born in and seen so little of.

Lara's House would never be or feel the same again. We returned to Connecticut while I mourned my friend. We had few visitors, and Winston as always looked after me. We did go back to Lara's for a couple of weeks, but I was lost. Bob worked my butt off, and Cloud found some more beautiful boys to train for eventual transfer into the Cloud's Machine. Paul turned up one day and asked if I would tour the European Cloud's with him. He had never been out of the Caribbean or North America and felt a little apprehensive.

"I think that would do me good, Winston. About a month, I ought to spend some time with Rick in London. You'll come as well won't you?"

"Charlie, I really should remain here this time. We have three refurbishments going on and the Connecticut estate needs some attention. Paul will look after you."

"Alright, I will only go for three weeks then, maybe not even that."

"Charlie, you will go for a month, and you will take it easy. Paul you are to make him slow down if he tries to do too much. You will take Ronald with you as well, Charlie, no argument."

Chapter 12

The time spent with Rick in London was worth the whole trip. He had lost a little focus, and results were off. I straightened that out, and after a week, we left for Paris, Rome and Madrid.

While in London, we stayed in the company flat. There were only two bedrooms, so I put Ronald in one, and Paul shared with me.

"Charlie, you and I haven't had sex for years. Is this intended to change that?" Paul said, pointing to the double bed.

"That depends on you, Paul. If you would like a romp with me, I am sure I would be very accommodating."

I said that with a twinkle in my eye, and Paul laughed merrily as he replied, "You know I would, Charlie. You may be 11 years older than the first time we had sex, but you are still awesomely sexy."

"In that case, I'll be the slave again, and you can orchestrate some hot sex."

"Seriously, Charlie, can I treat you like the slave you were when I was 18?"

"Yes, why not? I don't have a whip or paddle for you, but I am sure you can improvise if you need to."

"Mmm, I'm thinking already, Charlie, you might have a sore bottom when I am finished though, like you did 11 years ago."

"I hope not quite that bad, Paul, if I remember correctly, 50 slaps with bare hands and ten with a whip."

"Well, OK, I promise no whip and no more than half the slaps, how does that sound?"

"You devil, you've become a sadist as you have grown."

"No, I'm just thinking of a little corporal punishment to repay you for being cruel in Boston."

"Oh well, I probably do deserve punishing for that. Winston would probably have done it at Lara's House if Mac had not been ill. Shall we go out for dinner first and have sex later or do you want to rape and beat me now?"

"Shower first, then punishment followed by sex I think. You can undress us and pamper me in the shower."

Absolutely no problem for me to do that. Paul still wore the same style of cute hipster briefs in white. He had a monster erection on even before I touched him. As I pulled his briefs down, I kissed the end of his cock.

"No, Charlie, you are my slave at the moment. Don't touch until you are told. Now shower us."

"OK, meannie, I will be allowed to touch it as part of washing you I presume."

Paul smiled and with a twinkling smile said, "Oh yes, Charlie, and some."

Washing Paul was so erotic. I finger fucked him with a very soapy finger making him squirm with pleasure, gently masturbated his cock while washing it and generally behaved badly. I dried him off and then myself. When I walked out of the bathroom, he was seated on the edge of the bed in his briefs.

"Stand in front of me, Charlie."

He started playing with my already erect penis and telling me what was coming.

"For your infantile cruelty in Boston, I am going to smack your ass like a child's would be smacked, across my knee. After which, I am going to use my belt to punish you like an adult, doggy position on the bed before I fuck you hard." He looked at me and smiled. "Perky is going to be a naughty toy."

I laughed. I had just been transported back 11 years.

"Across my knee, Charlie, spread your legs."

My cock was as it had been all that time ago so my balls could be punished as well, I hoped that he wouldn't. The first slap was quite hard, which surprised me, and I yelped. He then set up a staccato of slaps with each hand catching one cheek at a time. He gave me about 20, but they were not too hard, and I found it very erotic, maintaining my erection throughout.

"Stand up, Charlie, you obviously enjoyed that. I had better try something else before I use the belt. Lie on the bed face up and pull your legs right over so that your toes touch the bed as wide apart as you can manage."

My butt was now facing the ceiling and Paul sat cross-legged close to my butt like an Indian and played my ass cheeks like a tom-tom. Very quick quite hard slaps, I was squirming half with pleasure and half pain. I only picked up ten of those before being told to roll over into doggy position. Paul struck me quite hard twice with a leather belt.

"Ouch, Paul, those two really hurt."

"Alright, Charlie, I am going to fuck you now then."

He did, slowly, exquisitely, my tingling bum just made it more erotic, and I came buckets well before he did.

We both rolled onto our backs, exhausted.

"Crikey, Charlie, you are still the best fuck I have ever had. Will you do me now?"

"Are you kidding, just watch."

I was hard again and inside him in no time. I had him doggy fashion and as I long stroked him with my cock, I let my hands wander all over his body. I leant forward and kissed my way slowly up his spine finally nuzzling his neck and whispering to him how much I loved his body and had done for 11 years. I sat up again and started caressing the cheeks of his ass each time I moved out of him. I could hear his breathing becoming ragged as he gasped at all the sensations running through his body.

"Oh crikey, Charlie, that feels so good. You know you have never made love to me like this."

I rolled him over, lifted his legs up onto my shoulders before re-entering him. He started to rotate his hips as I continued thrusting in and out, but now I played with his cock and balls, occasionally running my hands up his body to tweak his nipples. I pushed his legs further back so that his feet were resting on my shoulders and his knees were laying spread as wide as they would go. I massaged his perineum hard and rolled his balls in my hand. My hands were everywhere. This man was exquisite to handle.

"I'm cumming, Charlie, please fuck me hard."

So I stopped moving and held his hips firm to stop him moving as well. I leant forward and kissed him deeply.

"Sorry, Paul, I want this to last. You feel so good to be inside."

"Oh, Charlie, don't do this, no one else has ever come close to satisfying me like you do. If you make this any better, I am never going to be satisfied again in my life."

I looked into his eyes and realised he was telling the truth. I drove in hard then and almost immediately, we both had incredible orgasms. As he came down from his high, he started to cry softly. I was leaning on my elbows still inside him as my penis softened. I bent forward to kiss away the tears.

"What is it, Paul? Have I hurt you or done something wrong?"

"No, Charlie, that was wonderful. I love you so much. I think I have always loved you. I am so envious of Winston. I have never had a proper boyfriend, Charlie, because I only have enough love in my body for you; it has consumed me for 11 years."

He was crying very hard now, and I felt like shit. I had no idea. I knew several of the boys loved me, but they all loved someone else as well.

"What about Peter, he doesn't have a boyfriend either does he?"

"No Charlie. We both love you the same. We have threesomes sometimes because they can be fun but neither of us thinks of anything serious without you being part of it."

I was shattered. The most beautiful twins I had ever seen saved their love for me. I had a great deal of thinking to do about these two beautiful young men. I would need to talk to Winston as well.

I spent a long time gently caressing Paul and calming him down. I would want to make love to him again during this trip, but I would be very wary of making this situation worse before I had talked to Winston. I did talk to Winston, every night, and told him Paul was looking after me in every way. The worried tone came back into his voice.

"Charlie, this isn't going to get traumatic for us is it?"

"No, Baby, but I will have to talk to you about the twins when I get back. I have found out something that I can't leave, but can't solve without you. I promise you have nothing to worry about though. I will love you forever you know that. I am never going to work myself into a nervous breakdown again and put you through the hell I did over Jamie and Luke.

Paul and I made love every night we were in London. He was awesome. I suppose because of his love for me. It was gentle and loving and incredibly satisfying.

We moved on to Rome next, but I made sure we all had separate bedrooms this time. Of course Paul and I had a few romps, but I wouldn't let him sleep with me all night. He was getting too used to that, and once this trip was over, I didn't want a serious problem with him.

Ronald had never been to Italy, so I let him roam free for a few days while Paul and I went through Cloud's like a pair of white Tornadoes, well a black one and a white one. Very productive, and it proved the necessity for Paul's appointment. I allowed Paul several days with the Maitre D and the waiting staff just observing. He was very good, noticing the smallest detail. When he was satisfied, we moved on to the kitchen, and he watched me working. I would spend a couple of hours each night telling him what I had been looking for so that he could handle it by himself in the future.

Madrid was the same. I allowed Paul a day for the tourist bit while I went through paper work with the GM, the same as I had done in Rome.

"Each time you do this trip, Paul, you can take an extra day and expand your knowledge of each city. It will also be a good idea if you can pick up the basics of the language as well. It is the best compliment you can pay the staff in each location."

"I will, Charlie. Where are we going next?"

"Paris and then London again – in both those locations, I want you to do everything. I am just going to watch, and I will de-brief you each night, OK?"

"Of course, Charlie, and then home, yes?"

"Yes, Paul, I need to see my soul mate."

Paul blushed and looked away from me.

"I haven't caused problems with Winston, have I, Charlie?"

"No, Lover, you and Peter could never do that. You know how much we both love you two."

"I'm sorry, Charlie, Peter and I have both tried so hard to find someone else to love, but no one ever matches up to you."

"Shush, you mustn't say things like that. You will make my head swell." I said it laughing hoping to take the tension out of the atmosphere.

Paris and London were a complete success. Paul's knowledge of Cloud's was so good that our de-briefs were almost non-existent.

Almost exactly one month away as predicted. We both flew to New York and had a conference with David to fill him in on our trip. He was no longer on the board of directors, but he still owned 30% of the company. I left him with a full report of our trip and posted copies to all the other directors with my comments.

When we left David, I went straight to Connecticut, while Paul returned to Boston with Tom's copy of the report.

"Paul, after I have had a talk with Winston, I think it will probably be a good idea for you and Peter to come down to the estate for a few days. I may invite Tom and Jason as well and turn it into a planning session for future development of both companies."

"I would like that, Charlie, and I know Peter will. Thank you for the last month. You have been an awesome boss and lover."

He kissed me softly on the lips and was gone.

Winston and I didn't surface for 24 hours after I arrived home. I know that with Paul I had plenty of sex, but Winston was my true lover, and I had missed him. He was incredible. Taking charge most of the time and fucking me silly.

"Crikey, Baby, I think I like the new dominant you. I will be delighted to be your slave now instead of vice versa."

"I'm pleased, Charlie, because I intend to be master."

"Wow, where did that come from?"

"Now, tell me about the twins."

So I did.

"I don't know what to do about them, Winston. You know I have always loved those two – well, ever since we settled the business of Pinky and Perky any way."

"Why don't you retire to Lara's House, Charlie, take Peter and Paul, Jamie and Luke with you and set up a harem?"

I nearly fell off my seat with shock. I looked in Winston's eyes and saw the twinkle.

"Mmm, what a good idea, I hadn't thought of that one." Then I slapped him playfully and said, "Seriously, Winston, I can't leave this. You should have been in my place when Paul told me. We had just made love, and he was so emotional, it took me ages to calm him down."

"Jeez, I don't know. A harem really would solve the problem of those four, but I don't think I could share you on a permanent basis."

"How would you feel about a few foursomes with the twins and an occasional romp for me with them individually when I have to go to Boston?"

"I could live with that, Charlie, but isn't that just prolonging the problem?"

"Yes I suppose it is, but if Peter and Paul have not found anyone else to love in 11 years, what are the chances of it happening now. They have incredible exposure to beautiful young gay men. You would have thought one of them would measure up. I don't think I am that special."

"That's the trouble, Charlie, despite all the people that have told you they love you, there is a mental block on you accepting it. You are the most special person in the world to your potential harem and me. Darren and Ryan, Tom, the original four white waiters, any one of them would jump into my shoes tomorrow."

"Come on, Lover, that's a bit over the top. Darren and Ryan have been lovers for years. Tom and Jason still can't bear to be apart from one another for a night, which was why I moved the G.A.Y. Headquarters to Boston, so they could be together."

"I'm telling you, Charlie, any of them would leave their partner for you."

I truly was dumbfounded. A little male slut from East London, in 11 years had become a multimillionaire and had at least seven drop dead gorgeous guys ready to become his slave. Awesome, but also a terrible responsibility I didn't need. I had never intentionally hurt another person emotionally. I loved all these guys, but Winston was the only one I would die for.

"Oh Jesus, Winston, what am I going to do? I can't handle all of them. Peter and Paul will be difficult. What do I do about the remainder?"

"Charlie, I've always been able to share you because for seven years, I had to. Now I don't have to, but I love all those guys as well. Remember Darren, Ryan, Peter and Paul were my friends almost from the beginning. The four white waiters and Tom have been my friends for years. Tom and Jason have fucked me. I don't have any problems with any of them. You decide what you think is best, and I will go along with it. I love you, Charlie. If I live to be a hundred, I will still love you. Make your own decision, knowing that I am cool with it, whatever it is."

We remained in Connecticut for another week just making love and lying around. Winston supervised some landscapers he had employed to do a makeover on the grounds, but generally, we just chilled.

"Winston, my tour of the European outlets was very productive. I think I ought to do the same here. Paul will need to come. Will you come, too?"

"Why, Charlie, what can I contribute?"

"My peace of mind for starters, and for the company. On the commercial floor, you miss even less than Paul, so you can be good for him as well, professionally."

"OK, but you have to tell me what you are planning with Peter. I don't want you springing surprises on me."

"I'll think about it, Winston, I promise. I also think Peter should join us in Miami. Cloud's there is out of our mainstream supply line for beverages. We need to look at the whole set-up there. All four of us can go to G.A.Y. and see what we think of that operation. I know it is turning in good profits, but maybe it could do better, besides we haven't seen Ty for ages."

"Huh, no management consultancy fees to pay for G.A.Y., Charlie, but first class managers to consult. You are just as crafty as David when it comes to the profitability of your company."

"They are both my companies, Winston," I said very tongue in cheek.

"OK, Charlie, it sounds like fun. We can start when you like."

I talked to Peter and Paul – almost the same conversation.

"Come up to the Connecticut estate for a strategy meeting. Paul, Winston and I will start the grand tour, and you join us in Miami. Peter, does that fit in with your schedule?"

"It does, Charlie, but even if it didn't, for the opportunity to see you again, I would make it."

Confirmation of Paul's conversation with me.

They arrived together, naturally, and we settled them into adjoining suites in the house.

Dinner that night was a delight for me. Three incredibly beautiful young men sat with me. Almost certainly, we would make love together later.

"Charlie, tell me what you think of the wines. I bought them with me and have asked Ashton to serve them with dinner."

Ashton was my Major Domo and the first non-gay I had ever employed.

"OK, Ashton, bring in the wines."

By the end of dinner, I was goggle eyed.

"Peter, these wines are fabulous. Where did they come from, and more importantly, can we get enough of them at a respectable price to put into Cloud's?"

"Charlie, the price is unbelievable, and if you are happy, I want to buy the whole production from this vineyard in New Zealand."

"Do it, Peter, I don't even want details."

"Thank you, Charlie, it is going to be a heavy expenditure, but we have the storage space."

"Have you talked to Tom?"

"Yes, he said if you were happy, he had no problem, but like me he was worried about the initial cost."

"No problem, go for it."

When we finished dinner, I walked round the table, took Peter in my arms and kissed him softly on the lips.

"You have always made me proud of you. I know you will never let me down. Thank you." I saw his eyes start to mist up, so I kissed him again and whispered, "Don't cry, Peter, I love you, and I don't want you to cry because it will start me off as well."

He looked at me and laughed. "I still find it difficult to believe that anyone in the world can have as much love to give as you do, Charlie."

After dinner was great. We sat around talking and drinking coffee and liqueurs. When we were all ready to go to bed, I looked at Winston, and he nodded.

"Peter and Paul, Winston and I have a giant bed and we would love you both to share it with us tonight if it pleases you."

They looked at us both but directed their remarks to Winston. "Are you sure?"

Winston laughed. “Of course, Charlie is getting old, so nowadays, I need some young bloods in bed with me.”

I nearly fell off my chair laughing.

“I’ll show you who is old. I’m going to fuck each of you tonight. You first, Winston, for your cheek, then you can watch me make love to these two delightful creatures.” I stuck my tongue out at him and we all laughed.

It was magical. Winston was as delightful as always. Peter and Paul were unbelievable. Both of them cried like babies after our orgasms. That was when Winston realised the depths of their love for me. We fell asleep with the twins sandwiched between us. I couldn’t remember ever being so happy.

Tom and Jason arrived the next day, and we had a long meeting discussing both companies. The result was a commitment from me to Jason that we would expand G.A.Y. in the coming year by two more outlets if we could, and of course with David’s approval. Tom thought it was time to do the same with Cloud’s, and again I agreed.

“Tom, you have my shares to vote, and I am sure David’s as well, so the other directors can just be informed of our new plans. Jason, I will confirm with David on G.A.Y., but almost certainly, that will be a yes. I want you both to start the hunt for premises once you have decided on the cities, but I want final say on them before you start negotiations. Peter, Paul and Winston, I suggest you work your way down the coast going through each of the Cloud’s, and we will meet up in Miami. I am going to New York to see David.”

The meeting broke up, and while the others went off to talk to their deputies, I took Winston aside and told him the reason I needed so much time with David was that I wanted to sell Lara’s House.

“You can’t, Charlie, you love that place, you always run there when you need to relax and have an injection of happy powder. How can you even consider selling it?”

“It’s not the same place anymore, Winston, not since Mac died. There is only Cloud there now, and he can run this house for us.”

“Oh Charlie, please think about this. I don’t think David will be very happy about it.”

We all went our separate ways that afternoon. I called David, and he said I should stay at his apartment, so that evening I had a quiet dinner with him, and we arranged a full day of meetings for two days hence. That pleased me because I could have a thorough inspection of Cloud’s and G.A.Y. in the village. I had dinner with Julio at G.A.Y. and was fresh for the fray when I met with David in his study the following morning.

“David, the inspection of our European operations with Paul was immensely rewarding, as was my week with Rick. I think you are very quickly going to see improved figures for all outlets there. You already have my report, and I have mailed copies to all the other directors. I would like your approval to initiate searches for new premises for two more Cloud’s and two more G.A.Ys. I have already discussed the plan with Tom and Jason, who would like to go ahead with it. Peter, Paul and Winston are working their way through all the Cloud's doing what Paul and I did in Europe before we all meet up in Miami to sort the two outlets there. Peter has found some new wine from a New Zealand vineyard that is superb, and I have sanctioned the purchase of the whole lot. It will show up as a big debit on the balance sheet, but I am absolutely convinced it is a winner and will enhance Cloud's reputation for excellence. On the companies' front, David, that is it really."

"Well done, Charlie, you don't appear to be losing your edge, and I am happy for us to start expansion plans again. Do you need any input from me?"

"No David, I just need to be able to vote your stock in Cloud's and have your agreement for G.A.Y."

"You have it. Is there something else, Charlie?"

"Yes, David, I want to sell Lara's House."

I had never seen David shocked, but my statement really shook him.

"You aren't serious, Charlie, are you?"

"Yes, David, since Mac died there is only Cloud and Bob left, and I can employ them in Connecticut. It's lost something for me now."

"I'm sorry, Charlie, I don't know that I can say yes to that. I have my clause to stop it. Let me think about it, and I will get back to you. Better still, I am going down there for a few days after this meeting. Why don't you come with me, and we can discuss that and further talk about the direction we want the two companies to go in. You can fly back to Miami to join the others when they get there. We'll keep the jet at the airport on call."

"Alright, David, but I am not likely to change my mind."

After we arrived and had looked round the estate, Mac's replacement asked to talk to me. "Charlie, I am trying very hard to keep up Mac's standards here, but I can't. I love Lara's House almost as much as you and Mac did. Please find another estate manager to replace me. I will still remain as deputy if you will have me."

I was shocked, to give up a prestigious position like this without being asked must have taken courage and a love for Lara's I had not realised extended to the staff as well.

"I will have to think about that one, Thomas, thank you for being honest with me."

"I had to, Charlie, we arrived here on the same day, and I have admired you ever since."

"Really, that's funny because I never performed for you while I was a slave did I?"

"No, Charlie. I always wanted to, but I knew Mac never touched you when he could have done everyday, and as I grew older, he told me it was because of the respect we both shared for you."

I told David, and he just shrugged. But the next morning after breakfast, he asked if we could meet in the study. We sat in easy chairs around the coffee table.

"Charlie, I have a proposition for you. For this next week, you revert to slave status identical in every way to when you were 20. The only difference will be, no whip, but the paddle and chores book will be in existence. I will be very diplomatic when I inform the staff. At the end of the week, you will return to owner status, and we will go over the estate and decide what needs doing to bring it up to A1 standard again. The house already is, so no problem there. If at the end of those two weeks you still want to sell, I will give my blessing."

I looked at David as though he were mad. "You can't be serious, David. I'm nearly 32, president of two companies, owner of this estate. Can you imagine the humiliation of even walking around all the time in little shorts, never mind actually being used by the staff?"

"That is why I want you to do it. I think you need to be reminded of where you started this whirlwind that made you a multimillionaire. You love this place more than anyone, Charlie. I don't want you to do something you will regret."

"Sorry, David, I don't think that idea is a starter. I can just abandon it and walk away."

"Oh I like that, the loving caring, Charlie Fellows, throwing out all the loyal staff on a whim."

"Very funny, David, that was below the belt. I will have to think about this."

I went for a walk, talked to as many staff as I could. There were quite a few that I knew who had been here for years. They all told me how much they loved it and what a pleasure it was to work for me. I came back and did the same thing in the house with the same result.

At lunch, I told Cloud, David's proposal and asked what he thought. I shouldn't have. Cloud, my protector when he could be, the last of Lara's senior staff to fuck me, said, "I agree with Mr. David, Charlie. And if you do take up his offer I will take great delight in paddling you myself for your disloyalty."

I was fuming, Cloud, the one person on this estate who I thought would give me 100% support.

"OK, David, I'll do it. For the next seven days, I will be your slave again. I'll even sign a new contract to that effect if you want me to so that I can't wimp out if it gets a little rough."

I was amazed. He pulled a paper from his pocket and slid it across the table to me. It was worded almost exactly as my original contract but limited to one week, and the penalty if I failed to complete would be the forfeit of my whole fortune to charity. I signed, too stunned to do any thing else.

"OK, Charlie. Your white shorts are in your room. The same ones you had as a slave. Cloud will go with you and shave you. He will also give you an enema. In half an hour, I want you in the entrance hall where I am going to punish you as before and inform the staff of your new status. Oh and you will call me Master, and Cloud, Sir, as before. If you slip up, I will allow a member of staff to punish you in the gym, restrained and witnessed. You will be doing the cooking as well."

He got up and left, Cloud said, "Come along, Charlie, you have brought this on yourself with your stupidity."

I was shocked, but I was no wimp. So I followed him to my old room. It was very erotic having Cloud shave me. He played with me as well giving me a tremendous erection.

"Let me cum, Cloud, that feels so good."

I nearly went into orbit. He slapped my ass so hard with his bare hand I couldn't believe it.

"You will call me, Sir, Charlie, or I will give you ten more of the same."

I had done it again hadn't I? Put myself in an unenviable position out of stupidity.

"Enema time now, Charlie. I'm going to give you as many as necessary to see the water running clear."

Erection was soon gone. I really didn't like them, and how embarrassing!

When we walked into the entrance hall, the staff were all there looking surprised, embarrassed, angry and a dozen other emotions.

"Come here, Charlie, and face the staff. I have already told them what is happening. Some of them remember when you were a slave before and will fill in the details that I might have missed with the new boys. When we did this 12 years ago, I paddled your butt. Today, however, the two youngest members of the house are going to take turns. They have been told to put plenty of effort into it, and I will stop them when I think your ass is red enough. Now step out of your shorts Charlie and assume slave standing position only hands clasped behind your back instead of your head. Look at the floor, Charlie, you have not qualified to look these boys in the eyes yet."

David stood beside me playing with me and, as I got harder, I got redder. When I was fully erect, there were many gasps from the staff that had never seen my monster.

"Turn round, bend over, spread your legs wide and grip your ankles."

As I turned, I saw the two new pantry boys stood behind me dressed like me but carrying paddles. I marvelled again at how Cloud found such beautiful young men to fill their roles. My next thought was how old were they and would they like to work in a Cloud's Restaurant.

"Daniel, you can start with five good hard ones. Michael, you will follow with another five. Keep alternating until I tell you to stop."

My erection went very quickly. Daniel was definitely no wimp. He hurt, and by the time Michael took over, I was gasping. I broke at ten.

"Please, David, no more, that hurts so much."

"You will receive ten for calling me David, Charlie, in the gym lunch time tomorrow, and Thomas will administer them. Daniel five more from you will be enough for now."

I was sobbing by completion and feeling so humiliated.

"Stand up, Charlie, face the staff again."

"You will work out with Bob every day this week, Charlie, for at least three hours, some of that will be swimming and the gym sessions will take up an hour morning and afternoon. I want the beginnings of a fine slave again when you are finished. You have gotten soft in recent years. You will be available to the staff for two hours before dinner and all night if I don't want you. I have told Cloud, Bob, Robbie and Thomas that as heads of departments they are to set an example and shag you at least once this week and to paddle you if they feel at all inclined. They only need the excuse that you are planning to sell this place. The rest of the staff will do it as well. They will be encouraged to keep your ass glowing if you slack at all. Now I think you should see if you can remember how to cater for us. Away you go, take your shorts with you. The paddle and chores book are already in the staff restaurant with your routine pasted in. You need to note the contents as well."

I hurt, I was embarrassed, and I felt humiliated. The only humiliation David had not heaped on me was a finger fucking while he talked. I put my shorts back on and walked through the staff lines to the kitchen.

"Good morning, gentlemen, Robbie, I know you are the chef, so introduce me to the others please."

"Charlie, my deputy is Jack. He is Darren's younger brother. Brandon and Chris are kitchen assistants."

"Hello, Jack, if you are half as good as Darren, I will be stealing you away for one of the Cloud's Restaurants, and if you are as well hung as your brother, I hope you will be gentle with me if you summon me for chores."

I was laughing as I said it and shook all their hands.

"Let's cook up a storm for lunch, guys, and show them that Charlie hasn't lost his touch. Robbie, I don't intend wasting this week. I want you to understudy me in everything to do with the kitchen. If you have any input, I want to hear it, OK?"

"Yes, Charlie."

Lunch was a success. I noted that I had about an hour after lunch before I was due in the gym for my first session with Bob, and Robbie's name was in the book to fill that hour. I looked at him as I read it, and he looked me straight in the eye and said, "I need to get this out of the way, Charlie. I don't want to do it, but I am going to obey Mr. David."

"I understand, and I don't have a problem. I am going to have a shower, and then I will come straight to your room."

Robbie was naked when I got to his room, just finishing drying his hair. I looked him up and down while he was doing it and noted another beautiful young man. His groin interested me the most, of course, and it was mouth wateringly attractive. Thick, cut, about five inches soft and lying comfortably on a low hanging ball sac that I thought would fit nicely in my mouth. His body had a little hair, and his skin was that lovely light coffee colour that Winston maintained. When he had finished drying himself, he went to lie on his bed.

"Charlie, at the end of your week of slavery, are you really going to sell this place and put us all out of work?"

"That without any embellishment is about the score. Of course I will look after you all severance wise."

"So whatever I do to you won't matter very much will it because I am going to be out of a job anyway?"

"I guess not, Robbie."

"You know we all love Lara's House, don't you, Charlie? The same as you used to."

I was beginning to feel guilty and this was only my first encounter.

"I think I am going to punish you first, Charlie, for being so callous and then I am going to fuck you. Take your shorts off, get on the bed doggy fashion and spread your legs wide."

He took the paddle from me and positioned himself to lay into me. He was good. I was screaming at the end. He had truly hurt me.

"Stay where you are. I am going to fuck you now."

It wasn't until he entered me that I realised how big his cock grew. I was so pleased he had lubricated it and my ass.

"Oh God, Robbie, that feels enormous, please be careful."

"I will, Charlie, because I want you to enjoy this as well."

He was, and I did, cumming before him.

"Pain, pleasure and now humiliation Charlie, lick my cock clean. KY, my cum and your ass juices should be humiliation enough I guess."

When I had finished that disgusting action, he signed the book gave it and the paddle back to me and said, "I'll see you in the kitchen for dinner, Charlie, and will be only your deputy from now on. By the way, Charlie, you have a great ass."

I laughed as I replied, "Well thank you kind, Sir. You are a mix of moods, Robbie, aren't you? How long is your cock by the way?"

"The same length as yours. Cheerio, Charlie."

Gym next to an unhappy Bob.

"I can't believe you are selling this place, Charlie." He was shaking his head and looking very sad.

"I would like you to come to Connecticut with me when this is all finished, Bob. I still need to keep fit, which I haven't been doing for sometime."

"I can see, Charlie, take your shorts off and assume slave standing on the wrestling mats."

There were a couple of the staff in the gym, and they watched for the next hour fascinated and embarrassingly close.

Bob followed me out of his office and walked all round me noting every square inch of my body.

"Tense all your muscle groups, Charlie. Let me see how soft they've become."

He felt all over the relevant bits.

"Do me 50 push ups, Charlie, followed by 50 sit-ups"

I did, but I struggled.

"Hmm, not good, Charlie. Five minute warm up on the treadmill at 10 kph followed by 15 minutes at 17. Take your heart beat beginning and end."

He left me then and worked with the other two boys. When I stopped, he came back and looked at me frowning.

"When you were fit, Charlie, that little warm up would not have fazed you at all. Now look at you. You're a mess. This estate has spawned a bunch of beautiful fit young men to feed the Cloud's machine. You were the most beautiful in body and mind, Charlie, now look at you. Keep this up for another year or two, and even Winston will find you unattractive."

I moved over to look in the floor to ceiling mirrors on one wall and winced. Bob was correct. The body I had been so proud of and everyone had lusted after was a mess.

"I'm sorry, Bob, you are right."

"I ought to beat you for your idleness on this front, but I see someone already has. I won't add to your discomfort today, but I will if you don't give me 110% every session this week. Forty minutes left Charlie, just time for a good circuit."

Robbie behaved as though nothing had happened when we returned to the kitchen for dinner prep. The staff were fulsome in their praise of dinner, but comments I heard about me were not complimentary. David sent for me when he finished dinner.

"That was superb, Charlie, I had forgotten how exquisite your cooking was. I shall enjoy this week even if it is only for the food. I have talked to Winston. The boys are extending their time at each Cloud's and will probably be about six weeks before hitting Miami. I have also told him why you won't be calling him this week. His reply to that was. 'Don't hurt him, David, but please try to make him change his mind.' You might like to consider what you are going to do after this fortnight in the light of that news. When you have showered, Charlie, come to my room with the paddle."

"Yes, Master," was all I could think of to say. I was fuming at my stupidity and already sore from two paddlings today.

David had taken over my master suite, just to emphasise my position. As soon as I entered, he told me to get rid of my shorts.

"I am so sad at this turn of events, Charlie. I gave you Lara's House because of your love for it and its people. I know I am going to have to work with you for the foreseeable future, but I am still going to punish you at every opportunity this week, so watch yourself. The staff will do the same because I know they feel betrayed also."

David lay on the bed then and just ordered. "Pleasure me, Charlie."

I did but my thoughts about the future detracted from my actions, and David got cross. "Damn it, Charlie, I know you can make me squirm with the pleasure you give me sexually, but this is crap. I'll paddle you if you don't improve."

I was so distracted that I failed. David pushed me away got up and put on a pair of slacks, shirt and sandals.

"Come with me, Charlie. Bring your shorts and the paddle."

We went into the lounge, and David pulled the whipping horse into the centre of the floor. There were two young houseboys dusting and polishing knowing that the room was in use most of the day but hardly ever after dinner. When they saw David and me, they made to leave.

"You don't need to leave, boys, finish your work first. Charlie, over the horse."

I stretched myself along it, and David fastened my arms and legs, the same as before pushing my butt back to be punished. I knew this was going to hurt because I was already sore. He squatted by the side of me and talked while he finger fucked me.

"The two house boys are watching everything I do, Charlie, so Cloud will probably be on their backs tomorrow for not doing a proper job here tonight. As compensation, I am going to put on a show for them."

He moved further down my body and used both hands. One was finger fucking me while the other one played with my cock and balls. It was very erotic but a little embarrassing. When I was seriously turned on and dribbling pre-cum in an almost continuous stream, David stood up and said, "Let's see how quickly we can make that shrink."

I heard the paddle before I felt it explode on my buttocks.

"Oh God, that hurt, Master," I gasped as it sent shockwaves of pain through my body.

The second one was worse, and I screamed.

"Oh please, David, no more. That is unbelievable."

The third one was the same and accompanied by the comment. "You are not learning, Charlie. Ten more for calling me David. I think these two boys should administer them. What are your names, boys?"

"I'm Seth and this is Matthew, Mr. David"

"OK, I want you to come here and each of you is to give Charlie five licks with the paddle."

They were not particularly harsh, but my butt was already bruised, so I sobbed through all of their ten.

"That was good, guys, now I want you both to fuck him."

I couldn't believe David, but I could see they were both erect as they stripped, and David joined them.

"I don't want to hear you screaming or gasping, Charlie, so I am going to fuck your face while these two fuck your ass."

They were good. I came several times, and both of them used the lube and entered me gently. David was fucking my face while this was all going on, and I have to admit I loved it. I think that was why Lara's House had lost some of its charm for me. I liked the excitement of being used. I didn't like the punishment, particularly today where I had received way too many licks with the paddle. I determined to do better as a slave for the remainder of the week.

When they finished fucking me, David told them they could leave, but I guessed they would worry about what they had done to me.

"Seth, Matthew."

"Yes, Charlie," from two small voices.

"Thank you, I enjoyed you fucking me. You were very thrilling."

They left, and David patted my ass.

"That is more like the Charlie I love, but I think a little more humiliation is still required. For the remainder of the week you are to be naked at all times. I want all the staff to have the opportunity to see your bruised ass and your exceptional appendage."

"Oh no, David, that is too much, I'll never be able to look the staff in the eyes again."

"It doesn't matter, Charlie, as you intend sacking them all in another ten days."

He released me and sent me off to my own bed for the night.

The next event of note was the gym after lunch the next day when Thomas had to deliver ten licks for my calling David by his name. There were a few estate workers watching, and he hurt me. I was restrained over a vaulting horse, and after each one, he said to me, "I'm sorry, Charlie."

My ass was now seriously bruised, so I had to be very good for a few days, or I was going to be in physical difficulties. Bob realised as well and tailored my workout accordingly. He was very quiet, and when we were finished, he said, "Swimming pool now, Charlie, until you have to go back to the kitchen. I want you to do two lots of 50 laps with some naked sunbathing in between."

Despite my sore ass, I felt good while doing supper. Seth had his name in the book for me for the whole night, which surprised me.

I showered in my room. I was about to seek out Cloud to find out where Seth slept when there was a knock on the door. It was Seth.

"Hello, Charlie, can we spend the night in your room. I share with Matthew and only have a single bed?"

"I think that would be acceptable. What do you want to do tonight?"

"Oh nothing, Charlie. It's just that you have a very sore bottom, and I thought if you were with me, no one could add to your discomfort."

How sweet was that? I kissed him on the lips gently and told him thank you. I had some reading I needed to do and asked him if he minded. He didn't, and he snuggled up close to me with his head on my belly as I read. He slid my bedclothes down to mid thigh and said, "Charlie, will I distract you if I play with you?"

"Probably, Seth, but I don't mind. I like to be played with."

He gently caressed my cock and balls running his fingers back and forth from one to the other. When I was very hard, he started to use his tongue and lips finally taking the big leap and taking me in his mouth. As he sucked me, he started to run his hands all over my body. I was getting seriously worked up. I couldn't concentrate now, so I put down my reading and slid down the bed taking Seth in my arms and kissing him.

"How old are you, Seth?"

"I'm 18, Charlie. Matthew and I came here as houseboys a year ago."

"I have obviously been neglecting this place. I used to know all my staff and certainly any as beautiful as you and Matt."

I started to fondle his cock and balls. Already erect he gasped at my touch and said, "Charlie, will you make love to me?"

He was a delight, I hurt him on initial entry, but he wanted me to remain inside him while the pain receded, and then I fucked him gently bringing him to orgasm twice before planting my seed deep in his stomach.

Despite my sore bottom, I slept peacefully that night as did Seth who I had to wake as I was leaving for the kitchen. I kissed him softly on the lips and said, "Thank you for last night, Seth. I won't forget your kindness."

Thomas had his name in the book for my after lunch session of chores, so I trotted down to his cottage. He had taken over the one next to Mac's. Once inside, he told me to assume slave-standing position.

"Charlie, I never did this when you were a proper slave, but Mr. David has made it clear that I have to this week. I am not going to prolong this, so please just get me an erection, and then I am going to fuck you bent over the chair."

It was all over in less than ten minutes. He signed the book and gave it and the paddle back to me.

"I'm sorry, Charlie."

"Sit down, Thomas. I have some time, so let's talk. Firstly, you don't need to apologise. You know I have always been a sex hound, and you were very gentle. Next, are you becoming another Mac? I see that you have taken no holiday for years."

"I don't have any family, Charlie. My parents died soon after I was born, and I have no brothers or sisters, so Lara's House is the only home I have. I love it here, so I see no need for holidays elsewhere."

Oh dear, I was having another serious twinge of guilt.

My second session of the day with Bob was very productive, and I was beginning to feel good physically again. Bob joined me for a run and the swim after my workout, and it felt like old times.

"Do you remember the first time we followed this routine, Bob, after that new workout programme you brought in."

"Yes, Charlie, they were good times weren't they. You were the cutest, sexiest guy I had ever met with a body to die for and paddling you here was so stupid wasn't it. I just had to go through the motions. I suppose I should paddle you properly today, only because I am as disappointed with you as everyone else is. I had begun to think of Lara's House as my home."

"I'm sorry, Bob, and don't remind me about the body. It will take some work to get that fit and in shape again."

"No argument there. I would need you here for about three months to have you looking as good as that again. With the communication set up you have here, Charlie, you could do it, too, if you wanted to."

I looked at him and thought about it. We soaked up the rays for another hour before I headed back to the kitchen.

David sent for me after dinner. My heart sank, my ass was getting better, no one else had paddled me, and I dreaded another beating from David. I knew he was angry with me, so I didn't expect any mercy.

"Charlie, I want you to sleep with me tonight, and I want to make love to you."

What could I say to that except, "Yes, Master."

He pulled out the stops and made fantastic love. I was almost screaming with pleasure by the time he filled me with his seed.

"Oh God, David, I don't think you have ever made love to me like that. I nearly stopped breathing that was so fantastic."

"I'm pleased for you, Charlie, but now I am going to paddle you for calling me David again."

My look of shock and disappointment had David laughing.

"Only joking, Charlie, that was so good for me as well. I love you, Charlie, I have hated hurting you again, but you needed some shock treatment. Let's shower and then I want to cuddle you all night."

I felt like I had all those years ago when David was being tender and loving towards me.

Four more days left in which I knew I would have to take Cloud's monster and Bob's delicious one.

The gym was empty for my morning workout, and Bob took me over a vaulting horse. He was very gentle and took ages to cum.

"I want to savour this, Charlie, it is so long since I fucked you, and your ass is still incredibly cute even if you are a little out of shape."

I loved it of course. I was getting some great sex again, my ass was still a little bruised, but not sore anymore. I was feeling much better physically but still thought I ought to sell the estate.

Cloud sent for me after dinner, and he made love to me gently.

"I ought to paddle you as well as fuck you, Charlie, but faced with reality, I still love you even though I hate what you are planning to do. I won't work for you again after you sell Lara's House, so this is probably the last time I will have the pleasure of making love to you. I have never slept with you in my arms either, so I would like you to stay the night."

I felt protected spooned into Cloud and the feel of his cock against my butt sent me to sleep with an erection.

Nothing exciting the next day. I was fucked by several more staff but no paddling. I spent most of the time with a red face, embarrassed beyond belief at being naked all the time walking around the house and grounds. I slept by myself that night and did it badly.

Malcolm's name was in the book for the next day. Now I knew I was out of touch. I didn't even know we had a Malcolm.

"Cloud, who is Malcolm?"

"An estate worker, Charlie, we took him on temporarily to sort out a particular problem with some of the stock. He is leaving next week, job completed. I think Thomas would like to keep him, but he would be too expensive, and a high salaried specialist would disrupt the others."

Malcolm had one of the four man rooms that had been refurbished with just one bed making it very spacious, it was next to a bathroom, so Malcolm effectively had an en-suite double.

"Charlie, you are going to be blindfolded for the next hour because there are others who want a piece of the action but don't want you to see them."

"The staff all know there will be no come back on this, Malcolm, so they don't need to blind me."

"Nonetheless, Charlie, you will be blindfolded and stay like it until I tell you otherwise."

He produced a very effective mask that I could see nothing out of. The door opened again, and I could hear whispering from everyone except Malcolm who spoke normally. My guess was four of them all told.

"You can hold onto my shoulders, Charlie, and spread your legs as wide as you can."

In that position, I could feel bodies getting into position around me and then I felt the hands. My cock, balls and ass came under immediate attack. The cock and balls treatment was very stimulating, and I was very erect in no time. The boys had slicked up their hands already making all their touching very sensitive. There were definitely two working my ass because two hands pulled my cheeks apart and two separate lots of fingers started to penetrate me. When it reached four fingers in two definite pairs, I heard the whisper.

"Hook your fingers in like mine and see how wide we can stretch him."

They pulled quite hard stretching me as wide as they could go. It started to hurt a little, and then the hands came off my butt cheeks, and I could feel two more fingers trying to get in where I was being stretched. They succeeded, but I was grunting with the pain as they moved them about.

"OK, Charlie, I am going to guide you to the bed. Get on your back and in the centre."

As soon as I was there, my legs were pulled wide up and over so that my knees were close to my chest but spread wide. I felt a tongue on my cock, which was nice, and Malcolm said, "I am going to lube you with Crisco for this next bit, Charlie."

Something serious was going to happen for them to be using that, and I held my breath in anticipation of something nasty. It wasn't long in coming.

The whisper again. "You go first, you have the smallest fist. See how far up his ass you can get it and then I will follow."

Five fingers straight away pushing quite hard. I screamed as the knuckle went over my sphincter, but then the pain eased very quickly.

"Is he alright, Malcolm?"

The voice was worried and almost normal. I thought I recognised it and would listen very carefully when that person spoke to me again after this.

"Yes, it was only the initial entry. You are not to go in more than halfway up your forearm until he has settled down. Then be careful as you ease more in. The elbow is the absolute limit."

Whoever it was slid his arm in a little further and pulled it back again. He effectively arm fucked me for about ten minutes. I have to admit the feeling was incredible. He was being very gentle, but he was wriggling his fingers about, and I went ballistic cumming all over the place.

Both of my ass cheeks were slapped hard, just the once.

"You aren't supposed to enjoy this, Charlie. The boys are trying to punish you for selling their home. At the same time, they intend to get sexual pleasure out of you."

I could feel someone licking up my cum, and when he licked round my glans I was hard again.

"Another couple of inches to go for the whole forearm. That's fantastic."

So, I was being fist fucked by a small member of staff whose voice I knew.

The wriggling fingers continued driving me crazy again, and to add to that there were now a tongue and two hands working my cock and balls. The fist came out and another replaced it. Definitely bigger. This one was not so gentle, and I cried out as he powered in.

"Please, that hurts so much. Take it easy," I said to him as I gasped.

"Sorry, Charlie," was whispered at me.

I guess it was only a few minutes that this second fist remained in me.

"We are all going to fuck you now, Charlie, at both ends."

I was held in the same position, but with a continual change of hands as they rotated. My butt was fucked for a few minutes, and then someone else took over. The same thing with my mouth. I soon realised that they were going round in circles because I could taste the Crisco and my ass juices on cocks that I had to swallow. Utterly disgusting, and I cried in shame. When they had all orgasmed filling both my orifices with their sperm, I was allowed to sit up.

"All right, Charlie, on the floor kneeling. Good, now sit up with your hands clasped behind your back. Open your mouth and put out your tongue."

I felt a cock slide a few inches in and was told to wrap my lips round it hard.

"We are going to wash your mouth out now, Charlie, swallow it all or you will be beaten."

I wasn't given time to think about it. A sudden flow of liquid entered my mouth, and I had to swallow fast to stop choking. My head was held in place so that although I knew it was piss. I could do nothing about it. All five of them pissed in my mouth by which time I was crying harder than I had ever done. I was never going to feel clean again in my life. It was just too disgusting for words. When the last one finished, I had spilt quite a lot. My mask was pulled off, and I could see Malcolm's cock only an inch from my face.

"Lick it clean, Charlie."

I did, looking round for the others. They had all quietly left.

"On the bed on all fours, Charlie. Drop your head to the mattress and push your ass back with your legs spread. The others have said to beat you for spilling some of the piss and for selling Lara's House."

He stroked my ass running his hand through to my cock and balls before dishing out ten medium hard smacks with the paddle. No bruising I guessed but a lot of discomfort, and he had achieved the aim.

"You have a great ass, Charlie, and a fabulous cock. Watching and taking part today has been an incredible experience. Thank you."

That was it. I spent ages in the shower and drank gallons of water to try to clean my body and flush the urine out of my system. I scrubbed my teeth until they bled and went to bed still crying at my humiliation and degradation.

The next morning, I realised this was my last day of slavery and apart from the beatings and yesterday's disgusting session I had enjoyed the remainder. I had been screwed by many of the staff but taken no more paddling.

The chores book looked interesting. It was filled in as "The Kitchen Crew" for my afternoon session and "Pantry Staff" for after dinner. David told me that when the pantry boys had finished with me, I was to sleep with him again. Busy day and I guessed a sore ass internally at the end of it. I just hoped not on the outside as well.

Lunch finished, and Robbie approached me.

"Cloud has allowed us to use one of the guest bedrooms, Charlie, for the space, so after your shower, we are going to meet in the blue room."

When I entered, Brandon and Chris were seated on the bed with just their briefs on, and Robbie was standing, arms folded by the window cradling the paddle.

"Brandon and Chris want to fuck you, Charlie, but are too nervous, so I am here to help them. They want to paddle you as well but are afraid for their jobs even though you are throwing them out any way. Take their shorts off, Charlie. I want you to give them blowjobs, but don't let them cum. They are going to do that inside your ass."

More cute guys with more than adequate packages. I caressed them through their briefs first getting them hard. I slid my hand under the waistbands one at a time and pulled their briefs off. As the cock heads showed, I kissed each one. When I started to play with them swapping my tongue and mouth between the two they were wriggling like a couple of eels. I kept giggling like a kid at their antics. They were just plain delightful. When one of them was ready to cum, I would leave him, concentrate my mouth and tongue on the other, worrying nipples, licking perineum's, swallowing ball sacs. I loved it, so did they. I knew I couldn't keep Chris from cumming any longer, so I put some KY on his cock and my ass and whispered in his ear.

"I'm ready for you, youngster, if you do me doggy fashion, I can continue playing with Brandon."

"Thank you, Charlie," he whispered back.

He entered me very gently with no problem. He was only about seven inches and medium thick so he slid in easy, but I gripped him hard as soon as he bottomed out. I worked my butt and was soon feeling his sperm bursting inside me. He fell over my back and gasping for breath told me that was fantastic. I smiled, pulled my mouth off Brandon's cock and asked him how he wanted to take me.

"On your back, Charlie, and I want Chris to hold your legs a long way back and wide so that I can watch my cock going in and out."

I had to laugh as I replied.

"You little voyeur, Brandon."

He slapped my butt quite hard making me jump.

"You're a slave, Charlie, don't be cheeky."

Chris had wiped himself clean, and once I was in position, he asked me if I would suck him again while Brandon was fucking me. No problem, particularly as he hooked my legs behind his arms so that he could lean forward and suck my cock. He was a wonder, and I determined to have him again next week when I was the boss again. Brandon long stroked me trying to prolong his orgasm, but he was too young to exercise that control so Chris and I finished sixty-nining when Brandon pulled out. Wow what a lovely sex session.

"Charlie, while the boys paddle you, you can suck my cock. It will at least stop you screaming if they get too enthusiastic."

Doggy fashion on the bed with Robbie's cock in my mouth, and I waited.

Chris was first, he placed three soft licks on my ass, gave the paddle to Brandon and said to me, "I didn't want to hurt you, Charlie. I just wanted to see what it was like to beat you."

"Thank you, Chris, that was sweet of you."

I saw him blush and warmed to this young man. Brandon was a different case entirely. He had me squealing after six, he was vicious, and I knew I was going to be bruised. He finished with eight, but I was hurting. Robbie had cum in my mouth, so I guessed watching it all had him close before I touched him.

"Thank you, Charlie, I enjoyed watching." And all three walked out leaving me in a mess on the bed.

I remembered Ryan's Mum's salve and hoped the medical cupboard still had some. It did, and nurse put it on for me.

"You might avoid bruising if you are lucky, Charlie. Do try and avoid any further punishment today."

I laughed, "I always try to avoid punishment. I'm just not very good at it. Out of practice I guess."

Pantry boys and David and then I was boss man again.

I was disappointed with the pantry boys, they were lovely to look at, but they had no sexual finesse. They just shagged me.

"I think I am going to have to take you two to bed when I am the boss again and give you some lessons in love making."

I said it as I was leaving and they looked at each other before replying with broad grins on their faces, "Yes, please, Charlie.

Shower and then David's room.

"Well Charlie, what was your slave week like?"

"Interesting, David, you are crafty aren't you? Most of the boys were gentle with me but sad at my intended action. A couple were rough with me punishing me for my callous attitude, and Thomas was a revelation. I had no idea we arrived here on the same day, and he never touched me until this week. I will have to do some thinking this week."

"Mmm, and what did you just call me?"

"Oh bugger, sorry, Master."

"Drop your shorts Charlie and bend over."

I did and David touched my ass gently.

"It looks like someone has already damaged that today, Charlie. Perhaps I will spare you if you make awesome love to me tonight."

So I did. It was fun knowing that I was free tomorrow.

Chapter 13

David and I toured the estate the next day and I made copious notes on what needed doing. Thomas was with us, and I could see he was embarrassed.

"You have let it slide a little haven't you, Thomas? There is a lot of work to be organised here, David, before I put it on the market."

"You are still determined to sell then, Charlie?"

"I think so."

The next day I was in my study catching up on paper work when David walked in followed by another man who looked familiar. He sat down, and David brought me a sheath of papers.

"Look through those now, Charlie, will you?"

I did watching the other man occasionally. Where had I seen him before?

"This looks like the transcription of my notes of yesterday with a few additions, David."

"Charlie, that is the work of this man. He is an estate manager with a huge amount of experience, and first class lineage. This is Hamish Macdonald Charlie, Mac's younger brother."

I couldn't help it. I teared up, thoughts of Mac and shame at not recognising him for who he was. He had not been at Mac's funeral because he was abroad, so I had never met him.

"Under the belt, David … I'm pleased to meet you, Hamish. I loved your brother dearly. I'm sorry I didn't immediately recognise you. I should have done, you look so alike. He was a few pounds heavier than you though." We both laughed, and I liked him instantly. "So would someone like to tell me what is going on?"

"Yes, Charlie, Hamish will take his brother's old job if you will have him."

Of course, I took him on, and Thomas was delighted to be number two. The estate came alive again on the outside. Flowers and fresh fruit appeared in the house. Robbie produced better meals with the farm produce flowing into the kitchen, and all looked good again here in paradise. Staff smiled and walked again with a spring in their step even though they expected the axe to fall any day.

At the end of the second week, I asked Cloud to call a staff meeting for after lunch.

"I want everyone there, Cloud, in the staff restaurant, I will bring David."

"How long are you going to keep these boys, Charlie? You know many of them will be devastated leaving here."

"Just do as you are asked, Cloud."

Everyone was there when David and I walked in.

"David, Cloud, Gentlemen, as you know I came here two weeks ago to start the process of closing the estate up and selling it. Well I have finished my planning, so I thought I would let you in on it. Before I do though, I would just like to say that there were things missing in my life that had been part of Lara's House for me, that was the great sex I used to have here. You brought that all back for me last week, and I just want to say how good it was. I am remaining here for another four weeks to let Bob keep punishing me with his fitness programme. Miami for about a week after that. When I return, Lara's House is going to become my personal HQ. I will be running Cloud's and G.A.Y. from here. If you can forgive me for the stress and sorrow I have created in the last two weeks, I would like you all to stay here to look after the estate and Winston and me."

David was the first one to start the destruction of my back everyone was pounding it and shaking my hand.

"Thank you, Charlie," was on everyone's lips.

"I would like to see Brandon and Robbie in my study now, Chris same place in 15 minutes. Thank you everyone."

I was at my desk when they knocked and entered.

"Apart from David, you two were the only ones that were vicious with your punishment. I can't let you get away with that, so I am giving you both a choice. You can take severance and leave, or you can agree to a reciprocal punishment."

They looked at each other and shrugged, then looked at me and Robbie said, "We want to stay, Charlie."

"Alright, Brandon, you can wait outside until I have finished with Robbie."

When the door was closed, I whispered to Robbie, "You hurt me for the right reason, so I want you to fake your yelps and screams of pain as I paddle you."

I took the paddle and beat the back of one of my leather chairs. Robbie did a good job making it sound as though I was killing him.

"Brandon isn't going to be so lucky, so don't ever tell him I never touched you. Fetch him in for me, please."

"I want you to witness this Robbie as Brandon's boss. Brandon strip, buck-naked and then prostrate yourself over my desk with your legs wide apart."

I laid into him with the paddle like he had done to me. He was screaming after only a couple, and I had to get Robbie to hold him so that I could continue. After ten, he was blubbering like a baby.

"Stand up, Brandon, shake my hand, no hard feelings."

"I'm sorry, Charlie."

"OK, youngster, get dressed and go and ask nurse for some of Ryan's magic potion. He will know what you mean."

I wondered after they had gone if I had been too harsh with Brandon, but then Chris knocked and my thinking changed tack.

"You wanted to see me, Charlie."

"Yes Chris, I would like you to have your first lesson in lovemaking tonight. Will you sleep with me?"

His eyes lit up and a grin spread across his face from ear to ear.

"Oh yes, please."

"Alright, you come and find me when you are finished work. Bring your tooth brush with you."

David was next. He just plonked himself down on a chesterfield and looked searchingly at me.

"Well, satisfied?"

"Yes, Charlie, if you are sure."

"I am, I was stupid, seeing Hamish was the final persuader. I loved Mac so much, David. His death clouded my judgement with regard to Lara's House. Apart from Cloud and you, I doubt any friend I have for the remainder of my life will match that wonderful caring old bear." I burst into tears. "I'm sorry David, I miss him so much."

He almost flew round the desk, pulled me into his arms and started stroking me. "It's alright, Charlie, cry for him, cry for your loss, it's OK."

A lot of cuddling and a large brandy later, I was back in control.

"No wonder we all love you so much, Charlie, you care for all of us the same as Mac cared for you."

I burst into tears again and David laughed, making me do it as well. Laughing and crying, how stupid.

Chris found me in the lounge reading. He had obviously showered and changed into brushed cotton powder blue shorts, (Cloud's colour), with a very tight white T-shirt. He looked and smelt so fresh I could have raped him on the spot.

"Hello, Chris, you look beautiful, come and sit next to me."

I pulled him close to me and kissed him softly on the lips.

"I think you are going to be one of my special boys here at Lara's House, and maybe later in one of my Cloud's or G.A.Y. venues."

"Thank you, Charlie. I think I would like that. Are you going to make love to me tonight?"

"I am if you will let me, but you know how big I am."

"Yes, Charlie, but Robbie is the same size as you, and he has fucked me."

I was surprised.

"But you act so innocent, as though you have never made love."

"Robbie doesn't make love, Charlie. He just fucks me like I did to you."

"I'm sorry, Chris, you should be made love to. You are so delightful to be with. Come, it's early, but I want to pleasure you very much. We can do something else later if you want to."

I took him to my suite and slowly undressed him, kissing and caressing him as I uncovered more of his beautiful soft skin. I dropped to my knees to remove his shorts and briefs. His cock was rigid and sprang up to slap against his belly. I pulled it away and kissed the head before running my tongue over it. He gasped and stepped out of his shorts, spreading his legs wider for me to access him. I licked his balls and up his shaft to the head again trying to bury my tongue in his piss slit.

"Oh gosh, Charlie, that feels so good. Please don't stop."

I laughed softly.

"I have no intention of stopping, Chris. You are so beautiful."

"Thank you, Charlie."

I laid him on the bed and continued pleasuring him. I spread his legs wide and attacked his balls, slicking them up so that they would easily slip through my hands when I played with them. I bent his legs and pressed them to the bed exposing his hole more fully for my touch. Next were his perineum and then his love hole. Oh God, that was beautiful. I licked it slurped on it sucked it rammed my tongue as far into it as I could. It was unbelievable, the prettiest rosebud I had ever seen. I couldn't wait. I lubed his hole and my cock and eased into him, very gently, taking my time to feed him all of it. I watched his eyes carefully for any sign of pain. As soon as I bottomed out, I lay on him and continued kissing him and whispering to him.

"I'm sorry I have entered you so early, Chris, you were just too amazing to delay any longer. I promise I will be gentle with you now."

"Oh, Charlie, you feel so good inside me. Please fuck me for a long time."

I did. I slow stroked him stopping every time I thought I was going to cum. I never wanted to let my cock go soft and leave this boy. I played with him nonstop. His cock and balls I kept slick, I continually caressed and nibbled his nipples, kissed his neck, lips, eyes. I was going crazy with lust for him. I rubbed my belly into his cock rotating my hips to further stimulate him front and rear. I made him cum three times before I lost control and fucked him viciously for my last few strokes making him cum again and depositing what I was sure amounted to my largest semen deposit ever. I remained inside him as I went soft lying on his chest.

"Chris, that is the most exquisite lovemaking I have ever had. You are unbelievably sexy and lovely."

"Thank you, Charlie, I had no idea it could be this good. Will you do this to me again?"

"Of course. Shall we have a shower and go down for a night-cap before doing it again?"

"Oh yes please, Charlie."

We made love twice more before snuggling up together to sleep. He was delightful to cuddle all night. I knew I would want to do this again. We woke late, and I had to apologise to Cloud and Robbie for keeping Chris from his duties, but not before we had devoured a huge breakfast in the dining room. Chris was very apprehensive about eating with me, but I was reluctant to part with him.

I hung around the kitchen unnecessarily just to be near him before pulling myself together and going to see Bob. After lunch, I took him with me for my afternoon session at the gym and later to the pool where we lazed around naked. We were the only ones there, so I cuddled him on a sun bed when we weren't actually swimming.

"I am falling in love with you, Chris, and that can't be allowed to happen. I love Winston and to stop after all these years would kill him, but somehow you have to fit into my life here."

I made love to him there and marvelled at his allure. I could not get enough of this boy. He slept with me again that night. Just cuddling him was almost better than the sex.

The next morning, I entered the staff restaurant after breakfast just as Brandon slapped Chris hard across the face and called him a white man's whore. Chris screamed at him.

"I don't care what you call me, I love Charlie and I'll be his whore if he wants me to be."

"I don't want you to be my whore, Baby. I love you too much for that. Brandon, see Cloud, you are finished here."

"Please, Charlie no, he is my best friend. I don't want you to fire him."

I was surprised.

"Alright, Chris, both of you in my study now."

Seated behind my desk with the two boys standing in front, I addressed Chris.

"Give me good reasons why I should keep Brandon here, Chris, after he struck you and called you my whore."

"We grew up together, Charlie, he was always my protector from the bullies. He is like a brother to me. I don't know why he called me your whore."

"OK, Brandon, you tell me why you struck him so hard and called him my whore."

No answer.

"No answer is as good as confirming your sacking, Brandon."

"I love you as well, Charlie, I was jealous," he said softly with obvious embarrassment.

"Well, you're a fool, boy. I would have made love to you at some time. You must know that I sleep with other staff members if they want me.

Don't be stupid. Look after Chris for me. When I think you are worthy, I will take you to bed, but you have to prove your worth first."

"I'm sorry, Charlie, please forgive me."

"I'll forgive you when Chris does."

"Please, Charlie, I forgive him now."

"Alright, off you go, and both of you had better come and sleep with me tonight."

They both beamed at me before leaving, and I was hard pressed not to laugh. I had the feeling I was going to have an enjoyable night. I did, but it was slightly messed up by Cloud reminding me that I already had a lover.

As soon as they appeared in the lounge, both dressed as Chris had been the first night, I took them to my bedroom.

I wouldn't let either of them touch me because of my game plan, but I took over an hour pleasuring them jointly. Both of them had wonderful groin areas. Only a small amount of hair, long straight, thick cocks, nicely hung ball sacs and the most incredible hole on Chris with a very pretty one on Brandon. They were both 18 but looked about 15. I could have eaten them they looked so wholesome. As it was, I limited myself to eating their cocks and balls, and chewing on their asses as well. They were like a couple of worms wriggling around on the bed, gasping every time I hit one of their erogenous areas with my tongue or wet fingers. When they were both ready to orgasm I guided Brandon into Chris, emphasising the need to be gentle. They were like two beautiful young fawns cavorting in the forest. Brandon was so comfortable for Chris to take, he kept sighing as Brandon long stroked him. I talked him through it, making him rotate his hips to hit Chris's insides in different places on each entry. When they orgasmed, they were so far out of it that they made no noise, just slowly deflated. They kissed gently, and I could see the love they had for each other in their eyes.

I rolled Brandon onto his back and slid down between them cuddling both of them.

"Gosh Charlie, Chris is my best friend. I've never done that to him before. It was fantastic, and what you did to us was amazing."

"How about you, Chris, did you enjoy your best friend making love to you?"

"Yes, Charlie, that was so good. You first and then Brandon. He was very gentle, but also very exciting."

"Good, let's clean up and then Chris, you can do to Brandon and me what I did to you two. When we are both very hot, I am going to fuck Brandon, and if you stand in front of me I will give you another blowjob."

"Golly Charlie, that sounds awesome."

As I was entering Brandon, I told him I was going to do to him what I had made him do to Chris so that he could feel how good it was.

His orgasm was even more powerful than when he was fucking Chris, and Chris had a terrific orgasm as well filling my mouth to overflowing with his cum. I brought Brandon to another very quick orgasm. I had been hitting his prostate, so he was right on the edge.

"Clean up now boys and bed. With me if you like or you can go together."

"Can we stay here, Charlie? We only have single beds, and I want to cuddle you or Brandon."

Another wonderful night's sleep for me cuddling two beautiful boys

The next morning I had housekeeping put a double bed in the boys' room. They were delighted when they saw it and sought me out at the pool that afternoon to thank me.

"I want you to be happy together, but I hope you will occasionally let me make love to you both."

"Oh yes, Charlie, we would like that very much." And they were gone leaving me with no conscience problems when I called Winston that night.

"I miss you so much, Baby, even though life has been so eventful here. Why don't you leave Peter and Paul to it, and we will meet up with them again in Miami?"

"Charlie, you know I would love to because I miss you so much, but we really are doing a lot of very useful work together. If we finish this off now, we won't need to do it again for ages."

"OK, Lover. Are you getting any sex?"

"You should never ask me that, Charlie, I never have, and you know it. Would you be cross with me if I was?"

"Of course not, at least not if it is with Peter and Paul. I would be worried if it was with someone I didn't know."

"I'm pleased. I was going to tell you anyway tonight, but I was a little worried having never done it before. We had a threesome last night. I didn't mean to, Charlie. I think we were just very randy, and it became a bit of a dare. You aren't angry with me are you?"

"Of course not. You don't think I have been celibate, do you? Besides my slave week that is."

"No I guess not. Who?"

"The two kitchen boys. I am teaching them to make love to each other, and I have had a double bed put in their room so that they can sleep together. They are delightful, Winston, and only look about 15. Very sexy with the most beautiful asses."

"You sound like you are in love again, Charlie."

"No Baby, well maybe a little bit with the one called Chris, but you will always be my only true love. I really can't wait for Miami, I miss you so much. It seems like forever since you were with me."

"I feel the same way. I suppose that was why I made love with Peter and Paul last night. I was very naughty, Charlie, I fucked both of them."

"You lucky little devil, I've never had them both at once. Call me tomorrow if you have time and hurry it up wherever you have to go so that we can make Miami soon."

"OK, Charlie, at least another three weeks though I think. I love you, goodnight."

"I love you too, Baby, sleep tight."

I was getting the most incredible sex. I had overcome another falling in love episode by pairing Chris with his friend, so the last thing I needed was David's latest problem.

"Charlie, I have the most amazing young man for you to see. I am bringing him with me today. Ask Cloud to put him in a staff bedroom but with an en suite."

"What do you mean amazing, David?"

"I'm not saying anymore, Charlie, that will spoil the surprise."

David arrived at Lara's House and came to my study immediately with his surprise in tow.

"Hello, Charlie."

"Hello, David, is this your surprise?"

"Yes, does he remind you of anyone?"

"No, should he?"

"Come on, Charlie, how about you 15 years ago."

"Hmm, possibly, David."

"Well this will make you more convinced. Strip, Freddie."

The boy stripped, needing a reminder from David to remove his boxers. His look of anguish touched my heart and took me back 12 years.

"Oh crikey, David, I see what you mean. Does it get as big as I think?"

"Not quite, Charlie, your supremacy is intact, but only by about a half inch. His name is Freddie Smith, and he is a slave the same as you were Charlie for the same reason, only for two years against your ten."

Freddie looked amazed as he listened to the conversation.

"He doesn't have your talent, Charlie, and I can't keep him in New York. Can I leave him with you? I will start him off with the staff the same as I did you, and then leave his rota up to you. I have had him a month. I haven't beaten him, which was probably a mistake, and he isn't very good in bed. You might like to train him if Winston will allow it."

"Well, I suppose you can leave him here, David. I don't know that I particularly want to supervise a slave, but I can always delegate that task. No whip though and only senior staff to punish. I won't standby and have him brutalised like I was."

"That's acceptable, Charlie, just don't go falling in love with him."

"Come on, David, you know Winston is the only person I fall in love with now. He still allows me to fool around a little, so I might try him for you.

He is certainly very pretty, and the butt and box should keep the staff happy if we can teach him to be good at sex."

"I thought you might. Cloud can take him now, get him shaved and into shorts which I have brought with me. Nurse can give him a triple enema and organise him for one everyday. Staff in the entrance hall in half an hour if that is OK, with you, and I'll play with him for everyone to see and then paddle him."

"Alright, David, but I am not happy about the paddling."

"I know, Charlie, but embarrassment, humiliation and pain will show him his place and save you time and trouble later."

Freddie hated being shaved but detested the enema even more. The thought of that everyday was most unappealing. What would he need it for any way?

He soon found out when David introduced him the same as he had me nearly 13 years ago, only without the whip and punishment routine. Instead, he was told he would receive ten licks every week from a head of department or under their supervision. He was to call senior staff Sir.

"Now strip, Freddie, and stand with your legs astride and hands clasped behind your back."

A hard slap on his butt was required to gain compliance, and I could empathise with that.

David played with Freddie until he was erect, not quite as long as I was and not as impressive because it only rose a little above the horizontal.

"Turn around, Freddie, spread your legs and bend over, grip your ankles and keep still until I complete your punishment. If you move, I will start again."

The first one was such a surprise that Freddie jumped.

"I am going to start again, Freddie. You will receive ten without moving regardless of how often I have to start again."

By the time David had finished, Freddie was sobbing.

"Put your shorts on, boy, and go with Charlie, he will sort out a routine for you. Charlie, I have to return to New York immediately. We can talk during the week."

"OK, David, you really did mean a flying visit didn't you?"

"Yes, cheerio."

When we were ensconced in my study, Freddie stood in front of the desk while I looked him up and down carefully.

"You are almost too pretty to be a boy, Freddie. If we can teach you how to give real pleasure in bed, I am certain my staff will love it. I know they were a very happy bunch when I was a sex slave for them. Do you enjoy sex, Freddie?"

"Yes, Sir, but I know I am not very good at it."

"Well, my partner is away this week, so we might get in a few sessions, and you can workout with me everyday and swim as well. I don't intend to see much beating done, Freddie, apart from what David has specified, unless you are disobedient or lazy. Bob will work you hard in the gym as he does me, and I will work you at the pool. We are going to have to find you a job as well. What are you good at and what do you like?"

"I'm not very good academically, Sir, but I was learning massage and fitness training before I got in over my head with gambling. Were you really a slave as well?"

"Yes, Freddie, for six years. David let me off four years because I nearly died twice. I was brutalised with the whip as well as sexually. He gave me Lara's House, and we went into business as well. We jointly own two companies. I am president of both and run them from here because my partner and I love this house. Now, what we are going to do with you for a couple of days is have you shadow me. After that, I will let the staff have you for a couple of hours per day. Do you have trainers and sport socks?"

"No, Sir, I only have the clothes I came in and my new shorts."

"You are lucky then. You look about the same size as me. Come, let's find out."

We went to my suite where we found new trainers and socks, which fitted Freddie perfectly.

"OK, Freddie, let's see what Bob makes of you."

"Crikey Charlie, I'd like to see you two together when you were his age. I wouldn't bet on who was the sexiest."

"Yes very funny, Bob. Let's get on with my routine and see how he does."

"Shorts on or off, today?"

"On, I think, Bob, until we are used to him being around."

"Getting bashful, Charlie?"

"Oh come on, Bob, let's get on with it."

One hour later I was not feeling so chipper.

"The boy is fit, Charlie. That can only benefit my work with you."

"Good, if I am going to wet nurse David's new slave, it will be nice to get something from it. Swim now, Freddie, see you tomorrow, Bob. Better still, join me for dinner this evening at eight. Tell Robbie there will be three for the main dining room, but we can have the same as the staff."

At the pool, I stripped and told Freddie to do the same.

"I want you to get me excited and give me a blowjob, Freddie. Let's see how good you are."

"What here, Sir?"

"Yes, of course here."

"But what if someone comes?"

I laughed heartily as I replied, "Freddie, you will be having sex with an audience frequently, I am certain, while you are here. Get used to it."

The boy was enthusiastic enough, but he really wasn't very good. He took a long time to make me cum, and the orgasm was as weak as I could ever remember.

"Freddie, that was a one on a rating from one to ten. Now watch feel and learn. I am going to give you one."

It was a pleasure to see how he reacted to my touch. When he came, I could tell by the amount I swallowed that it had been good for him. The fact that he had been begging me to let him cum for ages before I took mercy on him emphasised that point.

"Oh God, Charlie, that was amazing."

He said it as he came down from his high. When he had fully calmed down he realised what he had said. "Oh gosh, I'm sorry, Sir, I didn't mean to use your name."

I laughed. "It's OK, Freddie, I don't much like being called Sir. I think I would prefer it if you continue to call me Charlie. Did you learn anything from that?"

He giggled and said, "Yes, Charlie, I learnt that I would like you to give me lots of blowjobs."

I laughed as well. He was beginning to relax, and I could see a happy character underneath the frightened little boy David had delivered.

"Well, I might have to give you a few more while you are learning, but don't get too used to it. I am going to fuck you for your next lesson and then you are going to give me a blowjob and fuck me the two sessions after that. I expect both to be very good, so besides getting enjoyment, I want you to learn as well. Time to go, I think. I want you to wear a T- shirt for Dinner tonight. You will eat with Bob and me at eight o clock."

Dinner that night was very pleasant. I don't know why I ate alone so often when Winston was away. Bob was good company as was Freddie. He appeared very relaxed in my company, and I liked the feeling. He was 15 years younger than I was, and his young body excited me. The combination of him and Chris was going to give me problems if I were not careful.

"Bob, the main reason for us being together at dinner is to discuss this young man. I don't know how long David is going to leave him with us, but while he is here I would like him to learn something useful. As you know, he is a slave in the same way I was. He is 18 and would like to become a masseur and fitness instructor. Can we work out a schedule for him that will leave him some time for slave duties but keep him occupied the remainder of the working day."

"That shouldn't be too difficult, Charlie. I don't have a training programme, but I can soon get one if you will sanction the expense. I can certainly teach him massage techniques. We can use you to practice on. I think you need regular massages while we bring you back to fitness."

"Good that's no problem. Set it up so that he has time at the pool to get a good tan and a couple of hours in the afternoon or early evening for slave duties. How does that sound to you, Freddie?"

"Thank you very much, Charlie, that sounds terrific."

Turning to Bob, he said, "I liked working with you today, Sir. I will try very hard to please you and Charlie."

Bob looked at me unhappily and said, "Does he have to call me Sir, Charlie? I'm not really comfortable with that formality."

"I don't think so, Bob. I don't know why David imposed that condition. I can understand it with Cloud and Hamish, but, Freddie, I think you can call everyone else by their first names."

"Thank you, Charlie."

After Bob and Freddie left me, I asked Cloud to join me for a night-cap because I wanted to discuss something with him. I was amused at how reluctant he was to sit with me in the lounge.

"How long have you known me, Cloud?"

"Twelve years, Charlie, why?"

"I was just amused at your discomfort. You have beaten me, made love to me and carried out incredibly personal actions on me. I would have thought sitting with me here would have been easy."

He laughed and said, "They were all different, Charlie, because I was ordered to do them as part of my job."

"Well so is this but never mind. I was wondering if you would feel uncomfortable if I invited staff to join me for dinner in the main dining room some evenings. I realised tonight with Bob and Freddie how pleasant the company was with Winston away again."

"Of course not, Charlie, anything you want to do here is fine with me, you are the boss."

"I know, Cloud, but you are the most senior member of staff, and I would not want you to feel uncomfortable with my guests."

"I promise that will not happen, Charlie."

"Thank you, Cloud, you know how much I value your friendship. I would not want to do anything to change that. I think it would be pleasant when Winston is away, and I have no other proper guests. We can start with you tonight if you wouldn't mind."

"OK, Charlie."

At dinner, I told Cloud I wanted an understudy for Robbie in the kitchen.

"Any particular reason, Charlie."

"Yes, we are too thin on the ground with only one chef. Jack really isn't good enough to train as a full chef. We can keep him on because I will probably be stealing Robbie for Cloud's. Usual criteria please, young, good looking, gay."

Cloud laughed, "What else?"

We both laughed, he knew me as well as anyone other than Winston.

Chapter 14

The next morning I bumped into one of the houseboys, literally, as I left my study.

"I'm sorry, Charlie."

"No problem, Moses."

He was almost out of my sight when I realised. "Moses."

"Yes, Charlie."

"Come here a moment and say to me, 'Is he alright Malcolm?'"

He didn't have to say it. The look on his face told me the answer.

"You were one of the boys at my blindfold session weren't you, Moses?"

Give him his due, he didn't try to deny it. He hung his head and whispered, "Yes, Charlie, I'm sorry. Vincent insisted we do that last thing. Oh gosh, I shouldn't have said that. He'll kill me."

"Vincent is your closest friend here is he?"

"Yes, Charlie, but he is a bit of a bully as well."

"Who else was there?"

"Oh please, Charlie, don't ask. I'll never be happy here again if they find out."

"Hmm, OK, go and find Malcolm and both of you come to my study, don't tell him why."

When they came in, I told them they could sit down.

"Malcolm, I know Moses was one of the boys at my blindfold session. I recognised his voice when we spoke this morning. I can work out the others by association, but I have a deal for you. I understand that you would like to remain here on the permanent staff, and I know Hamish would like to keep you, but your salary would not fit our staff plan. I can change that by creating a new job, stock manager, reporting directly to Hamish, and you would live in a staff cottage like Thomas. For the names of the others, I will do it."

"That is blackmail, Charlie, and much as I would like to stay, that act would destroy my credibility."

"I wouldn't tell. I would make it sound as though I had worked it out through association."

Malcolm's look of anguish told me how difficult this was going to be for him. Lara's House had cast its magic over yet another person. He looked at Moses then me, lowered his head and said, "What are you going to do to them if I tell you, Charlie?"

"I am going to make all of you do something as degrading as you made me do, if you want to keep your jobs that is."

"Crikey, Charlie, I don't know about that."

"OK, Malcolm, I'll find out anyway. It will just take me longer. The other boys will have the right to refuse when I find them, but if they don't accept my terms, they will be fired and join you in not working here. I can guess one other already. Moses' best friend is Vincent, only two others to work out."

"Hector and Jonathon, they always sit together for meals, so you catch one you catch them all."

"I will announce your permanent employment after we have sorted the degradation. I want you in my study again at 1330. Moses, you say nothing."

I walked into the staff restaurant at lunchtime and sure enough, my four villains were together.

"I would like to see you four in my study at 1330."

They looked shocked. I wondered if they had guessed why.

I had them lined up in front of my desks looking very apprehensive.

"You were given carte blanche to use me and abuse me while I was a slave. You obviously believed that the final act you committed would be construed as being way over the top, so you had me blindfolded. Unfortunately for you, my investigative skills are quite acute. A case of guilt by association, Vincent you work closely with Malcolm, the first boy to fist fuck me had a small hand. You four were just too perfect a fit. I am correct aren't I?"

They nodded.

"I respect you for not trying to bluff me, but I am going to take my revenge for that last act if you want to remain here. The choice is yours. I want the use of each of your bodies for one hour in the barn on the hill. Absolutely no holds barred, exactly the same as was the case with me. I will tell you when. You can go now if you accept my terms. Stay if you don't, and I will terminate your employment now so that you can leave today."

They all left, and I had all the time I wanted to work on a plan.

My priority at Lara's at that time though was Freddie. He was delightful. I was teaching him how to be good in bed, and he was an enthusiastic learner. I was coming back into shape very quickly, and I knew Winston would be delighted, which made me work harder. Freddie was the other reason, with a difference of 15 years, I was very conscious that to him I must appear quite old, but I wanted him to fancy me. Perverse I suppose when the only person I should be trying to impress was Winston.

With Freddie learning Bob's trade, it allowed Bob to pursue another train for his career.

"Charlie, in another six months, Freddie could take over my job here. I would like to take that opportunity to leave. I have saved a lot of money here thanks to your generosity, and I want to open my own gym in New York."

I was shattered. Bob was almost family. He had been with me so long.

"I don't know what to say, Bob. You, David and Cloud are the only family I have now. I would miss you terribly if you were to leave. If it is a case of money, I can increase your salary. I will hate losing you."

"No, Charlie, I will hate leaving, but I need to progress after all this time, and at Lara's, I will never be anything more than I am now."

"OK, let me think about this."

I called David.

"Hello, Charlie, to what do I owe this pleasure?"

"David, can I buy Freddie's contract from you?"

"Oh dear, Charlie, you haven't fallen in love with him have you?"

I laughed. "Of course I have, David. How could anyone as beautiful as him escape my love? That isn't the reason though. Bob wants to leave in six months and thinks Freddie will be good enough to replace him. I would like that to happen. Freddie is becoming very good at the job already. His personality is blooming, and he is popular with the staff, so the gym will continue to be used under him the same as it has been under Bob."

"You don't have to buy it, Charlie. I will gift him to you. My lawyer will send you the papers."

"Thank you, David, once again I owe you."

"Yes you do, Charlie, can I take it out of your body next time we meet?"

I laughed, which turned into a giggle as I formed my reply, "Oh yes, David, would you?"

He laughed, too. "You don't need an answer to that do you, Charlie?"

"No, David, I don't believe I do. Thank you again."

Bob was happy when I told him I would release him in six months time with five years salary as a pay off and transfer of his pension fund anywhere he wanted it.

"Charlie, that is too generous."

"No it isn't, Bob, think of the things you have done to help my life, think of the great sex we have had, think of the way you have kept me fit all these years. Five years salary isn't at all generous."

I gave him a big hug and told him he was always welcome here at Lara's, and if he got into difficulties, he was to call me. I made a mental note that I would have his business monitored to make sure he succeeded.

Next was Freddie.

"You are my slave now, Freddie. I want you to be ready to take over from Bob in six months time. I am going to move you into senior staff quarters, and you are going to dress like a proper physical training instructor. Your slave duties are over except as directed by me, as is the weekly paddling. I will have you paddled if I think you need it, and I will let staff have sex with you occasionally. I know how good I was for staff morale when I was a slave, so you can help on that front as well."

"Thank you, Charlie, I don't deserve it, but I will try very hard to please you."

"I'm sure you will. Would you like to start by going to bed with me tonight?"

"Oh yes, please, Charlie. I don't mind doing the sex slave bit. I get lots of really good sex from it."

I had to laugh. Here was another slut like me.

"You can still do it, Freddie, but now it will be voluntary most of the time. Just tell the staff how you want to play it."

Another happy customer.

I had no idea how good Bob's massage technique was, for some peculiar reason we had never gone that route. Now I was finding out. Freddie was massaging me under Bob's supervision almost everyday. Without touching my groin area, he was getting me erect every time, and of course even if a towel had covered me, which it didn't, it was obvious.

"You two get me hard. One of you gets rid of it before I leave this table."

"What a good idea, Charlie. You and I take turns, Freddie, agreed."

"Oh! Do we have to, can't I do it everyday, and you watch to make sure I do it right?"

All three of us dissolved with laughter.

"You cock hounds. Why don't you do it together?"

"Greedy as ever, Charlie, what is Winston going to think when he is here?

"He'll probably want to join in, Bob. Or better still, if he joins me for a massage you can have one each."

"Charlie, I think Freddie will freak if he ever has any kind of sex with Winston. He is the sweetest guy in the world and that includes present company."

Freddie looked totally bemused. "Gosh, Bob, is Winston really that awesome?"

"Yes he is, Freddie, this sex fiend here can't get enough of him." Pointing at me, he laughed, "Even if you do make love to everyone else on the estate, Charlie."

"Mmm and he has been away far too long, Bob. I'm off to Miami next week, and when we come back, I'm not going to let him off this island without me for a very long time. This is the longest spell apart we have had since I was ill."

Miami could have been the moon or anywhere else in the universe, I wouldn't have cared. I had missed my Lover, but it wasn't until I held him that I realised how much.

Our first night together, we didn't sleep at all. We talked or made love until breakfast. There were so many sixty-niners and mutual fucking, I lost count of the number of orgasms I had. I know the best two were when I fucked Winston the first time, and when he fucked me the first time. The remainder of the orgasms were merely heart stopping. Oh God, I loved that guy so much it hurt.

Peter and Paul spent the whole of breakfast taking the Mickey. I didn't care. I was so happy to be with my Baby again nothing was going to upset me.

Both venues were hard work even with four of us. They were turning in acceptable figures, but the atmosphere wasn't right in either place, and the menu and wine list at Cloud's were still not right. Peter and I worked on them together, eventually ditching both and starting from scratch. The result was pleasing to both of us. Winston and Paul with an interior designer presented me with plans for a makeover, which looked impressive, so we decided to close Cloud's, transfer the new menu to G.A.Y. while the refurbishment went on and then do a partial makeover of G.A.Y. without closing completely. Two weeks had flown by before we knew it. While the other three wrapped up the loose ends, I decided to take the company jet to Boston to brief Tom on what we were doing, and I would pick Winston up in Miami to return to the island while Peter and Paul took scheduled flights back to Boston.

My Baby was quite worn out when we arrived back, and I realised how much of a strain the last seven weeks had been on the three of them. I telephoned Tom and told him that Peter and Paul were to take at least two weeks off, no argument, starting straight away. They would be welcome at Lara's if they just wanted to unwind, and I didn't think it would be out of place for them to use the company jet.

Winston and I were chilling out by the pool, when I heard the helicopter coming in from the direction of the airport. I hoped it would be the Twins. A half-hour later, I had my wish as Peter and Paul walked into the pool area. Big hugs and kisses had the other swimmers looking in surprise. Many of the staff were new enough not to know how long P&P had been part of my life and where they had started. From pantry boys to high powered business executives in 12 years, not bad!

Freddie and Bob worked overtime for the next two weeks. Peter, Paul, Winston, and I had a workout, a sauna and a massage almost everyday and then chilled by the pool every afternoon, usually with Freddie present as well as other staff. I hardly let Winston out of my grasp, and Freddie was obviously fascinated at my devotion to him.

When he was massaging me one morning after my workout, he said, "Charlie, does Winston know that I am going to give you a blowjob after I have finished my massage?"

"Of course, Freddie, Winston knows everything I do sexually. Sometimes he joins in, but mostly he just wants one-on-one sex with me."

"That is incredible. Isn't he jealous?"

I laughed. "Of course not. He has nothing to be jealous of. It's all to do with conditioning. He knows I'm a slut, but for our first six years together, I had no choice because I was David's slave, and I had to do what you did for a few weeks. There were times when the best we had was a quick couple of hours in the afternoon, and when David was on the island, the only time I saw him was in the kitchen. He knows he can never match my sex drive, so he accepts that I screw around. We have had some memorable sessions with other staff who we love, but they are few and far between."

"Wow, Charlie, will I ever get the chance for sex with both of you?"

"Freddie, I think I am turning you into a sex slut like me, but the answer is probably."

Lara's House was becoming fun again. The next night, Winston and I fucked Peter and Paul. I don't think it's the best sex I ever had, but it was certainly the most fun. We had been together for so long, it was almost incestuous. The twins, even at 30 were still incredibly sexy. I fucked Paul because Winston, Ryan and he were as close to each other sexually as it was possible to get. Freddie was a different colour, but it was an attitude thing, and I could see him being part of the team soon. I thought how amazing it would be to watch Winston make love to him. I also wanted Cloud to have him. That was going to be very difficult to engineer, but I would succeed somehow.

The next internal problem to confront was the five piss artists. I hadn't told Winston, but it was such a dilemma, I eventually told him and asked for his advice. He was shocked and as always, when he hurt for me he cried.

"Oh Charlie, that is so disgusting. I would have fired all of them. If you intend to keep them, let me thrash them. I'll use a whip and put them in hospital for a long time."

"Whoa, Lover, let's not get carried away."

"Oh Charlie, I can't even begin to imagine how gross that was. Let me think, but they definitely need a thrashing, plus something equally as gross as the thing they did to you."

The next day he told me what he thought would be appropriate.

"Line them up on all fours, Charlie, invite about a dozen other staff to fuck them and as they go soft piss in their mouths, and then make them kiss each other while they are paddled, at least 20 times. I want to be the one who paddles Malcolm and Vincent."

"Crikey, Winston, that's pretty severe."

"No it isn't, Charlie. They all fucked you and had your belly awash with their piss. They are getting off light."

And so it was done. I couldn't believe how hard Winston administered the paddle. Both Malcolm and Vincent were screaming for mercy before he was halfway through.

Life was now very tranquil for me, and I came back to shape and fitness. Winston became quite dominant, telling me the reason was my incredibly sexy body. I wasn't fucking him as often, but I was getting plenty of fucking around the estate. Winston knew, but it didn't appear to bother him.

The six months of Bob's notice flew by, and with much bittersweet sorrow, he departed for New York. I had persuaded him to use the same lawyers and accountants that we did at Cloud's. They had both agreed to tell me if Bob ever got into financial difficulties but nothing else. I was satisfied. I would workout at his gym every time I was in New York and persuade as many of our friends as possible to transfer to it.

My first day with Freddie was a revelation. Bob had obviously told him of the things we did when I was a slave as well as a free man. I had always put myself entirely in Bob's hands. Whatever he wanted me to do, I did without question. Pretty erotic things at times, and a few times when I was being a bit obstinate or lazy, he had even paddled me and that as his boss!

"Charlie, I realise that I am still a slave and that I can still be punished by you any time you want, but I am going to treat you exactly the same as Bob did. If I think you will get more benefit from exercising naked, you will. If I think you are slacking, I'll paddle you, and I certainly won't hesitate to make any part of the programme erotic if I think the increased blood and adrenaline flow will benefit you."

I looked intently at him to see if he was serious. "Hmm, I'm not sure what to say or do about that, Freddie. I'm tempted to have you restrained over a whipping bench and given 20 with the whip or 50 with the paddle for your audacity in talking to me like that."

He looked frightened and in a very tiny voice said, "I'm sorry, Charlie, but I want to be as good for your fitness as Bob was."

I cuddled him and told him, "To make things easy for you, youngster, during my gym sessions, you can treat me as though I was still David's slave and you a senior member of staff. How does that sound?"

"Thank you, Charlie, I promise I will keep you very buff. And I won't paddle you very often."

He was grinning at me as he said the last bit. I laughed as well.

"My poor ass has taken so much punishment in the last 12 years Freddie, I don't suppose the odd paddling if I need it will do anything more than what it is intended for."

"Start as you intend to continue, Bob told me, so naked for exercise today, Charlie. First thing, I am going to take a whole range of measurements for comparison purposes. Then I am going to fix this to you to monitor your heart rate while you do some set piece exercises. I have already marked out a five-kilometre course round the estate, which I will run with you today. We are going to see how much time we can knock off it. You can run in a jock strap. It finishes at the pool where you will do 50 timed laps. That routine will only be three times a week. The other two visits will be callisthenics and circuit training."

"Christ, Freddie, I've heard of kill or cure, are you sure that is not going to be over the top for me?"

"No, Charlie, Bob and I discussed it, and he assured me it was OK. You should be able to handle that without problems. A double incentive for you will be a considerable improvement in your muscle tone and your stamina.

Also, if your daily record ever shows you slipping, I will give you ten with the paddle, before or after I fill you with my protein."

I looked stunned. This boy was going to make certain I kept focussed and fit.

"Right, Freddie, I am going to get in first on this one. Get naked and assume the position over the vaulting horse."

I opened him up with my fingers, gave him ten erotic paddles and when he was rock hard, fucked his brains out making him cum with me.

"Oh crikey, Charlie, will you do that every day?"

"Mmm, I might if you please me."

I cuddled him and we both laughed with the pleasure my little show had generated.

He was as good as his word. We finished at the pool with me about ready to drop. I struggled with my 50 laps but sure as hell enjoyed the next couple of hours improving my tan. Freddie rejoined me later carrying a laptop.

"Look, Charlie, I have your details on screen and all of your programme times. You get to see these on completion each day, so that we can both see your progress. I can do the same for Winston if you like. I also have some short programmes on computer if people like Peter and Paul want a little conditioning when they visit."

"Hey, Freddie, you're going high tech, yeah?"

"I have to, Charlie. I'm not like Bob. I have to justify everything I do as a slave."

It was certainly a revelation to me to watch my progress on a fitness level. Winston really didn't need to workout like I did, but he joined me some days and just carried out basic circuits and then the pool where he was usually very comfortable by the time I arrived.

We were both fully into the routine of running both companies with computers and the telephone. Video conferencing was our greatest boon, and we hammered that. I realised that Winston was doing a large amount of the executive work.

I thought a call to David was warranted.

"David, I am beginning to realise how much senior executive work Winston is doing. I would like to make him a VP in both companies. His remit is so wide, can we make him a VP without portfolio?"

"You must be a mind reader, Charlie. I was in Boston recently talking to Tom and Jason. I got the same input. They tell me you are only consulted on major issues, the remainder of the time they talk to Winston. Why don't you come up to New York for a few days, and we can do it officially? I'll get Tom and Jason, Peter and Paul down from Boston, and we'll make a party of it and use one event for some more publicity for Cloud's, please the shareholders, that sought of thing."

"Brilliant idea, we can surprise Bob in his new gym as well. We'll fly scheduled and come up tomorrow."

When I told Winston, he thought it was all a bit sudden.

"What are you planning now, Charlie? I always sense trouble when you make decisions like this."

"Nothing, Baby, David and I want to have a talk, so I thought we would both go. I'm going to take Freddie as well to give David some pleasuring and surprise Bob."

So we went and stayed at David's apartment leaving the company flat for the Boston boys.

David invited everyone for a formal dinner at Cloud's the first night with the press being alerted. Champagne was poured for everyone in the restaurant after we had all eaten, and David stood up in the centre of the floor.

"Ladies and Gentlemen, Cloud's is ten years old this year, and from its beginning most of my dinner guests tonight have been major movers in its success. One in particular has stayed in the shadow of Charlie Fellows, our president, but has been a major contributor to that success. Tonight, I would like to bring that young man out of the shadows and publicly recognise his great contribution to this company … Winston, you started here as a waiter. Now I would like you to accept the position of vice president without portfolio, not only of Cloud's, but of our sister company G.A.Y. Please everyone, raise your glasses to Winston Groves, our newest senior executive."

Winston looked at me almost begging me to rescue him. I whispered to him, "Make me proud, Baby."

He stood up, very shakily. "Ladies and Gentlemen, David Andrews and Charlie Fellows never cease to surprise me. They have been doing wonderful things for loyal employees ever since I first met them. I never wanted, or expected, public recognition for my work. Just being allowed to work alongside Charlie has always been reward enough for me. I will, however, accept these new appointments most gratefully, and kill David and Charlie for springing this on me. Thank you both for this honour, you know I will work even harder to justify your faith in me."

Everybody laughed, cheered, and sang, "For he's a jolly good fellow."

Winston dragged me off to the office as soon as he could and thanked me.

"You deserve it, Baby. You make my life complete and my work better for your presence, besides all the work of your own. I love you, Winston. I'll always love you, and I'll never be able to show you even half of that love or appreciation for just being you."

He dried his eyes and looked at me in wonder.

"Golly, Charlie, where did that come from?"

I punched him on the arm and laughed as I told him, "You know all that. You've always known that. I just don't tell you everyday."

He hugged me, and we joined the others who were all fulsome in their praise of Winston. Paul was crying quietly next to Winston, and I just picked up his whispered, "I love you, Winston, and I'm so pleased for you."

What a night. Completed by me making very tender love to my baby and having him snuggle up close to me using my chest for a pillow. Another occasion in my life where I wondered how I could be so lucky.

The business pages of the papers gave details of the appointments and a background profile of Winston. It looked very good, and Winston was almost preening himself after he read it.

We descended on Bob's new fitness centre after breakfast. All of us purchased a one year out of town membership and nearly suffocated him when we found him in one of the fitness rooms with clients. He was amazed and pleased to see us. We didn't do much working out, but we did find out that things were going well.

"Bob, when we are ready to leave, can you sit down with Winston and work out a corporate membership for Cloud's and G.A.Y.?"

"You know I can, and thank you, Charlie. You never give up helping us do you?"

I blushed. "I try to reward loyalty, Bob, and in your case devotion to me in the face of adversity. I am so pleased for you. Freddie, can stay as well? You may have some stuff here he can use, and you make sure you bill me for it."

"OK, Charlie."

The tone of voice told me I would never see any bill.

Back at David's, I joined him in his study and told him I had a surprise for him tonight.

"If you don't have a boyfriend to keep you warm tonight, David, can I suggest you take Freddie to bed?"

"Oh Charlie, thank you but no thank you. He was hard work and very unsatisfactory as a lover."

"Trust me, David, you will want him back as your slave tomorrow morning if you sleep with him tonight."

He looked at me cockeyed and said, "I'll believe that when it happens, but send him to me anyway. I can always send him back to his own bed."

That evening, we all descended on G.A.Y. and had a ball. I had forgotten how long it had been open, but it only seemed like yesterday when the barman came up to me and said, "Good evening, Mr. Fellows, Sir, what can I get you?"

"My usual please, Nick, and whatever these gentlemen want. Oh crikey, Nick, you're still here. That's amazing. Why?"

"Best bar job in town, Charlie, I'm not clever enough for anything else."

I got hold of Julio and told him Nick was to have a bonus of six months salary in his next pay packet.

The next morning at breakfast Freddie was seated with David who looked like the cat that got the cream.

"Charlie, you old devil, what have you been doing with this boy? He was almost as good as you."

"I had four weeks without Winston after you left him with me, so I did some training with him."

I could see Winston smirking. I had told him about getting Freddie into shape, and how much he was like me at 18.

"Thank you, Charlie, he was delightful. A little young for me to consider buying him back but very nice nonetheless."

We all laughed and Freddie blushed. I walked around the table and kissed him gently on the cheek.

"Well done, youngster, I'm pleased you didn't let me down."

He blushed scarlet, and his eyes as he looked at me told me everything.

We took the company jet back to Lara's House the next day and sent it straight back to take the others to Boston.

Settled by the pool that afternoon with a few members of staff scattered around, Winston slid onto my sun bed and cuddled me.

"You didn't have to do that in New York, Charlie, but you made me feel very proud. Am I really worth a vice presidency?"

"Yes, Lover, you probably deserve my job. You work far harder than I do."

"Thank you, Charlie, but I'm not clever like you. Cloud's and G.A.Y are you. I overheard David talking to one of his other company executive's one day. He said that neither company would be half as successful as they are without your inspired leadership and the devotion of the staff."

I was flattered. I loved both companies and the good they had done for so many of our friends.

In retrospect, I was quite amazed at how quickly I could slide on the fitness front. We had only been in New York for four days, but when I worked out the next day, I was lousy. Freddie came down to the pool after we had finished.

"Charlie, I would like to have a chat with you in the gym office now if it is convenient."

He looked serious, and I guessed he was going to bawl me out.

I slipped on a pair of shorts and a T-shirt and joined him on the walk back.

"What's the problem, Freddie?"

"I would sooner leave it for the office, Charlie. I am on home territory there, and I can assume you will honour your word to be subservient to me in my own environment."

I was definitely in for a rollicking. I wasn't looking forward to it. Freddie was going to be assertive over me, and I thought it might be amusing. Wrong again.

In his office, I noticed the second chair had been removed, so when he slid into the one behind his desk, I had to stand.

"Charlie, even making allowances for your four-day break, today's performance was pathetic."

He swung the computer screen round for me to look at. Every exercise was highlighted in red showing a worse performance than before we went to New York.

"That is bad enough in itself, Charlie, but if you check back it is over a month since you did worse than that. I have to assume that you were just being exceptionally lazy today for which I think you should be punished."

I was gob smacked. I was about to bluster but stopped myself, remembering what I had said to him when he took over from Bob. Being true to my word looked like it was going to get me in trouble again.

"For insulting me by not giving me the commitment I have earned from you, Charlie, I am going to humiliate you and for giving such a poor performance, I am going to paddle you."

I looked aghast at this boy daring to say or do either of those things.

"Now take your shirt and shorts off, Charlie."

What could I do but obey.

He came around his desk and started to fondle my cock.

"You look so much fitter and sexier than you did when I first arrived, Charlie, but we can't let you slack off now. Kneel in front of me and take my shorts off and then get me erect so that I can fuck you."

It was great to play with him and take him in my mouth but humiliating to do it this way. When he was very hard, he told me to get up on the desk on my back and pull my legs back as wide as I could manage. He grabbed a tube of lube and stood back so that he could see my ass clearly as he lubed himself and then me. He finger fucked me for a little while with four fingers while I blushed scarlet. Then he entered me in one smooth movement. I gasped. I hadn't been screwed by something as big as Freddie for some time.

"Humiliating isn't it, Charlie, being fingered and fucked by a slave who you had to suck first? I hope this part of your punishment alone will mean I never have to do it again, but I still intend to paddle you."

He was good, but he came too quickly for me to do likewise, so with a still raging erection, he made me turn over with my legs spread wide on the floor and my chest on the desk with my head cradled in my arms.

"Ten, Charlie, you can count them off for me, and thank me."

He wasn't soft about it, but he wasn't vicious either

"One, thank you, Freddie."

"Two, thank you, Freddie."

By five, I was grunting as each one landed and my erection had gone. By ten, I was sore.

"You had better grab a towel and slip through to the showers, Charlie, your ass is red and dripping cum. I will ensure that no one in the gym bothers you until you leave."

I felt so damned humiliated I didn't say anything. I just left. I went straight to my suite after my shower and lay on my bed on my tummy.

That was how Winston found me, asleep. When I woke I could feel a soft hand rubbing some ointment into my butt.

"I can't even begin to imagine what has happened here, Charlie, would you like to tell me?"

"I made a deal with Freddie when he took over from Bob that we would revert to the same roll I had with Bob when he first came here. If I slack off in the gym, I can get fucked and punished. He monitors my performance on computer. I was pretty awful today, and my punishment was a quick suck and fuck and ten with the paddle."

"You can't let him carry on with that routine, Charlie. He is a slave, and you are the president of two companies. It's humiliating."

"It's meant to be, Winston. I need keeping on my toes, or I am going to get fat and horrible. Don't you see? I want to remain looking sexy for you, and it is too easy to let myself go. Freddie did this today out of frustration. He wasn't vicious, and I'm not bruised, but I will be better in the gym tomorrow because I don't want this again."

My baby was not a happy bunny and looked with disapproval at Freddie when they passed in the corridor on our way to dinner.

Next day, I was actually apprehensive about going to the gym. Was this what made Lara's so attractive to me? I could stop being the high-powered executive here. I could spend hours being the subservient little slave that I had been and recharge my executive batteries for the next company challenge.

I had taken to wearing T-shirt, shorts, trainer socks and trainers around the estate but carrying workout jock and shorts for the gym. I still of course sunbathed naked even though I now allowed staff to use the pool all the time. The only exception was when I had quests who were not Cloud's or G.A.Y. employees.

In the gym office, Freddie was at the computer, and I noticed the second chair had been returned. I plonked myself down in it and tried to sound like yesterday was not in my thoughts.

"Hello, Freddie, what have you planned for me this morning?"

"Humph, strip for me, Charlie, naked."

He didn't look up or acknowledge me in any other way, and I started to get angry at his rudeness. When I was naked, he walked round the desk and felt my neck and shoulders ran his hands down over my buttocks and round the front to my pecs and abs.

"You are very tense, Charlie. I think we will abandon exercise programmes today. I am going to give you a deep tissue massage and then you can spend a half-hour in the steam bath and finish off with a swim before lunch. When your lunch has had an opportunity to digest, I would like you to take a gentle jog round our running course. Finish here so that I can have a look at you again."

He was right. I needed to unwind from New York and yesterday's debacle. Of course, I got incredibly hard during the massage, but Freddie ignored it. By lunchtime, I felt good, relaxed, unwound, just what I wanted to be. I did some paperwork in my study for an hour and then went for my run. Running shorts trainer socks and trainers no T-shirt. I bounced into the gym office feeling full of bon homme until Freddie said, "Strip naked again, Charlie."

I did, beginning to fume at his rudeness.

He felt me all over finishing by slapping my ass.

"Good, Charlie, back to normal tomorrow."

He still didn't look at me, just went back to his computer.

"Freddie, I want to see you in my study in half an hour. I want you showered and body shaved, get nurse to give you an enema, and wear only your slave shorts."

I turned and left, but not before I had seen the shocked look on his face.

I pulled the whipping bench out from the corner and put my large paddle on it. I cleared my desk and sat behind it hands linked across my chest. At his knock, I called, "Come."

I pointed to a place about six feet in front of the desk and said, "Strip, Freddie, then slave standing position."

As soon as he was compliant, I started, "I am very pleased with your training programme and how you enforce it with me, Freddie. What I am not pleased with is your rudeness. You don't look at me when you talk to me, you don't greet me when I arrive, and you haven't used the word please for so long that I think it may have left your vocabulary. If you were an employee, I would be issuing you a written warning concerning your behaviour. You aren't, you're a slave. I think it is time you were reminded of that. For the next 30 days, you are going to revert to full slave status. The chores and punishment book will be returned to the staff restaurant for them to use. All punishment and sex sessions will be held in the blue room, which I will have prepared and a notation to that effect will be placed at the front of the book. You will wear only your slave shorts, and you will address me as Master. At the end of 30 days, you will make an appointment to see me here and ask for your slave status to be reviewed, if you think you deserve it. I will not hesitate to beat you if your standards slip, and if you are bad enough, I will flog you in front of all the staff. Now I want you over the whipping bench."

I secured him making sure the restraints were adjusted to force his ass well out. On cue, there was a knock at the door, and Winston entered.

"I know you think Freddie has got above himself, Winston, so I thought you might like to witness this punishment and then have a rough fuck afterwards."

"Mmm, thank you, Charlie. If his ass isn't red enough after you have finished, I might administer a few more as well."

"I am going to administer ten hard ones now, Freddie, and ten more tomorrow. How many more you receive after that will be in your own hands."

I didn't spare him. I powered in with all ten reducing him to a quivering blubbering heap. When I had finished, both Winston and I fucked him to orgasm."

Winston winked at me as he left and whispered, "He is rather a nice fuck, isn't he, Charlie?"

I nodded. When I released him and had him standing in front of my desk I said, "Have you anything to say, Freddie?"

"Yes, Master, I'm very sorry. Please don't paddle me again that hurt so much. I promise I will try very hard to be a good slave."

"I will see about that, Freddie. In the meantime, you are not to change the way you deal with me in the gym. Do you understand? You are also not going to paddle me with anything like the power I used on you, are you?"

"No, Master."

"Good, off you go."

He picked up his shorts and was gone. Once again, I realised that using the paddle gave me a buzz, but I would still only use it where absolutely necessary.

I had a specialist in under the guise of a TV engineer and had six miniature cameras placed in the blue room with wide-angle lenses and a remote station recording everything. I was going to become a voyeur, but it was mainly to make certain that Freddie wasn't abused like I had been. Later on, I had a small room nearby converted and six screens installed that showed real time action. I thought it might be fun to watch all six screens together occasionally. Yes, I know, very voyeuristic. I guess I was getting kinky in my old age.

My next gym session was much better. Freddie was careful to be polite to me. When we finished and he had entered all the data, he looked up at me and said, "You lose your edge very quickly, Master, don't you?"

I replied, "How so?"

He swung the computer screen round and pointed out the red failure exercises. "There are only a few today, and they are not very far off, but before you went to New York, there had been a constant steady improvement in your fitness levels. Against the charts, Master, you are too fit to be 33, but your life style has helped that situation. If you had even less stress than now, we could probably get your fitness level to excellent for a 25 year old."

"Thank you, Freddie, for that vote of confidence, but I don't think anything will achieve that. Do you know why I make so many visits to Ronald?"

"No, Master, I have never felt it was my business to ask. I always thought it was because of your position and they had to look after you."

"It's because I lost the will to live some years ago when Winston left me, and I nearly died. I damaged my heart and probably other organs but not badly apparently. I'm monitored anyway just to make sure. That is why you had to get Bob's approval for my programme. I will never be as fit as I could be because I am not allowed to tax my heart too much."

He nodded his acceptance of my statement without question.

"I will see you in my study in 30 minutes, Freddie, same routine as yesterday."

I noted the look of disappointment on his face as I trotted off back to the house. When he entered my study, he was looking scared. I knew he still hurt from yesterday. It had been obvious from his movements around the gym.

"Strip, Freddie, and over the whipping bench."

His look of anguish would have melted my heart if I had not already decided on a different approach. I secured him and made a big show of positioning him correctly.

"Please, Master, I still hurt so much. Please don't paddle me again today. I promise to try hard to be a good slave."

"Oh you'll be a good slave, Freddie, I guarantee it."

I fondled his dick, but he was so terrified of another paddling, he didn't get hard.

I used Ryan's Mum's ointment. We had paid her for a stock of it. The Aloe Vera in it made it good for so many things it was amazing. Because it had come from the fridge it was cold and when it hit Freddie's butt, he jumped so hard he nearly broke the restraints. I laughed so hard I nearly fell over.

"Psychological warfare, Freddie. The ointment is a soothing cream that will take away the soreness very quickly. You aren't going to be paddled today. I am saving that ten to add to others on another day if you ever give me cause."

He cried, and being a sucker for a tearful boy, I released him and took him in my arms.

"It's alright, Freddie, you're OK. No paddling today."

I made love to him on my chesterfield, tenderly. I must have been truly angry to paddle him like I did the day before, but the effect was what I wanted. I hoped I would never have to do it again.

"Thank you, Master, you are amazing. I love it when you fuck me with so much affection."

I laughed and gave him a cuddle.

"Come and have lunch with me today, Freddie, and if you are free after lunch come down to the pool with Winston and me."

"Thank you, Master, I would like that."

Winston looked at me with raised eyebrows when I walked in with Freddie for lunch.

"Yesterday's session has had the most amazing effect on this young man, Lover. He has been a delight today. I think I'm falling in love with him, is that alright?" My eyes were twinkling as I said it.

"You remember what Paul did to you in London to punish you for what you did to him in Boston?"

I laughed, "How could I forget, I nearly blew my balls out through my cock."

Winston dissolved with me. When he could speak again, he said, "Well, if you don't behave yourself, I am going to let Freddie witness me doing it to you, and I won't be a pussy like Paul was."

We both fell about laughing, and Freddie just looked totally bemused. Even Cloud looked in to see what was going on.

"Freddie doesn't like the paddle, Winston, so he is being an incredibly nice boy. Would you like him to join us in a threesome after lunch?"

"Seriously, Charlie?"

"Yes, if you would like to. I promise you he is lovely in bed."

"Why not, he certainly felt good yesterday. Would you like to do it down at the pool?"

I nearly fell off my seat until I saw Winston's eyes. More laughter.

"One hour to let your lunch digest, Freddie, and then come up to our suite, OK?"

"Yes, Master."

Winston and I curled up together for a cuddle until Freddie knocked.

"I have had an enema Master and a shave and shower."

"OK, take your shorts off and come and lie between us. We are going to spoil you."

Winston and I competed to see who could make him squirm with pleasure the most. Freddie was delightful. At 18, his skin was like silk, stretched over a more than adequately buffed frame, every muscle group showing. His nearly 12-inch penis was lying along his tummy hard as iron and his ball sac dropped enticingly into the V between his legs. I lifted it into the palm of one hand and attacked it with my tongue. I pushed it up into the base of his cock and licked under it and down his perineum to his hole. Meanwhile, Winston was attacking his nipples and playing with the remainder of his torso, finding the ticklish spot, caressing the abs, anywhere that he could get a reaction. He slid his penis into Freddie's mouth and received a tongue whipping of his glans that had him gasping.

"Oh, crikey, Charlie, if you taught him, this why don't you do it to me?"

I came up for air and watched. “Sorry, Winston, that is a new one on me. I’ll get Freddie to teach me.”

I went back to my game.

“Oh God, Charlie, please, will someone fuck me, I am going crazy?”

Winston and I looked at each other and with wicked grins returned to our task. Eventually when I thought Freddie was going to have a heart attack, I lubed up his ass and Winston moved round to take him. I sat back and watched. The expressions on their faces were awesome. I don’t think I had ever seen Winston so turned on with anyone else. I fucked Freddie’s face for a little while and then left Winston to finish him. His orgasm was incredible and then Winston came, nearly screaming the house down. When he rolled off Freddie, I put Winston’s legs over my shoulders and fucked him for ages, long strokes, slowly delivered as I rotated my hips.

He came again and again, as I exercised incredible control. Freddie came down from his high and watched us. I kept going for ages but eventually powered into Winston delivering a mega load of my seed. He felt it and came again.

“Charlie, I love you so much.” And with that he closed his eyes and slept.

Freddie looked at him and then me. “Charlie, when my slave contract ends if you two will do that to me even once a month, I will sign another one for life. I have never been made love to like that. You and Winston are awesome. I love you both so much.”

I kissed him softly and rolled him into my arms. We all slept for a couple of hours.

The next day, I decided Cloud had to have some of this action. It took a lot of persuading but eventually he did.

“Charlie, thank you. That boy is nearly as awesome as you are, but so young. I felt truly guilty fucking him, but he was amazing.”

I laughed, “Maybe it’s time you and I had another romp, Cloud.”

“No Charlie, I don’t think I dare make love to you again ever. I would fear for my sanity.”

The next couple of months were manic. Winston and I were video conferencing almost every day. In discussion with David, Tom and some other directors, we decided to look at the idea of expanding both companies over to the West Coast. Because of the distance and our previous experience, we were going to do three Cloud’s and three G.A.Ys. at once. Tom and Jason, Winston and I were going out together and pairing up. We were going to hunt for locations in San Francisco, Los Angeles and Seattle. Tom and Winston took Los Angeles, (my baby wanted to look at Hollywood). Jason and I took San Francisco. We were lucky about the same time, swapped over to check locations and then all headed for Seattle. Again, we were lucky and in less than a month had our six locations secured with deposits. We sent out the architects that had done the two New York locations, and Winston and I returned to Lara's House. I rested up for a couple of days before returning to the gym. I didn't want Freddie to have an excuse to punish me for poor performance.

My third morning back, I bounced into the gym, still full of good feelings because of the success of the trip.

"Good morning, Freddie, how are you?"

"I'm fine thank you, Charlie. I have heard your trip was very successful. Are you back for long?"

"I hope long enough for you to bring me up to standard again. I have not exercised for a whole month, and we have all done far too much drinking and eating. Winston will be down in the next few days as well when he has tied up some loose ends, so you will be busy for a while."

"OK, Charlie, let's have a look and see how bad you are."

Warm up, a circuit, a run and a swim. Knackered at the end but satisfied at my work rate. The sun felt good on my body lying out by the pool in my usual naked state. A few of the staff who I had not seen welcomed me back. I was unwinding again, and the relaxation had me dozing when Freddie sat down beside me.

"Can we go to the gym office, Charlie, to discuss today's effort?"

"Is that necessary, Freddie, I am rather comfortable here."

"Yes it is, Charlie. The performance was poor again."

"I expect it was. We know I go off the boil quite quickly, but we both know my work rate was good today, wasn't it?"

"Yes, Charlie, but I don't think that's the point. I really would like to discuss this in the office."

"Freddie, you are being a pain, but OK. Let's make it quick. I want to soak up some more rays before lunch. I have a busy afternoon."

He had done it again, removed the second chair so that I had to stand. This looked ominous, and I was angry.

"We agreed that if your performance deteriorated, Charlie, I should punish you. If your work rate was poor I would humiliate you as well. Your work rate was good today, but I still feel hurt that you couldn't find a couple of hours a day to maintain your standard while you were away. I think you deserve both punishment and humiliation. Because the last session did not achieve the desired result, I think both should be more severe than last time. Strip please, Charlie."

I was seriously tempted to refuse and give him a good whipping, but he was still only 18 and learning his man management skills. I reckoned I was a big enough person to put up with it if it helped his confidence and motivation.

"I think you are wrong, Freddie, but I won't go back on my word."

I stripped and assumed slave-standing position.

"Strip me and suck me, Charlie." I did with relish, once a cocksucker always a cocksucker. I loved it even if it wasn't the way I would have liked it.

I played with his balls and ran my hand between his legs to tickle his hole. He was still delightful.

"Hmm, that is lovely, Charlie. I think I'll sit and let you bring me to orgasm."

Still delightful, but when he came he pulled off my mouth and shot his load all over my face. Now that was humiliating.

"Lick it clean, Charlie," he said pointing his cock at my mouth.

I did, really seething now.

"In the gym now, Charlie, on your back on a massage bench with your legs pulled back and spread wide"

"I presume the doors are locked, Freddie."

"No, Charlie, nothing in our agreement says I have to exclude other staff."

I did and fortunately, as it was morning, no one came in. He finger fucked me for ages occasionally slapping one cheek or the other. Not too hard, but after several I could feel it stinging. Eventually he lubed up and fed me all of his cock in one smooth movement.

"I should last for a long time, Charlie, as I have already cum. You can spend the time scooping up my cum and eating it."

He was really getting into this and giving me ideas. I thought this was all completely unjustified and would let him know in no uncertain terms later. He eventually orgasmed, and I could feel that he had been truly turned on taking me like this.

"Lick me clean, Charlie."

"That is disgusting and terribly degrading, Freddie."

"I know but I want you to learn from it."

I did and nearly threw up. He was building a big heap of resentment in me and that would cost him.

"Over on your tummy, Charlie, I am going to finish off with a beating. I found your old slave whip, so I am going to use that today."

The first one landed before I had time to comment, and it hurt. So did the next nine, and when he was finished I was writhing with the pain. I looked at my ass in the mirror. If Winston saw it, he would go ballistic.

"That's it, Charlie, I hope you have learnt your lesson today."

"I have learnt a lesson today, Freddie, and that is, your man management skills are deficient and your learning curve on that front is going to be extremely painful and humiliating. What you have done to me today was completely unjustified. I suggest you think about it and see me in my study after supper."

He looked frightened, and he needed to I was going to hurt him for this piece of stupidity.

He looked very smart and buff standing in front of me. His gym vest was immaculate and clung to him like a second skin. His shorts looked expensively tailored and with his jock strap on sat nicely over his abdomen, trainers and trainer socks to the same standard.

"Well, Freddie, tell me what your thoughts are now on today's session from the time I walked into the gym."

"You worked hard for the whole session, Charlie, achieving reasonable results considering your month off. The punishment was because I thought you could have shown more dedication to maintaining your standard while you were away and the humiliation was because I was frustrated at having to keep bringing you up to standard."

"So you still maintain it was justified."

"Yes, Charlie."

I stood up and dropped my trousers showing him my ass.

"Including this?"

He gasped, "Oh no, Charlie, I didn't mean to mark you like that."

"If Winston sees this before the bruising and whip marks have gone, Freddie, I doubt you will be out of hospital for a month. He will destroy your buttocks with the whip."

"I'm sorry, Charlie."

"You will be young man. You must learn to use your authority better. Your attitude needs realigning or you are going to be in serious trouble in your chosen career. You don't learn, Freddie, that's the problem. Perhaps more humiliation is necessary, pain by itself isn't working. I am going to have the whipping bench taken to the staff restaurant and placed by the door. You will be secured to it for the duration of the next two lunches. I will have a notice put above it inviting everyone to administer at least one solid smack with their bare hands."

"Please Master, no. I promise I will try harder to be a good slave."

"You have promised that before, Freddie, and you get worse. When are you going to learn that your position here is a privilege that I can withhold anytime I want to?"

"Now, Master, I promise now."

"No, Freddie, you are going to receive your full punishment this time."

Lunch was in full swing when I brought Freddie into the restaurant the next day, the first lunchtime. Every eye was on me when I told Freddie to strip and had him secured to the whipping bench.

"Freddie keeps forgetting he is a slave. He has a bad attitude that needs rectification. You would all be doing him and me a favour if you remind him as you leave today and arrive and leave tomorrow by giving him a good, solid smack like this."

I laid a stinging blow to his buttocks as I said it. Then I left. After lunch I went back to find a boy sobbing and showing an incredibly red butt. I slapped it again eliciting a spine-chilling scream. I took off his restraints and told him when he had calmed down to see me in my study. It was half an hour before the knock on the door came.

"Come," was all I said.

He hobbled in still crying and obviously in great pain.

"What have you to say to me, Freddie?"

"I'm sorry, Master, I really will try harder. Please don't let the staff beat me again tomorrow. The pain is unbelievable. I hurt so much."

"I'm sorry, Freddie, last time I prescribed two lots of punishment, I let you off one, and you've done it again. This time you will have both reminders. I will not tolerate your insubordination or stupidity in dealing with me in the gym. You are good at your job, and you have become a wonderful sex toy, but you may not speak to me as if I was a junior member of staff or punish and humiliate me to the degree you did yesterday. You almost crossed the acceptable line the first time. This last time was way over. In fact I would be cross if I heard you talking to junior members of staff the way you talked to me. That is probably why you hurt so much. The remainder of the staff are as fed up with your attitude as I am. Go and see nurse for some salve. I will see you in the gym in the morning."

He was standing behind his desk when I arrived the next day.

"Good Morning, Freddie."

The "Good Morning, Master" sounded very tearful.

"I assume you will be instructing this morning not indulging."

"Yes, Master."

He broke down then sobbing like a baby. "Please, Master, I am still in so much pain. Please don't have me punished again today. I will be so good from now on. I will do everything to the best of my ability all the time. I will never give you cause to punish me again."

I wanted to give in. I was so in love with this beautiful boy. If there were no Winston, I am sure I would be falling over myself to make him mine despite our age difference. He and Chris were a continuing source of agony. I wanted them both. I would happily have had four in a bed every night Winston, Freddie and Chris. God I would be a wreck after a week.

"Hmm, let me think about this while you work my butt off."

"Yes, Master. After your warm up, I want a basic circuit. I am going to stimulate you after that for some strength exercises, and I want to see what we can get out of you with adrenaline pumping."

Warm up and circuit were grist to the mill for me. I was barely breathing heavy at the end of it.

"That was fine, Master, slightly better time than your last one. Now take your shorts off. I am going to stimulate you almost to the point of orgasm, and then I want you to follow the programme that will come up on the big screen. I have laid out the equipment you need."

I stood in the centre of the gym with Freddie pulling out the stops to excite me. I was humming like a guitar string within a few minutes and gasping, almost cumming well before five minutes had passed.

"Stop, Freddie, I am almost there."

He left me and turned on the video.

The programme was a killer, but I was so turned on. The adrenaline gave me so much extra strength. Of course, it only lasted for a few minutes, but so did the programme.

In Freddie's office, we compared the results with previous ones of the same exercise. It was amazing, I was almost 25% better.

"We can't do that every time, Master, but it's an interesting exercise isn't it?"

"Yes, where did you come up with that idea?"

"I didn't, Master, Bob sent it down after talking to me about it in relation to you."

"Do you consult with Bob often, Freddie?"

"Yes, Master, mainly with reference to you. I am very careful about what I ask you to do."

"Do you care that much then?"

He looked at me with big baleful eyes and then looked down almost whispering, "Yes Master, I love you. I would never risk hurting you internally."

I was gob smacked. How the hell was I to continue his punishment? The problem was that if I didn't, he would almost certainly offend again. I really did have to make this punishment register, or I was going to be doing it every few weeks, and it would get worse.

"Very well, Freddie, I will see you in my study at 1230. Clean inside and out. I don't want your bowels emptying in the staff room."

I heard the sob, but I didn't look, I couldn't.

When he arrived, I told him to wait where he was. I would be back. I slid into my study toilet from the corridor and watched him through the door crack that I had left deliberately. He didn't move. I almost ran down to the staff dining area and got the attention of them all.

"Freddie is still extremely sore from yesterday's spanking. You are all as pissed off with his attitude as I am it would appear. I have to let you loose on him again today, but I will only bring him down for you to slap him as you leave. Be a little less enthusiastic than yesterday will you. I don't want him damaged too much more."

"OK, Charlie, half strength today," some wag piped up.

When I walked back into my study, I don't think he had moved.

"Looks like you have missed half your punishment today, Freddie, I was delayed. Off we go now though."

He was shaking, almost uncontrollably by the time I had him strapped down.

"He's all yours guys," I said, winking as I addressed the staff.

He was sobbing when I returned, but his ass didn't look too much worse than earlier.

"If I ever have to punish you again for something as serious as this, Freddie, I will have you strung up in the barn and whipped by a member of staff. Do you understand?"

"Yes, Master."

I took him in my arms then and kissed him gently.

"I love you, Freddie. Please don't make me hurt you again."

He looked at me wide eyed and just dissolved in great gut wracking sobs.

"I'm sorry, Master. I'll be good. I promise I'll be so good."

I half carried him to the couch and let him recover there. I knew my decision was correct, but I got no joy from it. I had to humiliate him now as well, and I really didn't want to, but again the lesson had to be well taught to make certain this would be the last time.

"I am going to give your butt a few days to recover while I think about the second stage of your punishment, the humiliation. Back to work when you are ready."

He was still on the couch watching as I set up the video link with the architect in New York. We discussed a myriad of issues for the new venues, it took over two hours, and I was so deep into it that I forgot Freddie. When I finished he was still there, looking at me slack jawed.

"Why are you still here, Freddie, no work?"

"Oh golly, sorry, Charlie, you are awesome in business as well as in bed, and I forgot the time. I had no idea you were so clever."

"Flattery won't affect my decision on your humiliation, Freddie."

"Oh no, Charlie, I didn't mean it to grovel. I meant it because it's true."

"OK. Off you go."

Little bugger, he was just making it harder for me. Of course, I was flattered. A little hero worship never hurt anyone's ego.

Winston heard about the staff restaurant incidents.

"What on earth did Freddie do this time, Charlie? I hear he won't sit down for a week."

"More of the same, Lover, he keeps forgetting his place. I have to think up some extreme humiliation for him as well, in front of plenty of staff. That's proving difficult."

"Why don't you do something along the same lines as David did with you when he invited friends in to watch and enjoy sex with you, Charlie? You can always make it even more humiliating if that wasn't bad enough."

"What a good idea, Winston. I'll choreograph it like you did my sessions with Ty and company and Jamie and Luke."

"Oh Charlie, we were never going to mention that again. I still feel so ashamed."

"I'm sorry, Baby, I know how you feel, but you shouldn't."

I got hold of Malcolm and told him what I wanted. Him plus the foursome who had me blindfolded, plus two of the larger estate workers, in the blue room after lunch the next day. I had the six cameras already recording, and I attended with a camcorder. I was dressed just in a pair of shorts because if I got really hot I was going to take part.

The boys were all there when I turned up with Freddie, and they were all naked. Freddie looked at them all and then with an anguished expression on his face looked at me.

"I told you I would humiliate you big time, Freddie, as the second part of your punishment. Learn from this because you will never have it this easy again, so think very hard about your behaviour from today onwards. I am going to record it all and let you have a copy as a reminder. Malcolm is in charge. You will do everything he asks you to, and you will obey him as you would me. You will be spanked at the whim of any of these boys, so I suggest you do everything in your power to keep them very happy for the next couple of hours. Do you understand?"

"Yes, Master, please don't do this. I promise to be the best slave ever."

"You will be, Freddie, because I promise you will not want worse than this to happen to you again. He is all yours Malcolm. You have two hours."

"Take your shorts off, Freddie, and stand in front of me. Now bend over and start sucking my cock."

Placing his hands on Malcolm's thighs for support, he started licking and then sucking his cock. As soon as he was into his stride, the other boys kicked his legs wider and took turns spreading his ass cheeks and finger fucking him. I had told them to use plenty of lubrication because they were all going to fuck him, and I wanted him humiliated not incapacitated. When Malcolm was rock hard Vincent replaced him. All of these boys were very well hung, particularly the two big estate workers, Vidal and Raul. Thomas had recruited them from the Dominican Republic. They were both blacksmiths and the size of their arms left no doubt about that. Their dicks were the same, even larger than Cloud. Freddie was going to hurt after these two had reamed him out. This rotation continued until he had sucked all of the boys for a while. Vidal and Raul got a bad deal here because Freddie could only lick the cockhead. His mouth was too small to get them in. He had struggled with mine, but it paled into insignificance against these two. Freddie looked at me and with a look of fear on his face said, "Please Master, don't let these two fuck me. They will kill me."

"A short life and a happy one, Freddie." Cruel aren't I?

The next action was to roll him up as they had me, and let Moses fist fuck him. While that was going on, the remainder wanked off over Freddie's face smothering it. I wiped his eyes clear because I wanted him to watch all the action.

Malcolm had positioned him such that he could see what Moses was doing in the mirrored wall. It was bloody erotic, and I was sporting a solid erection that the boys all ogled in between their other activities.

The next action was the circle-spit roast. Having to suck dick that had been up your ass was about as degrading as drinking another guy's piss. I had hated both equally, but the pissing was truly beyond the pail for me.

Freddie screamed in agony as Vidal entered him, but it was done gently, and he gave Freddie time to adjust before fucking him properly, not giving him his entire monster. I thought that both he and Raul were about 15 inches and at least as big round as master cock that David's New York staff had fucked me with.

Eventually as with me, they all came in one orifice or other. As they were calming down, Malcolm made Freddie scoop up all the cum on his face and eat it. The final act which I knew was disgusting was to lay him in the bath and all of them took turns emptying their bladders in his mouth and all over his body. Then they left.

I stood and watched Freddie slowly get control of himself, the gut wrenching sobs slowly turning to sniffles.

"That was foul, horrible, vile, disgusting and probably another hundred nasty things, Freddie. You have another year as a slave. I hope this lesson will be seared into your brain and the arrogant, unthinking little shit that was you will never surface again."

"Oh no, Master, I will keep my promise."

"Alright, Freddie, back to normal for you. P.Is. Dress and no more slave behaviour."

"Thank you, Charlie."

I was bleeding watching him trying to control himself.

"Hop out of the bath, let's wash away the last of the urine. There is a gallon of mineral water on the vanity unit. Drink as much as you can and wash your mouth out. Clean your teeth with that new brush and rinse with the Corsodyl, and then I'm going to give you a shower."

I treated him like Mac had me the only time he had ever made love to me. So gently, he was almost purring despite still crying softly. After I had dried him, I took him to the bed and cuddled him, stroking his body.

"Don't ever make me do anything like that again, Freddie. I want to love you not punish you and humiliate you."

He looked like a little puppy dog as he raised his head to make eye contact.

"I'll try so hard, Charlie, I love you, too."

I rolled him over, gently rubbed some soothing antiseptic cream into his very puffy anal entry. Slapped his ass gently and said, "No more work for you today, put on a pair of Speedos and join me at the pool if you would like another cuddle."

I explained to Winston, told him everything we had done to Freddie and how heartbroken he had been at the humiliation.

"Can we sandwich him in between us for cuddles if he comes down?"

"Yes, Charlie, if you like. You really do love the little chap, don't you?"

"He is very beautiful, Baby, and at 18 very vulnerable, much more so than I was when I came here. I was 20 remember and much more worldly than Freddie is."

I don't know who was more surprised that Winston and I took a large sun bed and sandwiched Freddie in between us for cuddles, him or the other staff that saw it. He buried his face in my chest and cried softly while Winston and I caressed his body.

"It's OK, youngster, it's over. Learn from it but otherwise try to forget it."

We had him join us for dinner as well and then took him to bed with us repeating almost exactly, what we had done before, except that after I had made love to Winston I let Freddie fuck me. He loved it and did a Winston. He bounced around the room like a schoolboy.

"Oh Charlie, Winston, you two are just so amazing! That was fabulous."

"Come here, you nut, cuddles before we shower and turn in for the night."

He did and promptly fell asleep.

"He's had quite a day, Charlie, hasn't he? He's very resilient, just like you when you were 20, bounces back from adversity very quickly. Don't destroy his spirit, Charlie, by being cruel, will you?"

"Of course not, Baby, I hope this is the last time I have to punish him. You know I'm a little bit in love with him don't you?"

"Yes, Charlie, I think I am going the same way. What do you think we should do about it?"

"Nothing, Lover, not as it stands anyway."

"You might have to give some more thought to a harem Charlie."

His eyes were laughing as he said it, and I laughed with him.

We eventually showered, and Freddie stayed the night. I was in the middle this time because I wanted to feel both my lovers as I sank into the world of nod.

Chapter 15

San Francisco was incredible, our two new venues had cost twice as much as our previous most expensive, Miami, but wow, were they ever impressive. Cloud's opening night was as successful as always, discerning eaters across America knew of our reputation. G.A.Y. was different. It was a successful opening but not outstanding. However, by the end of the first week, it was packed to bursting point every night. I left Winston, Tom and Jason to oversee the two establishments for the first month taking in Los Angeles and Seattle as well. Opening all three together was quite a strain, but it saved us a fortune in travel expenses and executives' time. We had trained the senior staff for all venues in New York and completed the staffing and training onsite. We were all old hands at this now, so there were no hiccoughs. I flew back early stopping in New York to see David.

"Charlie, I have the early figures for all six establishments, I can't believe you've done it again. They are amazing."

"Thank you, David, but I don't do this by myself you know Winston, Tom and Jason have worked incredibly hard for this success."

"I know, Charlie, but you are the guiding light. Nonetheless, I want to discuss bonuses for those three. Any ideas?"

"Yes, David, Tom should have a huge one accompanied by a substantial increase in salary. You know we haven't kept his remuneration in line with the company's profitability. He doesn't complain because his stock is so much more valuable. Can I suggest a $1 million bonus for him and a one hundred thousand-dollar increase in salary? For Jason, we have doubled his responsibility, so we ought to double his salary, but let's go 50% this year and if we agree he is worth it, the other 50% next year. He should have a good bonus as well, any suggestions?"

"How about a quarter of a million?"

"Mmm, I thought that as well. Can we make a little bit of a show doing it and at the same time announce new salaries for other senior executives like Peter and Paul and the GMs of all outlets, plus the chefs."

"Clever, Charlie, that takes care of all the old Lara's House people and the fab four white waiters from our first Cloud's. You still love all of them don't you?"

"Yes I guess so, David, but they have all helped to make you and me even wealthier than we ever dreamt."

"OK, Charlie, let's have them all here for the presentation of bonus cheques and salary announcements. We'll close Cloud's for the night and keep it a company do. We've not rewarded Winston, Charlie. You aren't going to tell me you don't think he is worth it."

"No, but he already has my fortune."

"That's yours, Charlie, we need to show him his worth. Stock or money?"

"Stock David, all the bonuses should be paid in stock. We keep a tighter control of the company if the boys are all shareholders."

"Crafty, Charlie. How much for Winston, same as Jason and the same salary increase?"

"That is incredibly generous, David. You'll embarrass him with that."

"I know, Charlie, but he does deserve it. Now are you going to pay your debt for Freddie tonight?"

"Sorry, David, I had forgotten about that, yes I would love to."

"Slave for the night, Charlie, so that I can be kinky and sadistic if I want to."

"I don't think I have any choice after what I agreed. I do keep letting myself in for trouble, don't I?"

"Yes you do, Charlie. I'm pleased to say."

We both laughed and I wondered what he was planning.

We ate at Cloud's and I went to the kitchen for a kiss and cuddle with Darren and Ryan. They didn't appear to change at all. They still looked 20 and were as much in love as they had always been. It would be wonderful to have a night out with them again, and all the other originals. We would have to do it the night of the presentation.

Back at David's apartment, he told me to see him in his study after I had showered, shaved and had an enema.

"My whole body, David?"

"Yes, Charlie, and only wear your little white briefs. You will call me Master from now until breakfast time as well."

"You're really going for it tonight then, David?"

"Yes, Charlie, and you've already chalked up a black mark calling me David."

I could sense trouble, and I wasn't disappointed.

"I'm here, Master, clean as a new pin inside and out."

I was grinning which prompted my first hint of things to come.

"I don't think you are taking me seriously, Charlie. Have you seen yourself in the mirror lately? You look as sexy and desirable as you did at 20. Lara's House has really been good for you this last year. Tonight, I am going to treat you as I did when you were 20. Take your briefs off and prostrate yourself over my desk."

David kicked my legs further apart and played with my ass, running his hand over both buttocks and down into my crack before lubing a couple of fingers and fucking me with them.

The next thing was David warning me of my first punishment.

"Ten for being cheeky and for calling me David. Count them off the usual way Charlie."

I couldn't believe it when the first one landed, it hurt.

"One, thank you, Master."

The next nine were nearly as hard. It certainly wasn't erotic and my erection had gone to prove it.

"Stay where you are. I have a present for you."

He showed me a 12-inch dildo. I realised it was the same shape as my real one. He pushed it all the way in before allowing me to stand.

"Now, undress me, Charlie, and get me very excited."

Knelt between his legs with the dildo up my ass felt very erotic, and I came to full erection about the same time as David. I loved his package. always had, so I was enthusiastic to please him even without the threat of another paddling.

When I had him gasping, he made me stop and climb onto his desk on my back, legs in the air spread wide. He fucked me for about ten minutes with the dildo playing with me all the time. When he pulled the dildo out, he told me to pull my cheeks apart as far as I could. He pulled up a chair, sat down close to me and started fingering me in a very humiliating way. He was using both hands and wriggling the fingers around inside me, finally putting both thumbs in and pulling my asshole as wide as he could until I screamed.

"Oh God, David, that really hurts."

"Move your hands, Charlie."

I did and he spanked me. Only four times but quite hard.

"Don't call me, David."

"Why are you hurting me, Master? I thought you wanted to enjoy my body not abuse it."

"I want both tonight, Charlie."

With that comment, he entered me and fucked my brains out. No finesse, just a very hard pounding. When he came, it was a very intense orgasm. He fell forward over me and kissed me.

"I haven't been that wicked since the last time I spanked you, Charlie. That was delicious. Now I am going to take you to bed and do this all over again only making love to you not beating and raping you."

He did, too. I was begging him to let me cum, I was so turned on by his lovemaking. When I did explode, he did, too, and the result was a half hour of silence while we returned to normal.

"Was that as good for you as it was for me, Charlie?"

"I don't know about you, David, but it was incredible for me. Experience tells, you were fantastic."

"So were you. It's a pity I have to paddle you again for calling me David."

"Not fair, you drive me crazy with your lovemaking and expect me to behave rationally afterwards."

"Mmm, you have a point. If my morning blowjob is good, I'll let you off."

A quick clean up and sleep. David spooned me into him and cuddled me all night. I loved it. His blowjob the next morning was great so no more paddling. At breakfast, I told him what I thought of the early part of the sex play.

"You're a bastard, David. I never intended for you to abuse me in payment for Freddie. Over the years you have paddled or whipped me several times without reason. Why?"

"It's that ass, Charlie. I'm sorry. I always have the urge to fuck it up as well as fuck it. It's just so damn sexy."

"Mac told me that once, but he thought it was an either or case not both."

David just shrugged and that was it. I returned to Lara's House and started organising the big do in New York.

I left it a couple of days before I went to the gym.

"Hello Freddie, I hope you are going to be the diplomat today, I haven't exercised since I left so my standard will have dropped."

Warm up and circuits, a run round my 5 km course and finish at the gym. Freddie already had the results on his computer by the time I got back.

"Not as bad as I expected, Charlie, but I still think you should be humiliated for ignoring my suggestion that you exercise while you are away."

I bit back the comment I was going to make to see what he intended doing.

"Very well, Freddie, what do you want me to do?"

"Strip and go and lie on the massage table."

I did and Freddie came in, gave me an incredibly good blowjob before fucking me gently and making me cum again.

"That sort of humiliation I can take anytime, Freddie."

"Thank you, Charlie, I just wanted to welcome you home and let you know I have missed you, Master."

The twinkle in his eyes made me laugh, and I pulled him to me for a kiss and a cuddle.

"It's good to be back, Freddie. Would you sleep with me tonight?"

"Oh yes please, Charlie."

I was definitely home. With no major projects on I was going to thoroughly relax and enjoy home for a few months, get my tan up to scratch and work with Cloud and Hamish to do some redecorating and redesigning bits of the house and estate.

The night after my first with Freddie, I went to see Brandon and Chris in the kitchen.

"Would you two like to come to bed with Freddie and me tonight?"

The grins that spread across their faces answered the question before they spoke.

"Yes please, Charlie."

"Good, so that you know what to expect, I am feeling lazy, so I want you to make love to me, Brandon, and Freddie is going to make love to Chris, OK?"

"Oh yes, Charlie, that is more than OK."

At the gym, I told Freddie my plan.

"Thank you, Charlie. Chris is very hot. I will be delighted to make love to him."

The scene was set. Although I hated enemas, I made the other three join me, and we all took them before showering. I had my plan, but it was more than possible I would change it as the night progressed.

We piled into my bed for a lot of mutual kissing and cuddling. Of course, we were all monstrously erect, so there was plenty of groping going on as well. This was not how I had envisaged it. I wanted some serious lovemaking, but we were all giggling like schoolboys. It did eventually sort itself out as Chris and Freddie really started to get it on. I was proud of Freddie. He was working on Chris so well that very quickly Chris was wriggling all over the bed. It was lovely to watch him kissing and caressing Chris all over making him alternately gasp and laugh. Chris's cock was bouncing around so much that I just had to take it in my mouth for a few minutes, sucking on it hard while I played with Freddie's monster. Brandon took his cue and started working on my lower parts. He had been practicing. He was only using his tongue and fingers. The tongue was nearly licking me to death while his fingers roamed over my belly and up to my nipples before descending and running down my inner thighs. I left Chris to Freddie and let Brandon pleasure me uninterrupted. I ran my hands over any part of his body, I could reach while keeping a watchful eye on the other two. Brandon didn't let me near his cock and balls for some reason, but he had me incredibly hot for fucking by the time he lubed my ass and his cock. He slid into me in one smooth movement then fell forward on his elbows to kiss me.

"I haven't let you touch me, Charlie, because I am going to remain inside you for as long as I possibly can."

He moved back onto his haunches just gently rocked in and out of me. The feeling was beautiful. I could feel every movement, and he was hitting my prostate regularly to the point where I had several orgasms close together. I was gasping, this was so erotic, being gently fucked by Brandon and watching Freddie doing the same to Chris. I was playing with two pairs of nipples hearing both Brandon and Chris gasp each time I nipped them. My lover had an incredibly ferocious orgasm but remained inside me for another much gentler one. I was in cock heaven. I didn't want to be without a cock in me all night. I was brought back to earth with a bump when Chris and Freddie orgasmed together. Chris's scream was ear piercing.

When he could speak, I heard him say to Freddie, "I have never had an orgasm like that, Freddie. That was beyond awesome."

I looked to see if Brandon had heard it. He had. Repair work needed here.

"Brandon, I think both of us have some work to do. I am not used to being second best."

He looked upset as he replied, “I thought only you made love to Chris better than me, Charlie. I love him so much I always give him my best.”

“I’m sure he wouldn’t want your loving to be any better, but if he does you only need to make love to him like you have just done to me, you were fantastic.”

“Really, Charlie?”

“Yes, Lover, that was awesome tonight. I think we all try to be better with outside sex than we do with our own lovers, but the feelings are different when it is someone you love like you love Chris. I’m sure he would agree.”

Honour satisfied, we all showered, and I asked them if they would like to spend the night and if so could we have a fuck sandwich with Chris at the front then me, Freddie and Brandon. I wanted to go to sleep with a cock inside me. They all thought that was great. We all lubed up and I slid into Chris, Freddie slid into me, and Brandon into him. It was bloody marvellous. When I told Winston, I was sure he would want to try it. I wondered how many of us could get into this bed together. Wow.

The next morning, I gave Chris a long slow blowjob while the other two showered.

“That’s because you didn’t sleep in cock heaven last night, Chris.”

“Oh, but I did, Charlie, I had you inside me the whole night. I love Brandon, but I love you more. Don’t tell him will you?”

I kissed him and blushed. Another boy who I could have anytime, frightening!

I worked hard on my body and my tan over the next few days. I was going to be the best for my baby when he arrived back on the island.

Chapter 16

"I'm coming home, Charlie. I miss you so much. I can't stay away any longer. Tom and Jason will fly home scheduled in a few days, but I am returning in the company jet today. I love you."

"I love you, too, Baby, stay safe. I'll see you for dinner."

I had been getting the most incredible sex from Freddie, Chris and Brandon, but nothing compared to making love to my baby. He really was the moon and the stars for me. He had seen me through all my traumas, stuck by me when anyone else would have given up. Nearly died for me, taken incredible humiliation and punishment when he thought he had humiliated me, nursed me through major and minor breakdowns and still missed me enough to want to come home early to be with me.

I told Robbie I would help with dinner. I wanted something special for Winston when we ate tonight. I worked hard for Freddie, had a great massage to relax me and several hours of sun to make sure I oozed health and vitality.

I called the airport to check the landing time of Cloud's Inc. private jet. Funny, they said they didn't have it. I was getting worried, and then I heard the chopper. I ran down to the landing pad expecting to see Winston emerge from it. Instead, it was David.

"Hello, David, what's going on? I am expecting Winston."

"Let's go up to the house, Charlie. I have something to tell you."

I felt ice crawling up my spine.

"Tell me now, David, what is it? Has something happened to Winston?"

I could see the tears in his eyes.

"I'm sorry, Charlie. The company jet crashed shortly after take-off from San Francisco this morning. There were no survivors. I'm so sorry."

I started to scream, and I don't remember stopping. In fact, I didn't remember anything for a week. When I awoke, Ronald was seated on one side of me and David the other.

I cried and I cried, and I pleaded with David to tell me it wasn't true. My Baby was dead, and I didn't know how I would live without him. I didn't even think I wanted to.

The shock of Winston's death caused a massive trauma resulting in me being partially paralysed. I was wheelchair bound. Freddie was an angel. He became my minder and my shadow. He went everywhere with me. I had an army of mother hens trying to get me interested in living again. They needn't have. Without Winston, there was no life. I couldn't even begin to imagine spending the next 30 or 40 years without him.

Freddie slept with me every night and just cuddled me. Of course, the other reason he stayed was everyone's fear that I would top myself. They were probably right. I would have done it. During the next few months, all my old crowd made the pilgrimage to Lara's House to spend time with me. They were probably doing more harm than good until Paul and Ryan arrived. They were inconsolable.

"Charlie, we loved him so much. What are we going to do without him?"

They were lost, 30 years old now and vulnerable like kids. I cried with them and comforted them. They were my little 18-year-olds again, looking to me for guidance and comfort. They were the beginning of my road back to life.

Cloud and Freddie were the first two people I really focussed on as I started to mend. The love and devotion they showed me was almost palpable – my oldest friend and my youngest.

Winston's money was so tied up with mine that no one had attempted to sort it out. I did. He was worth a shade less than $1.5 million. This was the first positive thing I did. I even started to race round the house in my chair. Freddie told me I would wear him out if I didn't slow down. I needed to be doing something for Winston was all I could think about.

Freddie and I took the new company jet to Winston's home island. I met his family for the first time and saw his father. This was what Winston would have looked like when we grew old together. I wept, and he wept with me.

"I know how much Winston loved you, Charlie. You were his whole life. He loved us, but he only had room for you in his heart. You were his sun and moon and stars."

I wept even harder, but I was healing. To die would have been a negation of all that he had meant to me and I to him. I had to live and I had to live to the full or tarnish his memory. I knew in my heart that he would want that.

I called Winston's father, Dad, when we sat down to talk about the will.

"Winston left $1.5 million, Dad. It belongs to his family."

"No, Charlie, it belongs to you. You made it for him. You should keep it."

"Dad, you have no idea do you? Winston was genuinely a very competent and hard working vice president of Cloud's, and before that the whole board of directors voted him a million dollars for his services. The money belongs to you and his mother and his brothers and sisters. Let me put it in trust and appoint trustees who will help you manage it. We will use my company people so that you will incur no costs and no rip-off artists."

"Whatever you think is right, Charlie."

I stayed with his family for a few days, and promised his two baby brothers that if they wanted to leave the island, I would employ them somewhere in my organisation.

"We aren't gay, Charlie."

I think that was the first time I had laughed since my baby died.

"I know, Billy, mores the pity, you are both so obviously Winston's brothers. I could fall in love with you without any problem."

I kissed them both as I left and saw the love for their brother shine through and accept me for who I was.

"Don't be strangers. You will always be welcome at Lara's House. I would like you all to see where we were so happy together."

The day we arrived back home, I walked for the first time since Winston's death.

The first business thing I had to think about was Freddie's status. His slavery had ended some time while I was out of it. He had made no noises about leaving, or a salary to stay or anything. He seemed totally devoted to bringing me back to health.

I gave it a lot of consideration. What I felt for him was love, not like the love I had for Winston. I would never feel that again, but I didn't want to lose this boy as I recovered. I would sooner lose him now and be done with it. I called him to my study after breakfast one morning.

"Come in, Freddie, sit down. We need to sort out your life. You have been out of slavery for several months. I will pay you for your free months and supply you with airfares anywhere in the world you want to go."

He started to cry softly. "I don't want to go anywhere, Charlie. Don't send me away. I want to remain here and look after you. I love you, Charlie. I'll still be your slave as long as you don't send me away."

I moved around the desk, sat next to him on the couch and took him in my arms.

"I'm not going to send you away, Freddie. I know how much you have protected me since Winston died. I would love you to stay and look after me. We can talk about a contract later. Thank you for protecting me from myself. I won't forget it."

I called David next.

"Charlie, how wonderful to hear from you. How are you?"

"I'm fine, David. I'm going to live. I think Winston would be very disappointed if I gave up because he is dead. I have seen his family and given them the $1.5 million that he owned. I will buy their stock if they want to sell it. I don't want strangers owning a chunk that big."

"You sound good, Charlie, I am so pleased. Would you like to come to New York to talk?"

"Yes, David, have you done the salary and bonus thing yet?"

"No Charlie, it was your brain child. I rather hoped you would like to do it when you were well again."

"I will work on it here, David, and let you have details before I arrive."

"That's wonderful, Charlie. By the way who is looking after you?"

"Why, do you think I need a minder?"

"Of course, Charlie, you always have."

"Very funny, David, but yes, Freddie is a free man now but is staying on to take care of me."

"I'm pleased, Charlie. He is a beautiful boy inside and out. I'm sure he'll be good for you and to you."

I summoned Freddie again. I knew what I wanted for my peace of mind.

"Freddie, I have come to a decision about your future. I would sooner lose you now than next year or the year after, so I have two choices for you. The first is simple. I will pay you one hundred thousand dollars and give you a first class air ticket anywhere in the world, but you leave today. Alternatively, you can sign this contract. It puts you into slavery again for ten years. In return for your signature on that document, I will buy half million dollars worth of stock in Cloud's and assign it to you. At the end of your ten years, you are free and the stock is yours. It will probably be worth between one and two million."

"If I can remain here with you, Charlie, I will sign the contract. I don't want the money. I just want to be with you always."

"Thank you, Freddie, but you will have the money because by the end of your ten years. I am sure you will have earned it."

The deed was done. At 34 years old, I had secured a minder for the next ten years.

My first workout was very gentle and followed by a long period at the pool tanning. Freddie, true to form hardly left my side. He was running the gym from wherever I was.

I worked on the plan for the presentation and realised how much I missed Winston's input for this kind of thing. More tears, I guessed it would be many years before thoughts of him didn't make me cry.

I talked to Tom and Jason about the get together, but not the true reason. I wanted to go completely over the top, so I told David and Cloud's other directors that I intended funding the do out of my own pocket so that I didn't have to justify the expense to anyone. All of the senior staff would fly first class to New York. I booked rooms for all of them at the Waldorf and arranged a fleet of luxury limousines. The only non-senior manager present would be Ryan. I had plans for him. I of course was staying with David, as was Freddie, who was like my shadow.

Freddie did a Winston on me when I had him in a tuxedo for the night. He bounced around our bedroom like a kid. Well, I suppose he still was really.

"Oh golly, Charlie, this is amazing. Thank you so much."

I have to admit he did look good. Another little Greek God like I had been when David first had me. Midnight blue tux with ruffed shirt and matching bow tie and cummerbund. He could have been a model. We had slicked down his unruly mop of hair, and he looked like someone out of a twenties song and dance show. I felt a twinge of guilt at my feelings. I hadn't had sex for six months, but I felt a tingle in my groin looking at him at that moment.

"You look incredible, Freddie. I could eat you."

"Thank you, Charlie. I wish you would. I love you so much."

Darren had organised the meal before joining us, and Peter had sent special wines and vintage champagnes down from Boston the week before to give them time to settle again. Jamie was the wine waiter here, and he brought me every wine during the evening to taste. He was as delightful as ever, and having him and Luke serving my table was a wonderful bonus. At the end of the meal, I had the champagne served, and all waiters except Luke and Jamie were asked to leave. I kept those two near me in case I needed them. I had David on one side of me and Freddie on the other.

"Gentlemen, Welcome to Cloud's New York and my apologies for bringing you here under false pretences. The real reason for this shindig is to inform you all personally, of some decisions David and I have made concerning you all. First and foremost, I want to thank Tom and Jason as COOs of our two companies for the work they have done in keeping us so profitable. I don't think thanks are enough without reward, so, Tom, this envelope contains a certificate for one million dollars worth of Cloud's stock."

There were gasps from around the room.

"Also, Tom, we consider we have been underpaying you, so effective immediately, we have enhanced your pension and increased your salary by one hundred thousand a year."

More gasps and Tom took the envelope whispering to me, "You didn't have to do this, Charlie, but thank you so much."

"Next is Jason, one of the first waiters in this restaurant, you have been an amazingly effective leader of G.A.Y. We would like you to have this cheque for a quarter of a million and an immediate increase of 50% in your salary followed by another 50% next year. We have doubled your responsibility. It is only fare that we double your salary."

He was crying as he took the envelope and whispered. "I love you Charlie, always."

What a bunch I had fostered, always crying around me. I felt so proud of all of them.

"All of the general managers and premier chefs in both companies are to receive salary increases of 20% effective immediately, and you can tell all your staff that their salary increases will be inflation busting ones. On top of that, I would like you all to have bonuses totalling 10% of your salary for each year you have been with us."

I was pleased that they all appeared to think I had been very generous. When the applause died down, I had one further announcement.

"Not everyone in this company rises to senior management even when they could. One such person is here tonight because of his loyalty to this company and his love for his partner that has stopped him moving on. Ryan, you are a credit to Cloud's and your love for Darren is awesome. I would like to reward that loyalty and love with a bonus check for one year's salary."

I couldn't believe it. Thirty years old and by the time he reached me to take his cheque he was sobbing like a baby. I hugged him hard and kissed him softly on both cheeks.

"Winston would have been so proud of you."

Wrong thing to say, both of us had to be led away to calm down. A large brandy each, and we were both laughing and crying at our own stupidity.

"Thank you, Charlie, I love you so much, I would work for you for free, so this is just too much."

Back in my place, I apologised for my behaviour and warned them it might happen again before I was finished tonight.

"Before I ask you to stand and toast each other for your outstanding performance, I would like to tell you about an initiative I have set in motion. One month ago, I placed ten million dollars in a trust fund. That fund will be called 'The Winston Groves Memorial Fund' and is to be used to help the brothers of all Cloud's and G.A.Y. employees with their university and college tuition and student expenses. Details of how to take advantage of it will be in all pay and salary envelopes this month. Any senior staff who would like to donate to the fund may do so. I know Winston would have loved me doing this."

That was it, more buckets of tears, and David and Freddie had me in a sandwiched bear hug as David raised his glass.

"Gentlemen, I give you a toast. To each other, you are two awesome teams."

Everybody did, and then David continued, "Most of all tonight, I would like you to stand and toast Charlie Fellows. We all owe him so much. To Charlie, live long, Charlie, we all love you."

That was too much, another brain overload and I collapsed causing pandemonium. A few cold compresses and I was conscious again. I apologised to everyone and suggested we retire to G.A.Y. where all of their drinks for the remainder of the night would be on my personal tab.

The newly appointed bar manager took my arm as I walked in.

"Good evening, Charlie."

"Hello, Nick. I wondered if you would ever stop calling me Mr. Fellows, Sir. How are you?"

I could see tears in his eyes as he replied, "I'm fine, Charlie, how can I ever thank you for my bonus. I never expected it. You know I am the highest paid barman in New York already."

"Of course I do, Nick, but that's because you are the best barman in New York, and I am not going to risk losing you."

He gave me a quick kiss on the cheek and was gone. What a shock, he had never done that before.

Tom and Jason hardly moved from my side for the remainder of the night, and their closeness was good for me emotionally. They, more than anyone other than David, knew how much Winston's death had affected me.

Cuddling Freddie in bed that night, I had my first erection since forever.

"Would you like me to do something with that, Charlie?"

"I don't think so, Freddie. Let's leave it, and if it is still there in the morning, we can have a rethink."

My best night's sleep since Winston died. Freddie told me the next morning after he had made me orgasm that I had been hard most of the night pushing my cock into his back.

"Charlie, you almost drowned me as well, quite obvious you have been saving up your cum."

We spent another couple of days in New York socialising particularly with Darren and Ryan, Jamie and Luke. I was so relaxed, at last. I should have taken them all to bed. I am sure that therapy would have been good for me, but I didn't.

Freddie and I did a ton of clothes shopping. I wanted him to have a descent wardrobe for when he travelled with me. I also wanted him to have lots of sexy slave shorts and personal underwear. The shorts were silk hip huggers, and he looked incredible in them. Looking in the mirror when he tried a pair on he said, "Oh my God, Charlie, I will get raped every time I wear a pair of these."

"Mmm, I think you probably will, by me."

I realised I was behaving like a sugar daddy, but I didn't care. It was lovely to see my man/boy enjoying himself.

"I would like to buy you a new watch, Freddie, and a gold slave collar."

He looked at me quite shocked.

The slave collar was a beautiful box choker in solid gold with a little gold padlock the key to it going on my personal keyring. He looked incredible in it. I added a very slim designer watch in white and yellow gold. He was so beautifully slim and elegant. None of the big chunky watches would have looked right.

The jeweller didn't know what to do as Freddie burst into tears, threw himself into my arms and blubbered his thanks with the usual comment, "I don't deserve this, Charlie, thank you."

I shrugged, paid and took my new baby home. Back on the estate, I made Freddie go and sort his department out.

"I don't need a full time minder anymore, Freddie. I need a full time trainer for my staff. Off you go. P.I. dress today, I will think about your sexy shorts some other time."

With a quick laugh and a "Thank you, Master," he was gone.

No matter how much I told the staff I was OK, they continued to pussy foot around me. Cloud was the worst.

"Cloud, if you don't stop treating me like a piece of delicate porcelain I am going to scream. I am OK. Winston is up there looking after me, and all of you are doing a terrific job down here. Please start treating me normally."

"I'll try, but you know how special you are to me particularly, and most of the remainder of the staff are grieving with you."

He did start to unwind and be normal with me followed by the remainder of the staff. Freddie was bringing me back to fitness, and Ronald was monitoring me all the time. He had resumed the routine we had followed when Winston and I were recovering from our comas. The first weekly examination where I got an erection was so funny. He pounced on it and took it in his mouth.

"I have to taste this, Charlie, to make certain it really is yours. I wondered if I was ever going to see this thing rise up again."

I was laughing so much I went soft again before he could make me cum.

"Sorry, Ronald, maybe next week."

"I hope so, Charlie. I have never ceased to lust after your cock."

The next milestone on my recovery was Freddie. When he told me we were going to do the whole nine yards the following day I planned for it. Warm up, circuit, run and finally swim. I told Hamish no one was to use the pool until after lunch the next day.

"I want you in slave shorts tomorrow, Freddie."

He said, "Yes, Master," and I knew he was apprehensive.

He was so completely transparent. Most of the time, he called me Charlie, but if he thought I was going to take advantage of his slave status, he always reverted to Master.

When I arrived in the gym, I told him to take his shorts off. He noticed I was wearing slave shorts as well, and he looked totally confused, especially when I also took mine off.

"Warm up and circuit naked, Freddie, shorts back on for the run."

He looked incredible as we started the run. I got an erection, which he smiled at. When we reached the pool, I told him, "Slave standing position, Freddie."

I started to play with him through his shorts, and as he got hard, so did I, and his smile got broader. I pulled his shorts down slowly and eased the waistband over his extremely hard cock. Licking it as I uncovered more, taking his balls in my mouth while I made him step out of the shorts. I licked and sucked nibbled and caressed him for ages.

"I think you should do the same to me, Freddie."

He did, but I was lazy. I stretched out on one of the large sun beds. When I was gasping, I pulled him onto the bed with me, kissed him passionately and then attacked his beautiful butt. I spread him as wide as I could and used my hands to further part his cheeks. I licked and prodded with my tongue, sucked until I thought I would suck his insides out. I played with his ball sac as I swabbed his perineum, and when he pushed back on all fours, I lubed him from the supply in the poolside table and slid into him in one smooth motion. He gasped.

"Crikey Charlie, that feels huge. I haven't had that inside me for so long, I forgot what it felt like."

I fucked him long and slow. I realised very quickly how horny he was. He was orgasming almost continuously until I came as well.

"Oh gosh, Charlie, I had forgotten how awesome your cock was. That was incredible. I love you so much."

"I love you, too, Freddie. Thank you for saving my life."

He would never mean as much to me as Winston had, but he was coming close. I felt so protective towards him. He was so young and such a beautiful man/boy.

I wondered if I would ever let him resume slave status to pleasure the staff. David had lost me letting that happen. I wasn't sure I was brave enough to risk it. Perhaps if my sexual appetite returned, we could have a few threesomes or even full-blown orgies. I had the feeling Freddie was quite prepared to be as big a slut as I had been.

That night, I showed him the orgy video that David had recorded when I volunteered a night of slavery for $2 million dollars when he invited his friends in.

I told Freddie how much I got for that night, and he didn't believe me. I laughed and told him how I reckoned I was paid the $2 million.

"Crikey Charlie, if they were all rich guys like David, I bet they would have paid you the same for that action."

"Mmm, how would you like to be the centre piece in a party like that?"

"Oh yes, Charlie, if you didn't mind, the sex looked amazing."

"Perhaps we'll do it with some of the young staff with me choreographing it, and later you do the same with me and older members of staff."

He did his Winston act again bouncing round the room.

"Oh yes, Charlie, that would be amazing."

He saw the tears pricking the back of my eyes.

"Oh Charlie, have I done something wrong?"

"On the contrary, Baby, you have reminded me of one of the very amusing things Winston used to do when he was happy and eager to do something I suggested. I'm in love with you, Freddie. I don't just love you. Winston enjoyed our threesomes and for the rest of my life, you and I will have threesomes at least because Winston is always going to be here with us. Do you mind awfully?"

“No, Charlie, I loved Winston as well. Even when he was mad at me for humiliating you, he was always nice, and when he made love to me he was the gentlest person in the world. You were so lucky to have him for nearly 14 years.”

I sent for Hamish and Cloud a few days later. I had the pantry boys bring fresh coffee and biscuits to my study.

When they knocked, I called for them to come in.

“Hamish, Cloud, please sit down.”

We all sat round the coffee table

“The refurbishment and new landscaping we discussed before Winston died should be started soon, don’t you agree?”

“Yes, Charlie, but we didn’t want to approach the subject again until we thought you were ready.”

Hamish looked at Cloud for confirmation and got a nodded agreement.

“Good, but I want some additions to that. Cloud could you share Hamish’s cottage with him and could we accommodate the remainder of the senior staff in estate cottages?”

“Yes, no problem, Charlie, we have a lot more space with the smaller number of staff that you manage with.”

“Good, and can we empty the remainder of the staff quarters by sending some on leave and moving the remainder into the annexe?”

“Of course, Charlie.”

“Good, Freddie and I will take off and go to Connecticut while this is all going on because I want all the staff quarters done in one fell swoop. Save a lot of disruption in dribs and drabs. But first I want you and Hamish to do me a big favour.”

“Anything for you, Charlie.”

“Good Cloud, I have $10,000 in cash here and the company jet is on the tarmac at the airport. I want you to take it to New York and spend at least a week there enjoying yourselves, buying each other presents and just generally chilling out and having a good time. You are booked into a double suite at the Waldorf and a limousine is booked for your exclusive use. Those bills are already taken care of. The money is fun money. If you need anymore, you are welcome to it, and David is authorised to give you another $10,000 if you want it. I would prefer you remained there for two weeks, but I am probably not going to get that without a serious fight. OK guys?”

“Oh no, Charlie, we don’t want to do that.”

“Cloud, you said you would do anything for me. Well, that is what I want you to do.”

Anyone would think I was sending them to a torture chamber. They were as bad as one another.

"Oh and you are booked at Cloud's for dinner tomorrow night. I have already signed the bill. Luke and Jamie will be your waiters, and they already have your wine order. I will however let you choose your own food."

Cloud laughed. "Are you sure you trust us to do that, Charlie?"

I laughed, too.

"Only just, Cloud. Now, off you go and enjoy yourselves. Freddie and I will look after things until you get back."

This would be the first time in 14 years that I had been at Lara's House without Cloud, and it felt different. It made me realise how much a part of this estate he was.

With Cloud gone, I started to organise the two orgies. First step was to talk to the people I wanted to participate – Robbie and his three helpers plus the two new pantry boys even though I hardly knew them. We turned them out so quickly for Cloud's that this was almost a temporary assignment, and Thomas who I thought might like to fuck someone who looked like I did 14 years ago.

For my session under Freddie's control, I picked the two estate workers who had the enormous cocks, the two estate workers who had fucked me at my kangaroo court hearing as a slave, Robbie again because he was such a great fucker, and Chris again simply because he was so damned cute.

With no Cloud to show disapproval, I set up the lounge for it. The whipping bench was already there, and I had the examination couch brought in from the nurse's station. I thought the stirrups on it might come in handy. I also had a couple of paddles handy and lots of lube and towels. Dustsheets over the furniture so that we wouldn't soak it in cum finished the transformation.

After dinner on the appointed night, I walked in with Freddie, both of us clad in our little slave shorts. I sat down with Freddie kneeling beside me.

"OK, guys for as long as you like you can use Freddie for your sexual pleasure. The paddle is available to ginger him up if you want to, but nothing heavy. If you are in to a little humiliation that will be allowed as well. I want you all to enjoy yourselves, and that includes Freddie, so keep your sadistic streaks reasonably well hidden."

They all laughed, but I could see they were a little nervous. I thought I would get the ball rolling.

"Freddie stand up and face me. Legs wide arms behind your head."

I played with him through his shorts and ran my hands gently over the rest of his body. When he was rampant, I told him to face the room and take his shorts off.

"He is all yours guys ready to fuck, suck or be fucked."

"I love your cock, Freddie, so if you would like to take my shorts off we can go sixty-nine in the centre of the floor." Brandon had now truly broken the ice.

In less than five minutes, the floor was a tangle of arms and legs as everyone grabbed a cock or an ass that they liked. Chris was the first to be entered by one of the pantry boys. I was determined to follow him. I looked to see what Freddie was up to, and he had Robbie up his ass and Brandon face fucking him with Jack wanking him. Good to see the kitchen crew working as a team again.

I was stripped, lubed and ready to go when Chris became a vacant possession. I slipped between his legs and caressed him. I played with his nipples and used the cum from his orgasm to lubricate his cock so that I could start wanking him. His groin was too gorgeous to resist, so I licked it all over. I knew his cum tasted sweet, so what the hell.

He watched everything I did and said just loud enough for me to hear, "Thank you, Charlie, I'm glad it's you. I love you very much. Are you going to fuck me?"

"Yes, if you would like me to."

"Oh yes, please. Do it now, Charlie. I want you inside me."

He was delightful. I fucked him with long slow strokes. As always, when I was inside this beautiful boy I never wanted to cum. I wanted to last forever and watch all the wonderful emotions that passed across his face. I know I articulated my hips and rocked on my knees, but I didn't think that was enough to cause this boy so many different emotions all of complete happiness.

Without any noise, he started to orgasm but despite his butt muscles working their magic on me with each spurt of his cum I didn't join him. I carried on, and on, and on. He came several times before I failed and had a magnificent orgasm. I fell into a torso smothered in cum and kissed him all over his face, licking up any cum that had reached that far.

"You are a wonderful lover, Chris. I'm not surprised that Brandon is one of the happiest members of staff. I love you, boy wonder."

"Thank you Charlie. Can I leave now? I think I want to sleep, thinking about your loving?"

"Of course you can. Let's go and shower together."

Brandon by this time had changed position and was fucking Freddie over the whipping bench with another of the pantry boys completing the spit roast. He looked happy, so I didn't mind leaving him for a few minutes.

Brandon looked at us as we were leaving, and I winked at him.

I soaped rinsed and dried Chris. He was adorable. If it were not for Brandon, I think I would have slept in a sandwich every night. A beautiful black boy on one side and an equally beautiful white boy the other. I slipped my shorts on again, kissed Chris good night and returned to the lounge.

Freddie was still across the whipping bench, restrained, but now Brandon was laying into him with the paddle. Freddie was screaming with the pain, and everyone else was standing looking aghast at the ferocity of the attack.

"You worthless piece of white trash, this is what you get for being a useless slut."

I pulled the paddle out of his hands and screamed at him.

"What the fuck is the matter with you? Why are you abusing Freddie?"

He looked at me in shock, completely deflated and burst into tears.

"I thought you had taken Chris away to make love to him. I can't compete with you, Charlie, and I love him so much."

"We have been this route before, Brandon. Security will keep you confined tonight and tomorrow morning you'll be escorted off this estate. You need help, and we can't give it here."

I called security and had Brandon taken away. Freddie was very distressed as I freed him. I took him in my arms and caressed him speaking softly to him.

"I'm sorry guys, Brandon has fucked this up for us, you are very welcome to remain and play with each other, but I am taking Freddie to bed."

I took him directly to the shower and pampered him.

"He hurt me so much, Charlie. I wasn't doing anything wrong. Why did he beat me so hard?"

"Shh, it's my entire fault. I went out with Chris for a shower, and Brandon thought we were sneaking off for private sex."

I plastered Ryan's Mum's cream over his ass and put him to bed. He was asleep almost instantly. I decided that the paddle would never again be used against him even for erotic pleasuring. He had just experienced something I got used to, beatings for someone's sadistic pleasure.

I went back to the lounge to check everything was OK, and nearly died laughing. The remainder of the boys had stayed and were in a suck circle. They all looked up at me and smiled, so I said good night and joined Freddie in bed. He buried his face in my chest and cocked one leg over my abdomen. I fell asleep cuddling him, and in the morning neither of us had moved.

I was about to slide out from him when I saw him wake up. He looked up into my eyes and I saw fear.

"I'm so sorry, Baby. I am never going to allow that to happen again."

"I still hurt, Charlie. No one has ever hit me that hard."

"I know, you stay there. Would you like some breakfast?"

"Just OJ and coffee please, Charlie."

I sought out Chris first and told him what had happened.

"I'm sorry, Chris. I can't let him get away with it this time. His attack on Freddie has left him very distressed. Why don't you take OJ and coffee up to him and sit with him until I come back."

It looked likely I would have two beautiful boys to look after today.

I found Brandon under guard in a spare bedroom.

"What do you want us to do with him, Charlie?"

"You will be escorting him off the estate later, Eric. I'll let you know details. Go and have your breakfast now and let me know when you are back. I will be in with him."

"Brandon, I am sending you to New York to be part of David's household. You will go and see a psychiatrist for some counselling. You have to learn to control your anger and your jealousy. If you get the OK from the doctor, you will be allowed back here, otherwise you are history. You are getting a third chance for only one reason. I love Chris very much, and I know he loves you."

"Thank you, Charlie. I will try very hard, but please don't send me away without Chris."

"This isn't negotiable, I am going to look after Chris, and you are going for therapy. The alternative is that you will not see Chris again on this estate."

"But I will die, Charlie. I know you will be making love to him. I can't stand that thought."

"That is why you are going. I am no threat to you. Freddie is my lover. We will make love to Chris because he needs lots of loving. Remember that because you should be the one doing it."

He broke down completely, and I decided to send a member of the security staff with him. I phoned David who agreed to accept him, and the case was closed.

I returned to my suite and told Chris what I had done. Another bucket of tears, so I left him and Freddie consoling each other. Three in a bed for the foreseeable future.

I gave Freddie a few days to recover and then before Cloud and Hamish were due back, I asked him if he would like to choreograph my night of slavery. No paddles, but light spanking was acceptable.

"Oh yes, Charlie, I love to see you with your legs in the air and a large cock protruding from your ass."

I laughed, "You kinky little bugger."

"You don't know the half of it, Charlie, but I'll try to show you. Tons of sex, humiliation and embarrassment. Is that alright?"

What could I say? He looked as though he was intending to show his true self without any inhibitions.

"Yes, I guess so, Freddie. I kind of got used to it when I was a slave, so I can live with it if it gives you pleasure. I need to make it up to you for what Brandon did as well."

I told the boys when I entered the lounge in just my little slave shorts.

"Freddie has Carte Blanche tonight, as do all of you. So I don't want you to feel uncomfortable with any of the sex, humiliation or embarrassment that your actions might cause me. This is my pay back to Freddie for allowing him to be punished so badly by Brandon."

"Alright, Charlie, in at the deep end. Take your shorts off and up on the examination table."

Bradley and Hector, my guards from my trial so long ago, put my feet in the stirrups and hoisted them, spreading them wide at the same time. I was wide open with all of the boys looking at me. I was only embarrassed because I realised Chris was there. Not my cleverest choice, I thought. Freddie lowered the table so that it was just the right height for me to be able to suck cock or take it up my ass. A little fine-tuning and I really was splayed out but not uncomfortably.

"Chris, you are the youngest so you get the first blowjob and the first fuck."

Chris stripped and fed me a very erect penis. Of course, I loved it and used my hands to caress the remainder of his body. Robbie had the other end and started to open me up. All eyes were on me and the hands soon followed, playing with my cock and balls, running over the rest of my torso and pinching my nipples. Bradley and Hector smacked my ass at the same time.

"Keep still, Charlie, or you will receive more of the same."

How could I? Robbie was hitting my prostate almost continuously and with all the hands playing with my cock and balls, rubbing my perineum and tweaking my nipples I was almost going ballistic.

"Stop everyone. Bradley, we need to bring him down from his high."

Brad stood at the bottom of the table and for about five minutes spanked my ass with both hands. Not terribly hard, but it was humiliating enough with everyone watching for me to lose my erection.

"OK, guys dive back in. Chris, time for you to fuck him and for you to get a blowjob, Robbie."

I could see what he was doing. I was going to be stretched gradually by ever increasing sized penises until it was time to take Raul and Vidal.

Chris, Robbie, Hector and Bradley all got sucked and fucked me to orgasm.

"Charlie, play with Vidal and Raul and then prepare to take their cocks. They are going to fuck you for five minutes each while you give the other's another blowjob."

I raised my head to watch as Raul positioned himself ready to enter me. His cock was frightening. Out of curiosity, Freddie had measured him and Vidal. They were both 15 inches long and nine inches round. The others had opened me up very well but three, roughly 12 by sevens couldn't prepare me for this. As Raul got over my sphincter, I screamed and everyone else gasped. It looked incredible as the pain eased, and I could look again. The others of course had a better view than I did until Freddie produced a mirror. I was stretched amazingly wide and I gasped at the sight. Raul eased into me then until he had about 12 inches in me. I felt so full it was amazing. He started to fuck me, and I gasped. I had never felt a sensation like it in my life. When he changed over, Vidal completed the penetration giving me the complete 15 inches. The pain was incredible, but once I had it, there didn't appear to be any point in stopping him from continuing.

Everyone else was slack jawed watching me and receiving more blowjobs of course. Raul and Vidal came on consecutive rotations filling me with incredible amounts of cum.

"When you others cum again, do it over Charlie's face. Then while he scoops it all up and eats it, I want you all to finger his ass."

I looked at Freddie who was grinning like a Cheshire Cat.

"Sorry, Charlie, I just love humiliation."

I wasn't amused, but what could I say. By the time I had scooped up and eaten all the cum, my ass was pretty damn sore on the inside.

"OK, Bradley and Hector release the stirrups and put Charlie over the whipping bench. I know he has been a great sport tonight and given us great sex, but I want him blindfolded, and as you all leave, I want you to give him up to ten slaps each on his butt to show what you think of him. Not just tonight but for anything he does or has done that you are not happy with."

I didn't like this turn of events at all.

The first one to go was Chris. I knew it was him because he whispered to me.

"This is for taking Brandon away from me, Charlie."

Ten slaps that hurt, quite a lot. He set the trend for Robbie. I was getting sore. The other four were gentle, only gave me a couple and whispered in one version or another their thanks for a great evening of sex.

Freddie took the blindfold off and fucked my face first, transferring to my ass to plant his seed. The whole thing only lasted a few minutes.

"I was so turned on, Charlie, I knew I would not last. Thank you. That really was a great session. If you want to punish me now, that is all right, Master. I had such a good time it would be worth it."

I stood up and in my most serious voice said, "I need to get the whip, slave, you are going to be restrained and take at least 20."

He looked so shocked until I giggled. "Oh crikey, Charlie, I thought you were serious."

We showered and went to bed happy. The sex had been awesome with Raul and Vidal fucking me.

I went to the Blacksmiths shop the next morning after breakfast and shook hands with the two guys.

"Thank you for the sex last night. You two have awesome cocks."

They blushed but almost in unison said, "Thank you, too, Charlie, you are pretty awesome yourself."

Cloud and Hamish arrived home the next day looking rested and happy and something else that I couldn't put my finger on.

"It's so nice to have you two back, did you enjoy yourselves?"

Nods of agreement and almost coy looks at each other.

"I guess it would be foolish to ask if your suite was OK, being the Waldorf."

Again, nods and the looks that seemed so out of place with these two. If it were Freddie and Chris, I might have expected it, knowing they would probably have used only one of the bedrooms.

"Oh my God, you two have become lovers."

Cloud went pale, and Hamish blushed such a deep red I thought he would explode.

"Charlie, please, we didn't intend to. It just sort of happened."

"Oh Cloud, it's fine. I am so happy for both of you. Oh golly, we have to throw you both a party this is marvellous."

"No, Charlie, no no, no. I would be so embarrassed."

"But, Cloud, everyone will know very quickly because I presume you are going to move into the cottage with Hamish?"

"Yes but we were going to do that anyway for the refurbishment, and I just wouldn't have moved back to the man house afterwards."

"Come on, Cloud, no one on this estate is that naïve. Besides your faces will give you away. They always do however careful you are."

"Charlie, what will the staff think?"

"I would imagine that every last one of them will be absolutely delighted. You are both respected and liked so much by the staff I am sure they will be upset if I don't throw a party for you."

Hamish spoke for the first time then. "Thank you, Charlie. I think we should allow it. Cloud, I want everyone to know that we are partners."

"Done, Hamish, we will have it before we start the renovations, etc., next week."

What a ball we had. I went back into the kitchen to help Robbie. This was going to be a buffet party to blow their minds. We flew in freshly smoked Scotch Salmon, Mediterranean prawns, New England lobsters and Scotch beef. Through Peter in Boston, I ordered the champagne and made sure that all the old Lara's House crowd would be here. It was difficult to keep it all from Cloud and Hamish, but on the lawns of the house on the day Cloud was rendered speechless by the food and the guests. It was fantastic.

Hamish and Cloud smothered me in kisses at the end of the day, and I cried with happiness for my oldest friend and his new lover.

Silly little queen, I was 35, nearly 36, and I still turned on the tap at the smallest excuse, but I really was truly happy for these two men.

There was so little for me to do now with both companies that boredom set in. Cloud's was spread over a distance of 8,000 miles, but with Rick in Europe doing a fantastic job and Tom in the U.S., I could leave that company alone and Jason despite covering both coasts was keeping G.A.Y in great shape. Our travel expenses had risen, but overall profits were climbing as the fine-tuning of the new outlets took place.

Almost a year after Winston's death, I took Freddie with me on a tour of the six G.A.Y. outlets. He loved Miami and was quite a celebrity the few days we were there. I spent quite a lot of time checking everything and every time I returned to him, someone was chatting him up. I would stand back to watch until he saw me. He always looked so guilty, so I thought I would broach the subject.

"He is very cute, Freddie, would you like to go to bed with him?" The subject of my comment looked on slightly embarrassed. "You know you can if you want to."

"Oh no, Charlie, we were only talking. He knows I am with you, and I told him I don't have sex with anyone else."

"Alright, Freddie, but would you like him to join us for dinner at Cloud's?"

"Yes please, Charlie, if he wants. His name is Callum Hudson."

"Hello, Callum, I'm Charlie Fellows. Would you like to join us for dinner?"

"Yes please, Charlie. Once Freddie told me he was your boyfriend, I stopped trying to pick him up, but he is nice to talk to."

"I don't have a problem either way, Callum. Freddie isn't tied to my apron strings."

Freddie looked upset.

"What is it, Baby?"

"Don't you love me anymore, Charlie?"

"What kind of silly question is that? You know I do."

"It's just that you have never let me sleep with anyone else if you weren't there."

"I've never stopped you."

He thought about it, brightened up and giving me a quick kiss said, "No of course, it has never come up, but I won't ever want sex with anyone but you, Charlie, or with you there."

I kissed him and laughed. "Alright, Lover, let's go and eat."

Glen was standing in for the Maitre D' and hugged me when I walked in.

"Charlie, how lovely to see you again. Don't worry, I haven't changed company."

"I'm pleased to hear that, Glen. I don't have any spare general managers hanging around at the moment."

"I'll get you seated and then call Ty, he isn't working tonight."

We ended up four for dinner. Callum was intrigued when the man who was GM of Cloud's joined us and gave me a big kiss and very effusive welcome.

"How lovely to see you, Charlie. Glen and I miss you so much."

"Thank you, Ty, this young man is Callum Hudson, he is a friend of Freddie's."

"Hello Callum, you are beautiful, are you going to be one of Charlie's new recruits?"

He blushed and said, "I don't know what you mean, Sir."

"Oh, isn't he then, Charlie?"

"Not yet, but you do have a point, Ty. Callum, by new recruit, Ty thought that because you are a beautiful young man that I was going to employ you here or at G.A.Y."

"Do you work for both places then, Charlie?"

"Sort of."

Ty laughed, "Charlie owns Cloud's and G.A.Y., Callum, and as you can see in both establishments, he only employs beautiful young men."

"Golly, Charlie, I would love to work for you. I have been trained as a waiter and a barman."

"Charlie, we are one short here on the waiting staff. If he is any good, I would take him happily."

"Would you be prepared to spend a month in the kitchen while Ty trains you to our waiting standard, Callum?"

"Yes, Charlie, anything to work on South Beach at Cloud's."

"OK, come and see Ty tomorrow morning, if you check out OK, he can take you on."

Freddie laughed, and with a wicked twinkle in his eyes said, "That's handy, Charlie, if I ever change my mind I know where to find him for a sexual romp."

I slapped his leg playfully and said, "Someone is asking for a paddling."

"Oh yes, Master, beat me, beat me, I am an ungrateful slave."

Callum didn't know what to make of it as three of us dissolved with laughter. Ty of course knew that Freddie was a proper slave.

"I am so pleased that you found Freddie, Charlie, you deserve to be happy."

Quick exit to hide my tears, I knew what he meant, but thoughts of Winston were still so painful.

I heard later the conversation that followed while Freddie came and comforted me.

* * * * *

"Why is Charlie crying, Sir?"

"My fault. I reminded him in a very stupid way that having Freddie was good for him after Winston died last year. Winston had been Charlie's lover for a long time and died in a plane crash a year ago. They nearly died for each other twice over the years, and we didn't think Charlie would recover from Winston's death. Freddie was the reason for him to live."

* * * * *

I came back to the table looking a little silly.

"Sorry guys, bad memories."

Ty gripped my hand and said, "No Charlie, I'm the one should apologise."

Everything settled. Freddie and I went back to our hotel after dinner, leaving Callum to wander back to G.A.Y. to finish his evening.

Washington for a few days then New York. David as always was pleased to see us, and we stayed with him.

David, Freddie and I had one threesome while we were there, and Freddie and I went to bed with Jamie and Luke. Both sessions were terrific, and it was truly lovely to snuggle up with Jamie and Luke for the night after we had made love.

"Do you love Jamie and Luke very much, Charlie?"

"Yes, Freddie, they are two very special young men."

"Why didn't you bring them back to Lara's to be your lovers then?"

"Because I had already found you, Baby."

He snuggled deeper into my arms and said, "You really do love me then, Charlie?"

"Of course I do, silly, why else would you be here?"

He grinned up at me and replied, "I thought I was just someone you could have orgies with and beat when you were upset."

"Mmm, I think it probably is time I gave you another beating. You are beginning to forget you are still my slave. You know David used to have me beaten by a member of staff every week to remind me."

"Oh no, Charlie, that was cruel."

"Maybe, but it kept me in my place. That is why I think I will start the same routine with you."

He looked shocked, and I realised I would never be able to beat him again, even keeping him as a slave was a waste of time. I would sooner lose him than keep him with me if he wanted to leave.

I laughed and saw him relax again.

"I shouldn't play with your emotions like that, Freddie. Winston used to get very angry with me when I did it in front of him. I had to let Paul beat me for doing it to him once. When we get back to Lara's, I am going to tear up our agreement. I don't want you as a slave anymore. I want you to be able to fly if you want to."

"Thank you, Charlie, but I never will."

Connecticut next and Freddie was amazed that I had another large estate besides Lara's House. He loved behaving like the Laird while we toured the estate. There was very little that needed doing as my estate manager here was first class.

Freddie liked the gym. It was much smaller than at Lara's, but then so was the staff. I only kept a skeleton staff here. If I intended staying for long, I would bring staff with me.

We settled in comfortably for a few weeks just relaxing and making love. We went up to Boston a couple of times to socialise with Tom and Jason, Peter and Paul. It was so pleasant to not be under any kind of pressure.

Home to Lara's for my 36th birthdays and Freddie's 22nd.

"You deserve a special present for making my life worthwhile again after Winston. How would you like to go on a world cruise? We can take a few months if you like, and when we come back, I might feel inclined to do some more serious work to justify my salary."

Needless to say, the answer was yes, and we spent over a month just planning how we would do it and all the alternatives if we wanted to spend a lot of time in one place.

Before any of that though, I took him to my study and handed over his slave contract.

"The money is still yours Freddie even if you leave tomorrow. Now I know 100% that you are here because you love me and that is all I am ever going to want from you."

He gave me back the contract.

"I want to be your slave, Charlie. When this contract expires, I will sign another and another forever. I want you to feel free to punish me if I step out of line or behave above myself. I know I have so much to learn and so much loving to give you before I can get close to Winston. Please let me."

I hugged him and tore the contract up any way.

"OK, voluntary slavery."

He giggled, and I loved him more. Then I cried. For the first time, I felt I was betraying my love for Winston by loving this young man so much.

"I'm sorry, Charlie, please tell me what I've done."

"Nothing, Baby, it's just me."

I told Cloud how I felt about loving Freddie so much.

"Charlie, I know Winston would be encouraging you if he could speak to you from heaven. He loved you so totally, he would hate you to be sad now. Love that boy with all your heart. You owe it to Winston. If you don't, all the love you had for him would be soiled."

I was shocked that Cloud thought of it this way, but it gave me food for thought. After a couple of hours thinking about Winston's attitude when he knew I loved people like Ryan, Peter and Paul, Luke and Jamie and of course, at the end Freddie, I had cried myself dry but realised Cloud was right.

Chapter 17

My life for the next year was as relaxed as I had ever known it. I attended a couple of board meetings in Boston, saw David in New York once and of course took Freddie on his world cruise. By the time that was all completed I was fast approaching 38 and Freddie 24. I was still incredibly fit and looked much younger. The same applied now as had done at 20, I had a butt and package to die for. Freddie on the other hand was infuriatingly not aging at all. Most people on the cruise thought he was about 17 or 18. I took so much ribbing from him.

"They all think you are my rich sugar daddy, Charlie. Have you heard the comments about cradle snatchers, etc.?"

"Yes I have, Freddie, and I don't need you to keep reminding me."

We both laughed, but it was amazing.

When we arrived home, we slipped into our old routine spending most afternoons at the pool where we were nearly always naked, and I was hard nearly all the time.

I thought of Winston often, particularly here where we had spent so much premium time, but now there were no tears. I hoped he was still looking out for me. I needed him to because Freddie wasn't maturing the way I hoped. He remained the cheeky little boy he had always been. Hamish and Cloud told me they had paddled him a couple of times, not hard but just as a reminder.

Wrong to go easy on him I realised a little while later. I had been delayed in my study on calls, and Freddie had gone down to the pool. About a half hour had elapsed when an estate worker knocked on my door and told me I had better come down to the pool, there was trouble.

I arrived just in time to hear Freddie,

"I don't give a fuck if he is one of your workers, Hamish. I still think I should be able to punish him for the state of this pool. You can't control your people perhaps I can."

Hector was there looking shocked, and Hamish was obviously very angry.

"You don't talk to me like that, Freddie. I have a mind to paddle you severely right here."

"Well think again because I'm not letting an incompetent paddle me."

Now I was angry.

"Yes, you are, Freddie, take your shorts off, bend over legs astride and grip your ankles."

"That's not right, Charlie. Hamish should be punished not me."

"Do as you're told, Freddie, or you will receive so much pain your mind won't believe it."

He did as he was told.

"Hamish, ten good hard ones. Hector you get ten as well."

Freddie was sobbing after only two, so by ten he was a real mess and by 20 he was almost falling down.

"Now go to my study and wait for me."

Hamish and Hector told me what the outburst was all about. Pathetic really. Hector hadn't removed all the grease from the side of the pool to Freddie's satisfaction and had blown up instead of just pointing out the offending area and asking Hector to clean it again. Hamish had arrived in the middle of it hearing Freddie's raised voice.

In my study, Freddie had dried his eyes and was looking defiant. I might have gone easy on him if he had looked apologetic, but this was too much.

"You are arrogant, rude, undisciplined and disrespectful. I am not going to tolerate it. You are going to suffer so much humiliation for this act you will not believe it. Your position on this estate demands that your attitude and your manners are impeccable. If you can't understand that, then I will either break you to my standard or make you leave. I am going to take my time thinking up the most humiliating things I can have done to you, but I can't think of any good reason why I should lose the services of my trainer, so punishment will be light. You will sleep in the staff quarters until I tell you otherwise. Get your toilet gear and ask Cloud for a room. You will not need clothes. You are going naked until I decide otherwise. Now leave me."

"I'm sorry, Charlie, I'll be good."

"I've heard it all before, Freddie, and don't call me Charlie. I am your Master and will decide your fate on that basis."

I left him stewing for three days. Cloud told me he was very quiet everywhere he went and Hamish told me he had been to see him, and Freddie apologised most profusely for his bad manners. He hadn't however apologised to Hector so that was where I started the humiliation.

I had Hamish put down a large plastic sheet poolside and place on it three large empty buckets, a further bucket nearly full of freshwater and some soap and a towel. After breakfast, I took the toy box down to the pool with Freddie in tow. All of the estate workers were stood round the plastic in a semi circle all wearing shorts and Hector was on the plastic holding a douche.

"Get on all fours Freddie with your ass facing the staff. Hector I want you to give Freddie an enema."

They both looked at me aghast and Freddie started to cry. When Hector had finished, I told Freddie to evacuate it into one of the empty buckets. I can't think of anything more embarrassing than having someone watch you evacuate your bowels. By the time he was evacuating his third enema, he was sobbing with the humiliation, and I had barely started.

"Use the soap and fresh water to wash your backside, Freddie, and keep pointing your ass at the staff. I want them to see that you are clean."

Everyone was fascinated at this exercise.

"I want you on your back now, Freddie, with your legs over your shoulders spread wide. You two come and hold his legs down."

Two of the workers jumped to it.

"Hector, Alex, I want you to start finger fucking him until you can get in a pair of fingers each, then I want you to stretch him further. The rest of you gather round so that you get a good view."

It was very erotic watching Freddie being finger fucked in his perfect little butt. By the time I called a halt he was stretched so far a good sized dick could go in the hole between Hector and Alex's fingers. I opened the toy box then and pulled out a 12-inch dildo that I lubed and pushed in all the way. He squealed but was immediately OK, again when the fingers were removed.

"Hector, you were the one Freddie was so rude to. I want you to give him ten slaps on each buttock, then remove the dildo, and fuck him with your dick, cumming in his ass."

When it was done, I let all of the others fuck him including Raul and Vidal.

"On all fours again, Freddie, let everyone have a good look at your cum dribbling ass."

"OK, guys, thank you, Freddie will clean up here."

Freddie was in a terrible state. I wondered if I had gone too far this time with the humiliation.

"Clean up here, Freddie, return all the equipment to Hamish and then go and shower. See me in my study when you are cleaned up."

I left him to get on with it but detailed a worker to keep a discreet eye on him.

It was over an hour later when there was a timid knock on my study door. Freddie came in looking very pink from having scrubbed himself clean, but his eyes were haunted. I had gone too far.

"Do you understand how seriously I take your behaviour?"

"Yes, Master," said barely audibly.

"Do you have any idea how the action I have taken today has nearly broken my heart?"

He looked up with an extremely bemused expression on his face.

"No, Master."

"I love you, Freddie. I love you so deeply I never believed it possible. After Winston died, I wanted to as well. You were a major factor in changing that thought. I love you so much now that some days it hurts just to look at you. To do what I have done to you has nearly destroyed both of us. You are my love, my life partner. The people that love and respect me have to love and respect you also if our life together is to mean anything. Do you understand now?"

"Yes, Master, please forgive me. I love you so much, but I forget myself sometimes. I'm not like you. You have so much love and respect for people. I don't have that. I don't have that capacity for loving, and everything I feel that is good is centred on you. I would die for you, Master, please don't stop loving me when I am bad."

I cried for this child, how could I have allowed such humiliation. I truly loved him to distraction now. He was more beautiful than any boy I had ever seen. He thrilled me beyond belief. He cried, too, and we hugged each other.

The emotional rollercoaster that was our life had to stop. I would destroy him and he, me, unless we did.

I chartered a large yacht and instructed the captain that crew were to stay away from us as much as possible unless we called for them. We virtually lived on the quarterdeck lying in the sun or chilling out in the main deck lounge. We ate very little, mostly fresh fruit and fruit cocktails. We drank no alcohol.

We did however spend a lot of time in our cabin showing each other the love we felt for each other. I realised that I had damaged this boy. This time I had gone too far. I had broken his spirit. He was quiet, almost withdrawn. Apparently, his only waking thought was to care for and please me. I died a little. This was not what I had wanted to achieve. How could I possibly reverse the damage, or perhaps it would heal itself if I lavished enough love on him. I cried for him frequently and that actually made matters worse because he understood why.

After the cruise, I toured with Freddie anywhere we could have light-hearted company. Boston was the final stop before returning to Lara's House.

I had a private meeting with Tom and Jason and explained about Freddie.

"I know you two have pledged your faithfulness to one another, but would you please break your vow and have a foursome with Freddie and me. I think if you make love to him, Tom and he sees you screw me Jason in the fun manor that sex has always been for us, it might just bounce him out of this ennui that he is lost in. I am dying a little every day watching this spiritless boy that I destroyed."

They didn't even have to consult.

"Of course we will, Charlie. Why don't you both come for dinner at the apartment tonight, and we will sort him out."

The two of them were seriously on form keeping Freddie and me in fits of laughter with anecdotal stories from the restaurant and G.A.Y. When we were so relaxed that nothing would hurt the mood, Tom started, "You know, Freddie, Jason and I have been together since the two companies moved their HQs to Boston, but we have always suspended our vow of fidelity for Charlie. We would love to extend that to you as well. Will you join us in bed together? I know Jason wants to penetrate Charlie, and I would like very much to see if Little Tom would enjoy you."

The look of concern on Freddie's face as he looked at me was a classic.

"Is that alright, Charlie?"

"Yes Baby, Tom is an awesome lover, and Little Tom is the most exceptional cock ever to penetrate me. Jason is pretty damn good as well. His cock is very familiar. He screwed me while I was still a proper slave."

All I can say is that it was fun and exceptional sex. Freddie reacted exactly the same as Winston had concerning Tom's kissing and then his cock action.

"Oh golly, Charlie, that was totally amazing. Can we go again?"

Tom and Jason nodded at me, and I replied to my lover, "Yes, Baby, but would you mind terribly if I let Little Tom get reacquainted with my love tunnel?"

"No, Charlie, the whole sex thing was fun."

He was almost bouncing off the walls as he said it, and I knew the therapy had been right.

Tom completed my evening when he whispered in my ear after filling me with his seed, "You are still the best fuck I have ever had, Charlie."

Jason piped up, "I heard that, Lover, and I agree. Charlie, you are just so amazing."

I blushed, Freddie giggled, and Jason and Tom cuddled. I was happy.

* * * * *

Lara's House and another re-evaluation of my life. There was no great enthusiasm to expand either company. Everybody was making lots of money, and the millions of investment required to expand was not forthcoming. I considered starting a new company with a different theme using my private fortune, but I was fast approaching 40 and not sure I wanted the hassle.

In retrospect a wise move. Less than a year later, I had my first heart attack. The doctors had been correct. When I nearly died after Winston left me, I had damaged my heart. Now I was paying the piper.

It was a mild one and did not affect my life that much, but I decided now was a good time to back off from my two babies. I had been the driving force behind Cloud's and G.A.Y. for nearly two decades. I resigned my presidencies of both companies and just became a consultant. David stepped back in and took both of them. A private meeting in New York to sort it, and for the last time, David took me to bed and made love to me.

"I never thought I would find a 40-year-old lover awesome, Charlie, but you are. You have always been. You are the only regret in my life, did you know that?"

I did, he had told me often how much he loved me and what a fool he had been to lose me. I thanked him because but for him I might have lost Freddie the same way.

Freddie wasn't clever like Winston, so I set up my will to put everything in trust, but all the income from it to be available to him. Lara's

House I left to Freddie for his lifetime, and if he had a lover, for the lover's lifetime as well. I sold the Connecticut estate. We had never really used it. I told Freddie everything, and he was shocked.

"I have also given six sperm samples to a sperm bank, Freddie. I suppose as we near death, we all seek immortality, and this is how I am going to get it. One year after my death, you are to find a surrogate mother to have my child. I want a son. You and David are to be responsible for his upbringing, and when you and your lover die, he will have Lara's House and my trust fund. Be good to him Freddie and love him as you love me."

"You aren't going to die, Charlie. I'm going to look after you."

He was still so annoying. Twenty-eight nearly and still looking like a teenager. He had matured at last. The old spark was there, but more controlled. He ran the estate with Hamish and Cloud – friends at last after all the traumas.

"You know, Charlie, he has at last grown up to be another you. We all love him now and will look after him for you."

"Thank you, Cloud, he isn't strong and clever like Winston was. He is going to miss me. Don't let him die will you?"

"No, Charlie, we won't, but you are going to live for years. Don't be so morbid."

"Don't kid a kidder, Cloud. We both know that attack was my wake up call. I might survive another one, but we both know I am not going to make old bones."

I was right. I did survive the next one, but it put me in a wheelchair. While I was recovering from that, Brandon was killed in a car accident on the island, and Chris became our project to bring back to health. He grieved for a year, but Freddie won in the end, and the two of them became lovers as well as my constant companions.

I was ready now. Freddie would grieve for me, but Chris would comfort him, and they would be strong for each other. I told Cloud I wanted to be buried by the side of the old barn on the knoll, facing the setting sun and looking down on the estate that had afforded me so much happiness. My final action before my last attack was to organise and see completed a large cottage for Hamish and Cloud with the provision written into my will that it was theirs for the remainder of their natural lives.

I regained consciousness after my last attack long enough to say goodbye to the second great love of my life and to tell him and Chris that I would turn in my grave if they didn't make each other happy when I was gone.

Forty-four was too young to die, but what a life I had lived.

The End

About the Author

Chris Johns is a 65-year-old retired helicopter pilot, living in Antigua with his partner of 27 years. He spends his retirement writing and sailing, the former a recent love, the latter an enduring one covering 50 years of his life.

ng in the park. He was wearing these really tight jeans, so tight you

earing any underwear. "Excuse me," I said, having a hard time looki

, but before I knew it, I had his rod in my hand, and mine was in his

nt to do?" he asked, his tone challenging. I knew exactly, and sank t

FILTHY NEVER LOOKED SO GOOD.
HOT HOUSE EXCLUSIVE
ROBERT VAN DAMME

ORDER ONLINE OR CALL 800.884.4687 FREE XXX PREVIEWS & iPOD DOWNLOADS
HotHouse.com